THE DARKEST HOURS

An unputdownable psychological thriller full of
breathtaking twists

MARGARET MURPHY

Originally published as *The Desire of the Moth*

Revised edition 2021
Joffe Books, London
www.joffebooks.com

First published in Great Britain in 1997
as *The Desire of the Moth*

© Margaret Murphy 1997, 2021

ISBN: 978-1-78931-744-2

For Murf

PUBLISHER'S NOTE

This psychological thriller is set in the mid-1990s, when the internet was in its infancy, mobile phones had yet to evolve into smart phones, and suspects still smoked in interview rooms.

PROLOGUE

A fat, gibbous moon skulked low behind the trees, following his movements in mute disapproval, or so it seemed to his heightened sensitivities, casting its jaundiced light over the dusty fields. Long shadows formed almost solid blocks in which to hide. In ten minutes, she would come, as she did every evening, down the path, which shimmered greyly from right to left three feet in front of him, walking her dog, an absurd brownish mop of snuffling, yapping fur. First the dog, then her. Swift, silent and final.

Ann had known him immediately. Even in the dark. Even with the ski mask covering his face. More importantly, she had known why. It had spared him the pain of explanation and it had afforded a vindication: since she had remembered, she had effectively admitted her guilt. She hadn't been afraid, not at first, but later she had learned to fear him.

1

The first had been reported as a disappearance in the local free newspaper, but Chris rarely had time to watch the TV news and never listened to local radio, avoiding it especially since she had started featuring on it herself. The second death made the nationals.

'What are you doing?' Ted May turned down the corner of his newspaper indignantly and scowled up at his colleague.

'I'm trying to read over your shoulder, but you're not being very co-operative.' Chris returned his scowl.

They were taking a break in the staff common room of the Child Development Unit at Hazel Mount Children's Hospital. The room took up a fifth of the floor space of the entire department, an imbalance frequently commented upon during the previous sweltering weeks by psychologists and speech therapists who were having to conduct interviews in inadequate little rooms and a torpid, enervating heat.

'Didn't anybody ever tell you it's bad manners to read over a person's shoulder?' Ted demanded.

''Fraid not. Lousy upbringing. I put the milk in first, as well. What the hell has got into you this morning?'

'The heat,' said Jo Dowling without looking up from the report she was reading. 'Be thankful you weren't here yesterday. He was insufferable by the afternoon.'

'Well you try assessing ADD kids in an airless room at a temperature of eighty-five degrees. See how far you get.'

'If you couldn't do it, nobody could,' Chris conceded. Ted had a reputation for inexhaustible patience with both parents and children. 'Now let me see the paper. I think I know her.'

'The social worker? Why didn't you say so?' He handed it over.

The banner headline read:

SECOND COUNCIL WORKER SNATCHED?

Below it, a picture of the footpath where Ann Lee had last been seen. It was cordoned off with striped police tape. Chris skimmed the text, absorbing most of the facts at first reading. Ann's little dog had been found on the pathway, strangled, its lead wrapped tightly around its neck. There had been no sign of its owner.

* * *

Ted secretly relished the chance to be so close to Dr Christine Radcliffe. Her perfume was subtle, understated, but he caught a hint of it as she leaned in to read. She placed one hand on his shoulder; he could feel the warmth of it through his shirt, and he willed himself to continue breathing normally. Chris's hair, neatly swept into a French twist, gleamed dull gold. She was lightly tanned, deepening her rather sallow skin tone to a healthy glow. She wore a discreet amount of make-up; just enough to flatter her best features — her expressive violet-blue eyes and her full, sensuous mouth. A light dusting of blusher accentuated her high, delicate cheekbones.

Frances Lowe was standing in the kitchen area of the common room. She turned away to the sink and dragged a paper towel from the holder. Dousing it in water, she patted carefully at her face. 'It's so bloody hot!' she muttered.

Ted glanced at her, then back to Chris Radcliffe, whose grip on her newspaper had tightened.

'What*ever* is the matter?' Frances demanded.

'The social worker,' Jo said, her eyes wide. 'Chris knows her.'

'Knew her,' Chris corrected, still reading. 'Professionally. We worked together for a while.'

'The one who's been snatched?' Fran asked, adding with a little shiver of pleasure, 'How *awful*.'

Jo frowned disapproval at the receptionist.

'What? I said it was awful, didn't I?'

'That's not the point. Anyway, she's *missing*,' Jo said. 'It's only the papers saying she's been snatched.'

Fran raised her eyebrows. 'Well, it wasn't *her* who strangled her dog, was it? And if she got away, where is she?'

'You really can be insensitive at times, Fran,' Jo said.

Fran gave her a pert look and clicked over to the coffee table on her high-heeled sandals, clasping a glass of water in one sweaty palm and a damp paper towel in the other. She placed the glass carefully on the tabletop and dabbed at her forehead with the paper towel; it lifted her fringe from her eyes, giving her a tousled, girlish look. Her fat pink cheeks dimpled in childish delight. 'Well, go on then — tell us all about her.'

Jo exchanged a look with Ted and rolled her eyes. 'You're the absolute limit, Frances.'

'Don't try to tell us you're not interested.' She held Jo's stare, looking into the speech therapist's grey eyes and daring her to deny it.

'There's nothing *to* tell,' Chris said with deflating finality. 'It must be ten years since I last saw her. We worked on some cases together. I only really saw her in review meetings.'

Fran pouted. 'Well if that's all, what's the point in telling us you knew her?'

Chris didn't answer, and Ted gave Fran a hard look that said, *Leave it*, but the receptionist lifted her chin in defiance. 'That's the second,' she remarked.

'Yes,' said Chris, apparently deep in thought. 'The second.'

'There was the mother of two, just up the road,' Fran said, with fake concern. 'Snatched on her way home from an aerobics class. Horrible, isn't it? To think — it could be any of us.'

Ted eyed Fran, doubtful that she had attended an aerobics class in her life. 'Hardly likely . . . I mean, going by the headline. Unless you've worked for the council in the past?'

Fran's face was blank for a second, then her fleshy lips formed a perfect 'O', and, making no effort to suppress her excitement: 'Oh! You think it's to do with that children's home thing?' Her eyes widened with malicious delight. 'Didn't *you* work for the council when that lot happened, Chris?'

Jo hissed at Fran, then turned to Ted for support, but he didn't respond.

Reading the pain and anxiety etched on Chris's face, he stood and moved close to her, keeping his voice low so that the others wouldn't hear. 'Are you all right? Do you need to talk about this?'

'I'm not a bloody invalid, Ted,' Chris answered, turning too quickly and colliding with him. Swearing softly, she bundled the paper into his hands and stalked out of the room.

* * *

Darren Lewis knelt on the gritty concrete and read the paper. He'd been using it to get a fire going — insurance job. Empty premises. Nothing nasty.

CALDERBANK CHILDREN'S HOME SCANDAL

The headline had hit him like a fist in the gut. He was getting into the news quite a lot lately, one way and another. First that shit-eating cow Hardy, then old Fishface Lee and now this. Children's home scandals, he thought. The press seemed to get off on this kind of thing: all that stuff about the beatings; kids being used like Lime Street prozzies. It didn't matter to reporters that those kids were people with feelings, had grown up into adults with reputations to keep. Child abuse was attention-grabbing and it sold papers.

Lewis felt suddenly hot and his eyes started to water. Just dust in the air, he told himself. 'I don't have to think about it,' he said aloud. 'They can't make me.'

He concentrated on laying the fire, a skill that required care and attention. Pack it down too tight and it can't breathe — worse, it can smoulder for hours without really taking hold, a disaster if some bloody nosy parker sees the smoke. But leave it too loose and it flares up and dies too fast to make any heat.

He paused, picking up the discarded newspaper again and taking note of the journalist's name. Milton. Maybe he'd give Milton a call. Or maybe he'd pay him a visit.

He folded the paper, twisted it into a tight wad and thrust it into the base of the fire.

* * *

When Chris finished the session, just after twelve, Fran was waiting outside the door — Fran knew better than to interrupt an interview. The look of quiet satisfaction on Fran's face said she'd got a nice morsel of gossip to share over her lunch break.

'Detective Sergeant Foster from Merseyside CID wants to make an appointment to see you.' Fran said, making it sound like an accusation. 'He left a phone number.'

Chris's stomach lurched. *So. They had made the connection.* 'I'll do it now,' she said, taking the slip of paper from Fran's moist grasp.

'Feeling the heat?' Fran asked airily.

'What?' Chris followed the receptionist's line of sight through to the small room where she had conducted the interview. Her jacket was slung over the back of one of the armchairs. *Mustn't let Fran rattle you*, she thought, smiling a little, reminding herself that the woman lacked the subtlety for ambiguity. Let her enjoy her little triumph.

She picked up the jacket and strolled through to the office she shared with Ted May. The curtains were drawn, and the room was in darkness, but she didn't turn on the lights; Ted was conducting an interview in the room beyond and the blind which normally covered the two-way mirror was up. Chris could see the mother sitting tensely on the edge of her arm-chair. Ted had his back to the mirror and was chatting to her in his usual disarming manner. She could hear nothing — the sound system was switched off. She turned her back on the scene, sitting at her desk to dial the number Fran had given her.

Sergeant Foster arranged to call that afternoon. Just routine enquiries, he assured her, but declined to explain further. A light breeze lifted the heavy black-out curtain a fraction and Chris closed her eyes, savouring its short-lived coolness.

'Sorry.'

Chris opened her eyes. Dr Silverman had come through from the adjoining office. She was the consultant neurologist in the unit and worked closely with the team, assisting in complex diagnoses and recommending treatment and therapy. 'Ted asked me to observe this one. Do you mind?'

Chris had lost count of the number of times she'd watched Ted — a big, lumbering bear of a man — somehow fold himself up small enough to crouch on a tiny child's chair next to his subjects, picking out tests seemingly at random, chatting all the time to the child and the parents, asking apparently innocuous questions, putting the most defensive at ease, and getting to know their problems in one hour more thoroughly than some of their caseworkers had over months or even years.

When situations came to an impasse, Ted was often called in, ostensibly to make an educational assessment, but actually to find a solution which appeased both sides. So, if Ted had called in Dr Silverman, then this family's problems must be worse than most.

'Sure,' Chris said. 'Go ahead.'

She reached below the two-way mirror and flicked a switch. Ted's voice boomed out suddenly. '. . . no problem?'

The woman shrugged. '*They* say not.'

7

The door to the interview room opened and a boy rushed in. He was eight or nine years old and red-haired like his mother. There was a frantic, almost manic quality to his actions. He went straight to the table in front of the mirror without acknowledging his mother's presence. He picked up toys and put them down, keeping up a constant barrage of noise — growls and shouts, but no real words. Then, noticing the mirror for the first time, he gave a yell of surprise and began grimacing and mouthing. His crooked teeth seemed randomly placed in his mouth, a physical manifestation of his chaotic mental state. He squinted and groaned at his reflection, even climbing on the table to get a better view.

His mother came over and called to him. He seemed not to hear. She crouched next to him and stroked his face to gain his attention. 'Jason, you shouldn't be here. I told you to stay with Daddy.'

The boy squealed indignantly.

'Go back to Daddy,' she said firmly.

The boy left reluctantly, only to rush in a few minutes later and repeat his previous actions.

'He doesn't use any words at all?' Ted asked.

'He did, until he had the meningitis, but since then, nothing.'

'And his hearing is normal?'

'According to the tests.'

Ted nodded. 'He seems to understand what you say to him.'

'Simple instructions.'

'And the school insists he's just a slow learner.'

Dr Silverman stood with her feet slightly apart, her hands deep in the pockets of her lab coat. She peered at the group in the interview room, blinking over the tops of her half-moon spectacles, her intelligent grey eyes switching from mother to child and back to Ted in quick movements.

'There are no other problems.' Ted was using one of his techniques, circling back to an earlier question that he felt had not been answered in sufficient depth.

Dr Silverman turned to Chris. 'He's at an MLD school at present,' she explained.

Chris nodded and looked at the woman through the glass, who had shifted her position in the chair and was watching her child.

'Depends,' the mother said.

'Right.' Ted left a pause, and when she didn't continue: 'And what does it depend on?'

Chris saw the woman's jaw tighten. Her son had pulled apart one of the dolls and now seemed distressed by the damage he had done. He rushed to her and thrust the toy into her hands, making urgent grunting sounds. She reassembled the doll with practised movements as she spoke: 'What does it depend on . . . ?' she echoed. 'The teacher. The time of day. The *weather.*'

Ted allowed the silence to lengthen, indicating he had no intention of hurrying her, but that he wanted to hear her side of things.

'They say he's *fine* — but can I meet them at the hospital because he's put his fist through a window. He's *no problem* — but he's punched a teacher or bitten a kid or broken a chair, or he's got into a rage and no one dares go near him—' She stopped, apparently surprised that she'd allowed herself to be drawn into such an unguarded response and a little apprehensive of the psychologist's reaction. Chris realised that the woman must be used to accepting the blame for her son's behaviour. Years of implied — and even explicit — criticism of her management of Jason had made her bitter.

Ted merely gave her an encouraging smile. He went on to try out some tests on the boy but had to abandon them after the child attempted to tear up the block assembly cards when he couldn't match the pattern in the book with the blocks Ted gave him.

'ADD?' Chris asked.

Dr Silverman nodded, fixing her with her intense gaze. 'But far more than that.'

The neurologist nodded, a gesture of approval, her loose grey curls bobbing in girlish enthusiasm. 'Attention deficit disorder, epilepsy, aphasia — brain damage after encephalitis. The poor child is in desperate need of help.'

'His mother, too,' said Chris.

'His mother perhaps more.' Silverman shut off the sound, preparing to leave, and apologized once more for the interruption as she left the room. A few moments later, the door to the interview room opened and Dr Silverman entered. A mime ensued in which Ted introduced the neurologist, who shook the mother's hand, then sat and talked to her.

Chris turned back to her PC and began typing up the notes of her own interview, but she found it difficult to concentrate. What did Sergeant Foster want?

The first to disappear had been Dorothy Hardy, a quiet, plump, matronly woman, an ex-teacher who at the age of thirty had switched from a deputy headship at a primary school to working on provision for children with special needs at the borough's education offices. Dorothy had been a rather shy individual who shrank from conflict and always went with the consensus on any borderline cases.

Mother of two, the newspaper said. The children must have come later. Dorothy hadn't mentioned children when Chris had worked with her.

Her musings were disturbed by a knock at the door: one of Ted's more endearing peculiarities was his custom of knocking at the door to his own office if he thought Chris was in there.

'I'm not interrupting, am I?' he said.

Chris looked round. 'There's just me in here. I was about to break for lunch.'

'So, um—' Ted twiddled with his watch and glanced up at the wall clock.

'It still says ten thirty,' Chris said. 'Has done for two months.'

Ted smiled weakly. 'I just wanted to say — to ask really — if everything is OK. About the newspaper article, I mean.'

Chris passed a hand over her face. 'I'm sorry I snapped at you earlier, Ted.'

'No — it was understandable. Jo and Fran gawking at you like that, me making things worse.'

Chris smiled. 'You expressed concern. I behaved badly. So . . .' After an awkward pause, Sergeant Foster's request for an interview shouldered its way into her thoughts again. 'Has Fran been talking?'

His eyebrows twitched. 'Does she ever stop? I haven't seen her since break. Why? Is there something I should know?' Beneath Ted's disorganized, rather woolly persona there was a powerful intuition which he used to great advantage — and he rarely missed verbal cues. He came in and closed the door behind him.

Chris deliberated. 'All right,' she said, after a minute. 'You might as well hear it from me. Someone from Merseyside CID is coming over later to ask me some questions. Don't look so *worried*, Ted,' she added, seeing his concern. 'It's only a routine enquiry. They're probably talking to everyone who might be able to tell them something about them.'

'But I thought you said you barely knew the Lee woman — and that was years ago. What could you tell them?'

'Can I use the office?' Chris asked, avoiding an answer. 'I always feel a bit insecure in the interview rooms. You never know who's listening in.'

Ted flushed slightly. 'I hope you don't mean—'

Chris gave a pained smile. 'Don't go paranoid on me, Ted. All I'm asking for is a bit of privacy.'

Ted frowned at her. 'I'll write you a "Do not disturb" sign if you like,' he said at last. 'You can hang it outside the door.' Then he left, closing the door with such meticulously controlled composure that Chris was left in no doubt that he was furious with her.

2

Detective Chief Inspector Alan Jameson was having to spread his staff very thinly. His superintendent had pulled him off an investigation into a number of arson attacks so that he could focus on the abductions, which left Ray Staines with the knotty problem of finding the arsonist. Jameson had sympathized but didn't offer to find more staff.

The second abduction had raised the possibility that some sort of vendetta was being waged against Calderbank borough council staff. His officers were currently interviewing friends, associates, present and past colleagues and clientele of the two women concerned, as well as making house-to-house enquiries on the estate adjacent to the park where Ann Lee disappeared. Others were cross-referencing records going back ten years, when Ann Lee and Dorothy Hardy had first begun working together. Given the combined caseload of the two women, the task was enormous. The computer records had been relatively easy to access, but the older files had not all been entered onto the council's database and that meant sorting manually through bulging files, trying to filter out names which could be linked with both Hardy and Lee.

Calderbank's superintendent had done all he could, making introductions, oiling the machinery of communications, even releasing a detective inspector for liaison, but their tiny local nick was even more stretched for staff than Jameson was, and as the women were both tax-paying residents of Liverpool, this was a Merseyside Police enquiry.

He surveyed the busy activity of the incident room with lugubrious disenchantment. Telephones rang and were answered smartly, clerks typed information from the older files onto a database, and officers dialled out or received calls, assiduously jotting down information on notepads, accessing data on computers, and exchanging comments and notes with co-workers in the hermetic atmosphere of air-conditioned coolness at the police headquarters.

'They're working like stink, guv,' said Sergeant Foster, appearing suddenly at his elbow.

Jameson nodded. 'But is it actually achieving anything?'

'We've eliminated some of the possible suspects—'

'And what if the association between the two women is purely coincidental?' Jameson interrupted. 'We will have wasted valuable time finding irrelevant links. We're not even sure the same man abducted these women — if, indeed, they *were* abducted. And if they are still alive, we can't afford to waste our efforts on fruitless speculation. Each unproductive lead means lost time, and it's Dorothy Hardy and Ann Lee who will pay for our mistakes.'

Foster was used to this fatalistic streak in Jameson; it had become more marked during the past year — understandably, he supposed. But what had in the past been a helpful circumspection — a careful weighing of the possibilities — was now an inclination to impede the initial progress of investigations with anxious equivocation. Still, once he got going, Jameson still had the old spark.

'We could narrow it down by interviewing only clients with form,' he suggested, trying to stave off Jameson's infectious pessimism.

Jameson lifted his chin. He had a determined, rather emphatic jaw, which might have conferred on him an expression of obduracy but for his sensitive mouth and, rarely

— generally in the presence of women — an almost diffident manner of speech. 'It may not narrow the field by much,' he said.

'Cynic.'

'All right, it's worth a try,' Jameson said, with a look of mild amusement. 'We'll still need to know all the clientele up to ten years ago, in case this line of enquiry turns up nothing, but I think it's a sensible compromise, Bob.'

'Right,' said Foster, feeling brighter already. He turned to leave, but Jameson checked him.

'While you're at it, you might ask for a cross-reference to Sunnyside Children's Home.'

Foster's eyebrows shot up. 'Did those two—?'

'According to their boss, yes. Ann Lee and Dorothy Hardy both had dealings with the children who were sent to Sunnyside in the mid- to late-eighties. And in my experience, people will wait a long time to settle old scores.'

* * *

Chris Radcliffe wandered about the garden of her new home, thrilling to the scent of honeysuckle; it was late evening, but the day had stretched on seamlessly into night, and she had only just caught up on the paperwork of her interrupted and unsatisfactory day. The lavender was beginning to show little clusters of purple, their flower heads nudging the stems of the standard roses. The roses were at their best now, deep mauves and dusty pinks in solid globular clusters at the end of each stem.

The flat she had shared with Hugh had been spacious and comfortable, but it had not been *hers*. Hugh had conveyed that message effortlessly, unobtrusively, but nevertheless emphatically. She had stayed with him in Wallasey long after she had become impatient to move away. He would have stayed for ever if he hadn't been offered a year's sabbatical in India, working on the biological control of pests in rice. He had even paid a retainer on the flat, rather than go to the inconvenience of putting his belongings into storage and having to find accommodation on his return. Hugh liked routine and order in his life, and towards the end of their relationship, it had driven her wild with irritation. He had told her quite dispassionately that she was free to stay, if that's what she wanted. A cold dismissal after three years together.

Furious with him, Chris had set about finding somewhere to live. This little cottage had been a chance find. She had got lost in the Cheshire countryside, returning from a pub lunch with an old university friend. It had beamed at her in the evening sunshine, its sandstone walls rosy pink. The 'For Sale' sign was slightly crooked, conveying an air of mute desperation. She had been puzzled by the owners' delight that there was no chain, but Ted had set her right on the disappointments of house-selling when she had asked him. An offer was negotiated, council planning records searched, documents signed, and contracts exchanged within a month, and now, with Hugh gone barely two weeks, this was home. She found the Cheshire countryside soothing, with its easy, gentle slopes and variegation of high green hedges giving onto wide open plains.

She sighed, returning her attention to the garden. The landlord at the old flat — she was beginning already to think of it in those terms — had reserved sole use of the garden for himself and his wife, and it was the freedom of the garden she relished more than the extra space, or the knowledge that her nearest neighbours were more than fifty yards down the road. Above the satisfaction of finally being a member of the property-owning classes (an idea that still made her laugh at herself when she thought of it), above the liberation of personal solitude, above *everything* she relished her garden. She was learning with delight the diurnal rhythms of scent and temperature and activity which demarcated the different times of day. Early morning was her favourite, when the flat, waxy leaves of the aquilegia retained a little of the night's dew, and water stood like beads of mercury on the grey-green leaves. The quietest time — a time to be still — it was ruffled only by aggressive bursts of song from territorial robins, or the more speculative ballad-like melody of a blackbird or song thrush. Evening, building to its crescendo of scent and sound, was busier, but in the slow, purposeful routine of nature: bees hummed around the borders, and the constant, steady sound of activity might be broken by the wild piping of a blackbird which had sighted the neighbour's cat slinking in the shadows of the trees at the end of the garden. But there was peacefulness even in this; a sense of winding up the day's events, of winding down to the coming darkness, and Chris found that the rhythm imposed itself on her. The people she had interacted with or assessed and counselled during the day were gradually allowed to become part of the background noise of the garden, and they slipped with the sun into night.

All except Sergeant Foster.

She supposed they had got off to a bad start. Fran, daring her wrath, had misdirected Foster to the interview room, where she had been trying to convince a rather defensive mother that family counselling would help her to modify her boy's destructive behaviour. She had had to break off to take the sergeant through to her office, checking that the blind was pulled down over the two-way mirror before returning to the interview room. Her brief absence had lost her the impetus of the previous hour's discussion, and there was nothing to do but schedule another meeting and hope to resolve the situation then.

The office door was open, and as she entered, she saw the sergeant standing with his back to her, his head on one side, filching a look at her case notes.

'Did I barge in on something there, love?' he asked, unembarrassed by her appearance.

Still fuming at Fran and frustrated by the waste of time, she found the patronizing familiarity offensive. She walked to her desk and closed the file Foster had been reading.

'Is there something particular you would like to ask me, Sergeant?' she'd said with icy formality. 'I am rather busy.'

Foster responded by taking out his notebook. 'Just a couple of questions.'

He was short for a policeman, she thought. No taller than her — a wiry man, sharply dressed in a pale grey suit with narrow lapels and a slim tie. His beard was neatly trimmed and his hair carefully brushed and cut above the collar line. The shirt was of a design which always made Chris think of salesmen: a boldly striped blue and a wide collar which mismatched the proportions of his jacket lapels. He had the manner of a salesman too — at least initially — the familiarity of address, the natty style in clothes; she had almost expected him to glance around the room and make some complimentary remark about the decor.

'You worked with both Mrs Hardy and Mrs Lee.'

Chris draped one arm over the top of the filing cabinet, and its coolness abated her ill temper somewhat.

Foster darted her an impatient look. 'Well?'

'I'm sorry, was that a question?'

Foster pressed his lips together, interlocking the carefully trimmed hairs of his upper and lower lips. 'Was there anything . . . unusual in the cases you dealt with during that period?'

'Not that I remember. But it was a long time ago.'

'Ten years, give or take.' Again, he had waited for an answer, and when she remained resolutely silent, seemed to decide on a more direct line. 'How long did you work with them?'

'Eighteen months — two years, perhaps.'

'And there was nothing that sticks out in your mind? No one that Mrs Hardy or Mrs Lee mentioned?'

'In reference to what?'

He shrugged. 'I don't know. A case. Someone getting stroppy. Someone they rattled.'

Chris eyed him with renewed interest. She had expected him to ask about her working relationship with them. Their associates, personal aspects of their lives — not that she would be able to enlighten him there — but he seemed to be

17

working on a more sinister line of enquiry. 'You think their disappearances are linked, don't you?'

He didn't answer her question but waited for a reply to his own, and he seemed willing to allow the silence to continue indefinitely.

'All right,' said Chris, 'let's see . . . Dorothy Hardy had very little direct contact with the children or their parents. She collated information and attended case meetings as a representative of the LEA's administration team. I don't think she's capable of rattling or otherwise annoying anyone. Or at least that's how I saw her then. But as I say, it was a long time ago.'

'And Mrs Lee?'

She shrugged. Ann Lee had completed an Open University degree in social sciences at the age of forty, divorced her husband shortly after, and from there had gone into social work. 'Ann had a reputation as a champion of hard cases. She could be somewhat abrasive — she drew strong reactions from people. The kids called her Fishface.' Foster raised his eyebrows. 'Thing was,' Chris continued, 'Ann didn't mind. In fact, she seemed to relish the nickname.' Chris remembered Ann's protuberant eyes, half closed against the self-induced fug of smoke that drifted constantly from the cigarette drooping from her downturned mouth. 'If a kid's an unmanageable bastard I tell him so — you've got to be able to take it as well as dish it,' she would say.

'I get the feeling you didn't approve,' Foster said, and Chris became aware that she had been silent too long.

'It worked for some,' she said. 'The trouble was, Ann only had the one approach, one method — and that was attack.'

'Why do you keep talking about her in the past? She *was*, she only *had*.'

Chris felt her colour rise. 'Oh. I — I simply meant that was how she was when I knew her. It was a long time ago.'

'OK.' Foster snapped his notebook closed. 'That's it, then.'

'For what it's worth,' Chris said, surprised into an unguarded observation by the unexpected curtailment of the interview, 'if you believe they've been abducted by a parent of one of their clients, it's far more likely to be a recent decision of the panel.'

'Why d'you say that?'

'The parents Ann and Dorothy deal with are often under a terrible strain. They may be desperate for a variety of reasons — the child may be tearful and distressed, or worse than that, angry and destructive, or they may simply be lost, swamped in oversize classes and floundering in National Curriculum demands that are far beyond their capabilities. Parents want what's best for their children. They want to see them happy, to make things right — and they don't always get what they think is best. Tempers do sometimes flare, but it's generally short lived; people want to get on with their lives. Most parents make the best of what they're offered.'

'And what about the kids? Do they ever get violent?'

She smiled. 'They're people, too. They have their own frustrations and fears and worries, just as adults do. But surely you don't think a child could have done this?'

Foster stroked his beard from throat to chin with the back of his hand. 'Kids grow up though, don't they?' Delivered in his catarrhal Liverpool accent and a belligerent tone, those words had echoed around in her head for hours. That children held grudges against what they must see as high-handed authority, controlling their lives and blighting their happiness, was hardly surprising. Chris knew all about bitterness carried into adulthood . . .

A sudden noise startled her, and she turned to see the latch being lifted on the old wooden gate into the garden.

'Sorry, Chris. I tried the doorbell.' It was Simon — apprehensive that he had frightened her, restless and excited and eager, and trying to hide all of these emotions with a nonchalance he could not quite carry off.

'It's OK, Simon. I was just musing a space. I can't hear the doorbell out here,' she said, smiling, then tugged nervously at her fringe, pulling a few strands over her left eyebrow, hiding the scar over her left eye.

'I could put an extension in for you.' This was said with the enthusiasm which bubbled constantly below Simon's inscrutable exterior, then, checking himself again, he added, 'If you like.'

Simon hadn't changed much in the last ten years. He still had the same elfin quality. He was clean-shaven, and Chris couldn't imagine he needed to resort to a razor more than once or twice a week. His skin was smooth and rather pale. The eyebrows had retained the shape they had had when she had first known him, a little thicker than the eleven-year-old boy's had been, an almost straight line of mousy brown, a few shades darker than his hair.

'Have you eaten?' she asked. Eating supper together had become one of their rituals, partly born of the fact that Chris often realized only when the doorbell rang and interrupted her work that she hadn't eaten since lunch time, and partly because she suspected that Simon sometimes also forgot to eat. Hugh had once asked, in a rare fit of pique, if there wasn't some psychological term for the way women felt the need to feed their men. She had dismissed it as jealousy, not so much of Simon, but of the work which took up such a great proportion of her time and her thoughts.

They ate out on the lawn, balancing their plates on their knees as they sat on the rough wooden seat within the rose arbour, the air around them rich with the scent of roses and loud with the buzzing of bees.

'I'll have to buy a table and chairs, I suppose,' Chris said. 'This house-owning lark's all a bit new to me, I'm afraid.'

'This is fine,' said Simon, smiling. He had intelligent eyes, more liable to assess than to enquire, but she knew she was not mistaken in reading an affection, a fondness for her in the grey-blueness of this shy contact. He hurriedly ate the chicken and spring onions she had flash fried for them.

'I looked up those references you gave me. The photocopies are in the car.' He added shyly, 'I got a couple of spin-offs from them.' He insisted on going to fetch them in and returned weighted down by several books and a whole stack of photocopied papers and extracts.

Chris had been researching her new book for just over a year. The victims would put forward their own experiences in their own words; she intended to collate them into themes, but she wanted the book to be more than a collection of case studies. She hoped to explain, at least in part, the disordered affective bonds that resulted in the type of psychopathy which made men into abusers. With this in mind, she had given Simon a shortlist of four authorities on the subject, beginning with Bowlby. She had suggested Wedge and Prosser and Wedge and Essen as texts which might yield insights into the causes of failure of affective relationships, and Rutter's more modern theories on the effects of maternal deprivation would provide a counterpoint to Bowlby.

Chris laughed at the huge pile of literature he had brought, and Simon grinned. 'Have I overdone it?' he asked, blushing a little.

'There are two things an academic can never have too much of,' Chris said. 'Time—'

'And research,' Simon finished for her. 'I'll carry them through.'

Chris collected his plate, which he had discarded on the grass, and followed him through to the dining room. He explained the importance of each extract — he had read them all and taken brief notes.

She gave a low whistle and he beamed at her. 'You know, you could be doing this for yourself,' she said.

'Me? On my second-rate prison education?'

Chris considered him for a few moments. Was this the right time to broach the topic of higher education again? But Simon had half turned from her, presenting his shoulder and profile, seemingly absorbed in the photocopied sheets, frowning as he paper-clipped each set. She sighed. Best not rush him.

* * *

DCI Jameson went home for an hour at six. He needed time away from the office, and the dogs had to be walked. He barely noticed their ecstatic welcome. He showered and changed from one rumpled suit into another, hoping that his wrinkled shirt was not too visible under his jacket. It hardly seemed relevant when two women were missing — possibly dead — and he had no leads, no suspects, no sightings. But *someone* must have seen *something*. The interviews with colleagues and associates of the women were going slowly — too damn slowly. They would have to continue the interviews into the late evening if necessary; Foster could take care of that.

He spent only twenty minutes in the park, arriving home without remembering having crossed the road. He let himself in and the dogs scrambled frantically to the kitchen, their claws slipping and clicking on the wooden hall floor. The grandfather clock sounded a muted and slightly discordant quarter. He glanced at its tarnished face as he went through to the kitchen. Seven o'clock.

The dogs were lapping noisily at their water bowls, edging the steel rims against the skirting board as they emptied them, ringing a persistent, two-tone klaxon. Jameson walked across the new red tiles which had replaced the original cracked and subsiding kitchen floor, and opened the fridge door. Its white interior gleamed emptily. He sighed. There were plenty of restaurants on Lark Lane he could try; perhaps he would go out later, if he got back from work before they closed. He turned to the empty kitchen. The old pine table was scrubbed, and the surfaces cleared of the morning detritus he had left. Mrs Delaney had been — one of her mornings, as she called them. She came three times a week, although with only him to make a mess she wasn't really needed. He hadn't the heart to tell her, and anyway, she saw to the dogs and he supposed it would be unfair to them as much as to Mrs Delaney to reduce her hours. So the house was kept ruthlessly clean. Clean and sterile, he thought.

The dogs sat looking up at him now, keen-eyed, expectant, licking their lips and panting, their jaws drawn back in a grin as though at some shared joke.

'What are you waiting for?' he asked. Their tails wagged in unison, clanging against the steel bowls, and their eyebrows moved in expressive supplication. He refilled their water bowls and set about opening a can of dog food. 'How you eat this crap, I'll never know,' he said, putting a bowl down for each dog.

Tizzy and Lizzy. Zoe had resisted all suggestions that such similar names would confuse the animals. It had proved quite helpful, in fact. They both answered to either name and each set an example in obedience to the other. Zoe had been vindicated.

'*Good God Almighty* — Zoe!'

He ran to the phone and dialled the international number.

'Roz? Hi, it's Alan.' His voice sounded strained to him, and he tried unsuccessfully to relax. 'Look, I've a favour to ask.'

'It's Alan,' he heard her say. She made no attempt to disguise her apparent irritation. His ex-wife's voice was vibrant, alive and so near that Jameson felt a surge of feeling for her, despite the coldness of her tone.

'Do you know what time it is?' she demanded. 'You haven't forgotten, have you, Alan?'

'I'm working on a case,' he explained. 'Two women have disappeared. It's been non-stop the last two weeks.'

'He's forgotten,' she said to her invisible companion.

'Is that Brian with you?'

'Who the hell *would* it be at this hour of the night?'

'Look, I would have sent her something. I had it all planned and then this came up.'

'Something always does.'

'I didn't do it deliberately, for God's sake!'

'Do you know, somehow that makes it worse?' she said, her tone clipped and overly polite. 'At least if it was deliberate, you'd have had to remember in the first place.'

'I told you, I *did* remember. It's just this case. I've been working sixteen hours a day—'

'Save it for the promotion board,' she cut in. 'I'm not impressed by your obsession with your job.'

There was a silence, typical of their telephone conversations these days — a rapid attack and a few sideways swipes from Roz, followed by a pause filled with all the hurtful things they wanted to say to each other but never would.

'We got her something extra,' Roz said at last. Generally, it was Roz who broke the silence; whether out of pity or a desire to get the phone call over quickly, he could not say. 'Just in case,' she added with a sneer of sarcasm. 'And it's exactly what she wanted — a pair of roller boots, to save you guessing — should you take time out of your busy schedule to telephone your daughter on her birthday.'

He exhaled, grateful that despite her blunt refusal even to attempt to disguise her dislike of him, Roz would still shield Zoe from his lapses. 'What do I owe you?' he asked. Money was another difficult subject for them, and he added with a glow of embarrassment, 'I'll send you a cheque.'

'Don't bother. Just make sure you call her.'

Then the line went dead and he was alone again in his polished hallway with only the ticking of the clock to alleviate the oppressive silence.

3

Philip Greer had just finished breakfast when the police arrived. Breakfast was the easiest meal of the day. The night before, he had set out a bowl, which was standing on a side plate, and next to it a knife and spoon. The sugar bowl was placed dead centre on the table, and in front of it, his tablets. The toaster stood ready on the work surface next to the kettle, which contained a measured pint of water. The mug and a teaspoon were positioned in front of the spout, in exactly the right place so that he could tip the kettle and the water would go into the mug without splashing.

He had prepared everything in the proper order: tea bag in the cup, switch on the kettle. This gave just enough time to toast two rounds of bread and place them diamond-wise on the plate, which could now be moved to the left and a little above the bowl. When the kettle boiled he poured the water to one centimetre below the rim of the mug and then dunked the bag one, two, three, four times with the teaspoon before lifting it out, squeezing it and throwing it in the pedal bin, concentrating hard, because his coordination wasn't brilliant and he needed to keep his balance to make the pedal work first time. He no longer had to wash his hands after using the bin, because Flip had told him that the germs couldn't get from his foot to his hands. Of course, he knew this, it was a scientific fact, but somehow, he had needed her reassurance before he could fully accept it. He added the milk to the mug and placed it top right of the bowl. He poured milk onto the Rice Krispies next, and listened for them to start crackling before returning the milk to the fridge. On good days, he felt a tiny spurt of comforting pleasure at what he called 'crackle commencement'.

Breakfast had gone well. He had timed it all just right. Everything was OK. It was Good. And then he had heard the knock at the door. A little pang of anxiety squeezed at his gut. He hadn't washed up yet. He was supposed to wash up next. He glanced at his watch. It was 8.25 and he was supposed to wash up by 8.30. He sat, rocking just perceptibly. Maybe they would go away.

Another knock.

'I'm BUSY,' Phil shouted, feeling the anxiety build. His voice sounded frightened, and this made him more afraid. He had five minutes to get it right.

'Phil, it's Dave. Can you open up? I need to talk to you.'

'I'm not READY yet,' Phil answered, turning on the tap and squirting in the detergent. A cold wave washed over him. Wrong order. Wrong order. The detergent was supposed to go in first. Everything was going Wrong.

'Phil, you have to open the door. It's important.' Dave was the warden — a word Phil didn't like. It sounded like prison. Like the name 'warder', the American name for prison governor. But Dave was OK. He was nice. Dave understood that he got worried about things. Dave helped him when things went Wrong. But now Dave was *making* things go Wrong and he didn't know what to do.

He stood in the centre of his little kitchen, clasping and unclasping his hands. The water was spilling out of the bowl. It was going into the sink. He turned off the tap and stared in horror at the suds slipping down the sides of the bowl and catching at the base. He was breathing raggedly, little whimpers of distress escaped him. Dave called again and he ran to the door and flung it open.

* * *

Detective Constables Nolan and Flynn took a joint step back at the appearance of the wild-eyed man at the door. The guy was taller than either of them and he looked like he could do some damage.

'Everything's gone Wrong!' Phil yelled.

Nolan gave the warden a nervous glance, but Dave Quinn, a foot shorter than Phil, and carrying a hell of a lot more weight, seemed unperturbed. 'We'll sort it, Phil, don't worry,' he said.

'But I have to go to WORK!'

'Phil works three days a week at the central library on a work placement scheme,' the warden explained.

Nolan couldn't give a toss where the big guy worked. All he wanted to do was ask his questions and bugger off. Jameson had wanted Greer interviewed for two reasons: his name had come out of the files as a case dealt with by Ann and Dorothy, and he had also been seen hanging around the council offices, giving Dorothy some hassle. He shot a look at Flynn, who raised his shoulders in a gesture of apathetic wonder.

'Phil, I can drop you at work,' Quinn was saying.

'But I always get the bus!'

The big guy had his hands clasped together and was rocking slightly at the hips. Nolan braced himself for a fight, hoping that Flynn would back him. But you never could tell with Flynn; it depended if he was in the mood.

Dave Quinn spoke again. 'These are Detective Constables Nolan and Flynn—'

'What do they *want*? I haven't *done* anything!'

'We just want to ask you a few questions, Mr Greer.' This was from Nolan.

'What about?' he demanded breathily. 'I haven't done anything!'

'It's about Mrs Hardy and Mrs Lee, Phil,' Dave explained. 'You remember you went to see them?'

'I haven't. I didn't see them. I didn't do anything!'

'Bloody hell, mate!' Nolan was becoming impatient with his constant protestations. 'Put a sock in it, will you?'

Philip stopped abruptly and stared in shocked disbelief at the constable. 'What does he mean?'

Dave explained that Philip was apt to take things very literally. 'He means that he wants you to calm down, Phil. They just need to ask you a few questions and then you can go to work.'

Perhaps he caught Flynn's stolid look of contempt, because Nolan saw a flash of anger in the warden's eyes.

'Ask your questions, will you,' he said, 'and then leave the poor guy alone.'

'We haven't touched him, mate. If he dives off the deep end it's not our lookout,' Flynn said.

'Look, it's just a routine call. Let's go inside and have a little chat,' Nolan suggested, trying to defuse the situation.

Quinn winced, and simultaneously Greer looked fearfully over his shoulder into the sunny interior of his flat.

'No! No!' he shouted. 'They'll touch things! Move things!'

Flynn roused himself to action with a resentful shrug of the shoulders. 'I think we'd better just take him down the station, Nol. Question him there.'

'NO!' Greer gripped the side of the door with both hands.

Oh, Gawd, Nolan thought, *there's going to be trouble.*

'I'm not going to the station,' Greer yelled, and Quinn stepped forward, his hands raised, trying to placate the man.

'Phil—' he said.

'I'm not! I didn't DO anything. It doesn't hurt to look.'

'Look at who, Mr Greer?' Nolan asked, elbowing past the warden. 'Mrs Hardy? Mrs Lee?' He placed one hand flat on the door, holding it open.

Philip shoved him square in the chest with one huge hand with such force that Nolan cannoned into Flynn and they both fell backwards down the first few steps of the staircase.

Quinn yelled and lunged forward, but the door was shut in his face and he could hear Phil frantically scurrying about the flat. Nolan picked himself up and limped to the top of the stairs. Flynn had been winded and took a little longer.

'Bloody crazy bastard!' Nolan growled.

'What d'you expect, scaring the living daylights out of him—' Quinn stopped, silencing Nolan's protestations with an angry gesture. 'Shit!' He ran past Nolan, almost knocking Flynn down again, taking the stairs two at a time.

'What the f—?' Flynn demanded.

'I think I've just heard a window open in his flat,' Quinn called back over his shoulder.

By the time the three men reached the back of the house, Philip Greer had gone, leaving his jacket with his wallet in it hanging on the rail by the flat door, and the breakfast dishes unwashed, the suds slowly collapsing to nothing in the sink.

4

Four men were crammed into Chief Inspector Jameson's office. It was a small room, which seemed to shrink further in the present atmosphere of exasperated disbelief. Jameson sat at his desk; Nolan and Flynn stood. Foster stood to one side, his arms folded.

Nolan was mortified by his blunder — he had only been working with Jameson for a month and not only had he missed a chance to impress, he had lost the chief suspect in the biggest case he'd ever been involved in. What Flynn felt, no one could gauge; his natural laconicism was part of an overall unreadability. He stared at the modesty panel of Jameson's desk, while Nolan tried to explain.

'I asked him to come down the station, like, and he went ape, didn't he?' Nolan looked to his colleague for support, without success, and wondered for the hundredth time why Flynn always left him to do the talking.

Jameson examined him as though measuring him up for a uniform — a traffic warden's uniform, if the look on his face was anything to go by.

'I've had a complaint from a Mr Quinn,' Jameson said. 'Remember him? He's the warden of the sheltered accommodation in Mansfield Street. He says you harassed Mr Greer.

He says that Mr Greer has learning difficulties. That he's on medication and that he left that medication behind when fled from an oppressive and threatening police presence.'

'Sir — honest — the guy come out yelling before we'd said a dicky bird,' Nolan protested.

'Don't know about learning difficulties. That bugger's out of his skull,' said Flynn. The others looked at him, waiting for him to go on, but he lapsed into an intractable silence.

'He's built like a brick shithouse,' Nolan went on, when it became evident that Flynn had said his piece. 'Must be at least six foot two and heavy built, like. Shoved me into *him.*' He jerked his thumb at Flynn. 'Knocked us halfway down the stairs and slammed the door. Next thing we know, he's jumped out the window.'

Flynn nodded, giving his approval to this version of events.

'Neither of you gave chase.'

'I twisted my ankle in the fall on the stairs, sir,' Nolan said, embarrassed.

'And I've done me back in.' Flynn showed no trace of embarrassment, annoyance or anything else. It was a statement of fact, no more.

Jameson closed his eyes briefly. 'Let's go back to what Mr Greer said when you mentioned our two victims.'

Nolan checked his notes. 'He said, "I didn't do anything. It doesn't hurt to look."'

Flynn nodded. 'He's been watching them all right.'

'Yeah,' Nolan nodded, 'No danger — I mean, that's tantamount to a confession, right there.'

Jameson studied him again with that uncomfortable, penetrating stare. 'The fact is, gentlemen,' he said at length, 'there may be a great deal of danger. Wouldn't you say?'

Nolan shuffled in an agony of distress and muttered an apology. Flynn maintained his fathomless expression.

'I don't suppose you found a photograph of Greer in his flat?'

'We had a look, sir—' Nolan began.

Flynn backed him up: 'No books, no pictures, nothin'.'

'Like a clinic or something,' Nolan elaborated, 'Clean — but nothing personal anywhere.'

'Anything in his wallet?'

'A fiver,' said Nolan, 'couple of library tickets, a travelcard — that's about it.'

'Is he on the database?' The question was addressed to Sergeant Foster.

He leaned off the wall and shot Nolan a disgusted look. 'Only his name and address, and the names of his caseworkers, past and present, so far,' Foster answered. 'I've requested his file.'

He turned his attention to Nolan a Quinn. 'D'you two think you could put together a photofit?'

Nolan nodded, bracing himself against Foster's stare.

'See if any of the people we've contacted so far know Greer,' said Jameson. 'If he's watching people, someone may have seen him hanging around. He may be watching someone else now, for all we know. And if there's a photo on file—'

'I'll get it straight to you,' Foster assured him. 'Have you finished with Laurel and Hardy here, sir?' he asked, fixing them with a gimlet eye. Nolan's shoulders slumped. If Foster used those names around the lads, they'd never let it go. A thousand lifetimes wouldn't be enough to live this down.

* * *

Foster had returned to Jameson's office an hour later with two photographs. One was from Philip Greer's police file, the other was a family grouping.

'He was done for assault,' Foster said. 'Little old lady. He was in a gang that snatched her bag. Cracked two of her ribs and put her in hospital.'

Jameson nodded and picked up the family photo. 'Where's this from?'

'I got it from Greer's long-term foster parents. Their names were on file.'

'How recent is it?'

'It was taken last Christmas.' In the background was a Christmas tree decked out in little star-shaped lights. Greer stood to one side, towering above a little olive-skinned woman, his hands on her shoulders. He was smiling uneasily at the camera. Either side, at shoulder height, stood two young women — one as dark as the little woman, the other fair skinned and fair haired, both smiling, relaxed.

'A happy snap,' Jameson commented.

'The little woman is Mrs Stevens, his foster mother,' Foster explained, savouring the revelation to come. 'The dark-haired girl is her natural daughter, Isabel, and the blonde is Dr Chris Radcliffe.'

Jameson glanced up sharply. 'Didn't you interview Dr Radcliffe yesterday?'

Foster nodded. 'She didn't mention him at all. In the light of his little set-to with Nolan and Flynn, I gave her a bell just now, to see if she could give us any information.'

'And?'

'She said no. Said she had no professional involvement with "Mr Greer".'

Jameson walked to the door and reached for his jacket. Foster noticed that his boss's shirt strained a little at the belly. How had he let himself get so out of shape? He cast a critical eye over his superior's suit. It was good quality — Foster could probably buy three of his suits for the same price, but God alone knew when it had last been pressed.

Jameson turned and caught him looking. Foster's eyes flickered away, but only momentarily, and then the two men were eye to eye. A conduit of understanding seemed suddenly to open between them, and Foster knew that Jameson had read every complicated emotion that had passed through his mind: contempt and respect, impatience and sympathy in a turbulent kaleidoscope of feeling.

Foster broke the connection.

'I don't like being pissed about, Sergeant,' Jameson said, with more vehemence than the situation warranted.

Foster nodded his head in agreement. He picked up the photograph and looked at it again. 'What does she think she's playing at?'

Jameson took the picture from him and slipped it with the shot from Greer's custody file into his inside pocket. 'I don't know — but I intend to find out.'

In the short drive to Radcliffe's office, Foster filled his boss in on his meeting the previous day, and the interview with Mrs Stevens. 'Apparently, Radcliffe went to them when she was fifteen and stayed until she started working.'

'Why was she in care?'

'Mrs Stevens wouldn't say.'

'It should be easy enough to find out from her records.'

Foster nodded. 'D'you think she's mixed up in this, sir?'

'I don't know, but she does seem to be protecting our prime suspect, doesn't she? What's her relationship with Greer?'

'She's like a big sister, I suppose. He trusts her. I got the feeling he makes everyone nervous — not just police constables who should know better. He stayed with the family until he was eighteen, just after his A levels, then he moved into a hostel.'

Jameson shot him a sharp glance. '*A levels?*'

Foster shrugged. 'He's not thick, just weird.'

They pulled up outside the Georgian terrace in Rodney Street at ten a.m. The traffic was still light and they had no trouble parking. The row was well maintained, gleaming in the July sunshine. The two men stepped from the car and outside a three-storey Georgian building. The windows, two to each storey, on either side of the glistening black door, were painted white. The first-floor windows were ornamented with glossy black cast iron balconies, and all of the window sashes were thrown open in the breathless heat. There were several brass plates to the left of the door frame, one of which bore Dr Radcliffe's name and title: Consultant Psychologist.

Foster had tried the hospital, but the receptionist told him she worked from her Liverpool office Wednesday to

Friday. She had practically fallen over herself finding the address for him.

Jameson reached the second floor slightly out of breath and Foster politely refrained from comment, waiting until Jameson had recovered before knocking. The office door was panelled — old, Foster thought, judging by the way it bellowed inwards. It was painted white and bore a discreet name plate: Dr C. Radcliffe.

* * *

Chris Radcliffe was talking to a new patient, a fourteen-year-old, who was refusing to answer to any name but Len. This distressed her mother, who could not think of her darling Helena in such sweaty, working-class *masculine* terms. Len, Chris had decided, was rather fun. She had disappeared for five hours the previous Saturday and had returned with her hair in dreadlocks and woven with ragged strands of coarse purple and blue wool, a stud gleaming in her nose and a whole crop of studs and rings in her left ear.

Naturally her mother had decided it was a breakdown; Helena would never have done something so wild and irresponsible if she were sane. She was a good baby, a model child and a darling teenager until the horror of the last weekend. Len lit a cigarette and puffed at it, screwing her eyes against the smoke and wincing with every tentative inhalation.

'Enjoying that?' Chris asked.

'What the fuck's it got to do with you?'

Chris smiled. 'The technique's still a bit rough,' she said, nodding at the cigarette.

'Kiss my arse!' the girl sneered.

Chris leaned forward, frowning, as though seriously considering the suggestion. 'Would you really like me to?'

Len flushed in alarm and then, recovering, tried a nonchalant puff on the cigarette and a hard stare.

Just then the door was flung open as the intercom on Chris's desk buzzed urgently. Chris looked up at the two police officers. Foster, she recognized, but the other, taller man she did not.

She reached across the desk and flicked a switch on the intercom. 'It's all right, Nicky,' she said over her secretary's explanations, 'I'll take care of this.'

'Detective Chief Inspector Jameson,' said the taller man, showing his warrant card. 'I think you know Sergeant Foster.'

The chief inspector was about her age, perhaps a little older, and running a little to seed, Chris thought. His brown hair was cut short and brushed forward in a style slightly at odds with his face. It was a face, Chris thought, carved by experience. She glanced at Len, who was watching the two men with avid interest, the cigarette forgotten between her fingertips. 'How can I help you, Mr Jameson?'

If Jameson was relying on his interruption of her counselling session to disturb her equilibrium, he would be disappointed.

She saw a flicker of annoyance cross his face, then he placed two photographs side by side on the desk in front of her. He seemed to be watching for her reaction. She looked back at him, her eyebrows raised in question.

'You told Sergeant Foster you didn't know Greer.'

Chris glanced at the trim, sharply dressed figure of the sergeant, and then back to his superior. Jameson really was sloppy by comparison.

'I told the sergeant I had no professional involvement. He asked if Philip was one of my patients. He isn't and never has been.'

She was aware of Len's wide-eyed scrutiny. She was seated at the side of the desk, and tilted her head, trying to get a glimpse of the photograph.

Jameson spoke again: 'Obstruction of the police during an investigation is a very serious matter, Dr Radcliffe.'

'Hm,' Chris said. 'And what does your little black book of rules and regulations say about bullying and terrorizing a vulnerable young man so badly that he takes flight?' She cursed herself, knowing that she had revealed too much.

Dave Quinn had rung her as soon as he could to let her know what had happened, and now the police knew that she was aware Phil had absconded.

The look of triumph on Jameson's face confirmed that. But he had the good grace to say, 'Perhaps we should conclude this interview in private?'

'And spoil Len's fun?' Chris said. 'That would be rather churlish having piqued her curiosity, wouldn't it, Mr Jameson?'

Jameson shrugged. 'If that's the way you want it. Do you know where he is?'

'No.'

'Have you any idea where he *might* be?'

Chris's mind flew to her old flat. Philip might go there. She had not been able to coax him into coming to her new house, yet, and Phil would perhaps go to the old place out of habit. What would he do when he realized he didn't know how to find her? He would feel totally alone. Would he go to Maria's?

'You've checked at my foster parents'?' she asked, to end a silence that was becoming oppressive.

Len's eyes widened at the words 'foster parents'.

'He hasn't been near the place, as far as they know,' the sergeant said. 'Mrs Stevens said the only one who could get through to him was Flip. That's you, isn't it?'

'Yes,' Chris said.

'That what he calls you?' Foster asked.

'It's what everyone in the family calls me. It's a family name.'

'What's it short for? Philippa or what?' There was a pause, during which Chris Radcliffe studied the sergeant closely.

'Does that have any relevance?' she asked.

Jameson said, 'You are our best hope of finding Mr Greer, Dr Radcliffe.'

'I suppose that's true,' she agreed. 'But I'm afraid I can't help you, Chief Inspector. You lost him. You find him.'

'We will,' he replied. 'We've contacted the local shelters and all the main hospitals. And this photograph will help.'

He retrieved it from her desk, and Chris gave an involuntary, sharp inhalation.

'You wanted to say something, Dr Radcliffe?'

'You don't plan to release that to the papers, do you?'

'Why do you ask?'

'Because if Phil sees his picture plastered all over the press he'll panic. He's terrified of policemen and the law and prison. Some pillock gave him a custodial sentence when he was twenty and he's never really recovered from it.'

'He was convicted of a serious assault, I believe.'

'He should never have been sent down,' Chris said.

'What would you have suggested?' Jameson said, his voice tight. 'A telling-off?'

She ignored the sarcasm. 'He isn't competent to serve a prison sentence; he should have been committed for psychiatric treatment.'

'In your professional opinion?'

Chris smiled sardonically.

'And you've no idea where he might have gone?'

'None.' Chris looked away, regretting it immediately. If Jameson was any good at his job, he'd know she was lying.

The detective turned to go.

'Mr Jameson,' she called.

Jameson turned back, a sour look of disapproval on his face.

'If you publish his picture, you'll never find him. And I will hold you personally responsible if he harms himself.'

Jameson nodded. 'If he gets in touch with you, perhaps you would be good enough to contact me.' He exchanged a glance with his sergeant, and they left.

Chris deliberated a moment, then reluctantly she got to her feet and, shooting Len an amused look said, 'Are you smoking that or is it just another fashion accessory?'

Len glanced at the crooked chimney of ash at the tip of her cigarette and opened her mouth to make some acid remark but closed it again.

Score one to Radcliffe, Chris thought.

'I'll be back in a tick,' she said.

She caught up with the chief inspector on the second landing. He stopped unwillingly. 'For what it's worth,' she began, with uncharacteristic uncertainty, 'Phil couldn't have killed the dog. He's terrified of them — he'd run a mile rather than even touch one.'

Jameson gave a curt nod.

'And another thing,' Chris added, feeling she was encroaching on the policeman's turf, 'you might ask yourself why the guy who *did* take Ann left the dog in full view. As though he wanted you to know he'd got her. These are not random crimes, but you know that, otherwise you wouldn't have sent Sergeant Foster to speak to me yesterday — you've already established a link between Dorothy and Ann. He isn't after money — you don't kidnap a council worker for that.' She paused, and Jameson turned fully to look at her.

'The longer they're missing, the less chance there is of finding them alive,' he said. His professional mask slipped for a moment and Chris could see worry etched deep into his face. 'I have to find them, Dr Radcliffe,' he said. 'If you know Greer's whereabouts, please *tell* me.'

She flushed. 'You haven't heard a word I've said, have you?'

'Don't you *care* what happens to those women?'

'If I had any idea where they were, I'd tell you, believe me.'

Jameson returned a look that said she was asking too much. The worry on his face had turned to anger. He began walking slowly down the stairs. 'If I find a shred of proof that you're shielding Greer, I'll have you prosecuted,' he said. 'And I'll press for the heaviest penalties — believe *that*.'

* * *

When Chris Radcliffe drove away from her office after her last appointment an unmarked car followed at an unobtrusive distance.

Chris sat in her car for twenty minutes under the shade of a lime tree opposite her old flat. It was six p.m. Mr and

Mrs Ainsworth would probably be eating their evening meal on the lawn at the back of the house.

She studied the building closely. There was no sign of activity on the top floor, which she had occupied until a couple of weeks ago. Hugh had left for India the weekend she had moved out. They had both been too caught up in their own affairs to say goodbye properly, which Chris now regretted. The wide windows at the front of the Edwardian house were all closed, even those on the upper floors — the Ainsworths lived in constant dread of burglary. 'One hears such terrible stories, my dear,' Mrs Ainsworth had said.

Chris caught a movement behind the low grey wall that bordered the property and sat up, craning to get a better view. Only a cat. It paused, watching her for half a minute, its tail twitching, before moving with arrogant grace to clear the wall and stalking past the front of her car. *A black cat crossing your path*, Chris thought idly. *Was that good luck or bad?* She never could remember. Finally, she decided on her story and, locking the car, she walked down the path to the back of the house.

They must have heard her footsteps, for Mr Ainsworth had half risen to his feet when she turned the corner. His newspaper slipped from his knee, and he swiped at it in an effort to catch it. Mrs Ainsworth had one hand to her throat, but she swiftly regained her composure, smiling a welcome.

'Oh, Christine,' she murmured, 'it's you, dear.' Mrs Ainsworth always called her Christine — the only person apart from her old headmistress who used her full name.

Chris stepped forward, smiling. They had just finished their meal and were sipping tea in the shade. 'I hope I didn't startle you,' she said, kissing Mrs Ainsworth lightly on the cheek, aware that Mr Ainsworth had clenched his pipe unlit between his teeth — a signal that he did not want to be kissed. Although affectionate and tactile in his interactions with his wife, Mr Ainsworth could not bear physical contact with anyone else. He smiled benignly at Chris, nodding his bald head, then, removing his pipe only to invite her to be seated, he buried himself behind his newspaper.

Mrs Ainsworth was fresh and pretty in one of her expensive, understated summer outfits — a simple sleeveless dress and a colour co-ordinated cardigan draped over her shoulders. Her hair, as always, looked freshly done, and she wore a single string of pearls.

'Now then, my dear,' she said with bright curiosity, 'I am surprised to see you so soon. Are you settling in all right?' Worry creased her strangely unlined face, and Chris hurried to reassure her.

'Oh, the house is lovely.' She almost added, *And the garden is my favourite part of it,* but stopped herself in time. Her landlords were not naturally selfish people, but they enjoyed their privacy, and Chris understood why they had reserved sole use of the garden for themselves: Mr Ainsworth suffered from the most crippling shyness she had ever encountered. When Chris had first moved in, the poor man had had palpitations at the idea that she was living in sin under his roof. For two months he disappeared in a flurry of embarrassment whenever he saw her. Frustrated, she had ambushed him in the hallway one morning, determined to make him talk to her. It had been touch-and-go for a few minutes, but she had blocked his escape route, and he had discovered with a kind of innocent wonder that she was not the brash, amoral hussy he had assumed her to be. Mrs Ainsworth had approached her later that evening, her eyes brimming with laughter. 'I hear you and Charles had a little chat this morning,' she said. 'You've made quite an impression on him.' Chris had asked whether he had ever tried to get help for his shyness. 'I'm afraid the idea of actually talking to someone about it might prove too much for him. Anyway, he thinks you psychiatrists and such are charlatans — voyeurs who trick the gullible into paying huge sums of money for telling you their sordid secrets.'

Chris had laughed at the look of comical ruefulness on Mrs Ainsworth's face. 'I see,' she said. 'You *have* tried.'

She understood perfectly that her exclusion from their garden had been necessary to Mr Ainsworth's tranquillity. It had been hard enough for him to concede to the economic necessity of letting half the house to total strangers, without having to share his garden with them as well.

'I loved it here,' Chris said gently, 'but I've always dreamed of having my own place, and Hugh and I . . . It really wasn't working out.'

There was an embarrassed silence, then Mrs Ainsworth surprised Chris with a mischievous smile. 'And it's *lovely* having a garden, isn't it?'

Chris heard the newspaper rustle and sensed that Mr Ainsworth was being teased. She smiled back at the old lady, raising her eyebrows in amusement.

'I'm pleased that you're settling well,' Mrs Ainsworth said, still a little curious as to the reason for the visit. Then, tentatively, 'You know that Hugh is away at present.'

'Actually, it wasn't Hugh I came to see,' Chris said. Then she used the excuse she had decided upon in the car on her way to the house: 'I was wondering whether you'd received any post addressed to me.'

'I thought you had redirected your mail.'

'I did, but one or two things have gone astray, I'm afraid.' This was true. She'd had to request a second copy of a psychological assessment on a child she was due to start counselling after it failed to arrive, and her monthly copy of *The Psychologist* had been four days late.

'Well, I'm afraid we've had nothing here, Christine. How tiresome for you. Are you waiting for something important?'

'Nothing special,' said Chris. 'Actually, it was just an excuse to pop in on my way home. Speaking of which,' she said, checking her watch, 'I think I should be heading that way now.' She had one more call to make before going home.

She thanked Mrs Ainsworth, who insisted on walking her to the front gate and waving her off. If Phil had tried here, he hadn't announced himself to her ex-landlords, and by now he was long gone. Chris waved back, turning the corner and accelerating off, unaware of the grey Sierra following a hundred yards behind.

5

The heat in the boot of the car was suffocating. Ann tried to slow her breathing, tried not to think what he would do next, tried more than anything not to cry, because the crying made her nose run and the tape across her mouth prevented her from opening it to breathe. She permitted thoughts only of these necessities for survival: slow, shallow breathing and no tears, forbidding herself any speculation on what he had done to Dorothy and what he intended to do with her.

He had seemed relieved that explanations weren't necessary, that she had recognized him and had known why he had come. For a time, while they had talked, she had thought that she might be able to persuade him to turn himself in, but . . . She stopped, unwilling to recall his reaction when she had tried to steer him towards letting her go.

It was dark. So dark, and yet outside it must be almost dawn. They had talked for such a long time about what had happened to him, circling each other's thoughts — she avoiding anything that might trigger an outburst, and he avoiding anything that might throw her into a panic. There was a tacit agreement between them that these things should not be said in plain terms; they both knew what had happened to him, and they both knew her part in it. All that was required was acknowledgement, and she had given it. It was enough.

There had been a gentleness, a compassion, almost a reverence in his treatment of her when the talking was over, and he had taken her back to the car. Perhaps, Ann thought, he won't do anything since it's nearly daytime and he won't want to risk being seen.

The car dropped into a pothole on an uneven track and Ann groaned as she banged her head. Then, silence.

She listened with every nerve in her body, sensing his presence, but hearing only the reverberating boom of the car in her ears, like the ghost of a memory. Five, perhaps ten minutes went by, then she heard a click and felt the car tilt slightly as he got out of the driver's seat. A pause, followed by the zip of a key being inserted into the lock, and the boot was flooded with light and sound and clean, fresh, seaweed-scented air.

She heard a slicing sound, then her legs were free. She obeyed his command to swing them over the rim of the boot and he helped her out. As they walked, she found herself looking about, hungrily taking in the sights and sounds: the flat marshes, faintly glimmering in the early light, stretching out to the mudflats on one side and fringed on the other by a dense cluster of unmanaged woodland.

The moon hung low, ready to set, ghostly pale now, transparent in the strengthening light of the dawn. The sky to the west faded from indigo to violet and flushed briefly pink, then a thin rim of gold appeared on the eastern edge of the marshes, spilling light into the silty gullies and onto the tips of the trees. A lark soared high, sending out a thin watery stream of notes into a sky the colour of washed denim.

A faint track led into the woods. They followed it, stopping at the top of a steep slope. A thicket of gorse and birch and brambles crowded the edge of the path, but there were breaks here and there in the shrubby growth. He slid his arm from under hers and Ann swayed a little, feeling vulnerable without his support. She turned to him, questioning. He smiled and she thought, it's going to be just fine.

Then he looked over her shoulder, down the slope, and something passed over his face — a stolid, determined look. She turned back to the ridge and saw what he had seen . . .

* * *

William Brown Street was silent in the early dawn. The city centre was not yet awake. A distorted shadow lengthened on the museum steps and paused at the library, huge, hulking, silent. The library building provided no dark recesses, no high walls, no safe haven, but he felt the need for somewhere familiar. The rotunda of Picton Library was flooded with pinkish chemical light. He was drawn to the oblong of shadow in the little lane at the end of the art gallery and stepped into its protective cover as from fierce sunlight to cool shade. For a few minutes he stared at the crenelated pattern of the brickwork sets, trying to work out the configuration of irregular hexagons, then a noise startled him into action and Philip Greer vaulted the low iron gate of the gallery's side entrance with the agility of a cat. A quick glance over his shoulder, then he hoisted himself over the balustrade on the right of the ramp. Below, the shrubby, secluded cover of trees and bushes seemed to welcome him.

6

When they got Sunnyside Home's work records, it turned out that several pages had been torn from Dr Radcliffe's file. Similar damage had been done to both Dorothy's and Ann's records. The dates these pages covered corresponded in each file: they seemed to cover the first six months of 1987, which could mean one of two things: that Dr Radcliffe had tampered with the files to cover up her involvement in the Sunnyside Home scandal, or someone else had removed relevant details from the three files. And that meant that Chris Radcliffe could be the next intended target.

Further checks had unearthed the files of one Christine Radcliffe, pupil of St Bernadette's Grammar School for Girls, who had been placed in the care of local authority at the age of fifteen. And since *Doctor* Radcliffe would not cooperate in his enquiries, Jameson felt justified in speaking to someone who could tell him the background of *Christine* Radcliffe — someone whose honesty he felt he could rely upon.

St Bernadette's Grammar School for Girls had managed to avoid the academic slide which had resulted from many of the comprehensive school conversions of the seventies. Now St Bernadette's High School for Girls, it had maintained a reputation for solid education and good discipline within a framework of Roman Catholic doctrine.

The school's main entrance faced onto a traffic-burdened A road up a dozen or so steps. The exterior was painted cream, but traffic fumes had deposited a film of oily black residue on the lower sections of the walls. There was nowhere to park at the front of the building, so Jameson drove left into Kinglake Road. A sudden gap in the sheer, windowless walls revealed itself as a roadway of sorts, and Jameson turned into the drive, a pitted and uneven surface which led through a set of tall gates into a courtyard which had been marked out with parking slots. Courtyard was too grand a title for so dark and seedy a place. Jameson could imagine it to be depressing in winter — a wind funnel and a cold sump, a place where the sun seldom crept and frost settled with the comfortable certainty of rarely being disturbed by the shrivelling heat of the sun. Jameson backed his car into the only remaining space and scanned his surroundings as he locked up.

The car park was closed in on one side by the high cream walls of the main building. There were no windows on the first two floors and, here and there, patches of fresh paint were evident — a dogged attempt to cover graffiti which, from the frequency of the bright daubs, was something of a problem. Opposite was a high wall, sixteen feet or so of rough red brick, topped by broken glass. Behind him were the gates of the car park, and ahead another wall with concrete steps mounting it and a red-painted handrail running up the side. A blue plaque, stencilled with white lettering, read, 'Girls' Entrance'. Jameson toyed with the idea of using the rear entrance: he was curious to know what lay beyond the brick wall, but he decided against it, not wanting to distress the girls by his sudden appearance on the school playground.

He carried his jacket over his arm until he reached the corner of the building and then put it on, for despite the heat he felt it would be unseemly to announce himself to the sisters in his shirt sleeves. He walked up the steps at the front of the building and obeyed the notice below the doorbell inviting visitors to ring for attention.

The first surprise of the day was that the door was answered, not by a nun, but by a small, beetle-browed woman in secular dress. He showed her his warrant card and she glanced up sharply; her eyes were dark brown, so dark that it was difficult to read an expression from them.

'I'd like to see Sister Aloysius, if she's still here,' he said.

The secretary sniffed. 'We have three Sister Aloysiuses,' she said unhelpfully.

Jameson raised his eyebrows. He hadn't anticipated rudeness. He looked down at the artificial curls of the copper-brown head. 'The lady I wish to speak to was headmistress here in the mid-1970s.'

Again, those dark, impenetrable eyes were fixed on him. 'You'd better come in,' she said, holding the door open.

He stepped into a low modern foyer. It gave the impression of comfort without ostentation. To his right, four pink upholstered chairs in a modern design clustered genially around a pale ash coffee table. Beyond this, walled off by a glass partition, was the secretary's office. The door stood ajar and she closed it to, throwing him an accusing look. Jameson let his gaze wander away from her to the walls, which were hung with carefully mounted abstracts, evidently produced by the girls. The quality was good. To his left, two shallow steps led to a wide alcove which housed grey metal shelving neatly stacked with exercise books ranked by form.

The woman disappeared up a set of stairs opposite, and Jameson moved to admire one of the paintings. It was a large canvas, reminiscent of a desertscape, but viewed from above; he felt an almost vertiginous sense of height. It glowed with oranges, golds and browns and seemed almost to emanate heat. Occasional flecks of grey depicted stones in three-dimensional realism, but the rest was abstract and alien, exciting in its intensity.

'One of our more mature talents.' The voice was strong, dark, well modulated, deep without sounding masculine.

Jameson turned. 'I should think she is,' he remarked, smiling. 'Sister Aloysius?'

'The same.' Sister Aloysius was the second surprise of his visit: he had expected a grey-haired contemplative, rather benign and perhaps a little ineffectual, someone the girls might treat with affection but little respect. She wore a habit of sorts — a blue pinafore over a short-sleeved white blouse. A stylized cross hung by a thin cord around her neck. She even wore a wimple and cowl partly covering her hair, but Sister Aloysius was much younger than his imagined old spinster. She was not tall but managed still to seem an imposing figure. Her hair was dark brown and curled frivolously from under her wimple. Not, he realized, that it was in the least contrived: it was a purely natural phenomenon, as were her forthright blue eyes and her somehow shockingly pretty mouth. She held out her hand and this time he was not surprised by her warm, firm grip.

'How may I help you, Chief Inspector?'

'I would like to ask you about a previous pupil.'

'A previous pupil?' She paused, and something flickered across her face.

'Do you have a moment?' he asked, wondering at her hesitation.

'Of course.'

Two girls, dressed in the blue-and-grey uniform colours, but in very differing styles, walked past. They murmured a polite 'good morning' to their headmistress and prepared to walk on, eyeing Jameson surreptitiously.

'I do hope you are on your way to the library, girls, since lunch break doesn't start for another ten minutes.'

Both girls blushed prettily, then smiled. 'Just on our way, Sister,' the taller of the two said. They crossed the foyer, their flat shoes making no noise on the grey carpet, into the alcove which housed the bookshelves, then disappeared around the corner. Jameson heard a door swing shut behind them.

'End of term, sixth form exams over, and such lovely weather. Who could blame them for the odd attempt at backsliding?' Her eyes sparkled with good humour. 'You haven't told me, yet, the subject of your professional interest,' Sister Aloysius looked at him with frank curiosity.

'Dr Christine Radcliffe.'

'Ah.' She glanced towards a glass door opposite the main entrance. 'Then perhaps we can make an excuse of the need for privacy and take a stroll in the convent garden.'

The playground was as he had imagined it, but the land at the rear of the building was far more extensive than could be guessed from the facade on the main road. The school was an untidy conglomerate of Victorian and Edwardian architecture which enclosed the playground and tennis courts on two sides; part red brick and part cream-painted rendering. At the far end of the courts a modern addition jutted out at right angles to the rest, partly hidden by trees. The gardens were terraced, and each level had its dry sandstone wall, each wall its requisite cascade of aubretia, which had been carefully clipped after flowering, and had given way to snow-in-summer and pinks, lamb's ears and saxifrage.

Sister Aloysius led the way, covering a surprising length of ground with her placid, unhurried stride. Now, Chief Inspector,' she said, 'what would you like to know about Christine Radcliffe?'

'Don't you want to know why?' Not, of course, that he would have given her the real reason.

Sister Aloysius half turned to him, and that look of high good humour barely under control again lit her eyes. 'There are two likely causes,' she said, preferring to divine his reasons than listen to some fabrication which would prove both unsatisfactory and insulting to her intelligence. 'The children's home scandal or these dreadful abductions.' She was sly, but not quite quick enough to cover the twinkle of amusement at his startled glance with the mention of the children's home. 'Presumably you're checking on anyone who may have worked with the women who have disappeared, and although it must be ten years or more since Christine worked at Calderbank borough council, she has rather brought herself to the front of people's minds with her new radio programme.'

'Dr Radcliffe was in local authority care for a time,' Jameson said, a little deflated, but determined to regain control of the dialogue.

There was a palpable silence. Apparently, the nun was assessing the pertinence of the question. 'And it may have been a "client" — isn't that what they call children these days?' Her disapproval of the term was evident. 'A *client* of one or both of the women who have disappeared who has done this?'

Jameson waited for an answer to his earlier question.

'You know that Christine was in care,' she said. 'Please don't waste my time, Mr Jameson.'

'Why?'

Her eyes narrowed. 'I must assume that you're asking why Christine was in care, and not for an explanation as to why my time is precious,' she said.

Jameson inclined his head; he hadn't been able to resist the tease — Sister Aloysius had had things all her own way in the exchange, so far. 'I'm sorry,' he said. 'Yes, I would like to know why a care order was placed on the doctor.'

'Of course, she was plain *Christine* Radcliffe then,' Sister Aloysius said, with a faint, mocking smile. She paused. 'If you know that Christine was in care, then you have access to the files which detail the reasons why. You don't need my version of events.'

Jameson walked on in silence. A sparrow chirruped somewhere in the shrubbery at the top of the terrace. The scent of the pinks was heavy, almost soporific in the strong midday sunshine, but it seemed the air had cooled by several degrees. He had seen no sign of vulnerability in Christine Radcliffe. Why was it, then, that so many people seemed to feel the need to protect her? First the foster mother, Mrs Stevens, and now her ex-headmistress.

'You keep in touch with your ex-pupils?' he asked.

'A few. Not all.'

'Dr Radcliffe, for instance.'

Sister Aloysius gave him a slow, appraising look.

'You knew she worked for Calderbank borough council,' he said in explanation.

'I was invited to her graduation. I haven't spoken to her since then — though we correspond occasionally.'

'Was her father invited?'

The question was asked casually, the response a laconic and unhelpful, 'No.'

'May I ask why?'

'You may. But I would have to answer that the question would be best put to Christine.'

'Who else was there?'

'Her foster parents.'

'No one else?'

'No one else.'

So, Greer hadn't been there. Had she asked him, Jameson wondered. 'Have you ever met her foster brother, Philip Greer?'

'No,' said the sister, frowning. 'Although Christine has spoken of him.'

'Spoken?' Jameson asked sharply.

'When she was still a pupil here,' the nun explained, sounding mildly irritated by the implication that he'd caught her in a lie.

'What did she say about him?'

Sister Aloysius sighed, glancing impatiently at her watch. 'Not a great deal. Perhaps you wouldn't mind getting to the point. Lunch break is about to start and I have a number of girls to see.'

'Both Mrs Lee and Mrs Hardy worked on Philip Greer's case at one time or another.'

'I see.' Sister Aloysius stopped at a heavy oak bench which stood beneath the inviting shade of a London plane, and sat looking down over the terraced flower beds, a blur of pink and white in the startling glare of the sunshine. She was calm and unreadable. Jameson sat beside her, sensing that this was not a moment to rush. At length, Sister Aloysius began.

52

'I owe you an apology, Chief Inspector. I had thought your questions prying and impertinent. I was wrong.' She considered a moment. 'Philip was only a toddler when Christine first met him — perhaps three or four years old. They were very close from the start. Christine has a real affection for him which goes far deeper than mere pity: the boy has learning difficulties, I understand, and has an obsessive nature.'

'Philip has disappeared,' Jameson said.

'Abducted?'

'Absconded.'

'Oh.' Sister Aloysius folded her hands and bowed her head. Jameson almost fancied her to be praying. He found the notion embarrassing and shifted uncomfortably.

'I take it Christine isn't being very helpful.'

No reply was necessary. A high, mechanical bell rang out across the still air from the building in three rapid bursts.

'Could she be deliberately shielding him?' Jameson asked.

'If you're asking me would she protect a kidnapper, I would say no. But if she believes Philip to be innocent—' She stood, smoothing the front of her pinafore. Girls slowly spilled out of the building. Jameson had not previously taken in the myriad of little doorways both at ground and basement levels.

He framed his next question carefully. 'You think she would protect a man the police want to interview?'

'If she truly believed him innocent, who could blame her?'

'I should have thought you would, Sister. After all, isn't it rather arrogant to assume that she knows better than the law — that she can dispense justice more fairly?'

'Christine Radcliffe is a highly principled woman. Her sense of justice is well developed, I can assure you. She is also a trained and respected psychologist. If she believes Philip Greer to be innocent of any crime, I for one respect her judgement.' Sister Aloysius shot Jameson an amused look. 'But aren't you making assumptions of your own, Chief Inspector?' In answer to Jameson's unspoken question, she

53

went on, 'You have no evidence that Christine *does* know where Philip is, otherwise wouldn't you have arrested her? So, this supposed arrogance and flagrant disregard of the law could be no more than mere fancy on your part.'

'I am not given to flights of fancy.'

'No, I don't imagine you are.'

Jameson felt perversely offended by her ready agreement.

She added, driving the point home with unnecessary force, 'A fanciful nature is not always a weakness, Chief Inspector.' She began walking down the pathway, negotiating the unevenly worn sandstone steps with more sureness than Jameson himself. 'If you want to know more about Christine Radcliffe, Mr Jameson, I suggest you talk to her. I've always found her a pleasant, communicative girl. Tell her your reasons for suspecting Philip Greer.'

But Jameson wanted more from the headmistress. 'The scar on Dr Radcliffe's forehead—'

Sister Aloysius waited.

'Did her father give her that?'

By now they were at the edge of the playground, which was well populated with girls from age eleven to sixteen. Some of them wore pale blue blouses over grey skirts, others, striped blue cotton dresses. The younger girls immediately took up rope games and a curiously regimented game which involved four people standing at each corner of one of the concrete paving slabs and moving in a complicated pattern of diagonals dictated by a girl in the centre of the square. Only the older girls, it seemed, were allowed in the gardens. The benches on each terrace were quickly filled by them, eagerly pushing up sleeves and rolling down socks to catch the sun.

Jameson stared into the headmistress's face, impatient for an answer, hoping to embarrass her into replying.

'I repeat, you have access to Christine's file,' she said.

'She never gave a believable account of what happened to her.'

'Christine never spoke directly to me of his violence. But I have no reason to disbelieve the social services' interpretation

54

of her injuries and her reaction to her father.' She paused, and Jameson had the impression that she was deciding how much to reveal. 'I visited Christine in hospital,' she said. 'This was shortly after her admission. I was convinced that she was being less than honest in her account of what happened. I assumed that she was trying to protect her father.'

'So *you've* read her file,' said Jameson.

He saw a muscle jump in her jaw. 'A painful but necessary duty.' They had reached the rear entrance to the building and Jameson became aware that the interview was coming to a close. Sister Aloysius took a breath. 'Why do you doubt her?'

'She said at first that she had been attacked on her way home from school.'

'She was afraid.'

'People act out of character when they're afraid, don't they?' he said.

Sister Aloysius hesitated. 'I want you to think well of Christine, Mr Jameson.' A group of girls dawdled past them, linking arms and talking quietly. Sister Aloysius took him by the elbow and guided him through the rear entrance to the top of the steps above the makeshift car park. 'I met Christine's father only once, and that was enough to convince me that he had indeed caused Christine's injuries. He came to school shortly after a care order had been granted, refusing him any contact with her. He threatened to kill us all if we didn't bring her to him.'

'What came of it?'

'The police were called. He was ejected. He didn't come back.'

'And that convinced you?'

'You may think that we religious types spend our lives protected from the seamier side of life, sheltered from difficulty and violence. To an extent you are right. But I have worked in the community. And I have met even here, in this civilized and cloistered environment, some disturbed and difficult people — both parents and children. Christine's father had a rage in him that was like a blazing inferno. A destructive maelstrom of uncontrollable urges and needs and wants and desires.' She stopped, then looked directly into Jameson's eyes. 'I honestly believe he would have killed Christine, if she had stayed with him.'

'The way I read it, he was in danger himself.'

Sister Aloysius folded her hands across her middle.

'It's a matter of record, Sister Aloysius,' Jameson said. 'Her father was treated for a knife wound the same night she was taken into hospital after what appears to have been a savage beating.'

'That doesn't make Christine a criminal, Mr Jameson. It doesn't mean she would abduct two women.' She tilted her head and regarded him with her bold, blue eyes. 'But you don't believe that any more than I do.'

'I think she's not telling us what she knows about the children's home connection. I'm *certain* she's shielding Philip Greer,' he said. 'I just wish I knew whether she's dangerous or *in* danger.'

* * *

The dogs had an extended walk that evening. Alan Jameson had fallen into the habit of crossing the wide arc of Aigburth Drive and letting the two border collies off the leash in the perimeter of Sefton Park, returning home after only ten minutes, but tonight he allowed them to run off, squabbling and chasing, rejoicing in the freedom of this rare treat. He followed them deeper and deeper into the park, across the broad pavilion and down into the quieter rhododendron-lined paths. They trotted ahead, quarrelling happily over a stick, seemingly oblivious to the teenagers on skateboards and rollerblades who roared past them at speed, down the tarmac paths towards the duck ponds. It was eight o'clock, and the day's warmth lingered like a heavy quilt, almost smothering breath in its stifling heat. There was no sign of a break in the weather.

Jameson pondered morosely that it reflected the status of this case, which stagnated along with the great globule of stationary high pressure which had stalled over the British Isles on its way to somewhere else more used to and better equipped for its unremitting sunshine and unforgiving heat.

Abduction or murder? Or both . . . If Dorothy and Ann had been abducted for money, why had there been no communication with the families? No ransom demand had been received, and that, Jameson knew, was a bad sign. He was suddenly frantic to be back at headquarters, even though there was nothing useful he could do; it was no more than an irrational feeling that his presence would have some catalytic effect.

And Greer was still on the loose. He recalled his conversation with Dr Radcliffe earlier that day. He remembered a strand of hair from her fringe quivering over her left eye as she had told him that Greer should not have been imprisoned. It was then he had noticed the fine white scar which traced the edge of her left eyebrow and then bisected it, ending in a hooked curve at the outer corner of her eye. She appeared unconcerned by it. Nevertheless, he thought, she does wear her fringe swept left across her forehead. He had found himself wanting to know more about that scar and how she got it.

Did Dr Radcliffe know where Greer was? She had paid a visit to her old flat after finishing at the office, which could of course be entirely innocent. But she had lied to him about not having any idea where Greer might be, he was certain of that. He whistled the dogs and they raced back, panting. He had reached the great grey wishing stone, a glacial erratic of small-grained granite, and was approaching the palm house. At the adjacent adventure playground, families still dawdled in little clusters here and there, and Jameson didn't want the dogs to start herding the children as they were apt to do if unchecked.

Why was Radcliffe so unwilling to help him find Greer? Was it concern for a man she regarded as vulnerable? Or in protecting him, was she protecting herself? It seemed unlikely — even preposterous — that the psychologist should be involved directly in the abduction of the women. But if Greer had acted out of a twisted sense of loyalty to her — if she and Greer had shared secrets about their past — who could say what she might do to protect him? Like tampering with the files, for instance? She had shared a foster home with Greer. Why was she there? Had her father really brutalized her? Since she had never spoken about the assault after the night of her admission to hospital, who could be sure? Maybe one of the women had turned up something in the records which Radcliffe didn't want generally known. If the one had told the other . . .

He shook his head. It was ten years since Radcliffe had worked with either of the victims — surely too long to wait to act on blackmail threats. Could one or both of them have been blackmailing her all that time? Could there be a connection with the radio programme? Being linked with the mismanagement of the children's home certainly would not do Radcliffe any favours with the media — and they would be itching to implicate some high-profile personality. What were the chances that she was simply protecting Greer, as she had always done? On the other hand, she might be entirely innocent — it could be someone else who had damaged the files. Did she already know Greer had done a runner when Foster had telephoned her to ask if she knew him? Protecting a friend — someone she thought of as almost a brother — was understandable. Even so, she was pushing her reticence to the point of obstruction.

And what of Greer? A contradictory character: he was better qualified than some of Jameson's own colleagues and could manage the classification system of a Liverpool central library with little formal training, and yet Dr Radcliffe had described him as having learning difficulties. Jameson had spent an hour reading through his file. Greer had been bussed to a comprehensive school outside the area, which had a special unit for children with language and communication disorders. He had left at eighteen with five GCSEs and two A levels — maths and physics — both A grades. It seemed that this model student's main 'learning difficulty' was his tendency to obsess about things, places, routines — and people.

Dorothy and Ann had taken care of him for ten years, but he had been assigned new caseworkers several months previously, after which he had been seen regularly outside the council offices in Pyke Street, apparently waiting for the two women. Eyewitnesses had seen him talk to Ann Lee on a number of occasions and to Dorothy Hardy once. Dorothy had seemed upset by the encounter and had been seen shouting something at Greer as she hurried to her car.

There was also a mysterious second man. Fair haired or blond, depending on the witness, he had loitered around the offices, occasionally talking to the women clerks. Called himself Dickens or something similar. He had asked a lot of questions, said he worked for a national newspaper but didn't name it. Surveillance of the premises since this report had come in had, predictably, turned up nothing. Either he was careful or he had achieved his goal and had moved on to pastures new. But if the abductor *had* moved on, then there were other people at risk and Dorothy and Ann had less chance of coming out of this alive, and he, Jameson, was powerless to help them.

Unless it really was Greer. Greer's obsessions formed a major part of his coping strategy — if his routines were disturbed, *he* was disturbed. He seemed to need the repetition of actions in a prescribed order to maintain his troubled equilibrium; any deviation provoked extreme responses. At what point, Jameson wondered, does neurosis become psychosis?

Perhaps Greer had wanted the two women to resume his regular sessions in order to rebalance his teetering stability. And when they had refused — as they must — did he lose control? But Dorothy was an administrator, a writer of reports: she wouldn't have regular sessions with Greer, so why would he fixate on her? Why did any lunatic fix on an innocent victim? They made their own fantasies and played by their own rules, Jameson reasoned. Greer was obsessional. He had concentrated the monumental intensity of his ideas, notions — and fantasies, yes — onto these two women for reasons Jameson could only guess at. He had a sense of time trickling away like water through his fingers, and with every drop Dorothy's and Ann's chances of survival were diminished.

* * *

It was frustrating not being able to do anything more tonight, but Chris calculated that she just had time to shower and change and drive back to Liverpool in time for the radio slot at nine. She packed a change of clothes into a George Henry Lee carrier bag and left it next to her briefcase, then she keyed into her office PC and made a note of her appointments for the next day. The last was at three p.m., which would leave her plenty of free time to try the squats Dave Quinn had suggested.

Dave knew her as Phil's friend, and he had been keen to help out. He had been surprised to see her and had begun explaining in some confusion what had happened the day before, until she had cut across his fumbled account to tell him that she knew all about the police foul-up and that she intended to find Phil.

'I'll try the library tomorrow,' she had told him, 'and the hostel where he used to live. He mentioned a guy he used to talk to there.'

'Could he be staying with friends?' Dave asked.

'Not that I know about. As far as I know, I'm his only real friend. He's got my new address, of course, but he's never been there, and I don't think he'd travel halfway to Chester on his own.'

Dave pulled at his lower lip. He had not shaved, and a fuzz of greyish shadow crowded the folds of his heavily jowled face, glittering dully in the evening sunshine. They were sitting on deckchairs with the looming shadow of Dave's high

Victorian terrace at their backs. The sun shone hazily over the wall at the end of the property onto the wilting stems of the sunflowers which sprang up in places near the wall, like Brobdingnagian apparitions in a bad dream. They foreshortened the little rough patch of grass Dave called a garden.

'If he's lucky he'll've found a squat,' said Dave, rasping one hand over his chin, then up over his short-cropped hair in a washing motion. 'Liverpool isn't a good place to sleep rough.'

'Can you give me any addresses?'

Dave nodded. 'I'll write them down for you.' He extricated himself from the low chair with remarkable agility for such a heavy man, then stepped directly from the narrow path that edged the house into his kitchen. Chris listened to him opening and closing drawers, trying to find pen and paper amid the chaos, while keeping up a constant stream of muttered obscenities.

He emerged a few minutes later, looking flustered. 'I'm not normally this disorganized,' he said, smiling apologetically. 'I've put some Birkenhead addresses in as well — you never know.' He studied her for a moment. 'Only . . .' he began diffidently. The sun was behind him; it flared in a halo around his head as he moved, and Chris raised a hand to shield her eyes.

'Leave it till morning,' he said. 'It's too dangerous going around these places at night.' He smiled a little, deepening the creases of his face. Chris had a fleeting image of a friendly Shar Pei, all wrinkles and folds, loose skin and placid temperament. 'And dress down a bit, eh?'

Chris looked down at her immaculate linen suit, her expensive shoes and the cream leather shoulder bag resting at her feet. 'Good advice,' she laughed.

It was Dave who had noticed her escort. 'Got protection, have you?' he asked.

'Not that I know of.'

Dave described the car, reading her the registration in a conversational tone while shaking her hand. She made a mental note and walked to her own Renault without a glance in their direction. They had followed her, two or three cars behind, all the way home. A man and a woman.

* * *

'Hey, gobshite! I'm listenin' to that, aren't I?' Darren Lewis threw a chip at his younger brother, who ducked and continued twiddling with the dial.

'It's only *talkin'*!' he snarled.

Lewis scraped his chair back and lunged at his brother, who immediately screamed for his mother.

'Get off him!' Julie Lewis landed a full-palmed smack across her son's ear, leaving suds from the dishes in the peach fuzz of his hair, which was all that remained after his visit to the barber's the day before.

'Frig off, 'eh?' Lewis yelled, spraying half-chewed chips and bread onto the kitchen table. 'I'm tryin' to listen to the programme!'

'Look at the bleeding mess you've left,' Julie said. 'You eat like a pig, throwing good food around. And you can stop your bleedin' swearin' an' all!'

Darren saw this was another row he couldn't win. 'I can't even listen to the bloody radio in me own home,' he grumbled, storming to the back door and dragging his jacket from the back of his chair.

'You don't live here no more!' his mother screamed after him, slamming the door with such force that the windows rattled in their frames.

He tuned in to Liverpool FM as soon as he slid into the driver's seat of his car, then he swung his legs over the gearstick and propped his feet up on the dashboard. His head rested at an awkward angle, half out of the open window, and the sun glistened on his hair like autumn light on wheat stubble.

'Our next caller is Jeff from Childwall!'

* * *

62

Chris Radcliffe sat opposite Jilly Henderson, surrounded by technical clutter and soundproofing and racks of CDs. She still couldn't get used to the cramped conditions of the DJ's studio. 'Go ahead, Jeff, you're through to Dr Chris.'

Chris sighed inwardly. She had asked for the 'Doctor' to be dropped, but Jilly was adamant that she couldn't speak with any authority *without* the title. Jilly was a pretty, long-haired twenty-five-year-old with a chirpy manner and a brittle smile. Only her towering ambition enabled her to quell a natural diffidence.

'Wor' I wanna know is,' Jeff began, and Jilly rolled her eyes, grimacing at Chris, 'how can Calderbank council have let them get away with the systematic abuse of children's rights for so long.'

Chris felt a thud of anxiety.

'You're talking about the Sunnyside Children's Home scandal, are you, Jeff?' Jilly asked brightly.

Chris drew a finger lightly across her throat, her eyes widening. 'I don't know the details of the case,' she said.

'You what?' Jeff's voice rose half an octave, immediately on the attack. 'You *worked* for them, didn't you? You must've read the papers. It must've went on for ten or more years, and you're saying *you didn't know?*'

'I'm sorry—' Chris began.

'Here y'are then.' There was a crackling of paper, during which Chris signalled to Jilly again, while Jilly gestured helplessly. 'I'll give you the details, shall I? Kids held down and pumped full of drugs. Locked in their bedrooms for punishment with no bedding — wearing only their underwear. Kept in solitary confinement, half starved and freezing bloody cold!'

'Jeff!' Jilly called, laughing nervously. 'I'm afraid we can't discuss this—'

'Boys beaten with a stick—'

Jilly pulled the plug and started playing the next record.

* * *

Lewis laughed till he thought he would choke, hammering the steering wheel, chortling and howling till the tears ran down his face. 'Christ! She near shit herself!'

Two girls walking past turned slightly to look back at him, smiles ready, willing to share the joke. 'What are you lookin' at?' he demanded, and their smiles froze. He stared after them as they hurried on, feeling a spurt of pleasure at the fear in their faces.

7

'Bloody hell!' Nicky exclaimed. 'You look like you've had a heavy night.'

'Do I?' Chris peered into the proffered compact mirror and shuddered. 'I suppose I'd better slap on a bit of make-up,' she said. 'I spent half of it trying to convince Jilly Henderson her career wasn't in ruins.'

'I heard it,' Nicky said, sliding her a sideways look.

'You did warn her about filtering out any questions on the children's home?' Chris put up both hands at Nicky's look of righteous indignation. 'I know, it isn't the sort of thing you'd forget.'

'I spoke to her at half seven, that's half an hour before she goes on air,' Nicky said, pained by the implication.

Chris apologized and put out her tongue, examining it in the mirror. 'God, I feel rough,' she said. 'What does it mean when your tongue's coated green?'

'Advanced liver rot,' said Nicky decisively. They had worked together too long and liked each other too well to allow petty resentments to cloud their relationship.

Chris groaned. 'D'you think coffee'd cure it?'

'It's got you rattled, hasn't it?'

'What? Dorothy and Ann?'

'That an' all — but I meant the children's home thing. D'you want to talk about it?'

Chris thought for a moment. Perhaps it would be good to unburden herself. Then reality reasserted itself. 'No. It was ten years ago, Nicky. Best leave it in the past.'

Nicky gave her a pert look and said, 'But it's not staying there, is it?' She took back her compact, clicking it shut. 'The *Herald's* doing one of those exposés.' She left Chris with the newspaper and went to make coffee.

At three p.m., Chris had changed into an old pair of jeans and a T-shirt. She slipped out of her shoes and into trainers. Catching her reflection in the mirror, she grimaced. 'Very authentic.' She turned her head better to appreciate her tidy chignon, then, removing the comb, shook her head vigorously and her hair fell free around her shoulders. She checked the mirror again, evaluating the effect. 'Better,' she conceded, then washed her face until no trace of make-up remained.

'Will I do?' she asked her secretary.

Nicky had been with her since she set up in practice on her own. She had come to interview fresh from college, actually bringing with her the RSA certificate in typing she had recently gained. Chris had seen her grow from a naive and rather serious teenager into a confident, able young woman. She had attended Nicky's wedding, seen her through her first pregnancy and had even shown up for the christening, despite her distaste for church ceremony. Nicky had her own style, owing more to the sixties revival than to the classic look preferred by Chris.

'You look almost human,' Nicky said, her lips pursed. Then a little frown produced two parallel lines between her neatly plucked eyebrows. 'Sure you don't want me to come with you?'

'You're needed here,' said Chris, 'to fend off queries from callers.' She checked the road below her window. It was a different car today, but they had been stationed outside since she had arrived.

'I've called your cab,' Nicky said. 'It'll pick you up in Roscoe Street, outside the auctioneer's.'

Chris slipped out the back way into Roscoe Street, picking her way around the mounds of black bin bags piled ready for collection, and crossed to the low, nondescript auction rooms of Turner and Sons. There was a strange stillness; on most days, summer or winter, a wind swept up the street from the river front, but today it crouched in the heat, emanating a festering air of expectation. Outside the auctioneer's a sign read 'SALE TODAY'. Auctions were held in the morning, but a few people still came and went, arriving in vans to pick up their purchases, leaving a couple of minutes later. The taxi driver seemed relieved to see she wasn't carrying anything.

'You'd be surprised what I've been asked to carry in this taxi, queen,' he said. He was further gratified when Chris told him that she had several calls to make. He was a neatly dressed man of indeterminate age, but judging by his smart appearance, he was probably one of the old guard who had gained their licences when there was still a dress code under the hackney carriage licensing laws, when Liverpool cab drivers still had to 'do the knowledge', and tips were measured in half-crowns.

Within minutes the driver had dropped her outside the central library in William Brown Street. He parked a little further up the road, opposite the grand, sweeping steps of the museum and read his paper while he waited for her.

No one could help her. Phil had kept pretty much to himself, as she had expected, and he had made no friends at work. The hostel was more promising, although the social worker was initially suspicious of her. The police had already paid a visit and he was clearly on edge. He must be new to the hostel — Chris had never seen him before.

'Phil and I shared a foster home for a time,' she said, handing him her business card. His hands were long and thin, the nails perfectly clipped and pale pink.

'Oh,' he said. 'You're Dr Chris! Heard you on the wireless last night,' the social worker said. 'Aren't you a bit young to be his shrink?' There was no hint of flattery, no suggestion of flirtation in this; he was merely making an observation. His face was gaunt, and his skin had the greyish tinge of a convalescent. Chris found it almost painful to look at him.

'We were fostered by the same people,' she explained. The social worker studied her more closely. 'Phil's like a kid brother to me.'

The social worker tapped his teeth with her card, then handed it back to her. 'OK,' he said, 'you want to talk to Jake — Jake Dixon. But he doesn't hang around the hostel during the day. Come back after six.'

Chris directed the taxi to the first of the addresses Dave Quinn had given her. He dropped her a couple of streets away — puzzled, but willing to enter into the spirit of the venture — and Chris walked the rest. It wasn't far from Phil's flat by Princes Park, and she reasoned that he was likely to go to the nearest place: Phil was fearful of new places, and anyway he had left his travelcard and money when he had fled.

It was a quiet, leafy street. The houses were large, detached or semi-detached and most were hidden behind high sandstone walls and mature trees. Chris looked up at the old building. The front door and windows were covered with corrugated iron. It had once been an attractive family home to a merchant or professional, but now its paintwork was flaked and peeling, the mock Tudor beams cracked and grey. There was a damp mossy smell about the place, despite the intense heat of the afternoon, and looking up, Chris saw that the guttering and downpipes had fallen or been ripped away in places and the brownish brickwork was stained in a wide green arc where rainwater had infiltrated the clay.

The tarmac pathway was slippery underfoot, though the moss had turned brown in patches where dappled sunlight penetrated the shade of the trees. There seemed to be no way in. She walked to the side of the house and discovered a 'For Sale' sign mouldering next to some old railway sleepers. Knotweed sprang up in tufts, pushing through the tarmac as if through soft loam. Chris brushed aside the tall growth to reach the rear of the building.

It, too, had been made secure, but Chris noticed as she scanned the upper floors that the attic window was uncovered, and she thought she discerned movement in the room beyond. She tried the window panels on the ground floor, but they were all bolted tight. When she pulled the back-door panel it gave easily; the bolts which seemed intact to casual inspection had been sheared or cut except for the top bolt. Chris swung the oxidized metal sheet at an angle. It groaned in complaint, then gave a little more, and she sidled through into the dark interior of the house.

It was pitch dark after the sunlight outdoors. Chris closed her eyes for a few seconds and then opened them, still able only to determine that there was little furniture in the room. Wishing she had brought a torch, she inched carefully forward with one arm outstretched. Ahead she could just distinguish the outline of a door. Presumably it led to the hallway and the stairs. She hoped to talk to whoever she had seen at the upper window.

The hallway was partly illuminated by a dingy grey light from the front door. The iron sheeting bolted to the exterior had been cut square, allowing a tiny segment of welcome light through the fanlight above the front door. The staircase lay to her left and two doorways to her right. She heard a small movement and whirled in the direction of it. The sound had come from the dark interior of the first room.

'Hallo?' she called, wondering how one introduced oneself in a squat. 'Anyone home?' She heard a snuffling sound like subdued laughter and stepped into the room, then tripped and fell.

'Friggin' 'ell, watch where you put your feet, eh, luv?' Chris apologized, although she was sure she had been tripped deliberately. 'Why can't you watch where you're going?' the man demanded.

''Cos it's as dark as an arsehole in here, that's why.' The second voice had a wheezing, gravelly deepness.

'Well you should know, Alf lad,' the first voice said. A rumbling, bronchitic laugh followed this observation; it came from the direction of the second voice.

The first voice seemed to have got to its feet. A dry rattling sound preceded the unmistakable rasp of a match being struck and a moment later the room was lit by a small globe of yellowish light. The first voice had lit a hurricane lamp. He held it to Chris's face, studying her closely.

'You're a bit lost, aren't you, girl?' said the voice, which was slowly resolving into a youngish man. He was bearded and wore his long dark hair — brown or black, she couldn't tell in the poor light — in a ponytail.

'I'm looking for someone,' said Chris.

'Your lucky day then, isn't it?' he said with a smile, ''cos you found him — the man of your dreams.'

'Lay off, Bollo,' the second voice wheezed. 'The girl's only askin' for help.'

'Who are you callin' Bollo?' the young man demanded, turning from Chris in the direction of the voice.

'I'm Chris,' she said, stepping over Bollo's bedding and offering her hand to the older man. He seemed taken aback at first, but took her hand, smiling at the novelty of it.

'I'm Degsy,' said the young man, anxious not to lose his earlier advantage. 'Short for Derek.'

'Short for dickhead,' grumbled Alf, his voice like gravel in a mixer.

'Fuck off!' Degsy yelled, lashing out with a foot and missing.

Alf chuckled. 'How can we help you, luv?'

'I'm looking for a friend.'

'Aren't we all?' said Degsy.

'His name is Phil — Philip. I'm worried about him.'

'They's no Phil here, luv,' said Alf.

'He may not have told you his name. He's very — shy,' she explained. 'But he's distinctive. Very tall. Early twenties, dark brown hair.'

She saw Alf shake his head in the gloom. 'Sorry, luv.'

'Give us your phone number, I'll give you a bell if I see him,' said Degsy.

'Maybe I can call back in a few days, if that's OK?' Chris peered into the darkness that swathed Alf.

'Any time, love,' said Degsy.

'Make it early in the morning, girl,' said Alf. 'Bollo here's still sleeping it off then. He'll be less trouble. I'll keep an eye out for your mate.'

'Thanks. Thanks a lot, Alf.'

'Hey!' said Degsy, affronted by the omission, 'Worrabout me then?'

Chris shook her head, smiling. She stepped lightly into the hallway and found her way easily through the large old-fashioned kitchen. There were two Primus stoves on the floor, and at the sink a small, slight figure was filling a bucket with water. She turned, startled by Chris's sudden appearance. She was a sickly-looking girl, pale and apathetic.

'Hi,' Chris said. 'Are you the girl I saw at the attic window?' The girl looked at her with big oval eyes; she shrugged but did not speak. 'I'm looking for a friend,' she said.

'I haven't seen him,' the girl said.

'Can't be easy washing nappies with no hot water.' A small mound of towelling nappies lay at the girl's feet.

She shrugged, defensive, a sulky look spoiling the delicate prettiness of her elfin features.

'At least you've running water,' Chris tried.

'Oh yeah,' said the girl, 'all mod cons.'

Chris tried to think of something to say which wouldn't offend the girl, but she reflected that there wasn't much she could say that wouldn't sound patronizing. She shrugged. 'Well, I'd best be off.'

The girl seemed about to say something, a spark of urgency lighting her face for a moment, but it was quickly extinguished, and she retreated into her sullen watchfulness. There was nothing more to be said. Chris left reluctantly, edging out through the barricaded door the way she had come.

Chris tried two other squats before deciding she had better get back to her office. The last was well organized, run along the lines of a commune. Two men and a woman were cooking dinner when she arrived. She had edged past the corrugated iron sheeting into the kitchen and had been greeted by a man carrying an axe. He relaxed when he saw her, but she had found herself subjected to close questioning before any of them would talk to her. Theirs was a relatively stable group, they had explained, but they did have contacts among the more transient sector of their community, and they were willing to pass the word. Chris was impressed by their organization: they had opened up the upper floors of the house to let in light, the place was clean and well lit — even the barricaded rooms of the ground floor — owing to the fact that one of their number had illegally reconnected the electricity.

The axe man had escorted her to the front of the house. 'Sorry if I frightened you earlier,' he said. 'There's a mad bastard loose, burning out squats. Insurance jobs, probably, but one commune had been served with an eviction notice a couple of weeks before. They were fighting it in the courts — seems the owner got impatient. This place is vulnerable because of the upstairs windows being unboarded. We're not taking any chances.'

Chris called in at the hostel on her way back to the office. Jake Dixon had been and when he'd heard she was looking for him, he had packed his few possessions and gone. 'He can be a bloody-minded bastard when he wants to be,' the social worker said. He looked even more tired than when she had seen him earlier. His pale blue eyes were shadowed and his shoulders slumped. He was a tall man, with thick, soft, short-cropped hair. 'I told him who you were,' he went on, looking somewhere over her shoulder. 'But he kept saying you were a front for the filth — er, police — and, like, he said he wasn't staying where he was going to be hassled.'

'Did you tell him I was trying to find Phil?' Chris asked, feeling a mounting desperation. Dixon was her best hope of finding Phil.

''Course I did,' he said, affronted. 'He kept muttering on about police harassment and . . .' He shrugged, apparently too exhausted to continue with the explanation. 'We're not a bail hostel. He's not a criminal. I couldn't force him to stay. Pity you didn't get here a few minutes earlier — you must've only just missed him.'

Chris had a sinking sensation in the pit of her stomach. 'Blond bloke? Spiky haircut — rides a motorbike?' She had seen him leave.

'Superb bike,' the social worker said longingly. 'Honda Goldwing, a classic. Makes you wonder, though. What's a guy like that doing dossing down in a hostel? I mean, when he can afford a dream of a bike like that?'

'Do you know anything about him?' Chris asked. 'Does he have any friends or family? What's his background?'

'He spent most of the time chatting up Phil. Latched onto him just after he came here. Phil's a bloody mine of information if you don't mind the way he goes on. Jake'd only been with us a week and at that time he was being pretty friendly with everyone — a bit nosy, like, but OK, you know. To be honest, I thought he was getting a bit restless. I didn't expect him to stay much longer. We were having dinner and Jake said something about going to see his social worker the next day, and Phil started reeling off names and departments, ID numbers and Christ knows what. He narrowed it down to one of two possible workers. It was eerie.

'Jake seemed dead impressed and made some joke about Phil knowing more about Calderbank council than the director of finance. Well, you know Phil, he never gets a joke, so he says, "Peter Brannigan? Room number 503." He even reels off his phone extension. "I know much more than Mr Peter Brannigan." Jake says something like, "You know what you are, Phil, mate? Buried bloody treasure!" They were always together after that . . . funny thing.'

Chris waited for him to go on, but he seemed engrossed in the idea which had just struck him, trying to make sense of it. She prompted and the social worker came to, like a sleeper from a dream.

'Well, I was thinking about him after you went. You know, the Goldwing and that. I don't know how the hell he got a place here. Talked nice — not your average Scouse scal — in fact, I don't think he's from round here at all. No criminal record that I know of. Seemed to have plenty of cash, not that he flashed it around, like, but he had one of them fancy little Macintosh PowerBooks — and they don't come cheap.'

'No,' said Chris. 'They don't.'

'Must have something to hide, though, eh? I mean, running off like that. Mind you, I didn't think he'd stay long after Phil got that sheltered accommodation. He hung around the new feller for a few days, but Sean — that's the new guy — didn't take to him. Said he asked more questions than a copper.'

Chris already knew the answer to the next question but felt compelled to ask it. 'He left no forwarding address?'

The social worker smiled, staring again at a spot somewhere over her shoulder. 'Sorry.'

Chris sighed. 'I just wish I'd got here half an hour earlier.'

'I doubt he would've spoke to you,' the social worker reassured her. 'He was pretty narked that you'd been in at all. Said if Phil wanted to go off on his own, it was his business.'

'He said that?' she asked, frowning.

'"It's his life" were his exact words.'

Chris had visited Phil during the months he had been in prison, watching his disintegration from an articulate, if more than usually neurotic and obsessive young man, to a paranoid, psychotic wreck. She had eventually persuaded the prison authorities that he was not fit to complete the full term, but not soon enough to prevent a breakdown. His placement in the hostel had helped to restore some stability to his life, but he was made constantly anxious by the intrusions of communal living and had only begun to make a real recovery since he had been allocated the warden-controlled accommodation. While he had continued living at the hostel he had remained in a volatile emotional state, still fighting with night terrors and a daily dread which most people would find intolerable. How could a man who knew or cared about Phil credit him with the ability to make a free choice about where he lived?

'Just one more thing,' she said. 'Who was Jake's social worker?' She wasn't surprised to find that the hostel supervisor had no idea.

* * *

Jake watched from a safe distance. His bike was hidden in a side entry a couple of hundred yards down the road. Dr Radcliffe. Caring Chris. Her name had come up too many times in the last few weeks for coincidence. He had known that Phil's beatification of her was too good to be true; Dorothy's less saintly version was more believable, and Ann had pulled no punches at all. Then the radio programme — the caller from Childwall had really rattled her with the question about the children's home.

Dr Radcliffe was definitely a woman he might find useful.

* * *

Chris began the journey back to the office at six thirty, trying to think while grunting in the right places at the taxi driver's patter.

Why had Jake Dixon been so angry that she had been to the hostel? He had latched onto Phil. Why?

'Now some cabbies'd pull their face at a fare like this,' the driver went on. 'They'd prefer bimbling and picking up the short runs, know worramean?' He squinted in the rear-view mirror and Chris nodded absently.

Jake was supposed to know — and like — Phil. How could anyone who knew him truly believe that Phil would disappear out of personal choice? Wouldn't he know that Phil would only have left in that way if he was in serious trouble and in desperate need of help? The taxi driver was staring at her. Chris looked about her. The taxi had stopped and they were outside Turner and Sons. She paid up, crossing to the back gate of the building that housed her office and used her latchkey. The bin bags were still piled high against the walls of the backs of the houses, a little riper and emanating the accumulated heat of the day. She walked up the fire escape to the first-floor entrance and let herself in, then she opened her office door wearily, wishing she was home.

'You looked bushed,' Nicky said.

'Just plain pissed off,' said Chris. 'What are you doing here? You were supposed to lock up and go at five.'

'And worry all night if you got back safe?' said Nicky. 'Anyway, I've been fending off queries, like you said.'

Chris groaned. 'Not the intrepid chief inspector and his sidekick?'

'Just the intrepid one. He phoned just after five. I told him you were busy till eight — I thought I'd better give you some leeway. He left a number for you to ring.'

Chris shoved it into the pocket of her jeans. 'Is Rick looking after Tommy?'

'Yes. Why? Do you need me to do something?'

Chris laughed. 'I'm supposed to be the workaholic around here! Go home, Nicky. And you needn't start until eleven tomorrow. I'll manage my morning appointments without you.' Then she added sheepishly, 'But when you do get in, could you see what you can do to trace Jake Dixon? He's tall, blond, green eyes. A bit flash. Try the flat agencies, estate agents, whatever you can think of.'

'Who is he?'

'Jake Dixon is probably the best chance I've got of finding Phil.'

'If you think he's got a record, I could have a word with one of my cousins, see if they've heard of him . . . ?'

Chris could've hugged her — at least four of Nicky's cousins were police. She'd been hoping Nicky would suggest it but hadn't wanted to impose on their friendship and would never have broached the subject herself.

8

The evening was hot, and Chris drove with the windows down, letting the wind ruffle her hair lightly. She arrived home at 7.40, let herself in, elbowing the door open and bending to scoop up the letters from the doormat. 'Junk,' she muttered. She propped her briefcase against the meter cupboard and, heeling the front door shut, slipped out of her shoes and padded through to the welcome coolness of the kitchen tiles, carrying the bag which contained her now grimy jeans and T-shirt.

She tossed the letters onto the table and opened the fridge, pouring herself a large tumbler of lemonade before emptying the carrier bag into the washing machine and switching it to warm wash.

The house was stuffy; not as warm as outside, but there was a breathless quality to the air, and she went around opening all the windows before taking a shower. The cool water felt good against her skin, and she turned her face full into the stinging jet. Barely a sound came through the open bathroom window; the garden was strangely quiet, as though the heat had left everything exhausted. Standing under the shower, Chris was unwilling to leave the refreshing wash of the spray, delaying to the last possible moment the call she would have to make to Chief Inspector Jameson.

* * *

Jameson waited until 8.15 for her call. He had left both his direct line and home numbers. The increasing impatience he felt was only due in part to frustration with the case; he found himself wanting to explain to Dr Radcliffe his reasons for releasing Philip Greer's photograph to the press, and this unreasonable compulsion added to his growing irritation.

He had shaken hands with Sister Aloysius at the top of the concrete steps which led down to the staff car park. Sister Aloysius's eyes had searched his, then she had said, 'She's a good woman, Mr Jameson, and a moral one, although I suspect not religiously inclined, and rather unorthodox in the application of her morality.'

The appeal was disconcerting in that it seemed she was making it directly to him. Sister Aloysius was pleading Chris Radcliffe's case to him as a man, not as a police officer. But as a man, he had certain feelings of attraction towards the doctor which he knew were likely to impair his objectivity, and he quelled these feelings angrily.

* * *

Chris put off the telephone call while she watered the tubs on the patio. She had changed into a pair of pale cream shorts and wore a sleeveless blue tunic over them. Her hair, brushed back from her forehead, dripped deliciously down her back. The heat was stifling. She could hear the washing machine thrumming rhythmically, a lulling sound on the evening air. She delayed further by dead-heading the roses, then turned on the sprinkler, returning to the kitchen with some reluctance.

Still she couldn't bring herself to make the call. She rummaged in the freezer, feeling no hunger but recognizing the need to eat. She found a microwave meal, but even the meagre preparation of puncturing the film lid seemed a trial — it was too damned hot! She returned the packet to the freezer and took a wedge of cheese and some flaccid lettuce from the fridge, adding sweet peppers and tomatoes to complete the salad, then sat out in the garden to eat.

The phone rang.

'Have you listened to your phone messages yet?' It was Maria. She never announced herself, expecting everyone to know her by her voice. They generally did.

'Not yet.'

'Chris—' Her foster mother's tone cut through her stupor, sending a tingle down her spine.

'Is it Phil?' she asked.

'He was on Granada Reports.'

'Phil?' The notion seemed absurd.

'His picture. The one the police took away. They said they want to question him about the kidnappings. Oh, Flip, what'll this do to him?'

'That bloody bastard Jameson! Why couldn't he wait?'

'Flip—' There was a silence of muddled feelings and embarrassment.

'Say it, Maria. Whatever it is, just go ahead and say it.'

'I was thinking . . . I mean, I know you think you're doing what's best, but—'

'Maria,' she interrupted, 'I don't know where he is.'

'Then God help him!'

In her mind's eye Chris saw Maria cross herself. 'But I'll find him,' she said. 'I know I will. First, I have to talk to Chief Inspector Jameson and find out what's going on, OK?'

Maria agreed and she hung up. She set her video recorder for nine thirty, when the BBC regional news would be on, and on her way to the phone remembered where she had put the slip of paper with his number on it. Cursing, she turned the washing machine to its spin cycle and retrieved the slip of paper, still in one piece, but washed clean of ink.

'Bloody sodding hell!' She picked up the phone and dialled the police headquarters in Liverpool. She was told that Chief Inspector Jameson wasn't there at the moment and no, they couldn't give her his number, but if she'd care to leave a message—' She hung up.

Sod that, she thought. If she left a message, Jameson would have to call her back, and waiting for him to phone would put her at a disadvantage. Then a thought occurred to her: if he had telephoned her at her office, maybe he had also tried her home number.

She played back her messages. Maria's, sounding frantic and exasperated that she wasn't in; one from a colleague at Manchester University; one blank, from someone who had become tongue-tied when faced with a machine and a limited time to leave a message; Sister Aloysius had left a succinct and non-committal message, nonetheless unmistakable as a warning; a friend had telephoned to say how much she had enjoyed the show. 'Give me a ring, if you ever get around to taking a day off — we'll meet for lunch, dinner, whatever. I don't care. Just ring!' The next recording was Jameson.

'DCI Jameson here. Look, I really would like you to get in touch . . .' He left both his direct line and home numbers and she jotted them down, dialling out immediately.

* * *

Jameson had just got in from walking the dogs when the phone rang. He had jogged part of the way and was dismayed by his poor level of fitness. A spark of unease went through him. Then he remembered he had promised to phone Zoe at ten, British time, as she always finished school early on Fridays. He still had plenty of time.

'I hope you know what you're doing.'

It was a woman's voice.

'Who is this?'

'Chris Radcliffe.'

'I suppose you're referring to the photographs I've had circulated.'

'Broadcast would be a more accurate term. You'll make him desperate, Chief Inspector. I hope you can live with the consequences.' Jameson didn't answer and Chris, aware that she had sounded pompous, uttered a grunt of disgust. 'Can't you get it into your head that Philip isn't the man you're looking for?'

'Who said we were looking for a man?'

She didn't answer straight away. But after a moment's silence, she said, 'If you're not, then why splurge Phil's picture all over the TV news?'

'Because I would like to know what made him run.'

'I've already told you.'

On impulse, Jameson said, 'Perhaps we should talk this through.' If Sister Aloysius was right, he should try talking directly to her.

'I'm listening.' The voice on the other end of the line was cautious, perhaps even mistrustful.

'Not over the phone. I'll come to you.'

She hesitated.

'Dr Radcliffe?'

'All right. You're invited. Alone.'

He noticed that she hadn't given him instructions to find her. Did she assume that police intrusion extended to knowing the names and addresses of everyone in the country — or could she have she spotted the two officers who had followed her home?

* * *

Chris had tried Simon's flat to put him off coming round, but there was no reply. He arrived five minutes later with more articles and extracts, and with brief summaries of each typed up. 'I thought it might help, with you being so busy,' he said shyly.

Chris fixed him a plateful of sandwiches and explained Jameson's visit as he ate. He paled at the mention of the police, but Chris reassured him. 'He's a nice enough bloke,' she said, surprised that she really meant it. 'But he's fixated on Philip as a suspect for the abductions and—'

'Maybe I should go before he gets here.'

'Finish your meal. For heaven's sake, he's just a man — a bit of a walking disaster, in fact.' She laughed. 'If you want to overcome your fear of the law, Alan Jameson's the man to do it for you. One glimpse of the food stains on his tie will convince you he's just another bloke with problems.'

'Bit of a slob, is he?' Simon asked, between mouthfuls.

'Not a slob, exactly. But he's careless of his appearance. You'd almost expect him to be an academic.' Strange, she thought, that Hugh, who was so immersed in academic life, should be so unlike this paradigm of scholarship. Stranger still that she should find herself drawn to the chief inspector, who was so unlike her former lover.

Simon left minutes after Jameson arrived. Jameson stared at the door some moments after Simon had disappeared through it. 'Is he always so jittery?' he asked.

Chris shot him a wicked look. 'Only around the police. Simon was locked up for a while for arson. He hasn't quite got over it.'

'And you feel safe with him?'

'Perfectly. We're all prone to a little madness from time to time, Mr Jameson.' She collected the plates from the kitchen table and put them into the sink. 'In fact, I think it's an entitlement. If things had happened a little differently, *I* might be in Simon's position now. Or worse.'

'Oh?' said Jameson.

Chris turned to the sink, filling it with water, squirting washing-up liquid as a form of diversion. 'Lots of people make mistakes, do things they're later ashamed of. Some get away with it and some don't. Simon didn't. But he did come through it, and I think he's going to be just fine.'

She felt his scrutiny and turned her back to the sink, favouring him with a dazzling smile. 'Find it all right?' she asked, wiping her hands on a tea towel. 'It's a bit off the main drag.'

'You didn't give me the address before you rang off.'

She slipped him a sly look. 'I didn't give you my home phone number either, which as you now know, is ex-directory.' She led him through to the back garden where the lavenders and roses exhaled a heavy scent on the solid stillness of the evening air. A faint mist of water arched from the sprinkler, creating a curtain of prismatic colour in the westering sun.

Jameson seemed mesmerized for a moment, then he followed her to the paved area, where the sun still played on one corner, and a cluster of folding wooden chairs huddled as if basking in the golden warmth.

'You wanted to talk,' she said, when they were seated.

'I spoke to your grammar school headmistress today,' he said in reply.

'I know.'

Jameson's eyebrows twitched. 'Don't you want to know what she said?'

'I'm guessing that she advised you to speak to me.'

'She did.'

Well, that was honest, at least. 'About what?' she asked.

'About why you think Philip Greer is innocent.'

She lifted her eyes to his, amused and a little curious. Jameson was not like any detective she had ever met. She shrugged, resigning herself to a repetition of something she felt she had already explained. 'Philip can't bear any alteration to his routine. He dresses in the same order every morning. He owns a limited range of colours and designs of clothing, so he doesn't have to make difficult choices. He eats his breakfast in a pre-arranged pattern. He always washes the dishes before he leaves for work. He has to put the washing-up liquid in the bowl before the turning on the tap. The dishes go in a certain order. He *has* to do this or he is seized with a terror neither you nor I could comprehend nor imagine. He falls apart if the bus is five minutes late to work.'

She paused. The chief inspector seemed puzzled, but he was listening — trying at least to understand. 'Philip couldn't vary his routine to the extent of putting the cutlery into the washing up bowl before the crockery — I don't see how he could vary it to the degree of abducting two women, Chief Inspector.'

'You're telling me he couldn't have done it because he couldn't be bothered to change his routine?'

'You're not listening!' she exclaimed. 'It's not a case of *bothering*. You would have to know Phil to understand how terrifying such a diversion from his habitual practices would be to him. I meant it when I said he's not capable of deception. He needs sameness. He can't take any alteration to his ordered rituals.'

'But he's been away from this ordered environment of his for two days already.'

Chris felt a spasm of worry. 'Yes,' she said. Philip had never been set so adrift before.

'Perhaps if the impetus were strong enough, he might change his normal patterns.'

She found it difficult to hold Jameson's gaze. 'Wherever he is, Phil will have reinstated as many of his rituals as he can. Change is not exciting for Phil in the way it can be for most of us. It isn't irritating or irksome if it cuts across his daily routine. It's frightening. *Terrifying.*' She saw Jameson's look of scepticism and tried again to explain. 'Phil has trouble making sense of the world,' she began. 'It has little comprehensible order for him. It doesn't make logical sense. You know how it is when you're feverish? You feel distanced from your surroundings, everything seems distorted. You can't understand what people are saying to you, and you can't relate to people as you would normally. Try to imagine that distortion applied to the emotions, interactions, language, time — even the objects of everyday life. That's how it is for Phil. So he imposes meaningless routines in order to try and *make* it make sense.'

'Yes,' Jameson agreed. 'And when two women he has known and relied upon for years are diverted to other cases, he reacts.'

She shook her head. 'No. Not Phil. He wouldn't — he couldn't hurt anyone.'

'Loyally spoken,' Jameson said. 'But when my officers questioned him, he lied about going to the council offices.'

'What did he say? "I never did anything. I didn't mean it," something like that?'

'It intrigues me that you are so near the truth, Dr Radcliffe.'

'No trick. I haven't spoken to him, if that's what's going through your mind. "I never did anything. I didn't mean it," is what Phil always says when he's in trouble. He's totally transparent. And he doesn't understand shades of meaning or the difference between a minor misdemeanour and a criminal offence. He'd say the same if he'd broken a dish or been caught shoplifting. It's either Good or Bad. And he's not capable of *that* kind of bad. He'd never deliberately hurt anyone.'

'Don't those two statements contradict each other?' Jameson asked. 'If he doesn't understand the true nature of right and wrong, how can he be expected to make valid moral judgements? How could he be expected to know that hurting someone is a great wrong?'

'You're right,' said Chris, and saw that she'd caught Jameson off-guard with her directness. 'It is contradictory.' She fell silent, wondering how best to explain.

'It's hard for me,' she said at length, 'as a psychologist, to assess my own relationships with any objectivity. Even harder in this instance, because I grew up with Phil. But I honestly can't remember any time when Phil deliberately hurt anyone or anything. He seemed aware from quite a young age that he was physically stronger than the rest of us, and he made compensations for his size and strength. Even when the other kids would move his things. He was the only child to have his own room — had to because he would get so upset when

86

anything was moved or touched — but he was only ever violent towards himself.'

A picture of Phil at ten years old, sitting on the floor of his room rocking a little and keening like an abandoned puppy and biting his arm until it bled.

Jameson must have seen something in her face. 'How did this violence manifest itself?'

'That isn't relevant,' Chris answered, more sharply than she had intended.

'And if he did hurt these women — perhaps unintention-ally — wouldn't he see that as a bad thing and try to cover up?'

'He doesn't have the imagination. All Phil understands are literal facts. He knows when he's done a bad thing and his reaction is to run away.'

'As he ran away from my officers?'

She stared intently into his eyes, willing him to under-stand, to believe her. 'He ran away because they had pre-vented him getting to work on time. Because they wanted to get into his flat, to touch his things. He can't cope with that. He was afraid because he had pushed them, and they fell, and he knows what assault is. He's terrified you'll send him back to prison.'

Jameson returned her look. 'If he's innocent, he has nothing to fear.'

Suddenly the tension, the intensity was gone, and she relaxed, straightening up as she did so; she even smiled a lit-tle. 'Can you say that, Chief Inspector? Can anyone say that with absolute certainty?'

He hesitated too long. She had expected the usual plati-tudes, the reassurances, the stock trite, transparent, disingen-uous phrases. But he seemed reluctant to coerce her with the usual lies, and that gave her the confidence to try again — to make him understand.

'The dog clinches it,' she said without elaboration, forc-ing Jameson to ask her to explain.

'People with — with Philip's type of disorder.' The detached psychologist in Chris, the part of her which was never off duty, noted her reluctance, even inability, to label Philip's condition. Let others call it a language and communication disorder, or Asperger's syndrome. To her, Phil was her foster brother. Labels were useful tags for treatment regimes, educational provision or the payment of benefits, but they couldn't define Phil as she knew him. 'They often have an abhorrence of dogs which amounts to a phobia. Phil will walk half a mile out of his way to avoid walking past a dog — even if it's on a leash. He used to have hysterics if one of the children in nursery school brought in a toy dog.'

'If you know where he is—' Jameson said.

Chris threw up her hands and began pacing. 'What will it take to convince you I'm not mixed up in all of this?'

'Turn in Philip Greer.'

She faltered in mid-stride and stopped, dimly aware of the scent of crushed thyme drifting up from beneath her feet. 'I told you, I don't *know* where Philip is.'

'But you wouldn't tell me if you did.'

She smiled, mildly chastened. And the anger seemed to flow out of her with that smile, with the exchange of honesty between them. She sat down opposite him and leaned forward, searching his eyes with her own.

He leaned towards her, closing the gap, and Chris realised with an irrational burst of irritation that this was textbook interview technique, mirroring her actions, designed to make her feel that they had something in common. It was unreasonable, she knew — hadn't she used the same stratagem thousands of times in her work? Even so, she settled back, resting her hands on the arms of the chair and looking at Jameson through half-closed eyes.

'You're welcome to search my house,' she said. 'I won't even insist on the formality of a warrant. You know my office hours if you want to check my workplace, but please don't make a habit of interrupting consultations: patients find it disturbing.'

Chris was surprised to observe that Jameson was disconcerted by this last sally. He gave a slight shrug. 'I should apologize for barging in like that,' he said.

'You needn't. I think it's done wonders for my street cred, being busted by the filth.'

She saw a half smile. 'Still, it was unsubtle. I hope it hasn't set your patient back in her therapy.'

Chris suspected that his discomfort was caused by the unsubtlety of the interruption, rather than through any real concern for her patient. 'Len will be all right. I think the dreads and the weaves and the nose stud are what's helping her through.'

'You can't approve—?'

Who sounds pompous now? Chris thought. 'For Len, yes, I do.'

'Well, it's obvious you don't have any children, Dr Radcliffe.'

She smiled into his eyes. Hazel. *Nice eyes for a prig*, she thought. 'You got me. It's the lack of grey hairs, isn't it?'

'It's the lack of respect for convention. Parenthood is about setting down guidelines.'

'Oh? I thought it was about loving and nurturing, building confidence and helping children become independent.'

'Sounds neat and tidy in the abstract. It's rather more complex in reality.'

'Isn't that what makes it interesting?' Chris asked.

'And you'd know of course,' Jameson said with sudden venom. 'Textbook ideals and fifty-minute fixes aren't what it's all about.'

Ouch. 'No doubt you'd be happy to enlighten me.'

'It's about responsibility. Pushing your own needs to one side. Never going out together because you can't get a babysitter — and when you can you're too knackered to be bothered. It's about the tedium of taking them to Brownies when you'd kill for a chance to sit and watch TV. It's putting their needs first. Always. You claim to understand situations, people, but you barely know—'

89

'No doubt you're the perfect paradigm of fatherhood, Chief Inspector,' Chris interrupted. Fatigue had frayed her temper. She was tired. She was sick with worry about Phil, and Jameson was lecturing her about parenthood. 'With your twelve-hour days and your twenty-four-hour on-call status. How many birthdays and Christmases have you *actually* shared with your family?'

Jameson stood, and Chris realised she'd hit close to home.

'I'd better be going,' he said.

'Are you going to take his picture out of circulation?' she asked.

He deliberated for a few moments. 'Greer must be found.'

'I know that — and I'm willing to help you. Only not this way.'

For a moment, only for a second or two, he seemed ready to relent, then he said in a tone of finality, 'I'm sorry.'

'Bullshit.'

Jameson's eyebrows shot up. 'What?'

'You're just too pig-headed to admit you made a mistake. So you'll find Phil, drag him in screaming, keep him for a day and then tell the public he's been ruled out of your enquiries. Because you will find no evidence against him. But, hey — it'll give you some breathing space until you've found a better lead—' She laughed abruptly. 'What am I saying? Until you've found any kind of a lead!'

She finished breathlessly and Jameson stared at for a moment, holding her gaze unwaveringly.

'We've found three sets of diary entries and notes that have been tampered with. They may or may not be associated with "in care" records of children placed at Sunnyside Children's Home during 1986 and 1987. We're looking into that possibility.'

'Whose diary entries?' Chris asked, feeling a quickening of her pulse.

'Dorothy Hardy's, Ann Lee's and yours. You could be in danger yourself—'

The emphasis on the word *could* was insulting. 'And I *could* be as guilty as sin — is that what you're saying, Chief Inspector?'

Jameson said nothing.

'Look,' she said, 'I profoundly regret what happened at Sunnyside.' She shook her head impatiently. Words could never adequately describe her feelings. 'I became a psychologist to try and help children. I'm ashamed to have been associated with what amounts to institutionalized abuse.' Her voice wavered, and she cleared her throat before going on. 'We were supposed to be there to protect damaged kids, not prolong the nightmare—'

The telephone rang and Chris got up to answer it, grateful for the interruption. It was for Jameson, and when she handed the receiver to him in the hallway, she saw that he was quietly fuming. Had he thought that she was about to break down? Make a confession?

The call was short, his replies were monosyllabic.

He was pale when he hung up, and his hand shook as he replaced the old-fashioned receiver on the hook. It jingled merrily, mocking the seriousness of Jameson's expression.

'Two bodies have been found within yards of each other in Sawrey Woods,' he said. 'Both female.'

Chris took a breath and held it.

'Now will you believe that this is not a game?'

9

Foster was the first to arrive. A golden light played on the mudflats; the tide was out and the sun setting. A warm breeze blew salty air from the estuary to the woodland, stirring the trees to a conspiracy of whispering. In the gully, darkness was falling and already lamps and generators were being rigged up, but the pale yellow of Dorothy's frock and the burnt orange of Ann's blouse seemed almost to luminesce, creating a pulsing after-image on Foster's retina.

The bodies were fully clothed and were so close together that one of Ann's arms lay across Dorothy's corpse as though to protect or comfort her. He had to scramble down to them, grabbing at whippy shrubs and tufts of grass to keep from falling. The young police constable who had been set to guard the bodies stood a few yards off, staring back up the slope with an expression of determined stoicism on his face.

The stench and the persistent sound of insect activity reached Foster from halfway down the slope — the forensic entomologists would have a field day with these two. He had braced himself for this, coming down the hill, thankful that the day's heat had quelled his appetite and that he had settled for a light salad for his evening meal.

'All right, mate?' he said.

'Sarge,' the officer returned.

Foster understood. The lad was concentrating on keeping his dinner down; sometimes the simple act of speaking was enough to make you lose control. Foster edged past the constable to where the women lay.

'Oh, Jesus.' He had thought he was braced for the scene, but he always found that when it came right down to it, you were never really ready for the callous disposal of human life.

At his exclamation the constable half turned and saw again what he had been avoiding for the past half hour. There were signs of animal activity, gnaw marks on the flesh. Foster recalled that the bodies had been found by a man walking his dog, and his stomach heaved. He turned away and saw the constable stumbling some distance off, retching. He forced himself to look again: Jameson would want a report when he arrived. Stab wounds by the look of it — both of them. Under the skin there were sinister rippling movements.

'Christ!' he muttered and turned abruptly to watch the constable, who was returning, wiping his mouth with a handkerchief. He looked no more than twenty, maybe just out of training.

The young constable muttered an apology, then blurted out, 'He's just dumped them like a bloody sack of rubbish — left them where anything can get at them. He never even covered them up.' He bunched his fist and then, not knowing what to do with it, thrust it deep into his trouser pocket.

'This your first, lad?'

The constable nodded dumbly.

'There's some'll tell you it gets easier — that you'll toughen up. Well, if it stops you puking your ring up, that's fine — the forensics lot aren't exactly sympathetic with officers who've got a tendency to throw up all over their crime scenes. But keep the anger. Sometimes I think it's the only thing that keeps us human.'

* * *

93

The discovery of Ann and Dorothy's bodies was the main feature of the morning news on local radio. Chris went to the living room and turned on the TV; it was in the national bulletins there, too. She had called Maria immediately after Jameson had left the previous night, thinking it best that she heard the news from her. She had expected Maria to be in a panic — her foster mother had a keen sense of the dramatic, and Chris was prepared for that — but she hadn't been prepared for her doubt.

'He's been missing since Wednesday,' she said, 'and now those poor women—'

'I know. I'm looking for him, Maria. I'll find him before the police do. I know where to look.'

'Well . . .' Chris heard a long exhalation at the other end of the line. 'Maybe you should tell *them* where to look,' she said.

'Maria, if the police find him first Phil could take fright. He might hurt someone or get himself hurt. He wouldn't be in this trouble now, except he panicked when they called at his flat.' The line went quiet and Chris spoke her foster mother's name.

'I'm still here.' Her voice had an edgy quality. 'Chris—'

'I'm listening,' Chris said, feeling faintly sick, half afraid of what Maria was about to say.

'What if he—'

Chris pressed the earpiece harder against her ear, as though afraid that someone might overhear. 'Maria, you can't think *Phil* killed Ann and Dorothy?'

'No . . . It's just . . .'

'Just *what*, for God's sake?'

'Well, he has been difficult these last few years — and that assault—'

'We've been through all that. Phil was a bystander. A bystander who got caught.'

'He was with those boys, Chris. You can't call that being a bystander.'

94

'The victim didn't even recognize him in the line-up! If he hadn't admitted to being with them there'd have been no case to answer.'

Silence. Chris knew she sounded belligerent. Given the weight of circumstantial evidence pointing towards his guilt, her insistence on Philip's innocence was an abnegation of the obvious, and she knew Maria was quite capable of drawing the same conclusion.

'You've always stood up for him, and that's good,' Maria said after a few more seconds. But if he did—'

'He *didn't*,' Chris interrupted, angrier at herself than at Maria. 'He could not and did not hurt those women. Not Phil.'

'You have to remember,' Maria said gently, 'that we had to ask him to leave after he'd done his A levels.' Chris remained stubbornly silent. 'All right, love,' Maria had said. 'You think about it. But that chief inspector seems a good sort. He knows his job, I'm sure. If you'd just talk to him—'

'I wish I could agree with you, *Marisita*.' She had used Maria's family name as a tacit apology. She had sat cradling the receiver for a long time after Maria had hung up. If Maria doubted Philip — Maria, his mother, or at least as close to a mother as Phil would ever have — how could she hope to persuade Jameson that he was innocent? Chris wasn't sure she could convince even herself anymore. Maria's reminder had made her uncertain. Phil had become unpredictable. 'He doesn't know his own strength,' Maria had said, but the platitude had only partly masked her fear of Phil. 'He needs a place where he can lock the door against intrusion. Where he can feel safe.' She might also have said, 'Where *we* can feel safe.'

The silence enfolded her, stifling all action, until the plaintive digitized voice of the operator had cut across her thoughts. *Please replace the handset and try again* — a wheedling, persistent, lonely voice pleading with her, the unseen caller. Chris had jumped up, hurriedly replacing the receiver, and walked with agitated steps to the back of the house and out into the garden. Here, the night sounds were a soothing medley. It was after eleven, but there was still a faint glimmer of light on the horizon, slowly fading in the yellow light of the rising moon, and she listened as the restless flutterings in the oak trees in the field beyond her boundary fence grew more infrequent until they were finally stilled. It was still oppressively warm. Chris sat on the old wooden bench, careless of moss and bird droppings. She stared at the moon and was startled by the sudden fleeting silhouette of a bat; it was there and gone in a moment, incongruous, like a cartoon animation against the parchment yellow disc. It returned several times and Chris followed its rapid, twisting flight, discovering its methodical patrol up and down the margins of the trees, in search of lacewings and moths.

She'd walked to the edge of the lawn and stepped into the shrubbery to get a better view. A violent flurry of movement at the end of the garden made her jump. She had disturbed something. Twice in the week since her arrival she had seen a fox pick its way daintily through the shrubs to the compost heap. Apparently, the previous owners had been in the habit of leaving scraps for the foxes. Chris laughed at her own nervousness and stepped noiselessly back onto the lawn, settling onto the old bench to wait, but the fox had never appeared.

The early morning news depressed her and she reached for the remote control, then she saw Chief Inspector Jameson and her thumb hovered uncertainly over the Off button. He was standing in a field with the dark backdrop of Sawrey Woods behind him. His suit looked more rumpled than the previous evening, and she guessed that he'd had about as much sleep as she'd had. He was coherent, professional, but Chris read in his face a deep personal sadness. It was probably tiredness, she knew, but at that moment she felt that Jameson blamed himself for the deaths. She felt almost sorry for him.

A reporter's voice called out as he finished answering a question: 'Ralph Milton, Chief Inspector, the *Herald*. Are you still looking for Philip Greer? Are you any nearer finding him?'

The question seemed to perplex Jameson for a moment, then he roused himself and turned to face to the questioner. 'We are looking into a number of possible leads,' he said. 'We need to interview Mr Greer in order to rule him out of our enquiries.'

Carefully phrased — for Philip's benefit or for hers?

'What about reports that he had been shadowing Dorothy and Ann before their disappearance?' The same reporter — apparently, he intended to make full use of his advantage.

Jameson stared at him a full five seconds. 'I can't comment on that.'

* * *

Foster knew what was on his boss's mind. The look on Jameson's face was enough to tell him that.

'It didn't come from the team, boss.' They were on their way back to Hawksley village police station, where an incident room had been set up.

'You're sure about that, are you?'

'Yeah.' In his present combustible state Jameson was like a firework that refused to go off — you were never quite sure whether to go up to it in case it blew up in your face. *Fuck it*, he thought. The team had pulled their tripes out the last few weeks, checking, filing, logging stuff on the computer, half of which he'd bet his salary to a sackful of shit was irrelevant. He'd even got volunteers to recheck the files for damage after the discovery that someone had tampered with Chris Radcliffe's file. And they had already shifted and sifted a mountain of paper. Volunteers fulfilling the roles of professional staff on a police inquiry into major crime — and what thanks do they get?

'It wasn't anyone on the team,' Foster repeated, knowing he sounded sullen.

'Check it and report back,' Jameson said. He was sitting hunched in the passenger seat, his hands clenched on his knees. He hadn't looked at Foster since they got into the car.

'*You* do it,' Foster said.

Jameson's head swivelled. 'What?'

Foster ignored the menacing calm in his voice. 'You don't trust your own sodding team after the way they've worked for you. You can tell them — 'cos I'm fucked if I will.'

Jameson didn't raise his voice, but the temperature in the car rose by a few degrees. 'You'll do as you're damn well told,' he said, softly.

'They've half killed themselves trying to find those poor women. They've got a right to some consideration. And what about their families? They've got families to think about.' He was too angry even to try and remove the emphasis on the word *they*. 'Families they haven't seen for nigh on ten days except to say good night and crawl off to bed and maybe a quick cup of tea in the morning before the whole bastard grind starts up again. And you—' Foster knew he was going too far, but he couldn't stop himself now. Jameson hadn't stood next to the stinking corpses for an hour. He wouldn't have the reek of death in his nose and clinging to his hair and clothing for days. Foster was sickened by the sheer wallowing self-pity of the man. 'You've hardly given them a second thought,' he said. 'It's all *you* can do to say good morning. Well, you can do your own dirty work this time.'

'All right, Sergeant—' Jameson began.

'No, it isn't. Half the team isn't even getting paid for this, but they've been here on their days off, after their regular jobs, putting hours in we've no right to ask of them. They're really carved up about this.' *I've started so I'll bloody finish*, he thought, with miserable certainty that this would end in suspension. 'They feel bad enough with how it's ended — and you're gonna put the bloody boot in, calling their professional conduct into question!'

'Are you finished?' Jameson asked.

'No,' Foster said. 'I suppose it's never occurred to you that someone down the borough offices gave the media that little gem?'

Jameson's answer was quiet and firm. 'As a matter of fact, it had.'

Foster turned into the car park of Hawksley station, already regretting his outburst. He pulled up next to a traffic division car and yanked the handbrake on too hard with a metallic rasp. Jameson was looking at his hands, and Foster's surreptitious glance confirmed they were no longer clenched.

They sat for another few minutes in silence. Foster caved in, unable to bear the tension. 'Oh, fuck it,' he said. 'You might as well say it. I'm suspended, aren't I?'

'You bloody well ought to be.'

'OK.' He thought all of the anger had gone, and then a fresh bubble rose in his chest at the injustice of it. 'But I'm *right*, boss.' It was only after he said this that he heard the levity in Jameson's voice, and turned to look at him. He wasn't smiling, but the amusement on his face was unmistakable.

'I had a bad night last night,' Jameson said. 'I suppose I was looking for a cat to kick.'

It took Foster a few moments to come down from his excitedly indignant state. 'What about your dogs, then?'

'They'd bite,' Jameson said. He ran a hand over his chin. 'I don't know, Foz,' he sighed. 'Check the council offices first. If no one coughs to passing the information to the press, *then* I'll approach the team.'

The bad night had as much to do with Roz as with the discovery of the bodies. At first she had refused to let him talk to Zoe, since her party had begun and she wasn't about to drag her away for a phone call that was over an hour late. It was only because Roz had raised her voice and Zoe had come into the room, guessing the cause, that they had finally spoken.

Zoe was thrilled to hear from him. She always was. She *loved* the roller boots, but how did he know? He was the *best* dad in the world, she had said. And he had imagined Roz listening to all of it, that bitter look on her face, and the worst of it was knowing that she was right: he was a selfish, unthinking bastard.

* * *

The office was strangely quiet when Chris arrived, just after nine. The place always seemed empty and drab in Nicky's absence; without her bright dresses and suits, her extravagant hairstyles and her often outrageous make-up, it was impersonal, formal, dull.

Chris was tempted to cancel her appointments, but the notion was a fleeting one. Her patients needed constancy, reliability; she couldn't let them down, even for Phil. Besides, Nicky would worry if she arrived to find the office empty.

Her thoughts kept returning to Foster's words the first time they had met — of course he had been trying to spark some kind of response from her — but whether or not she believed what he had said, the possibility remained that Dorothy and Ann had been murdered by someone they had dealt with professionally. The more Chris thought about it, the more sense it made that it could be linked with Sunnyside — they had all worked together on that one, at least at first. She would go back to the council records office after lunch. Wayne would help. She could just fit in a couple of hours before her final appointment at three thirty.

Nicky breezed in at eleven, as pretty as the icing on a cake, and wafting perfume with every movement. Her pale foundation contrasted strikingly with her glossy pink lipstick. She had backcombed her hair and it frothed becomingly, giving an impression of impermanence, as though it would collapse like candyfloss if touched. This was the sort of style she kept for special occasions: it was a difficult and time-consuming operation.

'Wow!' said Chris.

Nicky smirked. 'Like it?' She primped recklessly.

'It's — spectacular.'

'Rick's taking me the pictures straight after work. Me mum's gonna look after Tommy so's we can have a pizza after.'

'One piece of advice—' Nicky shot her a knowing look, then perched one hand on her hip, ready. 'Don't sit in the front row with that hairdo,' Chris said.

Not a flicker. 'Why d'you think I spent half the morning getting meself up like this?'

'The lengths you go to, just to get him in the back row!'

As Nicky busied herself with preparing tea, Chris went into her office to read through her notes on the next patient.

Nicky carried the cups through and plonked them down on Chris's desk, then perched her neat buttocks on the edge of it. Chris ignored her for some minutes, but Nicky, unabashed, sipped quietly at her tea and refused to budge.

'Can't you take a hint?' Chris said, when she could bear it no longer.

'Yeah, and you needn't look at me like that,' Nicky said. 'Even psychologists need to talk things over sometimes, you know?'

'I know. We have counsellors for that.'

'"Big fleas have little fleas upon their back that bite 'em."'

'"And little fleas have lesser fleas and so *ad infinitum*,"' said Chris. 'You know, you never fail to amaze me.'

'Was in our maths book at school. There was a little quote at the start of every chapter.' Nicky screwed up her eyes, conjuring the memory. 'That one was on . . . infinity.' She shrugged. 'Something like that. It was the only bit of the lesson I enjoyed, like. The rest was boring.' She sized up her employer for a moment. 'Well, are you gonna mention it, or am I?'

'OK, OK, I give in. Yes, I did see the news.' Chris had also picked up a selection of newspapers on the way in. One opportunistic tabloid journalist had found a useful hook on which to hang the story. The headline read:

MUNICIPAL MURDERS

Chris looked at the byline: Ralph Milton — the man who had quizzed Jameson on the TV news.

'Why d'you suppose he dumped them both together?'

'I don't know.' Chris had spent half the night wondering about just that.

'Can they find out much from the bodies? I mean, they said Dorothy Hardy's body was badly decomposed.'

Chris shuddered involuntarily. 'Do you mind if we don't talk about it, Nicky?'

Nicky coloured. A soft pink glow rose beneath the smooth patina of foundation and powder. 'Sorry, Chris,' she said. 'I was trying to help.'

* * *

Chris reached Calderbank borough council's records office at one thirty. The hostel supervisor had found out from some of the clients the names of the two social workers Phil had come up with as possibles for Jake's caseworkers. One had been Ann Lee, the other Joe Zwane. If Joe did know Jake, then she might find his file in the records office, and through Jake, trace Phil. If, on the other hand, Jake Dixon had no social worker, she would at least have learned that much more about him.

The frosted glass window was firmly shut and a stencilled sign, blurred but clearly readable through the glass, read, '*Closed*'. Chris went to the door to the left of the window, knocked lightly and walked in.

Wayne almost fell off his chair. He had been sitting with his feet up, his chair tilted at a precarious angle.

'Friggin' 'ell! Can't you bloody read? The sign says closed.'

Chris grinned. 'What's up, Wayne? Did I interrupt some erotic fantasy?'

'Mind your own!' He got grudgingly to his feet, an attempt to reduce the perceived disadvantage rather than an old-fashioned gallantry, Chris thought. He was taller than her by a head, but the advantage was lost because of a tendency to stoop.

'Could've broke me neck.'

Chris beamed at him. Wayne reminded her of some of the boys she had taught in her first job: he was difficult, likeable, sharp, naive, obtuse, clever, tough and vulnerable and quite unable to reconcile himself to any of these facets of his personality — as interesting a mixture of contradictions as she had ever met in her professional dealings. He wore the neatest beard she had ever seen, more than likely trimmed daily, and had the messiest hair, kept under control, at least at work, by an elastic band. He was dressed incongruously in a suit — the office requirement was shirt and tie, smart trousers (no jeans). It was as if he had decided to go one step beyond what was required in order to demonstrate his contempt for the petty work regulations.

'How're the gigs going?' Wayne had played in a band evenings and weekends for ten years, ever since she had known him. She had been to a few of his performances and had liked his style, which was somewhere between blues and rock. After a decade of pub gigs and disco spots, youth clubs and the occasional students' union — even after two changes of drummer and three lead guitarists — he still had an unshakeable belief that one day they would make it big.

'You're not getting at the files,' he said.

She frowned. 'Did I miss something? I don't see the connection — gigs, files — sorry, Wayne, you'll have to explain.'

He refused to be drawn, doggedly returning to his theme. 'I've been told not to let any files out of this building without phoning for confirmation to the office requesting it or to the police incident room.'

'Well that's all right then.'

He scowled mistrustfully at her. 'Fair enough. Off you toddle.'

A slow grin spread across her face. 'I didn't say I'd *leave*. But I won't take any files out of the office, never mind the building, and I promise to put them back where I found them.'

'I don't know . . .'

'Oh, come on, Wayne! Don't give me that more-than-my-job's-worth crap. Where's the possible harm in it?'

Wayne was affronted by her sudden loss of patience. 'Well *someone's* been dicking about with them,' he said defensively. 'How'm I supposed to know you won't go tearing great bloody wodges out of them while you're down there?'

Her response was a little too slow, a little too flip to convince. 'Now, would a convent-educated girl do a thing like that?'

'I told you, I'm not supposed to—'

'If you don't trust me, chaperone me,' she cut in. 'You're on your lunch break, aren't you? Lock your office door and let me into the basement.'

He did, with bad grace, returning to the office ten minutes later muttering darkly about the waste of his time. He came down twice in the next hour, once waving her away. She darted to the next aisle just as a second figure appeared. A uniformed PC.

'Thanks, Wayne,' she said later, as she was leaving.

'Only saving me own neck. You get sussed, I get sacked.'

'Chivalrous bastard.'

'Chival-wha'?' But he couldn't suppress a grin. 'You'll get me shot one of these days.' As she turned to leave, he said, 'Anything useful?'

'Dates and times, Wayne. Just dates and times.'

* * *

She couldn't make out her escort in the heavy Friday night traffic. She watched for them in her rear-view mirror as she pulled out from the kerb on Mount Street. They were invisible as she turned right into Rodney Street, past her office and onward, skirting the edge of the city centre. The traffic was snarled at the lights at London Road, and she had plenty of opportunity to look back along the long line of cars, but none seemed likely. It was strange; in just two days, she had developed a feeling for her trackers. Whether it was their studied disinterestedness or the absence of conversation between driver and passenger, she wasn't sure, but there was something which set them apart from the other, ordinary punters on their way home from work. It was with a sense of relief that she saw the blue Fiesta slide in behind her at the tunnel entrance. A woman or possibly a slightly built man — it was difficult to see through the tinted glass of the windscreen. A smallish car for police work, she thought, but perhaps it was supposed to blend in more successfully. Her escort was alone, but she was sure that it was the police. Resources would be stretched by the events of last night.

She analysed her anxiety with a detached interest. Why was she so nervous? As she had told Wayne, so far all she had were dates and times. The ones that were missing from the files. But all of them related to her employment in the borough's Educational Psychology Service, which meant the connection between her and the two murdered women was closer than she had imagined. Of course, Jameson would have made the same observations, but perhaps with a slightly different slant. To hell with him — he wasn't her concern. The damage to her files, Wayne had said, corresponded to the records and dates removed from Dorothy's and Ann's files. She wished she had had time to look through the records of a few other people she had worked with during that time, to see if their files had been tampered with. Perhaps she would be able to persuade Wayne to let her take a look at them on Monday.

The dates that were missing covered a six-month span, but only selected dates had been removed, which suggested that the killer had taken out any reference to himself — or *her*self? It was possible, but if it was a woman, she would have to be strong to have kidnapped and murdered Dorothy and Ann, and then dragged the bodies a hundred yards from the road to the woods. Unless they walked there themselves and she killed them there. She shivered, despite the heat. The key to finding the killer had to be in the files, but the problem was the files were incomplete.

She would check through her old diaries — they might tell her something, spark some recollections. Soon she would begin putting names to the dates and faces to the names. She hadn't been a borough educational psychologist long enough for the faces to blur into one amorphous mass; one of the long-standing borough psychologists had said that he could present the WISC tests half asleep after an all-night poker game, and with a stinking hangover. Children were seen, assessed and shifted to some other agency; neither the time nor the resources were available for follow-up or follow-through. And for some, the result was a work weariness, a business approach that bordered on callousness. She had finally left the service because she had begun to detect the same characteristics in herself.

Nicky had wanted to know all about her expedition to the records office when Chris returned, but had contained herself until her three thirty appointment had left. 'Well, go on then,' Nicky said. 'Don't keep us in suspense.'

She was fascinated to hear that someone had been at the files.

'What for?' she asked.

'To remove any reference to themselves?' Chris said. 'But why not destroy the whole file?'

'If they're anything like our files, they'd be a bit obvious, trying to walk out with them tucked under their jacket.'

Chris slapped her forehead. 'That's why you're such a good PA.'

'Is that PA as in personal assistant, or PA as in piss artist? 'Cos if it's PA as in personal assistant, I want a pay rise.'

'In that case, I'll stick to calling you a receptionist in future,' Chris said, but her mind was not on the banter. 'They're too bulky to remove. And if they had been booked out, everyone would know who'd done the damage. And anyway, as long as you see a buff folder with Ann Lee's or

Dorothy Hardy's name on it, you assume their work log is intact. The disappearance of a *whole* file is far more likely to excite interest.'

'Doesn't that mean it's got to be someone from the borough?'

'Or someone pretending to be someone from the borough.'

'Or someone pretending to be the police. Or someone like you, who knows someone on the records office staff.'

'In short, any bloody bugger,' Chris said, suddenly deflated.

'So what's missing?'

Chris shook her head. 'I wish I knew.'

'You wha'? Six months' worth of diary entries diddled with? Come on, Chris! Something must've happened. It's six months of your life — you can't just forget that!'

Chris avoided Nicky's eye, knowing she would read exasperation and incredulity there.

Nicky tried another tack. 'OK. You left at the end of that year — why?'

Chris closed her eyes. Nicky was like a pit bull when it came to worrying the truth out of a situation. 'I got sick of the self-perpetuating misery passed down like a genetic disease from one generation to the next. The inevitability—'

'Do me a favour! I'm not one of your radio listeners, you know. Just tell me the truth!'

Chris flushed angrily at the interruption. 'I'm trying to—'

'Well give it to me straight and save the bullshit for Wednesday nights.'

Chris bit the side of her lip. 'It was lots of things,' she began reluctantly. Ann Lee, for one, smiling at her in that knowing way and welcoming her to the real world. 'It was the compromises and the financial constraints and consider-ations; it was the workload and the lack of resources and the impossibility of follow-up and follow-through.'

'The bottom line, Chris. What was the final straw?'

'Sunnyside, OK?' Chris said it before she had time to think. So now Nicky knew. It was Sunnyside that finally made her quit.

Nicky nodded, satisfied, requiring no further explanation, no expansion. 'What about Jake Dixon?'

Chris blinked, stunned to have been let off the hook when she would have told Nicky the whole story, if she'd asked. 'It's like he never existed,' she said. 'There's no file. And I spoke to Joe Zwane — he'd never heard of him.' This was another source of anxiety. Dixon had managed to get a place in a local authority hostel but wasn't listed anywhere in the files. And now he had disappeared, and his disappearance coincided with more than one other. 'I don't suppose—?'

Nicky shook her head. 'Nothing yet. Shouldn't you tell Jameson?'

'Jameson is quite capable of working that out for himself.'

'You have got off on the wrong foot, haven't you?' Nicky raised a perfectly sculpted eyebrow.

Chris shrugged. 'The man has fixed ideas. He's too bloody stubborn to admit when he's wrong.' Nicky didn't comment. 'And you needn't look at me like that, I didn't start it. And I tried to talk sense to him last night, but there's no bloody talking to *that* guy.'

Nicky had remained resolutely silent on the matter, except to say on her way out to meet her husband, 'If you want my opinion, you're as bad as each other. Me mam'd say you want your heads knocking together.'

Chris had paid little attention: Nicky's mam based her philosophy on a variety of proverbs and horribly clichéd phrases. In many respects she was rather like Maria, except that Maria had also picked up a morbid tendency to superstition from her immigrant Spanish mother, which she wove easily into the cloth of her devout Catholicism.

The answer lay in the files. It had to. Otherwise why risk recognition, even apprehension? If her own file had been there it would have helped, but Jameson still had it; she'd checked that with Wayne. Jameson didn't trust her. That was evident, and it was hardly surprising, given her refusal to help him find Philip, but it made things damned difficult. Except for the tail. She had to admit that if Jameson's mistrust of her meant that her police escort would continue, then she would rather keep it that way. She glanced in the mirror. The blue Fiesta had dropped back behind a truck and was barely visible through the windscreen of his car. She wouldn't be playing any games of hide and seek tonight; let them keep her in sight all the way home. She needed the reassurance of a police presence.

* * *

Darren Lewis had no such apprehensions, however. He walked past the building on the other side of the road. Better view that way. He slowed his pace to a cocky swagger, aware that his clean white T-shirt and his carefully sculpted muscles would attract attention. He liked that kind of interest, but he wasn't so vain that he'd be willing to jeopardize a job for it, so he took care not to stare too openly. Just a few quick, darting glances that took in different facets of the squat.

Nothing doing downstairs. All corrugated iron and steel bolts, but the upper floors — *Christ! They're wide open!* he thought. They'd taken down the metal sheets, and some of the windows were even open. He loved occupied houses. People were more of a challenge. There was a chance of being caught — and if this lot caught him, they'd kick his head in. Somehow this possibility made the whole thing a more satisfying prospect.

He carried on to the end of the street. No alleyway. The gardens of the houses in the next street were back-to-back with these. Each garden had high brick walls on three sides. The only way around the back would be down the side of the house. Lewis smiled to himself. The risk was an added enticement. He felt a tingle of excitement in his groin. If the mingebags nobbled him he'd say he was looking for somewhere to get his head down. He never took his gear with him on a recce.

He completed the circuit and trotted silently in his Reeboks up the side entry of the house. More corrugated sheeting, but he knew the score. He lifted the oblong of metal by one corner and peered inside. A kitchen. Dark. And empty.

10

Jameson and Foster were sitting in a corner of the recreation room of Hawksley Police Station, which had been cleared out to serve as an incident room. Extra desks and chairs had been brought in, together with several computers and modems. The billiard table, which was too large to be moved out, had been shoved to one side and covered with old sheeting, but the rest of the room looked functional enough. It made local enquiries easier, setting up on site, rather than working from Liverpool; Jameson had even managed to get a couple of hours sleep between giving his statement to the morning news programmes and talking to his superintendent at eleven.

They sipped their tea in silence for some time, reluctant to return to the heat of the afternoon sunshine outside. The thick sandstone walls of the building insulated the interior from the worst of the day's heat, while the small windows, set high in the walls, let in a welcome breeze, together with sudden liquid bursts of birdsong.

Jameson imagined himself for a moment in this idyllic setting, twenty minutes' drive from Liverpool along the coast and a thousand miles from the snarling aggression of the city.

'How would you like a cosy little billet like this?' he asked.

Foster flipped him a wary look. 'Nothing ever happens in a place like this, does it? The odd case of wanton vandalism, disputes over public rights of way, a bit of rowdiness down the local on a Saturday night—'

'And a double murder in that nice little patch of National Trust woodland down the road.'

'Haven't got the patience to hang about forty years for the odd double murder,' Foster said. 'Anyhow, I'm a bit like you, boss.'

Jameson looked askance.

'Too ambitious.'

So, Foster saw him as ambitious. Jameson found this gratifying — Foster could be abrasive, strident even, but he was always honest, and ambition was a part of his own make-up. He was paying Jameson a compliment, in his way.

'I couldn't stick a place like this,' Foster went on. 'Full of woollybacks with no . . . whatchamacallit?' He clicked his fingers. 'No . . . aspirations.'

Jameson smiled. 'There are perks — woollybacks notwithstanding.'

Foster looked as though he doubted that. 'What, you mean like the glorious sunsets and tea made in a proper pot, served in a proper mug and brought to you by apple-cheeked WPCs . . . ?'

'The glorious sunsets don't sound so bad,' Jameson said. 'And I do enjoy tea which approximates to drinkable — nothing perverse in that, Sergeant.' He had to admit, though, Foster had a point. This wasn't the place for a man with a low boredom threshold.

He sipped hot, strong tea from a chipped green mug and turned his attention back to the case. He had two chief suspects: Radcliffe and Philip Greer. Both had links with Ann and Dorothy. Radcliffe had always protected Greer. Greer was missing. And Dr Radcliffe wasn't talking.

'Anything on Greer yet?' he asked.

'Sod all,' Foster said. 'I've got Nolan and Flynn checking out the squats.' He must have caught Jameson's look of amused enquiry because he said, 'Won't do them no harm to get their hands dirty, and anyhow, they've seen the bastard — they know what he looks like. That's got to be worth more than a photo.'

'Absolutely,' said Jameson. They stared at each other for a few seconds, Jameson wondering what was going through Foster's mind. Giving up the task, he returned to a question that had been troubling him for some time; 'Why start now? Why suddenly start doing all this? The abductions — and now murder?'

'Settling old scores? Disgruntled parent?' said Foster. 'Not a kid — least not one of their current cases — too young. And anyway, if their parents've got nothing to carp about, why should they?' Jameson felt there was something wrong with the sergeant's reasoning but didn't interrupt. 'Could be Dorothy and Ann knew something that might be damaging.'

'Blackmail?' Jameson considered this.

'It *could* be coincidence that the children's home story broke at about the same time,' Foster said. 'But if Dr Radcliffe *was* mixed up in it, well, it certainly wouldn't do her career much good.'

Jameson acknowledged this with a slight lift of his chin. 'Or,' he suggested, 'what about a one-time case on the panel's list? Someone with a care order, or in a home. Which brings us back to the Sunnyside connection.' He thought again that the way ahead would be much clearer, things much simpler, if he knew he could trust Dr Radcliffe. 'Maxim Regis is acting for the majority of the former care-home residents, and he's telling them to keep their mouths shut.'

'He wants doing for obstruction,' Foster growled.

'Still, the killer is hardly likely to be someone who's suing the council — he or she seems to want to extract a more biblical recompense.' Seeing Foster's puzzled expression, he added, 'Eye for an eye.'

'Well, that helps.'

Jameson wondered if Foster was being sarcastic, but the Sergeant went on: 'We can cross anyone who's taking legal action off the list. That leaves us with former residents who haven't come forward.'

'Good,' said Jameson, 'let's do that.' He allowed Foster time to feel a warm glow of satisfaction, then asked, 'How're we doing on the clients with violent histories?'

'There's a few we haven't been able to trace,' Foster said. 'The ones we have found are a mixed bag. Some seem to've got their lives together, but there's a some seriously screwed up bastards in the bunch.'

Jameson rubbed a hand over his face. 'Yes, but at the risk of repeating myself, why wait till now to start bumping people off?'

Foster leaned forward in his chair, attentive. 'Start? You don't think there's going to be more, do you, boss?'

'At the moment, I don't seem to be doing any bloody thinking, only reacting.'

There was a silence. Jameson focused his attention on a coffee ring on the low table in front of him. After what seemed a long time, he met Foster's eye. 'If this character's got something against the council and its education service, I can't see why he'd stop at two.'

Foster had to swallow hard on that one. 'So, like you said, why wait till now? Unless he was too young, or too small, or too sane before. Or—'

'Or,' Jameson chipped in, 'he was too securely banged up to do a bloody thing about it. We need to recheck criminal records and flag up any recent releases.'

* * *

'I seen Daz the other day,' said Gary.

'Daz who?' It seemed that George Maddox was in no mood for small talk.

'Daz *Lewis* — you remember.'

Maddox grunted, exchanging money for powder over Gary's scuffed kitchen table. 'I thought he didn't do drugs.'

'Everyone does drugs,' said Gary, looking up from the money, flashing the large, bloodshot whites of his eyes at George. 'Legal, illegal, smokable, edible, injectable — pills, powders, herbs — don't kid yourself.'

'You wha'?' George gave him one of his sharp, don't-fuck-with-me looks.

Gary looked back mildly. Maddox didn't scare him. Not while his German shepherd was curled up under the table, his head on one paw, growling softly just to let him know he was listening. Gary didn't make Georgie line up outside with the rest of the punters out of respect for the time they had done together, but it wouldn't take much to make him change his mind. He didn't owe Maddox a thing, and as a dealer he had plenty on Georgie boy — not least the withdrawal of his good will. 'He takes a bit of shit from time to time,' Gary said, returning to Lewis.

'Don't we all.' Maddox relaxed, even smiled a little.

'Wanted somewhere to get his head down,' Gary went on. 'Kept going on about that children's home thing.'

There was a just discernible change in Maddox. It was hard to define: perhaps a slight alteration of stance, a lowering of the head, a hunching of the shoulders.

'You went to Sunnyside, didn't you?'

'So?'

'Just wondered if any of the stories was true, like.' Gary looked past Maddox, over his shoulder, avoiding his eye. He sensed that Maddox was coming over all dangerous again. He'd never met a bloke so defensive about being asked a straight question. He thought about it and decided he'd had enough dicking about and raised his eyes to George's, deliberately hardening them to an impenetrable stare. George gave in first, which surprised him.

'D'you read about the Municipal Murders?' George asked.

Gary stood slowly to avoid startling the dog. He didn't answer straight away, for fear of making Maddox clam up.

He fetched two tumblers from the tarnished steel drainer and reached for a bottle of whisky from one of the grimy kitchen cupboards. 'Know them, did you?'

George smiled slowly, accepting the whisky. 'About time someone made that fish-faced fuck shut her hole,' he said, fiddling with the little packet of white powder.

'You wanna do that now?' Gary asked. He'd get more out of George if he was comfortable, sated; if he stopped for the night.

'I can wait,' said George, with such menace that Gary was offended. They locked gazes again, this time duelling for a full thirty seconds. George won the round. 'Sure, mate,' Gary said. 'Just trying to be the good host.'

George stared a few seconds longer. 'No sweat,' he said, his voice in resonance with the dog's low growl.

* * *

A faint hint of blood red light still lingered in the sky, and Darren Lewis smiled. He would create his own sunset soon. The roadway was deserted. He'd parked his car an easy one-hundred-yard sprint further back. In his left hand he carried a brown paper bag. In his right trouser pocket he felt the comforting weight of his gold lighter. One side was engraved with *Light my fire!* A present to himself, from his first ever commission. He slipped his hand into his pocket, felt the rough texture of the lettering under his thumb. He walked round to the back of the house, nodding to an old man who shuffled past. For one, or maybe two, minutes he listened outside, breathing in the stink of privet blossom and rotten wood, stirring a memory of some summer past, before he had started lighting fires. There was an undertone of mouldy carpets, and an overwhelming sense of safety wrapped up in it. He shook his head to free himself of the notion, listened again. There was no sound from the kitchen. He peeled the brown paper from the container and removed its cork, took the rag from his pocket, dampened it with the fuel from the flask: chemical flasks shattered more easily than wine bottles and were therefore more effective. Then he stuffed the rag in the mouth of the flask and lit it, holding on to it a second or two longer, just for the hell of it, then lifted the iron sheet and tossed the flask in with an underarm action.

A cry of alarm warned him, and he began to run. There were screams now, and he could see in his mind the fire taking hold. Thick black smoke coiling in oily strands from pools of hot liquid. Sharp spikes of flame on the tips of the shattered flask where beads of fuel formed. Lazy rings of blue-tinged flame. And all the time he was running. Somebody screamed at him as he turned the corner of the building. They were in one of the upstairs rooms. He did not turn to look but ran like fury with fire racing through his brain.

* * *

The sitting room was a mess. Chris had brought down the boxes of files and old desk diaries which Simon had lugged up to the loft when she had first moved in. Fortunately, the previous owners had installed a loft ladder and the roof beams had been covered with thick plywood, so the operation was relatively simple, if rather dusty. She felt guilty that another night's work had been cancelled, but she couldn't very well ask Simon to look over records referring to his own case, so she'd had no choice.

Her 1986 and 1987 diaries lay open on the floor, and next to them what seemed to be a jumble of document wallets, some of which had been opened and their papers spread out.

Chris sat cross-legged on the rug; the polished beech flooring was cooler, but harder on the buttocks. The sun had set two hours ago, but the French windows stood open. The room had cooled by a few degrees, worth the occasional irritation of a night-flying insect, battering itself against the lamps.

She was surprised that she had seen so many children in just under eighteen months, and appalled that so many

117

of them were now no more than names to her. She held in one hand a list of the dates missing from the files she had rifled earlier that day — or the day before, since now it was surely well after one a.m. She was checking these against her own diaries, looking for names and finding, frustratingly, that often the only names she had entered were those of colleagues she would need to consult or meet with on any particular day.

She looked with growing dismay at the great pile of multi-coloured wallets; she would have to plough through all of them, cross-checking for dates. They were her personal notes; she had thought about offering them to the borough when she left — strictly speaking, they were LEA property — but LEA records had to be presented on the correct colour-coded, set-format sheets. Borough administrators had neither the time nor the patience for background information or academic conjecture; they required half-page summaries, the miseries of years of neglect or abuse distilled into a few dispassionate words. Chris couldn't bring herself to hand over her notes knowing that they would be destroyed, so they had gathered dust for ten years, moving with her when she changed addresses because she had formed an idea that at some stage she might use them to write a book.

Each file contained a brief résumé of a child: their date of birth, date of referral, the names of their key workers, a summary of their problems, family and health history and her own impressions, together with her recommendations. But most importantly, there were dates — of interviews, assessments, panel meetings — and these could be matched against the dates that were missing from the borough's files.

A faint buzzing drew her attention from the papers she had begun sifting through. Chris looked across to the standard lamp, where a large moth with bright orange-red underwings seemed determined to beat itself to death against the bulb. She caught it, careful not to damage its wings, and took it outside into the garden. The flags were cooling now, and she closed her eyes for a moment, breathing the scented air and enjoying the drop in temperature. The moth beat its wings frantically, fluttering madly in her cupped hands, but she held it until she was halfway down the garden. The moon was a thin crescent, no more, and it occurred to her that the bright light of her sitting room must shine like a beacon in the crowding darkness of the country night. She lifted her hands and slowly opened them. The moth burst from its prison and was gone in an instant. Her unadapted eyes could not follow its flight into the darkness.

It was unnaturally quiet and suddenly Chris felt vulnerable standing alone, in the open, in the dark. She walked quickly back to the house, shutting the doors after her and returning to the heaped piles of records on the floor, but the darkness felt like a solid presence at her back and she returned to lock the doors and draw the curtains closed.

'Idiot,' she told herself, the sound of her own voice breaking the mood. She worked for another hour, whittling down the pile to something more manageable before calling it a night, but the problem niggled at her, robbing her of all but a few snatches of sleep. In her dreams Ann and Dorothy tried to help her sort through the files.

'Shall I take the pastel shades?' Dorothy's voice, remembered from ten years ago, was timid, afraid of giving offence. 'Sorry.' She smiled apologetically, anxious not to seem bossy.

She always did go in for pastels, Chris thought. Blouses and skirts in matching two-tones, and little flowery frocks in pink and palest yellow.

Ann was impatient, as always, telling her to just bloody well get on with it instead of apologizing for her sodding existence. But when she tried to pick up some of the files, they had slipped from her grasp and all three had looked in horror at the stumps of her arms, which truly were bloody.

Chris turned in her sleep with a low sob. Ann was screaming, trying to protect her head as an axe swung at her. She woke as the sharp, moon-blue blade made contact, heard distinctly the *snick* of metal slicing flesh. Chris lay for a moment, eyes wide, heart pounding, then allowed herself to relax. A dream. Just a dream. She closed her eyes briefly, listening to the thin, high song of a skylark trickle through the open window from the fields beyond her garden.

Then she was up and running, tugging on her dressing gown, taking the stairs two at a time. Front door bolted. Throwing the bolts. Into the still fresh morning air. Down the path, her feet slapping on the cool stone. Out through the gate. It closed behind her with a quiet *snick*.

The same *snick*.

The road was empty. No sign of her escort. In the distance, the sound of a car moving away from her. She returned to the gate. Opened it. Let it swing shut. *Snick*. Too early for the post. Too early for any bloody thing, she realized, having glanced at the hall clock. Five a.m. and no prospect of any more sleep.

Five hours later she was eating breakfast in her kitchen. Showered, refreshed, and with a list of fourteen names on a sheet of A4 paper in front of her. She had read through each of the files belonging to the fourteen names. Four girls, the rest boys. Next to each name she had written a date of birth, chronological age, and a short summary. She marked with a cross those who would now be under eighteen. An arbitrary decision, perhaps, but she couldn't conceive of a younger child having murdered Dorothy and Ann. The under-eighteens added up to five — two girls and three boys. The rest she looked at again.

David Trask, ESN, placement in a school for children with moderate learning difficulties. She didn't remember him. ESN. The abbreviation made her wince a little: 'educationally sub-normal' was not a term that would be acceptable today. More likely the all-encompassing 'learning difficulties' would be employed. She checked back through his file. He had been placed at the special school within eight or nine months of referral. Good going. It wasn't likely him, or his parents would have cause to quarrel with their treatment.

She looked at the next on the list. John Emerson — ADD, EBD. He had been sent to a special unit for children with behavioural problems. A vague memory of a little, shrew-faced boy. Hyperactive, yes. And destructive. He had been referred at the age of eight, having attacked his form teacher and then thrown a chair at his headmaster when he had intervened. Chris wrote a question mark in the margin next to John's name.

Laura Smith — orphaned. Foster placement. She remembered Laura. A tiny scrap of a girl with shining, black hair cut into a short bob. At nine years old she had nursed her mother through the terminal stages of cancer. Nobody knew about it until she failed to turn up for school for several days and the school, unable to get an answer by phone, had sent an outreach social worker to check on her.

The social worker had found Laura sitting by her mother, holding her hand as she raved in pain and delirium. Laura had given her mother her injections, just as the doctor had instructed, but they weren't helping. Laura's mother had died later that day and Laura had not been there — she had been taken to a children's ward at the same hospital, dehydrated and malnourished, and had been sedated because she kept trying to get out of bed to go home.

When Chris had interviewed her two weeks later, the child was withdrawn and resentful. She had refused to co-operate, saying only that her mother was dead, and she might as well be, too.

The ward sister warned her. 'Little Scouse tiger,' she said. 'Watch your eyes if she loses her temper.'

'Leave me alone!' the child had cried after a few minutes of Chris's gentle but insistent questions. 'I just wanna die!'

'Your mother wouldn't want that, Laura,' she said.

The little girl screwed up her eyes. ''Ow do you know?' she demanded. 'Youse lot never knew me mam.' She chewed the side of her index finger, nibbling avidly, like a mouse. Then the hand came down and she burst out, 'If they'd never give her them needles she'd've been OK!' Tears sprang into the child's eyes. 'They only give them her to stop her screamin'.' Her hands hooked over the edge of the chair and

121

she gripped it fiercely. 'I didn't mind!' she said, as though denying an accusation. 'I never! She would of been OK if they would've just left us alone.'

Chris put from her mind the image of this little black-eyed girl trying to comfort her mother who was beyond comfort, beyond help, beyond human thought in her agony. Her own emotional reaction would not help Laura. 'No,' she said, with quiet firmness. 'She wouldn't. She would not have been OK. Your mum died because she had cancer. No one could have saved her. I know you wanted to be there, Laura. I know you wanted to be with your mum when she died, but the doctors were worried about you. Little girls need sleep—'

The attack was sudden and shocking. Laura flew at her, fists flailing. She screamed over and over. 'I'm not a little girl. I'm not. I'm not. I'M NOT! I hate you. You bloody killed her! Yis all killed her, you bloody bastard *murderers*!'

Laura had stayed another week at the hospital and had then been placed with an experienced couple, but she had stubbornly refused any suggestion of adoption and she would not co-operate with any of the counselling sessions which were arranged. Even Ted had been rebuffed.

Chris had felt it a terrible failure. If she had handled it better — if she'd had more experience. 'Where are you now, Laura?' she asked the empty air.

The next two on the list she discounted — one child was dyslexic — late diagnosis. Withdrawal had been arranged for a structured reading and spelling programme to be taught in school. The other was a child who had suffered a spinal injury and had been allocated to a school with wheelchair access.

Then, Simon Webster. Simon's case had become something of a crusade for her, but the next boy on the list had been the real problem — Darren Lewis. It had been a few months after she started at the borough offices. Both referred at the same time, after an arson incident at the school in which she had taught before qualifying as an educational psychologist.

Simon was quiet, reflective and, beneath the bravura, sensitive. Always in trouble, though he never gave her any, always getting into scrapes. He reminded her of Phil — apt to follow the crowd and end up taking the blame.

Darren had been the leader on that occasion. He had filched the caretaker's keys from his office. He purchased the matches and lighter fluid, had even chosen the basement as the place where they were least likely to be disturbed. It was Darren who had given the instructions to bundle some rags and old newspapers in the corner, and Darren who had lit the thin line of fire to start the blaze.

Simon had watched, and then — afraid for the other children — raised the alarm. But he had been willing to take the blame for the older boy; Chris remembered how Simon had reacted, seeing her alongside the other members of the panel. His eyes kindled when he saw her, but he quickly extinguished the light in them, assuming a cocky stare which failed to convince even himself. And she remembered a haunted look about the child, remembered feeling a desperate need to help him, together with an absolute conviction of her powerlessness to do so.

The panel had decided that, since the school had chosen not to press charges against Simon, he should go back to his family. She could not analyse why she had been disappointed by their decision — Simon never actually said anything to her — but there was something in him, something which reminded her of herself, a kind of desperation to get away from home. From his parents.

She had recommended a placement away from his family for further evaluation. It was refused, although Darren had been placed in care. She had risked suspension in pushing the case for a care order, but the decision had gone against her and Simon had returned home. Chris shrugged. She was older now, less sure of her own infallibility. Simon had set other fires and eventually had been caught and given three years' youth custody. 'It took me four years to pluck up the courage to set the fire which put me away,' he had told her recently, 'but I had to do it to get away from home. Who'd've thought three years' prison could change a life so completely for the better?' She closed his file and slung it to one side. No point in allowing herself to become side-tracked. For Chris, reading case notes was like thumbing through an encyclopaedia or surfing the Net: sometimes you ended up miles from where you expected to be.

Darren Lewis was as different from Simon as it was possible to be. A weasel-faced teenager, it was difficult to like or indeed to feel any sympathy for him. He was a fourteen-year-old thug with spiky blonde hair and crooked teeth which gave him a wolfish menace when he smiled. It came as a surprise when he confessed — probably as a result of his mother's constant haranguing. Darren's mother, at thirty-five, looked fifty; there had been a spark of quiet triumph in her eyes when she finally told them what had happened. One less to worry about, one less to control. He had been placed in the care of the local council. Yes, she thought, Darren was worth checking.

The last name on the list was George Maddox. His Chinese mother had died when he was just five years old. His father, old and unable to cope with a demanding and tearful infant, had left him to his own devices. Kicked out with the cat in the morning and, like the cat, coming home only to eat and sleep, George had quickly discovered that on the street, violence was power. He had used violence to achieve his goals. He used it dispassionately, as a means to an end — he was not sadistic and he gained no pleasure from inflicting pain — but he would use whatever extremes necessary to gain the respect which he felt was due him. When he realized that his superior strength could also be used to material gain, he was pleasantly surprised, and was quick to learn to exploit his new-found talent.

As George's confidence increased, and his reputation became established on the estate where he lived, the old man became fearful of his son. He would go out in the evenings to avoid him, so George had the run of the house. The arrests followed shortly after. The first was for extorting money out of younger children on the estate, the second for mugging a businessman as he left the bank in Castle Street, in Liverpool city centre. Short spells in children's homes did no good. Thus, within a year, he went from truanting to bullying, from bullying to extortion and from extortion to mugging. And then to drugs. At the age of fifteen, George had had more arrests than any of the other boys on the estate, and he wore them as a badge of pride. He had a reputation to maintain.

When his father arrived home from the pub early one night, George was entertaining two girls with a few of his mates. The girls were naked, and the boys, in various stages of undress, were stoned.

'He flipped,' George had told her. 'Bastard smacked me with a beer bottle. He was screaming at the girls, calling them tarts, whores — stuff like that. My head was bleeding and he was calling me names — "Slant-eye", "Chink" — same old stuff. Said me mam was an easy lay, you know, like she was some kind of prozzy. Said I wasn't even his son. Called me a bastard.'

'The girls was crying, like. And then he grabbed me by the hair.' George's dark eyes glittered with indignation at the remembered humiliation. 'He was *embarrassing* me in front of me mates!' He fell silent, shaking his head in disbelief.

'And what happened then, George?' Chris asked.

George regarded her with deep suspicion.

'I had to stop him saying them things about her. He said she sold it for cash. He said filthy, disgusting things about me mam.' George looked down at his hands. 'Me mates'd gone, taking the girls with them. I knew it would be all round the estate the next day about me dad chucking them out. They'd be *laughing* at me, telling them what me dad'd said about Mam! He always was braver after a few bevvies — and he'd had a skinful that night . . . He kept needling me.' He'd glanced into Chris's face, his eyes anguished. 'I just wanted to stop him saying them dirty things about Mam. So I squeezed his scrawny, greasy neck—' He had looked up at Chris, eyes bright with anger at first, but gradually that had faded and he looked bewildered, almost surprised. 'Until he stopped.'

For some minutes there were only two sounds in the room: the slow ticking of the wall clock and the quiet sobs of the boy. 'I should've never been left with him,' George said, feeling for the first time the bitter injustice of it. 'I should've been took away.' Poor George. He knew then what his life would be. And he knew it could have been different.

Simon had been sentenced to youth custody. A secure unit. Chris wrote in the margin next to his name. *Is he out?*

Ruling out Simon, the list comprised John Emerson, Laura Smith, Darren Lewis and George Maddox. Where should she start looking? They'd be off the child protection register by now. Some of them could even be married with children of their own. And what of George? He would be in prison by now, she supposed, if indeed he was still in custody. Was there some sort of register? Could she call Her Majesty's Prison Service and ask for the location of a prisoner? Where would she find the number? They were hardly likely to be listed in Yellow Pages.

She went into the hallway and dialled 192. 'What prison do you want?' The operator's voice was professionally distant.

'No specific prison,' said Chris. 'It's a general enquiry.'

'That'd be the Home Office, wouldn't it? Don't they deal with all the organization?'

'Sounds right.'

'I'll give you the HQ.'

The line went dead for a second and then a recording gave her the number. No point calling at the weekend, Chris decided. She would get Nicky to try on Monday, and with a bit of luck her trawl of the flat agencies might have turned up something on Jake Dixon, the guy at the hostel who was friendly with her foster brother. In the meantime, she had promised old Alf a return visit.

11

Chris left her car in Birkenhead and caught a taxi through to Liverpool; she wasn't taking any chances. Traffic was heavy by the time she reached the top end of Smithdown Road, and the fumes and the heat were beginning to give her a headache. She stopped off at Tesco to make a few purchases, then joined the steady grumble of noise, turning right onto Ullet Road and making quickly for the quieter avenues around Sefton Park.

It didn't take her long to discover that the police had been busy. She was asked for her warrant card at each of the four squats she visited. At the well-organized commune, the rooms still blazed with light and she could smell chicken roasting in the oven, but a lookout had been posted at one of the front windows and two men — one of them the axe man of her previous visit — sat guarding the iron doorway at the rear of the house.

'What did you want to send them here for?' It was the woman who had spoken, her face closed, hostile.

'Who?' Chris asked.

'The bizzies, who d'you think?'

'If someone has tipped off the police it wasn't me,' Chris said. 'I want to get to Phil before they do — why would I tip them off?'

'I just hope you find your friend before you get us kicked out,' said a small and rather beautiful South Asian man.

'I'm sorry if you're being hassled—'

The woman broke in with a shout of harsh laughter. 'Hassled!' she said. 'We get that every day of our lives. We can take *hassle*.'

She turned away suddenly, and Chris looked from one angry face to the next, surprised, increasingly aware of an undercurrent of fear and grief. 'Something has happened,' she said.

The man put one hand lightly on the woman's shoulder and Chris saw that she was crying, shaking with silent tears. 'Friends of ours. Last night,' the man said. 'Their squat was firebombed.'

Chris searched his face. He nodded. 'They put the fire out, but Kirsti was already badly burned. She got splashed with the fuel.'

* * *

Alf seemed untouched by events. He knew about the fire-bomb attack, even speculated as to the motive, but somehow it seemed remote from him, as though it had no direct bearing on his own situation. He offered to take a stroll in the garden, but they abandoned the idea when he tripped over some barbed wire that had been dumped after being cut down from a gate or doorway. The grasses and dock and knotweed had hidden it entirely. Chris caught him before he fell, but it triggered a coughing fit that left her watching help-lessly until gradually it subsided and his breathing returned to its more familiar rumbling wheeze. He sat down on a large sandstone block in the sun to catch his breath.

'Wait there,' said Chris. She returned a few minutes later with a carrier bag.

'Brought your lunch, 'ave you?' Alf wheezed.

'Something like that.' She dived into the bag and pulled out a medicine bottle.

Alf looked at her, amused. 'Cough medicine?' he said. 'It's something stronger I'm wanting, girl.'

Chris grinned. 'Thought of that, too,' she said, taking out a bottle of whisky. 'Only, will you do me a favour, Alf?'

He laughed, a gravelly rumble in his chest. 'Take me meddy first, eh?'

She shrugged, still smiling.

The rumble grew louder, sounding like an elderly car engine turning over, but not catching. 'Ar' ey, girl — you're blushing.' He took the bottle from her hand and downed a swig. 'Got any sarnies in there?' he asked, rustling the bag.

'As a matter of fact . . .'

'Should of brought me bucket an' spade,' he said. 'We could've gone to New Brighton beach and had a picnic.' He gave another wheezy laugh and patted her hand, then stood unsteadily and walked with a slightly rolling gait to the back door of the house.

'Where are you going?' Chris asked.

'Back in a tick.'

He returned with two mismatched tumblers, both rinsed and wiped. Chris held the glasses while he poured each of them a shot. 'Can't have you drinking out the same bottle,' he said. 'You don't want what I got — and I don't drink alone.'

Chris sat next to him on the sun-warm sandstone, surrounded by rank weeds and the detritus dumped by generations of squatters. Chris sipped at her whisky, thinking she would rather have a glass of cold water.

'Only problem with this doss is the damp. But I'll be OK.' His dark eyes searched her own. Chris looked into his genial face and felt ashamed.

He patted her hand again. 'Now, this friend of yours—'

'Phil?' Chris said, trying to control her excitement. 'Have you seen him, Alf?'

'Not personally, like, but I know someone who reckons he might know where he is. Might take you to him.' He stopped, seeming momentarily embarrassed. 'For a price.'

'Anything!' said Chris, reaching for the cash in her back pocket.

'No! No . . . Not like that, girl. Play it cool. Let him think you're not that interested. Put a couple of fivers in your side pocket and make it look like you're having trouble getting the cash together, right?'

Chris nodded and Alf smiled, satisfied, turning his full attention to the food Chris had brought. 'Good scran this, girl. I'll take you round when we've finished our picnic, OK?'

* * *

Alf led her to a crumbling parade of shops off Myrtle Street, under the greying lintel which braced adjacent buildings as if to keep them from brawling, into a narrow, paved square. More oblong than square, it was grimy, run down and depressing. Chris sat as instructed at one end of a vandalized bench, Alf at the other. Shoppers, mainly women, scuffed through the square, their faces hungry and exhausted, their eyes avoiding the bench where Alf sat, staring out at them with bloodshot eyes.

Chris was surprised when a small, round man sat next to her. He wore a pale grey suit with shoes to match and he brought a startlingly white handkerchief from his pocket to wipe his tanned and polished forehead.

'I can't swear it's him, you understand,' he began without preamble. 'But he's very like the photos on telly. Nervy as well.' He was soft-spoken and retained a hint of a Liverpool accent, long suppressed.

'Where?' Alf asked. They had agreed that he would do the talking.

The little man shrugged. 'Gazzer's—' He stopped, embarrassed.

Alf nodded to Chris and she dug into one pocket, then the other and drew out a couple of crumpled notes. The man took the notes and smoothed them out before folding them and tucking them into the inside pocket of his jacket.

'Gary Tighe is my, um, provider.' He coughed. 'I saw your young man at his place a couple of days ago. I *could* give you an address . . .'

As they walked back to Alf's squat, having parted with more cash, Chris asked, 'Can I trust him?'

'He's a businessman,' said Alf, with evident distaste for the breed. 'You can't never trust that sort. But he thinks there could be a chance of making' more money, and that'll make him more reliable.'

'How does he expect to do that?'

Alf grinned. 'Told him you worked for one of them agencies that looks for missing persons and that, didn't I? Soapy bastard wouldn't mess up the chance of screwing a bit more cash out of you.'

Chris was rather touched by his gallant effort to curb his language. 'You don't think there'd be any point in going to the house now?' she asked.

'Wait till tomorrow, girl. Go when he told you. Your mate won't be there now. And you won't see him for dust if you warn him by swanning in there ahead of time.'

Chris gave an impatient sigh. 'I know you're right, Alf. I just hate hanging around while the police are looking for him.'

The sun was high and hot and the distant traffic sounds swelled and faded, humming like a lazy swarm of bees. They walked in the shade, an incongruous pair; the tall, cool blonde trying to moderate her pace to the shambling old man's shuffle.

'Alf,' she said suddenly, 'I don't suppose . . . Look, tell me to sod off if you want to, but—'

The humorous brown eyes crinkled at her. 'What?' he asked. Chris chewed the side of her mouth, wondering whether to shut up and let the matter drop. 'Go on, girl. You might as well get it off your chest.'

What the hell . . . She took a deep breath and launched in. 'Would you be offended if I suggested sorting out accommodation for you? A flat, bedsit, hostel — whatever you want?'

'Yeah.'

Chris flushed and mumbled an apology.

''S all right,' he said, grinning suddenly. 'It's been a long time since a good-looking girl like you looked out for me.' Chris laughed and he shrugged. 'I like the freedom. I'll be off down south soon as the leaves start to turn. Bath, London, Bristol. Better dosses for the winter. I've got mates all over.' There was pride in this. Alf shrugged. 'I can't explain it.'

'I take it it'd be no good offering you money, either?'

Alf glanced across at her and gave a short, coughing laugh. He put his hand on her arm, gesturing for her to stop. Liquid gurgled painfully in his lungs. Chris waited for him to recover, pushing him gently onto a low wall where he sat wheezing for several minutes, his chest groaning.

'At least let me find a doctor who'll treat you!' she blurted out.

'I won't be stayin' that long, girl. This place'll finish me off if I don't make a move soon. Now let's get back. That whisky's calling to me.'

The pale girl Chris had seen on her previous visit was loitering in the back garden when they got back. She sat on a lump of sandstone, feeding the baby from a bottle and pretending not to notice them. Alf greeted her with a rough, 'All right, girl?' She scowled at the baby, hunching her shoulders, and Alf shrugged. 'Suit yourself,' he muttered, shuffling inside.

The girl waited until the iron sheet had squealed into place behind him before she spoke. 'Some feller was looking for you.'

Chris had been watching Alf, anxious that he might fall on the uneven step. 'What?' she asked.

The girl's features were immobile. It was as if she hadn't spoken.

'Who was looking for me? What did he look like?'

The girl gave her a crafty look from under her lashes, then slowly returned her gaze to the baby.

Chris sighed and dug into her jeans pocket. 'Who?' she repeated, holding up a five-pound note.

The girl snatched the money from between her fingers. 'Didn't say his name. Asked if you'd been around, asking questions.'

'What did he look like?'

The girl stared at Chris as she balanced the baby's bottle with her left hand and pocketed the money with the right. Chris took out another note, holding it at a distance this time. 'Description,' she said.

'Tall. Blond. Not bad looking. Nice eyes.' She reached for the money, but Chris twitched it away. 'Nice eyes,' she said. 'What colour?'

'Greeny, sort of.'

'Police?'

'Not *him*.' The girl came close to a smile but gave up on it before it broke, and instead held her hand out for the money.

* * *

When she got home, Chris went straight to the dining room, where she had left her notes from Wednesday's session with Simon. She should do some work before he was due to arrive at four. She needed something to take her mind off the meeting with Phil tomorrow, something to help time pass, but she could not concentrate and rose impatiently from the table after reading the same passage over four or five times without any of it making sense to her. She telephoned Nicky. In the background she could hear the TV sports round-up.

'Remember that guy named Dixon who disappeared from the hostel just after Phil did a runner?'

'I haven't turned anything up on him yet. Why?'

'What colour were his eyes?'

Nicky hesitated. 'I'm only going on what you said—'

'And I'm going on what the social worker told me.'

'Green, wasn't it?'

Chris felt her stomach roll. 'That's what I thought,' she said, sickly.

'Well, are you going to tell me what's going on, or what?'

'I think he's following me,' Chris said.

'Call the police.'

'The thing is, I think *they're* following me, too. They'll think I'm paranoid.'

'Yeah? Well, just because you're paranoid doesn't mean they're not out to get you.'

'Thanks,' said Chris. 'That's very reassuring.'

'I'm not trying to reassure you. Tell Jameson about it — 'cos if you don't, I will.'

Chris hung up.

What the hell did Dixon want? Who was he? She realized that she was tugging at her fringe, pulling strands over the silver thread of scar tissue above her left eye and left off, exasperated and annoyed with herself. Next, she'd be biting her nails. Perhaps she should try and get the girl at the squat to set up a meeting, if he were to call again. But something told her Dixon would not be back. She jumped to her feet in an effort to dispel the panicky feelings rising in her chest and went out into the garden.

After wandering aimlessly up and down the curving edge of the lawn, she went to the small shed next to the greenhouse and took out a hoe, spending the next hour needlessly weeding. In the baking heat, scarcely a seedling had appeared anywhere, but she moved in an anticlockwise arc from the greenhouse to the shrubbery, trying to control the almost unstoppable urge to drive straight back to the address Alf's contact had given her. 'He won't *be* there,' she told herself, working on, jabbing the sharp edge of the new hoe into the dry dust of the sandy soil. She had almost resolved to speak to Jameson, to tell him what she knew about Dixon, if not what she feared. Then, slowing, leaning on the hoe, she bent to pick up a bright tube from the base of the laburnum. A Smarties tube. She lifted the lower, whippy branches and moved at a crouch, deeper into the dense tangle of leafy shade. St John's wort, azaleas and rhododendrons crowded together, but a space had been cleared beneath the rhododendron and the floor was littered with sweet wrappers. Chris looked back across the lawn to the house. There was a clear line of sight through the French windows and into her sitting room.

She stood up too quickly, catching her eye on a twig. She yelled and swore, then forced her way through the bushes onto the lawn, ran along the side path and through the gate. The blue Fiesta was parked fifty yards up the road. She could just make out the silhouette of the driver. The oppressive rhythm of pop music throbbed on the heavy afternoon air.

She heard the gate close behind her with a quiet *snick* and the invasion of her privacy seemed even more immediate and more monstrous than before.

She walked towards the car, hoe still in hand. She could barely see, through her watering eye, the outline of the driver (male or female?) but saw a violent movement before the engine roared into life. The gearbox groaned as the car was thrown into reverse. It moved away from her at crazy speed.

'Hey!' Chris screamed. 'I want to talk to you!' The car backed into her neighbours' driveway, clipping the corner of their wall. Chris broke into a run, yelling, but the car turned and accelerated away.

'Bastard!' she shouted. She hurled the hoe like a javelin after the car, but it landed well short of its target and skittered harmlessly off the road and onto the grass verge. She stood looking after it, fists clenched, unable to make out the registration through the water still streaming from her eye. Slowly, she became aware that she was being watched. Her neighbour, Mr Alsop, stood next to his car with a sponge in his hand and a startled expression on his face. Chris wiped the moisture from her eye.

'All right, dear?' he asked, tentatively.

Chris gave him a rueful grin and ran a hand through her hair, discovering bits of leaves and twigs and pulling ineffectually at them.

'Road hog,' she said weakly. Then, patting the sandstone wall, she added, 'Still, no real damage.' Mr Alsop nodded cautiously. They looked at each other in uncomfortable silence until Chris coughed. 'I don't suppose you got the registration?' He stared blankly and she decided it would be best to retire quietly. 'Mustn't keep you,' she murmured. She retrieved the hoe with as much dignity as she could muster and walked back to the house muttering, 'Bugger, bugger, bugger . . .'

Detective Chief Inspector Jameson's answerphone was switched on. He wasn't at his office, either. She was still staring at the phone as though she held a personal grudge against it, when the doorbell rang.

She flung it open to find Jameson himself standing on the doorstep. Foster stood beside him, looking sharp and faintly gangsterish in sunglasses.

'Dr Radcliffe,' Jameson said. 'I'm afraid I have some bad news.'

Her fears for her own safety fled, replaced by something far more immediate. She felt herself pale and unconsciously gripped the door frame.

'Phil?' she said.

The two men seemed uncomfortable. She looked from Jameson to Foster, willing them to speak. 'Your father.' Jameson had spoken.

An immense and terrible conflict of emotions swept through her, but when she spoke, her voice was firm. 'What about my father?'

'Can we come inside?'

'What about my father?' she repeated.

'He's dead.' She glanced sharply at Foster, suspecting him of having enjoyed giving the news. Again, Jameson saw the same conflict of feelings flit across her face.

'I thought you should know,' he said, seeming apologetic for Foster's bluntness.

'Thank you,' she said, knowing the response was inappropriate. 'Where?'

'The city mortuary. There are some details: formal identification, personal effects. And arrangements for—'

He hesitated and she realised that he had almost said 'for disposal of the body' but he changed this to 'For burial.'

She realised that he was waiting for an answer, and said, 'Now?'

He nodded. 'If it's not inconvenient.'

'Yes,' she said, 'of course. I . . .' She turned to the telephone and dialled Maria Stevens's number with trembling hands.

* * *

Jameson stepped inside uninvited, signalling Foster to return to the car.

'Bel?' he heard her say. 'Yeah. The police are here. No. No sign as yet. Listen . . .' She sounded incredulous, and enunciated the words carefully, as though it was important there should be no mistake about what she was saying, as though she was almost trying to convince herself. 'They say my father has been found dead. They want me to go to the mortuary.' There was a pause. 'I know. Could you?' Jameson thought he heard a hint of vulnerability in her tone, then she turned to him and asked for directions. She relayed the information and hung up.

Jameson insisted on driving her to the mortuary, seating her in the back of the car so that he could watch her in the rear-view mirror. She seemed pensive rather than upset.

'When?' she asked, as they turned out of the country lane and onto the A540.

'A few days ago. He was found on Monday afternoon.'

'Found?'

Jameson watched her steadily in the mirror. 'He fell down the steps of St Luke's church at the top of Bold Street.'

Jameson studied her anew. No surprise, no shock or sorrow registered on her face, only a speculative, almost calculating evaluation. She muttered something: 'Drunk,' or possibly '*A* drunk.' Jameson couldn't be sure. It was stated quietly and with no discernible bitterness.

'His blood alcohol levels were high,' Jameson said.

She fell silent, and Jameson concentrated on the road as they negotiated the lights at Bromborough. He glanced up into the mirror a minute later and saw her frowning.

'Why wasn't I informed on Monday?' she asked.

'The only ID he had on him was a marriage certificate,' he said. 'The local police tried to trace next of kin via the register of births and deaths, but it's a messy way round of doing things. It was pure coincidence that someone heard your show on Wednesday and thought there might be a connection.'

'Strange thing to carry around, a marriage certificate,' she observed.

Jameson considered this — it had seemed strange to him, too. 'They went to your old address and got no reply,' he said. 'They went back today and were given your new address by your old landlord.' He didn't add that some bright spark at her local nick had contacted him with the news, and Jameson had dissuaded them from going to inform her that morning. He wanted to deliver the news personally so that he could watch her reaction.

'You weren't at work on Monday, Dr Radcliffe,' Foster said.

'No.'

Jameson let the silence hang for a few seconds. 'Where, precisely, were you?'

She gave him a surprised look. 'Oh, I see. You're asking me where I was when he died.'

And when Ann was abducted, he thought, but contented himself with saying, 'If that's how you want to see it, yes.' He glanced away from the road and their eyes met briefly in the mirror.

'I was at home,' she said. 'I've just moved in. I had things to sort out.'

'Alone?'

'Yes. Alone. All day and all night. Sorry, Mr Jameson, I can't give you an alibi to crack.'

Her callousness was shocking.

'No doubt you will think me unfeeling and hard,' she said. 'But since you know fuck all about it, don't presume to judge me.'

When he glanced in the mirror, she was eyeing him coolly.

* * *

The woman called Bel was waiting outside the mortuary when they arrived. Jameson recognized her as the girl in the family photograph; she had stood on one side of Greer, and Chris Radcliffe on the other. Bel's hair was very dark and silky, her eyes, hazel rather than brown, were large and curved upwards at each outer corner. She wore no make-up but, despite her obvious anxiety, she glowed with health and energy.

'Isabel Stevens,' Foster breathed appreciatively.

She nodded to the two men then moved forward with the poise and grace of a dancer and took both Chris's hands. They exchanged a look and Bel put her arm around Chris's waist. It was an easy, sisterly movement, and Jameson, standing behind them, saw their heads touch briefly. He felt a sudden pang of guilt at the intrusion on their privacy and turned quickly to ring for the attendant. He showed his warrant card and they were admitted immediately.

'Where is he?' Jameson asked.

'We've put him in the chapel of rest,' said by a short, rather round man in a green plastic apron. He introduced himself to Chris as Dr Connolly, the pathologist who had performed the post-mortem. Jameson guided the two women to a door to the left of the cheerless little waiting room. He eyed the small man's clothing. 'Busy?'

'No rest for the wicked.'

'Don't I know it.' He had hoped to turn something up about Chris Radcliffe by talking to her father. And now he was dead. Just as two of her former colleagues were dead.

They made a curious tableau around the trolley: two policemen, the pathologist and the two lovely young women. The Stevens woman looked more upset than Radcliffe, Jameson thought. She kept throwing her foster sister anxious glances, and she had never let go of her hand. One arm was still curled around her waist. Radcliffe, he thought, looked strained, tense, but not upset.

The attendant drew back the sheet and Chris gave an utterance of disgust or distress. Turning quickly, she left the room.

* * *

The air outside was heavy, and it seemed the stench of mortuary disinfectant followed her into the bright afternoon sunshine. Chris Radcliffe walked rapidly, needing to put distance between her and the building, stopping only when she heard Isabel calling her.

Bel slipped an arm through hers and they walked on more slowly for a few minutes. 'Are you OK?' Bel asked.

'I don't know.'

'What's going on, Chris?'

Chris shook her head. 'I don't know that, either.'

'Dr Radcliffe?' Jameson was standing a few yards away from them, oddly diffident. Chris turned to face him. 'I'm sorry,' he said. 'I have to ask. Is that—'

'No, Mr Jameson, it isn't. That isn't my father in there. My father died a year ago, just as you described. A fall — at his home, not at St Luke's — he hadn't sunk quite that low. But he *was* drunk, and he *did* die as the result of a fall. He fractured his skull.'

* * *

Jameson was beleaguered with questions and requests as soon as he set foot across the threshold of the ops room. Several ex-clients of Dorothy and Ann had recently been released from prison. All had previous or current convictions for GBH. The files were waiting on his desk. There had been numerous calls from local and national newspapers asking for comment on the status of the investigation, plus two requests from his superintendent to contact him urgently.

Jameson retreated to the relative solitude of his own office for ten minutes. He paced the tiny room, wishing for the hundredth time that he could let in some air — real air, not the carefully temperature-controlled and humidity-moderated fluid which circulated in endless hermetic cycles through this building, but good, honest-to-god air. Even the tainted and noisy fumes of the Dock Road on a Saturday would be preferable to this climateless segregation.

When he had regained some of his composure he buzzed through to Foster's desk. 'Find out where the super is, but if anyone asks, I haven't arrived yet.'

Foster came into his office a few minutes later. He was wearing a nicely starched short-sleeved shirt which persuaded Jameson against removing his own jacket. A frank exchange of words in the car on the return journey to headquarters had resulted in an uneasy silence between them.

Foster could not understand why his boss hadn't arrested Chris Radcliffe for wasting police time, whereas Jameson secretly admired her courage in going to the mortuary. On the other hand, Jameson could not fathom Foster's hostility towards the doctor. She could be next on the list: after all, her files had been tampered with, as had Dorothy's and Ann's. The same time period, the same kind of damage. He reflected that if he were Dr Radcliffe, he would have wanted to look at the body for himself.

Foster was unconvinced. As far as he was concerned, he'd said, Radcliffe was a lying, conniving, smart-arsed bitch who was protecting a murder suspect.

They had agreed — but for very different reasons — that the surveillance on the doctor should be maintained.

'The super's at home,' Foster said.

'Good. He can wait.' Jameson wanted to acquaint himself with the men in the files before facing his boss. Jameson loosened his tie and unfastened the top button of his shirt, then picked up a file from the top of the mound on his desk and shoved it at Foster. They worked through the files, taking notes.

Darren Lewis, arsonist. The first was an attack on his school at the age of eleven. Given counselling. Two arrests each for theft, burglary. One conviction. Arrest for demanding money with menaces. Charges dropped, but a care order granted. Placement in Sunnyside Home. Several arrests for assault while acting as unofficial bailiff for slum landlords. No convictions because the victims refused to press charges. Imprisoned in 1990 for an arson attack on a restaurant. At first, they had thought it was a racial attack, then it turned out the landlord who held the lease on the place had wanted to sell, and a Mr Singh, the tenant restaurateur, had decided to sit out the lease. He had lost more than his business in the attack: Lewis apparently was careless of whether the building was occupied when he set the fire and Mr Singh had suffered thirty-per-cent burns to his upper body and face.

Jameson took Wilson's file next. He found it unproductive reading. Wilson had moved from petty crime — shoplifting and handling stolen goods — to involvement in a benefits fraud which had put him away for eighteen months. His one conviction for GBH had been on another pupil at his secondary school. Jameson tossed the file to one side. 'How's yours shaping up?' he asked.

'Heavyweight,' said Foster. 'A total of—' He flicked back a few pages and did a quick reckoning. 'Ten arrests up to the age of fifteen. Spells in children's homes, including Sunnyside. Then he topped his dad — manual strangulation.'

'Oh?' Jameson said. 'Now, that *does* look interesting.'

Foster smiled, it seemed that the acrimony of their discussion in the car apparently forgotten. This was typical of the sergeant: he could be forthright and blunt to the point of rudeness, but disagreements were quickly forgotten.

'George Maddox,' Foster went on. 'Convicted of GBH aged thirteen, when he ruptured another lad's spleen in a fight. Sent to a secure children's home. Murdered his dad ten days after he got out. Committed to a young offenders' institute, released on licence at the age of twenty-one, back inside after six months. Aggravated burglary. He's got a drug habit. Still in Avonlea, but he's allowed out odd days and weekends.'

Jameson made a note on the pad on his desk. 'Check the dates of his days out, would you?' He paused, glancing again at Darren Lewis's file.

'Lewis is evidently a poisonous piece of work,' he said. 'The sooner A Division get him on that spate of arson attacks, the better. He's another Sunnyside resident, by the way.'

Foster smiled without humour. 'The old school tie,' he said. They pored over the other files: Michael Doyle — links with fascist groups. Jailed for a gang attack on an Asian boy after a football match. The boy lost an eye and (although this was not in the report) the confidence to walk the streets alone.

Shane Reid, arrested for a violent attack on a teacher. Charges dropped. Arrested for car theft. Probation. Further arrest for car theft. Short youth custody sentence. Further arrest for manslaughter — hit and run.

Kyle Banister. Smackhead. Several convictions for theft and burglary. Beat up a woman who cut in front of him in a row of traffic. He'd stamped on her so hard that his boot print could be matched with the bruising on her stomach and back. It had taken half a dozen officers to subdue him when he was arrested.

Jameson buzzed through for DC Ryman, who had been given the task of whittling down the thirty or more files to the more manageable few Jameson and Foster were dealing with. While they waited for her, he asked Foster's opinion. Foster smoothed his moustache. 'Maddox, definitely, along with Lewis. Banister, maybe.'

'Agreed.' Jameson broke off to admit Mary Ryman. She sidled into the room as though nervous she would knock something over. Her tall and rather gangling appearance and her constant, nervy activity had won her the nickname 'Thyroid Mary'. She was wearing a sleeveless blouse in a dogtooth check pattern, which emphasized her flat chest and waistless body and gave her the appearance of a gawky

143

schoolgirl. The similarity began and ended in her appearance, for Mary Ryman was respected as an able officer.

'What can you tell us about Darren Lewis?' Jameson asked.

'I know that A Division have linked him to a series of arson attacks.' Ryman's voice was deep and rather husky. A smoker's voice. 'Landlords trying to get non-payers out, owners clearing properties of squatters, one or two possible insurance fiddles. He's slippery. Always seems to have an alibi.' She paused. 'You should know — someone was injured at one of the squats around Princes Park last night. She may die.' This was said dispassionately, but she gave an involuntary shudder. 'Lewis was questioned. Says he was with Gary Tighe all night.'

'Have we got an address on him?' Jameson asked, reaching for Lewis's file.

'On Tighe, yes. He's a pusher. But Darren flits about a bit. There's a flat in the Albert Dock and a house in Penny Lane—'

Jameson's eyebrows shot up at the high-priced property address.

'Yeah,' she said. 'Crime pays.'

'Get onto A Division, just as a matter of courtesy,' Jameson said. 'Tell them we're about to upset Mr Lewis. And before you go, have we got anything more on Maddox?'

'Rumour has it he brings bags of goodies back with him to Avonlea after home leave.'

'Jelly babies for the kids?' Foster asked.

'More like sherbet fountains,' she said. 'He finances his habit by dealing inside.'

Ryman left and Jameson slouched in his chair sunk in thought. 'Look into the Sunnyside connection between those two, will you, Foz?' he said. 'And find out the name of the journalist who's covering the murders in the *Herald*. He might know something of use.'

* * *

Bel had insisted Chris come back to her mother's house. But Chris had been restless and irritable, and after an hour or so remembered that she had arranged to work with Simon that afternoon. She phoned him, but there was no reply. 'He must've left already. I'll have to go.'

'Simon's a big lad, he can look after himself.'

'I know that, Maria, but I do have a lot of work to do, and I'm just making everyone miserable prowling around the house, so . . .'

Maria's mouth set into a disapproving line, but she didn't argue. Once Chris had made up her mind, she would not be swayed.

Simon's Mini was parked at the front of the house, but there was no sign of him. Chris called out and heard rapid steps along the path at the side of the house.

'Chris! Thank God!' It was Simon.

Chris marvelled at the fact that he had been worried about her but seemed unconcerned that she had wasted two hours of his time. As she made sandwiches and poured glasses of beer for them, she told Simon about the discovery of the drunk's body, and the police coming to inform her that the victim was her long-dead father.

Simon had remained silent for a few minutes, finally asking, 'Why would anyone *do* that?'

'A threat?' Chris said. 'A warning? Showing me he knows there are a few skeletons I'd like to be left undisturbed?' She piled the sandwiches onto plates, feeling a mounting rage and a parallel inability to act. 'He just won't leave me alone,' she muttered, throwing the knife into the sink with a clatter.

'I don't know what to say to you,' Simon said, almost as she had decided he would say nothing.

'I don't need comforting words, Si,' she said. 'You know how I felt about my father.' In a year of almost nightly meetings in which she gathered testimonies of adults who had suffered abuse as children, there had been no room for coyness about her own past.

'That's just it,' he said, glancing sideways at her in that shy, almost furtive way he had never entirely grown out of. 'I know I'm not a psychologist or anything, and I'm certainly no Einstein, but I do know from what you wrote in *In the Name of Love* that you must've had a lot of issues to deal with when he . . .' Simon shook his head, unable to say the word. 'Whoever planted the ID on the body is trying to mess with your head. I don't know how you can take it so calmly. If it happened to me—'

Some form of intuition told Chris that Simon was ready to talk about his own unhappy childhood, but although she had unconsciously been working towards this moment since he had started researching for her nearly two years ago, she felt unequal to the task. Her mind was drawn back repeatedly to the corpse lying in its own sickly-sweet aura. She turned away from Simon, breathing hard through her nostrils, trying to rid herself of the stench of the mortuary.

She turned back, trying for bright unconcern, and said the first stupid thing that came into her head. 'I didn't know you'd bought my book. You'll have to let me sign it for you.' She saw him flinch and instantly regretted the acidity of her comment. 'I'm sorry, Simon. You're right — it's affected me more than I like to admit. I'm just not ready to talk about it yet.'

12

Sunday afternoon traffic was light, and Chris Radcliffe had to wait until she reached Liverpool before trying to shake her police escort. When Phil turned himself in, no doubt Jameson would call off his hounds, but for now she would have to keep checking over her shoulder. A picture of the sweet wrappers on the ground under the shrubs in her garden flashed into her mind, and she felt a pang of fear followed by a surge of anger. If one of Jameson's men sent to find out who she was entertaining had left the sweet wrappers, she was safe and could indulge her anger.

But another possibility kept pushing itself forward, that whoever killed Dorothy and Ann was watching her. Or maybe Dixon was making a point: *I know where you live, so lay off me.* Maybe Dixon was the murderer. She was so taken by this thought that she almost ran into the back of the car ahead when it stopped at the lights.

To hell with this, she thought. *I have to think straight if I'm going to find Phil, and I can't do that if I'm fantasizing all kinds of wild scenarios.* She needed to focus on finding Phil safe. She just hoped he would turn up at the address she had been given.

And her father? Chris's stomach gave a sudden lurch and she had to pull over to the kerb. She felt winded. It had been so long ago, so very long ago, that she had almost believed that she'd left her father in the past. But there were issues she had never dealt with, aspects of her father's behaviour which she had never come to terms with. The body that had turned up at the mortuary had confronted her with those same issues all over again. For several minutes she rested her head on the steering wheel, eyes closed, trying not to think. But an image of her father's face superimposed itself onto the face of the nameless derelict and resolved like a developing photograph on the back of her eyelids. What had hurt her most was the peace — the total serenity — in her father's expression when she went to identify him. He had found that perfect, utter oblivion he had sought for so many years in alcoholic stupor, leaving her to deal with all the unresolved questions and emotions. He did not deserve such peace, and she would have kept him from it if she could.

A bead of sweat crept between her shoulder blades and slithered down her back; the afternoon temperature was well into the nineties, but still she felt cold. Ted had said it more than once, and she could not deny the truth of it: sooner or later she would have to get to grips with her father's death.

But not yet. I can't — I can't face it yet! She shoved the car into gear, revving the engine, coordinating the clutch badly and crunching the gears, muttering 'Fuck it' under her breath as she moved off. Glancing in her mirror, she saw the grey police Sierra slide into position a couple of cars behind her.

She headed for Scotland Road, driving at a sedate pace all the way to County Road, past the shuttered shops, slowing where the road narrowed as though she was in no hurry, hoping her pursuers would assume she was heading for the Rice Lane flyover. They hung back as she slowed for the lights at Kwik Save. They showed green but a few pedestrians stood either side, waiting for them to change. She checked in her mirror and caught the lights turning amber. Cutting right, she followed the narrow curve of Mandeville Street, then took a second, sharp right, heading onto the wide boulevard of Walton Hall Avenue, passing its sudden green expanse of parkland. At the first opportunity, she turned off and made for Norris Green, a maze of forties and fifties council housing, losing herself for a time in its crescents and closes. She eventually found a way to loop back, crossing Queens Drive a second time and risking a mile or two along Green Lane to get to Wavertree and the address that John J., Alf's contact, had given her.

Chris checked the time on the dashboard clock: 3.15. She was early. She parked at the top end of the street, hoping to get a glimpse of Phil when he arrived, but the street was deserted except for a black dog, one paw folded under its body, panting in the meagre shade of a low boundary wall.

It jumped up as she approached and glared at her, blocking the pavement, but side-stepped at the last moment, sniffing the air as she walked by. Chris walked on another fifty yards, wondering why no children were playing in the street. It was unnaturally quiet, the only sounds an occasional booming of voices from an open window: Sunday soaps distorted by high volume. Once, she heard the distant and oddly reassuring clatter of a train, hidden by a high wall and an embankment at the far end of the street, so that only its sound carried to her, declaring its presence indirectly.

Curtains twitched, and again it seemed strange in such an ordinary — even run-down — street, for people to show such an interest in the comings and goings of their neighbours. The prickling at her back was more than just the heat, she knew, and she was relieved to be able at last to turn in at a shabby-looking house with a faded green wooden gate. The hinges were perished, and she had to lift the gate to open it. It complained as though it was rarely opened and Chris was reminded uncomfortably of her own home — her parents' home — with its low wall and its broken gate; mostly, as a child, she had jumped over the wall rather than risk her father's accusations that she had caused the damage by forcing the already rickety wood over the dull, cracked red tiles of their doorstep.

The grimy windows stared blankly at her, and Chris sensed a presence behind the yellowed nets: the place had a sinister atmosphere. She quelled an urge to turn and walk away. There seemed to be no knocker or bell, so Chris rattled the letter box. A frenzied barking resonated through the house and Chris took one step back. Surely Phil couldn't be living here, not with the hound of Hell?

A fox-faced woman answered, opening the door a crack. It was on the chain. She did not speak but jerked her head once in an aggressive interrogative.

'John J. sent me,' Chris said, giving the message as she had been instructed. The woman withdrew her snout and slammed the door shut, but Chris heard the chain rattle and the door was flung wide. Chris peered past her, into the gloom of the hallway.

'Well, come in, if you're coming,' the woman said, then, following Chris's line of sight up the uncarpeted stairs towards the source of the barking, she snorted derisively. 'He's locked in one of the bedrooms,' she said, slamming the door shut again as Chris stepped inside. She jerked her head towards the dim passageway behind her. 'In the back.'

'Who's using the front door?' It was a man's voice.

The woman sulked, shrugging at the fury in the man's voice. 'I dunno, do I? Says John J. sent her.' The dog's barks had moderated to a protesting woof at the sound of his master's voice, then Chris heard the rapid click of its claws on the bare boards overhead, followed by a dull thud as it flopped down in some corner of its quarters, still offering small protesting growls and whines.

The owner of the voice appeared in the shadows at the end of the narrow hallway. He was tall and rangy, and even in this poor light, Chris could see that he had large, protruding eyes. 'John sent you, did he?'

Chris nodded, holding his angry stare.

'I'll fuckin' burst him, sending punters round the front! The fucking neighbourhood watch is all over us like flies round shit!' He reached out, flicking a light switch, and stopped, momentarily surprised by her appearance. 'What d'you want? This isn't the Adelphi, you know. You'll get no five-star service here, girl.'

'John said I would meet a friend here—'

He flashed a set of large white teeth at her. 'I'll be your friend.'

'Hey! We're not a friggin' dating agency, neither!' The fox-faced woman had been jerked from her sulking by a sudden flame of jealousy. 'Now d'you want something? We've got punters waitin' outside.' This last comment was flung at her partner with a snarl.

Chris got as far as the kitchen door before the man caught her, digging his bony fingers into the flesh of her upper arm. 'Where d'you think you're going?' he demanded.

Chris turned back and looked up into his gaunt face, quelling her fear, fighting to give an impression of unreadability, if not confidence. 'John told me a friend of mine would be here now. All I want to do is find him and leave.'

'And if he doesn't want to be found?'

Chris looked down at the fingers curled around her arm; she would have a neat circle of oval bruises on her arm tomorrow. She hoped he couldn't see the pulse throbbing in her throat. She looked past him to the fox-faced woman who was eyeing her jealously. 'You know the two women that were murdered?'

She felt his grip tighten, then ease.

'The police want him for that. Now do you think it's wise to keep a customer like that on the books?'

Doubt flickered like a candle flame in the pusher's muddy eyes, but he maintained his grip.

'Let her go, Gaz!' the woman said. 'We don't want to bring the pigs down on us.'

The kitchen door opened onto a back yard, which let a little light into the greasy squalor of the room. A trestle table had been pushed against the opening where a little queue of people stood in an untidy line while a stocky man with a bristling bull neck took their money in exchange for small squares of folded paper. To the left of the man was a cardboard box, filled with a jumble of blister packs and bottles, and paper strips of innocuous-looking picture transfers.

'Will you stop farting around an' giz a hand, Gaz?' the stocky man called without bothering to turn around.

Chris singled out the second man in the line. He had lost weight, even in this short time, and he was unshaven. Chris felt his distress — Phil's daily grooming ritual was as fundamental to his well-being as food and drink. She spoke over the big man's head.

'Hello, Phil.'

The man at the trestle table glanced back and gave a low, appreciative whistle. 'Whatever you want, darlin' — it's on the house.'

'Move the table, would you?' Chris said. She held Phil's frightened eyes with her own, while he stood rooted to the spot, torn between terror and delight. The little line of customers was becoming restless, demanding to be served.

The big man turned to her, a leery grin on his face — he had heard the faint tremor of uncertainty in her voice — and Gary Tighe took a step towards her, still unsure whether to let her go without a firm reminder that it would be inadvisable to take what she knew to the police. Chris sensed the movement behind her and tensed. Phil wavered. If she didn't get to him fast he would bolt. Her heart hammered in her chest. Tighe was crowding in on her and the fat man was thinking about more than the cash she had in her pocket. Forward or back? Back, and she would have to get past both Tighe and the girl — losing Phil in the process. Forward, then. Past the fat man. Forward to Phil. Chris summoned what she hoped was a cool, haughty look.

'Why don't you piss off?'

The fat man opened his eyes wide, ready to laugh, and Chris lifted one corner of the lightweight table and unhitched the stays in one swift movement. It collapsed, and the white packets slipped to the floor.

Chris jumped lightly over the mess onto the untidy strip of concrete which led to the back gate. The babble of voices as the customers scrambled for the stray packets was drowned by a simultaneous roar from the pusher and the resumed frenzy of the dog's barking. It echoed through the house and boomed out into the alleyway beyond the spiked brick wall at the end of the yard. Chris took Phil's hand, and although he flinched, he did not pull away. 'Let's go,' she said.

The big man followed her, treading on the flimsy plywood of the table. Chris heard it give with a loud *crack!* under the weight of his boot. He pushed two of his customers out of the way and Chris gasped as he grabbed her shoulder, spinning her round, but Phil put his free hand in the middle of the man's chest and shoved. The man fell backwards over the collapsed table, cracking his head on the floor, and they were off, running.

Dogs barked in the alleyway, and in the distance, Chris could hear another train approaching. They were nearer the railway line now, and the noise seemed hurried, urgent. Chris tried dragging Phil down the alleyway towards the top end of the street, to where the car was parked, but he planted his feet firmly either side of the gutter which ran down the centre of the cobblestoned back entry and refused to budge.

'Phil, come on!' Chris begged. She could hear raised voices in the yard behind them; what she feared most was that Gary would send the dog after them.

'Not that way!' Phil shook free of her hand. Chris looked into his troubled face and knew at once what was wrong. Phil would always choose circular routes for journeys. He hated taking the same route home as the journey out, even to the extent that he would travel out of Liverpool and catch a second bus back in to take him home after work.

'Which way, then?' Chris asked.

'I always go back that way.' Phil pointed back down the alley.

Chris sighed, reaching for his hand again, but this time he jerked away. She wondered if she would ever get used to it — the rejection of physical contact was for her the most difficult aspect of Phil's condition. She could cope with his anxieties, his compulsions and obsessions, but his abhorrence of simple expressions of affection was hurtful. Even though she knew that Phil could no more help this morbid disgust of physical contact than alter his rigid daily rituals, it pained her. It felt like rejection. It was a reminder that Phil's affiliation to her and his need to be with her was perhaps only another manifestation of his obsessive nature, and that she was no more than a useful fixed point of reference in his chaotic universe. At times like these, Chris understood why Maria and Pete Stevens, both caring, affectionate people, could not give Phil the same patience and understanding they had shown dozens of other difficult and disturbed foster children. 'Nil returns,' Pete had once commented with uncharacteristic terseness. Neither he nor Maria wanted, nor expected, gratitude or remuneration beyond that which was necessary for their foster children's comfort, but they did need to feel that they were doing some good, and that the children they cared for returned some of their emotional commitment and uncompromising love.

'We'll go your way,' she said, trying not to sound aggrieved. They walked side by side, the gap between them a great void to Chris and a reassuring distance for Philip, past the open gate of the house they had just left, where the two pushers were engaged in a row with the remaining customers. Gaz looked up from his wrangling to yell, 'Fucking bitch!' but he did not move from the safety of his back yard.

Phil did not register the pusher's remark. His mind seemed to be working on some problem which claimed all his attention. He plucked agitatedly at the flesh of his left arm, pinching it and pummelling it. They walked on.

'Where have you been?' Chris asked, to distract him from the injuring squeezing and nipping of his already bruised flesh. 'We've been worried about you.'

'I have to get my tablets!' The exclamations worried Chris. If Phil panicked now, and took to his heels, she might lose him for good.

'We can get them from your flat.'

For one terrible moment she thought he was going to run: he stood shuffling from one foot to the other, glancing up and down the alleyway, wondering which way to bolt.

'Flip, I can't go there! The police came! I can't go back!'

'I know.' Chris waited, then repeated, 'Phil, I know you can't go there.' She ached to stay the destructive movements of his fingers but feared it would precipitate his panic. 'We'll go in my car and you can hide around the corner while I get your pills, OK?'

* * *

In the event they had to get a taxi, leaving Chris's car on the other side of Liverpool, because whoever had told Philip that he could get the pills at Gary's had also warned him not to go down the street but to use the alley. This instruction had become one of his obsessions. Phil had always been fascinated by black cabs and was happy to chat to the driver about the various hackney carriage designs from 1900 onwards, while Chris went to retrieve his medication from his flat.

Dave let her in using his pass key. She gave the spartan rooms a cursory appraisal, with the warden following her, curious that she should turn up again. Phil's few books on the shelf in the sitting room had been placed out of order, and one of the kitchen drawers had not been shut properly. The dishes he had abandoned in the sink still sat in the bowl under a filmy slick of dishwater, the bubbles long gone; she would have to sort this out before Phil returned.

'Anything in particular you're after?' Dave asked.

Chris studied the soft folds of his wrinkled face. He could be trusted, she knew that, but it wouldn't be fair to Dave to involve him in this.

'Just wondered if there was anything that might give me a clue to his whereabouts,' she said.

He regarded her silently for some moments. 'No luck at the squats?' he asked after a long time.

'The police have been round, giving them grief,' she said, avoiding a direct lie. 'One of the squats has been firebombed.'

'I heard it on the radio,' Dave said. 'They'd better catch that one before he kills someone.'

Chris sighed.

'What?' Dave said. 'You're not saying he already has?'

'The woman who was injured is in a bad way.' A silence followed, and to break it, Chris said, 'Why don't you check through Phil's filing case?'

Dave looked at the blue metal box pushed into one corner of the room. He raised his eyebrows and his mouth twitched in a suggestion of irony. 'What am I looking for?'

Chris shrugged. 'Needle in a haystack,' she said.

Dave hoisted the box onto the coffee table and sat with his back to the bedroom door which led off the sitting room. Chris returned within seconds.

'No luck,' said Chris.

'Me neither. I reckon the police will have searched this lot pretty thoroughly.'

Chris looked at the short, pear-shaped figure of the accommodation warden. His sad eyes showed concern — as much for her as for Phil. Twice he started to say something and twice he changed his mind.

She smiled. 'Thanks, Dave.'

It was enough to break his inertia. 'People have gone to prison for less,' he said. 'I hope he appreciates what you're risking.'

Chris frowned. '*If* I find him, the plan is to get him to turn himself in.'

Dave searched her face. 'Tell him I'm here if he needs me,' he said.

Chris nodded.

He opened his mouth to speak, then stopped, a look of puzzlement on his face.

'What?' Chris asked.

Dave shook his head. 'You're probably right. Best if I don't know,' he said, opening the flat door and seeing her out.

The taxi driver was, by now, bored to death and beginning to seem uneasy about his knowledgeable passenger. He greeted Chris effusively on her return. 'Where to now, love?'

Chris stared blankly for a moment. Where to? Where *could* they go? Not back to her house — the police might be watching it. And she couldn't implicate Nicky in the obstruction of a police investigation. Her old flat came to mind as a short-term hiding place, but she quickly dismissed the idea — Mr Ainsworth would find the intrusion intolerable.

'Where can we go?' Philip asked, putting her own uncertainty into words.

The taxi driver's meagre reserves of patience were running low. 'Come on, girl — I haven't got all day!'

'Home,' she said, with quiet firmness.

13

Philip Greer was backed into a corner of the Stevenses' sitting room. A high-pitched keening rapidly gave way to screams when Jameson took a cautious step forward, murmuring reassurances. Greer threw his head backwards against the wall and Jameson flinched, stepping away in alarm, then Greer bit into his own arm, breaking the skin.

'Back off.' Chris Radcliffe spoke quietly, with an unnatural calmness. And Jameson, with all his experience of drunks and weirdoes and street violence from his years as a beat bobby, found himself a spectator to what followed.

She went to the video player and inserted a cassette. Jameson watched, vaguely horrified by her calm acceptance of what was happening. She sat, cross-legged, watching the TV screen and humming the opening bars to the introduction of *The Jungle Book*. Within minutes Greer subsided. He uncurled himself and crept from his corner to sit next to her. He barely noticed when Maria Stevens arrived unbidden some minutes later with a small metal box which had once held tea but now functioned as a first aid kit. She left without a word. Jameson could not fail to see the strain in her face, the powerless frustration at the unrelenting regularity with which this kind of thing happened. Her weariness with it all.

Dr Radcliffe shot him a look. It was a challenge but also a question. She cleaned the wounds on Greer's arm as he watched the screen, layered the bite marks with gauze — some were bleeding — and wrapped bandage over the gauze, an intense concentration on her face. Occasionally she winced, but Greer seemed oblivious to the pain, impervious to any stimulus but the film.

After a while, she began talking to him in a soft, crooning voice, reassuring Greer that she would stay with him, that he, Jameson, was not going to hurt him or lock him up.

'I didn't hurt anyone, Flip,' Philip said. His eyes, still shining with tears, were fixed on the screen, but he was calm, able now to communicate. 'I just felt so lost when they changed the caseload and I was off their rota. I used to see Ann once a month, on a Thursday at three o'clock in room 2.11. I got so upset — Ann said she'd try and get me back with her. She didn't mind. Mrs Hardy didn't understand. She started shouting at me. I really only wanted to talk, but I think she was frightened. I didn't mean her any harm.'

Jameson readjusted his assessment of Greer. Listening to him, it became possible to reconcile the compulsive behaviour with the intelligence. The two, he was beginning to understand, were not as interdependent as he had thought. After a time, Greer lapsed into silence and became once more entirely absorbed by the action on screen.

'How do you cope with that?' he asked.

Dr Radcliffe smiled a slow, sad smile. On the television set, Bagheera lounged indolently on a tree branch, his tail twitching faintly, as he counselled the young Mowgli. 'You cope because you have to,' she said. 'Because sometimes he can't.' She studied Jameson for a few moments then quickly glanced at Greer, who was still absorbed in the film. 'Let's go into the garden where there's a bit of shade.'

Jameson began to demur, but the psychologist smiled. 'Philip won't move out of this room until the final credits have rolled.'

So, Jameson followed her through the hallway and into the kitchen, where Dr Radcliffe paused to give her foster mother a hug. Maria Stevens was standing at the kitchen table, chopping vegetables for a salad. The tension was still there, between the shoulder blades, but she reached up with one hand and patted Chris's arm.

'Where's Bel?' Chris asked. 'Rehearsing?'

'The show starts tomorrow,' Maria replied, immediately becoming more animated. 'Last minute run-through. Isabel is in the chorus of *Les Misérables* in Manchester,' she explained, turning to Jameson with a smile of undisguised pride.

Jameson nodded, unsure of what to say.

Chris smiled. 'If she passes on any freebies, I'll see you get a couple of tickets, Chief Inspector. Unless that would be construed as a bribe.'

'Flip!' Maria scolded. 'Don't tease the chief inspector, he doesn't know you're joking.'

'Who says I am?'

Jameson found himself smiling. As a matter of interest . . .' he began.

'The nickname?' Maria said, shooting a mischievous glance at Chris, who telegraphed a return warning, but Maria went on recklessly: 'Christine Radcliffe — raised a good Catholic girl — was so foul-mouthed when she first came to us we used to dread the parish priest's visits.'

'Only because they were so boring,' Chris interjected.

'We had to find something for her to stay instead of all the f-words and blasphemy—'

'And I used the alternative so often I ended up being called by it,' Chris finished. 'Satisfied, Maria? Happy? I've spent the last two weeks trying to build up a mystique with the police to hide my sordid past, and now you've blown my cover entirely.'

Jameson saw that this must be the kind of banter they often engaged in, but it surprised him that the doctor was so sanguine about her personal history being discussed. Perhaps it was relief at having found her foster brother. Chris seemed to notice him glancing back through the open door into the hallway. 'Could you go and sit with Phil, Maria? Mr Jameson thinks he's going to bolt again.'

'Oh, no,' said Maria in all seriousness, 'not while *The Jungle Book* is on!' She shrugged, an expressive, expansive gesture. 'But if it makes you happy.'

Chris reached into the fridge and pulled out a couple of bottles of lager. She tossed one to Jameson. He caught the bottle with a quick reflex action.

'You're not going to say something priggish like "Not when I'm on duty," are you, Chief Inspector?'

'Have you always been so subversive?' he asked.

They sat on the garden bench under the shade of a rowan tree. Chris relaxed, one arm draped over the back of the bench. She took a mouthful of beer and let her head fall back, closing her eyes. When she opened them again, she caught Jameson looking at her and she returned his gaze, her eyes twinkling with amusement.

'Lots of successful people are obsessed to some degree,' she said, disconcerting him, for he had been wondering how anyone could function with Greer's level of obsessive behaviour. 'What else motivates musicians to practise eight hours a day, or academics to wrestle with abstract theories every waking minute of their lives?' She slid him a sly glance, then added in an undertone, 'It's been said that even policemen can become obsessed with certain cases, to the exclusion of home, children, wife, life.'

Jameson was needled into retaliation. 'I'm sure psychologists aren't beyond a bit of obsessive overwork,' he said.

'Precisely,' she said, the sparkle not diminishing one jot. She refused to be hurried, but took another swig from the bottle, nodding as she picked up the thread of her thoughts. 'When Philip came to us, the prognosis was poor. He had virtually no communication skills, he would only have anything, *do* anything, on his own strictly prescribed terms. He made it through school; although it was a struggle, Maria and Pete kept him in mainstream education. He's got two A levels, he can converse, even with strangers, he holds down a job at the central library and he lives in his own flat, paying his rent on time and doing his own shopping.'

There was something of an elder sister's pride in the way she had said it which prompted Jameson. 'Are you sure you're not related?'

Chris laughed, a gale of uninhibited, joyful laughter. 'My obsessions aren't on such a grand scale as Phil's.'

'I meant,' said Jameson, 'your obvious devotion to Mr Greer.'

Chris's amusement moderated to a broad grin. 'I've never gone in much for the selfish gene idea,' she said. 'I'm closer to this family than I ever was to my own.'

Jameson looked into those luminous blue eyes, with their humour and sadness and infinite, ungrudging compassion, and felt an unfamiliar emotion: hope. If she, who had been so betrayed in early life by those who should have protected her, could learn to trust again, and could have the capacity for so much love, then perhaps, after the bitterness of marriage and the impotent rage of separation and divorce, he too could begin again.

Her smile faded, and she seemed for a moment uncertain. 'It was good of you to agree to this,' she said.

'I'm not a monster, Dr Radcliffe. I've no desire to terrorize someone who is unable to stand his own corner.'

They had lapsed into silence, listening to the thrum of traffic on the main road fifty yards from the house, basting like the Sunday roast in the unreasonable heat of the early evening. Jameson, feeling that he had too sharply rebuffed a friendly advance, said at length, 'So you've known Philip since he was young?'

'Phil was about three when he came here. We arrived within weeks of each other.'

'And you were what? Fifteen? He must seem like a younger brother to you.'

'Yes,' she said, smiling a little at the thought. 'He does. He is.'

'You didn't find it difficult adjusting to a new situation, a new family, so soon after your mother's death?'

Chris threw him a quick glance, her eyes dancing with humour. 'Is this an interrogation, Chief Inspector?'

He pursed his lips. 'Interest,' he said. The doctor's attraction was beginning to work on him again, and he had to admit to a genuine curiosity about her past.

Chris shrugged, as if to say, *What the hell?* 'I blamed her for a time,' she said, and seemed surprised at her own frankness. 'I suppose the kind of fear Mum lived with day after day, month after month, all her married life . . .' She looked away, towards a beetle hurrying purposefully across the parched and tangled brown mat which was all that remained of the lawn. 'It eats away at you, and not just spiritually. So, it didn't surprise me when she told me she had cancer. At the time, all I could think was *You're leaving me alone with him!* It seemed almost that she was taking the easy way out.' She smiled over at Jameson. 'Children can be selfish brutes. Poor Mum. She never had anyone to lean on, not even at the last. It's funny, he never touched her in the last few months of her life.'

'Even the worst of people have some humanity.'

She shook her head. 'It was more a kind of superstition. Like when some people are afraid to say the word *cancer*. Such a big word. He was fearful of some kind of contagion. I don't know, perhaps he thought he'd caused it.'

'And your father transferred his violence to you after your mother's death?'

Chris frowned. 'Transferred is the wrong word. Intensified is more like it.' She shivered and her face took on a wounded, haunted look which made Jameson ashamed that he'd made her think of these things. She continued with difficulty, but as though determined to finish.

He leaned forward, encouraging her to go on, yet unwilling to speak for fear of losing the moment. His eyes played over her face. The thin white scar over her eye which she bore with unconcerned, almost jaunty indifference suddenly became more vivid to him, and he saw it for what it was: a mark of the violation of trust her father had enacted upon her, an insult to her childhood innocence.

'I felt frail, physically, as a result of my injuries when—' She paused. 'But also, emotionally. There was nowhere to be quiet here. Maria was, and is,' she said through a laugh, 'loud, ebullient, full of life, and her children were as voluble — they seemed to rejoice in family squabbles.' Chris gave a self-deprecating smile. 'I was trained from infancy to passivity and stillness, conditioned to obey promptly and without questioning. So I sat in the midst of all this noise and clamour, mistaking their robustness for aggression, and feeling afraid and dismayed.

'But Maria is sensitive, for all her volubility — she started taking me for long walks along the coast — Formby, Ainsdale, Hawksley marshes and Sawrey Woods, showing me places where I could be quiet.' She smiled at the memory. 'For such an impulsive woman she was surprisingly restrained; content to wait until I chose to talk, opening up opportunities but never pressurizing me.'

'And did you? Open up, I mean.'

She glanced quickly at him, keenly assessing, then he saw a kind of mental shrug and she went on. 'I think I rather frightened poor Maria. I told her everything. What he had done to us both. Not just to our bodies, but in here.' She tapped the side of her head. 'All the bitterness I had stored up against my mother, my anger at being so cowed, so *kept down* for such a long time.' A sudden burst of birdsong took her interest and she stopped, listening.

'Did it help? Talking about it, I mean?' Jameson was suspicious of analysis, believing that many people's problems were magnified by endless re-examination and assessment.

She frowned, concentrating on the question, as though considering the idea for the first time. 'I felt, after a time, that I could forgive my mother for what she had allowed him to put us through. I began to feel compassion for her suffering, too.' She dipped her head, raising one shoulder. 'Does that answer your question?'

'More than adequately.' But Jameson noted that Dr Radcliffe had not once mentioned her father by name.

* * *

It was after five when Chris arrived home. Simon was sitting on the low wall in front of her house. The windows of his battered old Mini were open and he was listening to the radio. He grinned and waved as she drew into the driveway. She threw him a guilty look as she got out of the car. 'I know,' she said. 'I'm late — again.'

'No sweat.' He pushed himself off the wall and ambled towards her, his thumbs hooked in the pockets of his jeans. 'I've been smelling the flowers, catching the rays, listening to the top forty countdown. Pure bliss.'

'I can explain.'

'No need.'

'I want to.'

He shrugged. Chris wondered if it was fear of being rebuffed again which made him unwilling to ask for an explanation, so she told him everything as they sat at the kitchen table, eating the salad she had made indoors because she had turned on the sprinklers. The garden was drenched in a fine spray which strayed onto the paved area by the house and even drifted like a cool mist in through the open windows. She told him about her finding Philip, that the police thought the murders represented some kind of vendetta against Calderbank Council staff, and about her suspicion that the police thought she was somehow involved in the murders.

When she told him about the arson attack on the squat, Simon paled. 'They can't think you had anything to do with it?'

Chris shrugged.

'If I was Jameson,' he said, 'I'd be looking at recent case histories.'

'He is, but the records are incomplete.'

'Mislaid or—?'

'Or,' she said. 'Definitely *or*. And of course, I had access to files while I worked for the council.'

A pained look flashed across Simon's face. Chris wondered whether she should tell him about the sweet wrappers she had found in the garden, but the idea of saying it aloud seemed ludicrous, and she told herself she was being paranoid. The wrappers probably blew in from somewhere.

Simon was watching her with intense concern. She laughed uncertainly. 'I did have an inkling that the police might be following me, but I should think they'll let up now they've found Philip.'

'*Following* you?' For a few minutes he toyed with the food on his plate, then, apparently summoning up courage, he said, blushing, 'I'm always here if you need me.'

Chris reached across the table and squeezed his hand. 'Thanks,' she said, 'but if it comes to needing protection, I'll get a big dog.'

Simon did not return her smile. 'I mean it,' he said. 'This could be dangerous.'

'Crossing the road is dangerous,' Chris said. 'Riding in a lift is dangerous. There's an element of risk in most things we do.' It sounded flat, unconvincing — even a little pompous — and Chris, feeling the need for reassurance, added, 'Anyway, I can't think why I'd be on anyone's hit list.'

'Penny to a pound that Ann and Dorothy couldn't, either,' Simon said.

14

Darren Lewis sat nursing a pint in the dim interior of the Rose pub. The saloon was half empty, most of the clientele having taken their drinks outside. He'd had to step over and round them in the car park and on the shallow steps at the entrance. Lads in jeans cut off at the knees, girls in little frocks. Clean limbed, smooth skinned, glossy and groomed. Their self-assurance was an insult to him, their loud, confident voices on the night air summoning a slow-burning rage within him which he neither comprehended nor attempted to quench.

He checked his watch. Half an hour he'd waited. Two girls at a table nearby looked over as he set down his pint and drummed impatiently on the tabletop. He reached for his fags and stared at the two of them as he lit up, resting his elbow on the table and positioning his arm so that they could see the dragon tattoo on his forearm. The blonde one smiled shyly and blushed, looking away. Normal girls. Not like the smart-arsed Charlottes and Helens lounging outside supping pints and acting like they owned the bleeding shop.

He took a drag and then folded his hands, palms down, on the table. He'd give it five more minutes and then he was going. Only fear had made him wait this long. Unconsciously, he flexed the muscles in his forearm, making the flame shimmer and flicker from the dragon's mouth.

'Is anyone sitting here?'

Lewis glanced from the boy who had asked the question to the blonde girl, who smiled shyly at him, to the empty stool next to his table.

'You trying to be funny?' he asked. The boy blinked, smiling, perplexed by the question. 'I mean, are you blind, or wha'?'

'Look, I just—'

'What are you studying, like? At *uni*?' He mimicked the student's accent.

'What do you mean?' The boy smiled nervously.

'English? History? Something *useful* like that?'

'Social sciences. Look — do you think I could—?'

'Social sciences!' Lewis had met more than enough social science graduates in his time. 'You'd think with your privileged education you'd be able to work out when a chair's empty, wouldn't you?'

The boy laughed, trying to defuse the tension. 'OK, thanks,' he said, moving to pick up the stool.

Lewis snapped one hand out and gripped the boy's upper arm. Soft. Too much time spent in libraries and exam halls. He leaned close so the boy could see the white patch on his eyebrow where the hairs had been singed off and had never grown back. 'Did I say you could take it?' he breathed. The boy looked wildly over his shoulder and Lewis saw the barman staring over, his eyes narrowed, his jaw set. 'Did I?' The boy started stuttering an answer, but Lewis cut in, 'Didn't they teach you no manners at boarding school?'

He caught a movement to his right and glanced over at an advancing figure. He recognized the man immediately, but resisted the temptation to slacken his grip, and went back to staring at the boy who was sweating now and wincing with pain.

'I'll get one from somewhere else,' the boy said, trying unsuccessfully to keep the rising panic out of his voice.

'You do that.' The voice was warm, deep, a trace of a Liverpool accent, mellowed by years of association with the business class.

Lewis shot a look at the man who had spoken. His boss. He heard the implied threat behind the pleasant tone. It wasn't directed at the boy. He hesitated. There wasn't much Lewis was scared of, but when you flirted with fire as he did, you understood power and you learned to respect it — or you got burned. He released the boy with a shove that sent him staggering. 'Where've you been?' he demanded but didn't dare look into the newcomer's eyes.

'That wasn't very civil.' The man sat opposite him, sweeping the stool into position one-handed.

Lewis felt himself grow hot under the hard stare. He risked a quick look and saw that he had gone too far. 'I hate bloody students,' he muttered apologetically, letting his gaze travel as far as the green polo shirt of his boss.

'What's the problem?' The warm tone of his boss's voice was edged with a chill of cold anger.

'I need somewhere to lie low for a bit.'

The man stood suddenly, and Lewis looked up, startled. He walked to the bar, rested one foot on the brass rail. Tailored, cream-coloured trousers hung crisply over his beige canvas shoes. Not much older than Lewis himself, but a businessman, with all the trappings of respectability. Lewis looked at his back. He was not tall, but he commanded attention and was served immediately. The businessman returned, smiling, and Lewis, knowing it meant trouble, averted his gaze and stared resolutely into his drink.

'Why,' the businessman asked, 'would you need to lie low?'

Lewis shifted uncomfortably. 'The pigs are all over me. They pulled me in tonight.'

'Why?' The quiet repetition made Lewis think of blue-tinged flames curling from a bowl of methylated spirits. Deceptive, seductive and dangerously explosive.

'I never told them nothing. They wanted to know what I was doing on the fifth and the eleventh.'

'You gave them your alibis, didn't you?' The business-man sipped benignly at his gin and tonic, smiling at the top of Lewis's fair head.

'Yeah,' Lewis frowned in an agony of indecision. 'But they're not soft, are they? Give them enough time, they're bound to suss me.'

'And you'll be in the clear. If . . .' The businessman waited until Lewis raised his eyes as far as his chin. 'If you hold your nerve and don't give them any more reasons to pull you in.' He took another sip from his drink and his gold signet ring sang against the glass. Lewis chanced a look into his face. Sun-tanned, youthful, sure of his position and his power. He glanced away quickly, but the businessman caught the look and laughed indulgently.

'Take my advice,' he said, in a tone of command. 'Go back to your flat and get rested. They tell me the view over the Mersey is very calming. You'll feel different about it in the morning.' He stood to leave but remained for some time, looking down at Lewis, asserting himself, making Lewis squirm. Just at the point when Lewis felt he couldn't stand any more, he spoke. 'Go home,' he said. 'Say nothing without your solicitor present. You've got an alibi — stick to it.'

Lewis nodded dumbly, humiliated.

'And if I were you, I'd find a back way out,' the business-man added. He took a couple of ten-pound notes from his wallet and placed them on the table. 'Take a taxi — pick up the car in the morning. This is a student pub. Your student friend is hardly likely to be on his own, and his mates might have taken exception to your belligerent little outburst.'

15

Jim Bradbury made his way across the parched grass of Sawrey Moss, listening to the swish of knapweed against the fabric of his trousers and worrying about the state of the ponds. They were dug from the heavy clay which had been used in brickmaking for centuries, until the inconvenience of salt blooms on the walls of fishermen's cottages and the introduction of modern methods had overtaken the small kilns of the area, and the pits had fallen into disuse. He could see as he crunched along the path that the clay of the upper reaches of the marsh had begun to fissure, and with every week of drought the water levels in his little haven had shrunk a fraction lower. He skirted the edge of the woods and walked on with long, loping strides, past the ponds for half a mile or more to the edge of the stable marsh, and looked across the wide expanse of reedy grass and sea asters, noting with pleasure that the tide was coming in. The deep gullies of the salty mudflats teemed with waders snatching their last chance of a meal before the high tide washed over the mud and the marsh with fluid stealth; dunlins hurrying with quick, darting, almost nervous movements before the ever-encroaching waters, oystercatchers crouching, heads down, rather jaunty in their black and white plumage, keen eyed for any tasty morsel, greenshanks and redshanks which he could never tell apart without his binoculars — he made a mental note to bring them with him tomorrow. A flock of lapwings rose up as one, their glossy plumage flashing green and mauve in the sunlight; they circled once and then made for drier ground. Jim looked out over the mudflats and, seeing the faint glint of blue on the shallow pools, turned his face to the pale blue sky and felt the sun's warmth on his face. Even here, on the windy border between marsh and dry land, there was scarcely a breath of air, but mercifully, the heat of midday was hours away yet; it was early morning and the day was at its freshest, the tide had washed in a faint whiff of the sea, and the curlews' calls far out on the marsh seemed mysterious and poetic.

Jim was surprised, on making the slow journey back to the hidden sanctuary of the scooped-out ponds, that someone had already set up and was quietly munching on a sandwich. Familiar. He'd seen him somewhere before. Maybe at the ponds, even. Funny, Jim thought, he didn't look the type. Not that there was a type as such, these days. You were as likely to see dreads and hair weaves, goatees and nose rings as elderly veterans like himself, kitted out in pork pie hat and green fatigues. Still, better here than causing bother on the streets, he thought, giving the fisherman a nod of acknowledgement, more inclined to expansiveness because his own favourite peg was free, and as he didn't seem to be wearing one of those blasted Walkman things, perhaps he wouldn't be any bother.

* * *

Two events happened simultaneously: while Jameson was being told of a third possible murder victim, Sergeant Tully was being asked to confirm the identity of an officer requesting access to files at the council offices. Tully was wiry in a more than usually literal sense of the word. He was tall — over six foot two in his stockinged feet — and thin as a pipe-cleaner. He was also uncommonly hairy, having a course, unruly thatch which twisted and bristled, refusing to lie flat on his head and which, to his surprise and annoyance, had faded to a steely grey almost on the day he turned forty.

'*Who?*' he demanded, wondering whether this was a wind-up. One or two heads turned. Tully was known for his irascibility and some of the younger lads treated Tully-baiting as a kind of sport — bloodless, but lively, even dangerous at times.

'What the hell are you on about?' he growled. Grinning faces appeared over monitor tops. Glances were exchanged. 'Is this some kind of joke? 'Cos if it is, I'm not laughing.' He scowled around the office and heads ducked down below the firing line. 'Who did you say you were? Right. And he says he's—' He glanced angrily at the few who dared to stay in sight. 'If youse lot're trying to pull a fast one—' He waved a finger at DC Potter, who raised his hands, palms up.

'Who's down at the council records office?' Tully demanded.

'Dunno, Sarge. No one, as far as I know.'

Tully held the receiver by the mouthpiece and used it to punctuate his speech with aggressive jabs. 'If I find out yiz've been pulling my plonker—'

Potter looked pained at the very idea. Tully put the receiver back to his ear and spoke briefly. 'Tell you what, Mr Orrell, you keep him talking and we'll send someone round to check him out.' Sergeant Tully grabbed his jacket from his chair and motioned Potter to follow him.

'What's up, Sarge?' Potter asked as they waited for the elevator down.

'Apparently,' said Tully, with a corrosive edge that banished from Potter's mind any thoughts of laughter, 'I'm at Calderbank records office even as we speak!'

'You what?'

Tully nodded, punching the elevator button impatiently. 'That was the records clerk. Apparently, I want to look at their files.'

* * *

'*Warrant Sergeant* Jim Bradbury?' Jameson said in disbelief.

'You know him, Guv?' Foster asked.

'Knew him,' Jameson corrected automatically. 'Yes. Every beat bobby around Liverpool city centre knew Jim Bradbury.'

Foster lifted his chin in the beginnings of a nod, but his face remained at a tilt and he stared into the middle distance, a slight furrow developing between his eyebrows.

'What?' Jameson said.

'Nothing, boss,' Foster said. 'I just never knew you were a plod.'

'Did you imagine I arrived fully formed behind this desk?' Jameson demanded.

He caught the look on Foster's face and realised that the sergeant had tagged him as a fast tracker: degree, CID, quick promotion to easy street. *Well, well.*

In reality, nothing could be further from the truth, but Jim Bradbury, more than any other cop, had helped him to achieve his ambitions — not because he'd taken Jameson under his wing, that wasn't Jim's style. But Jim Bradbury had taught Jameson everything worth knowing — first, about being a good police officer, and later, a good detective.

Jameson stood at the window for some minutes, trying to compose himself. The Mersey, glimpsed between the transformed warehouses of the Mersey docks and the harbour board offices, glinted pacifically in the morning sunshine, kingfisher blue substituting its usual drab greyish brown. He had always thought the cormorant a curiously apt emblem for the city, with its oily sheen and its bedraggled black feathers. The city, viewed from this silent height, had taken on a Mediterranean stillness. Half the population seemed to be strolling along the waterfront, oblivious or uncaring that something sinister walked with them, unseen, indiscernible from the happy crowds idling away a few hours in the unaccustomed heat.

Their short drive out to Sawrey Moss was conducted in silence, Foster concentrating on the road, which was already clogged with traffic, and Alan Jameson immersed in his own thoughts.

Jim Bradbury. Uncle Jim, as he was affectionately known. A big, rumbling bear of a man. Strong, too. Bastard must have caught him off his guard.

Christ! he thought, *what would Lily do?* Lily, who had waited all those years, biding her time, patiently counting the years and months and finally the days until Jim would retire and she wouldn't have to worry any more as he went off at the start of a shift, or if he came home a little late at the end of one.

Jameson had attended Jim Bradbury's retirement party a few weeks before all this madness had started. Lily had poked Jim in his wide, comfortable belly and said, smiling, 'Says it'll give him more time for fishing, but I've got other plans.'

'We're booked in on one of those "New England in the Fall" holidays,' Jim had told him, winking. 'There's good fishing to be had up on the lakes in Maine, so I'm told.' His retirement gift had been a fishing rod made of some sort of carbon fibre, one Jim had been promising himself for years, but for which he had somehow never seemed able to justify the expense.

'You won't get the chance, my lad!' Lily had said.

'You could come with me — you're not such a bad angler yourself.' Jim had paused, waiting for Lily's 'How d'you mean?' before adding, 'You lured me with the first cast of your line and landed me before I'd a chance to wriggle off the hook.'

When Lily had slapped his belly, it reverberated like a drum and Jim had hugged her, grinning like an idiot. Jameson tightened his jaw, trying not to think about Jim and Lily's holiday. He struggled to think of Jim as a murder victim, not someone he knew and loved in his own imperfect way, but as a body, the deceased — a thing to be treated with respect, certainly, and to be afforded the dignity that had been callously snatched from the living Jim — but something which could safely be viewed as evidence, at arm's length, and dispassionately. Sometimes the trick worked and sometimes it didn't. The body as evidence. Emotion would not undo the wrong, but vigilance might at least achieve justice.

'Sir,' Foster roused Jameson from his reverie. They had arrived at the narrow strip of unadopted road which ran alongside the moss, terminating at a five-bar gate held together with rope and twisted lengths of rusted barbed wire. He followed the uniformed officer on duty at the gate down to the ponds, which were in a depression, fringed by trees and shrubs, where the scene of crime officers were already busy. He braced himself and then walked to the far side of the pond, where Jim's body, which in some obscure way seemed not quite so large in death as in life, lay face down in the dirt.

The big man lay with one hand in the water. Jameson thought he saw it twitch, but it was only the gentle ripples on the water's surface, carp or maybe tench circling in the mud-brown depths, curious. Pond skaters skimmed the surface skin of the water in short, jerky bursts. A brilliant blue damselfly darted in, landing briefly on one bobbing finger and then dashing off on a zigzag course.

'How?' Jameson asked, looking down at the body. The body. He nearly had it now. It was a body he was looking at, not his old colleague, Jim Bradbury. A body. And he had seen enough of those to be able to preserve a detached professional interest when it mattered.

The man to whom he had addressed this question, a great, square rugby player of a man, who virtually burst out of his white overalls, extended a hand, insisting upon the observance of formalities. 'Good morning, Alan.' A clear, sonorous tenor's voice. 'I saw your fifteen minutes of fame on the box the other night. Looks like you've another on the books now.' He ought to know — Dr Dillon Etherington had performed the post-mortem examinations on both Dorothy and Ann. The forensic pathologist enjoyed his work hugely and had revelled in the challenge of carrying out his preliminary examination of the bodies on a seventy-five-per-cent gradient. Etherington was a man to whom people reacted instantly, and the emotions he provoked tended to lie at opposite extremes.

Jameson understood that police surgeons and pathologists and forensic evidence all helped to catch criminals, but he could never quite understand, nor could he bring himself to trust, the type of person who derived intellectual satisfaction from probing into the grislier aspects of death. For him, that kind of interest held a kind of prurience which he found unwholesome, even distasteful. If he had thought about it more deeply, he might have drawn a parallel between this abhorrence for the rummaging in the unpleasant details of sudden death and his squeamish dislike of psychological assessment and counselling. *And what the* hell *sort of name was Dillon anyway?* he thought with unreasonable testiness.

'Can we turn him over?' he asked.

A flicker of something passed over the doctor's face: triumph, curiosity or a macabre amusement, Jameson wasn't sure which, and for the moment he didn't much care. Etherington quickly regained his composure and nodded. 'Gently though.'

Jim Bradbury looked once more with sightless eyes at the eggshell blue of a cloudless sky. Jameson flinched from the terrible gaping wound in his chest. 'The knife?' Jameson asked, maintaining his composure. Just.

'No weapon found. As far as I can tell, he was stabbed from behind. Like this—' Etherington demonstrated by moving behind Jameson and reaching over his shoulder, bringing his fist into Jameson's chest. 'I'd say the assailant was right-handed, or rather that it was a right-handed attack and that he was smaller than Jim. This gash—' he pointed to the wound in Jim's chest — 'curves up to the right and gapes at the upper end, as though he has overreached himself and the knife has been pulled out a little.'

'Wouldn't Jim have been sitting down when he was attacked?' Jameson asked. 'He was fishing, after all.'

'Yes, and this is hardly fly fishing,' Etherington said, with just discernible disdain. 'But he was broad-chested — a bit like me.' He laughed: three musical notes. 'As the knife went in, he probably began to stand. A smaller man might be lifted, and the knife be dragged from the wound by the force. The knife had caught the left ventricle, however, and the poor devil would have keeled over onto his face even as he tried to stand. No blood pressure, you see. Messy job,' he added after a pause, and with the disapproval of an expert viewing an amateurish piece of work.

Jameson turned abruptly, needing to get away, almost toppling Foster into the pond. Apologizing, he blundered past, finding himself on the log stepping-stones which linked this to a larger pond only yards away.

Foster followed him a few minutes later.

Jameson was acutely aware the impression he must give to the sergeant, shirt-sleeved and sweating, with one hand clamped over his mouth. He moved his hand up over his forehead and pushed his fingers through his hair.

'Where does this lead?' Jameson asked, his voice sounding hoarse to his own ears. He indicated a path which skimmed the edge of the pond and then climbed uneven steps to the top of a gorse-crested grassy bank.

'That one goes straight out onto the marsh,' Foster said. 'There's two other entrances which run adjacent to a bridle path down to Sawrey Woods on one side and a wild-flower meadow on the other.'

Jameson glanced curiously at his colleague and Foster shrugged. 'Used to fish here when I was a lad.'

Jameson raised his eyebrows; he'd had Foster pegged for a Scouser, born and bred.

Foster had clearly read the surprised look and said, appalled, 'We didn't *live* here. Me Dad used to bring us out of a weekend and holidays and that.'

They emerged through the untidy and stunted tangle of gorse onto the broad stretch of marshland where, hours earlier, Jim Bradbury had breathed the salt air and had anticipated a good morning's fishing. The sun was already high, and the marsh shimmered with a million dazzling reflections. Sailing boats bobbed cheerfully a couple of miles away at Calderbank. By now the marina would be busy with enthusiasts sailing or surfboarding on the still and silk-warm waters. To the east of the marina, on the low hills of the Lancashire coastline, untidy rows of white houses cluttered the marginal area between sand and farmland. If it weren't for the brackish brown foam the water fetched up with every pulsing wave, and the occasional scum of household sewage thrown up from the outfall near the marina, this might be the Normandy coast.

16

'Darren Lewis has done a runner.' At the sound of DC Ryman's slightly hoarse tones, the two men looked up. She had angled the top half of her etiolated torso around the door frame, interrupting Jameson in conference with Detective Superintendent Compton.

'Sorry, sir,' she said, jarring her elbow in a hasty attempt to retreat. Compton waved her in.

'Not to worry,' he said. 'This is a personal call.'

Ryman looked even more dismayed.

'But if Lewis has disappeared,' the superintendent went on, oblivious to her discomfort, 'I'm as keen as the next man to find out why.'

'And where,' Jameson muttered.

Ryman recovered her composure and brought the rest of her lanky form into the room. 'I just got back from A Division,' she said. 'They've got people out looking for him now, guv.' She addressed this information to Jameson, and he realised that she was avoiding having to confront Compton's remarkable eyebrows; they were wild and bushy, and he made no attempt to control them.

'Have they any theories as to what spooked him?' Compton asked.

'He was interviewed here yesterday evening, sir,' Jameson intervened. 'I conducted the interview myself. He seemed edgy, but he gave the impression that he was concerned that he was being held up. Like he had something important to get to.' Jameson felt a spasm of unease at the thought that Jim had been murdered early in the morning after Lewis had shown such impatience to get away from the police station.

'How did he come across? Does he know anything about the murders, do you think?'

Jameson clenched his teeth. 'He's a cocky little bastard, sir. Wouldn't tell us anything of use.' He recalled the self-satisfied smirk on Lewis's face when they had asked him what he had been doing on the night of the abductions, the arsonist's elated look when he gave alibis for both days. 'He was too glib, in my opinion. Didn't need to check the days against a calendar. In retrospect, I think he was relieved. Maybe he thought we'd pulled him in for something else.'

Compton scowled, drawing his unruly eyebrows into a thick 'V'. 'And his alibis?'

'They checked out.'

Compton harrumphed and turned to the window. 'Obviously, it would be useful to have him account for his actions between the time he left the police station until early this morning,' he said.

'Obviously,' Jameson said, with rather too much emphasis, and drew a sharp and bristling glare from his superior.

'It may be worth checking if A Division want to talk to him about anything specific since we were last in touch.' Jameson directed this suggestion to Ryman.

'Ask A Division to keep us bang up to date with developments,' Compton added, then, with an effort: 'Well done, Constable.'

Ryman left, clearly glad to escape.

Jameson stared after her, remembering something Jim's wife had said. He shook his head. 'I keep thinking about Lily,' he said.

Compton's eyebrows suffered a brief convulsion. 'Waiting all those years, worrying herself sick that someone's going to do for him, and when he finally does cop it, he's fishing for bloody carp. That's bitter, Alan. It's bloody—'

'Jim tried to phone me yesterday,' Jameson interrupted. 'Lily's not sure why.' Did he think he had seen something, or was it just good old Uncle Jim, wanting to help out as usual? 'It occurs to me that the woods where we found the bodies are close to the ponds. I keep coming back to the idea that Jim may have seen something.'

'You'll have to speak to Lily again,' Compton said.

Jameson grunted in disgust. 'I know,' he said. It was the kind of thing he did every day, probing into private lives, intruding on grief.

Compton observed him closely, then, his eyebrows quivering with emotion, he said, 'You don't feel it until it's one of your own.'

'No, sir. Was there anything else, sir?'

Compton seemed affronted by the irritation in Jameson's tone, but he looked into Jameson's face and his expression softened. 'Find him, Alan,' he said. 'Find the lunatic who's doing this, then maybe you'll be able to get some sleep.' He paused, his eyebrows stilled for a moment, then he permitted himself an ironic smile. 'Correction,' he said, admitting to more than he was generally willing to, 'then maybe we'll *both* be able to get some sleep.'

* * *

Wayne proved more than usually obstructive when Chris arrived at the records office after work. She was pushing it for time, she knew, but she thought that the official records might provide more detail than her own personal notes. Perhaps she had missed someone — or something — important. She had destroyed her own records relating to the children's home after she had left the borough, and the children's home could be the link. Dorothy had disappeared just after the story broke.

Both she and Ann had worked with some of the children who had been given placements there. Chris's own involvement was something she would examine more closely when she had seen the records; Dorothy and Ann might have been murdered because of their part in it, and she regarded herself as no less guilty. Nicky had begun a trace on the boys — they would be men now, she had to keep reminding herself — putting in train a series of contacts who would eventually find them. Chris had suggested contacting the Home Office, but Nicky had snorted derisively. 'When d'you want this? Christmas?' Then she had telephoned an uncle who worked as a clerk for the Police Authority and two hours later had contacted Chris at the hospital clinic with the first address.

Laura did not seem to be on the Home Office register, and for this Chris was thankful: perhaps there was some hope for Laura, that she had made some kind of life for herself.

'Office is closed, luv,' Wayne said.

Unusually polite, Chris had thought, but blundered on unthinkingly. 'It's fifteen minutes to closing, Wayne, and I need to look up a file.'

Normally, such a remark would have invited some crude proposition, but Wayne rolled his eyes and said tensely, 'Come back tomorrow. It's too late to be looking for files at this hour.'

She should have sensed something amiss, but it had been a long day which had followed a difficult weekend and she was not at her most perceptive.

'File, Wayne,' she said, 'in the singular. It'll take two minutes. Laura Smith.'

'Got any ID?' he asked with a vehemence bordering on aggression.

'*ID?*'

'You could be anyone, couldn't you? For all I know, you just walked in off the street. How do I know you even work here?'

Chris noticed, at last, the sheen of sweat on Wayne's forehead and realized that the records clerk was in a state of mild terror.

Her eyes opened wide as awareness of the situation began to break in on her consciousness. She mouthed 'Shit!' and began a rapid back-pedalling which she knew would not prevent the inevitable fall at high speed. 'Well,' she said, 'I'll just have to come back tomorrow. I've left my ID in the office. It'll take ten minutes to get there and back, and I don't suppose you'd be willing to hang about—'

A tall, sour-faced man who could only be a policeman appeared at Wayne's back. He had been listening behind the door to the record office stacks. 'Lucky *I* brought me ID, isn't it, love?' he said, showing his warrant card. The counter stood as a barrier between them and Chris considered making a run for it, but Wayne was in enough trouble, without leaving him to explain her presence, so she waited while the policeman lifted the hinged flap and took her by the arm.

* * *

Jameson looked drained. He sat opposite her in an interview room, his hands resting on the black acrylic surface of the table, fingers laced, a look of ancient weariness on his face.

'What other information did you get from him?' he demanded.

'What do you mean "other information"? The bloke refused to hand over the file. Sergeant Tully will confirm that,' she said, with a glance to the big man on Jameson's left. 'Go ahead — ask him.'

'I already have.' He studied her for some moments, drawing out the silence, but Chris, who used the same tactic in her own work, held his gaze, wondering if the intense weariness was caused by the case or by some other factor.

'You've been there before though, haven't you, Dr Radcliffe?'

She shook her head. 'No.'

'Do you know Mr Orrell well?'

'Is that his name?' Jameson didn't answer. 'No, I don't know him at all.'

'You called him by name,' Tully said.

Chris looked up into the gargoyle features of the officer who had arrested her. 'His name's on his ID badge,' she said.

'You must have good eyesight.'

She shrugged.

'Good God!' Jameson exclaimed suddenly. 'This isn't a game, Dr Radcliffe! You have committed a serious offence.'

Chris frowned. Perhaps it was the tiredness that made him sound so pompous. 'Since I didn't gain access to any files, have I committed an offence at all? It's not as if I was impersonating a police officer.'

The silence was palpable. Then Jameson asked, 'What do you mean by that?'

Chris speculated whether she could risk throwing the question back at him, but decided on a more direct approach. 'Is that why you were there? Because someone has been dipping into the borough files? Is that how he knew where Ann and Dorothy lived?' Of course, she knew the answers to these questions already — Wayne had told her on her previous visit — but this was her first, perhaps her *only* chance to discuss the likelihood with Jameson that the murderer was someone that she and Dorothy and Ann had all known.

'Has Mr Orrell been helping you for long?' Jameson asked, unblinkingly.

She hesitated as though uncertain who Jameson was referring to, and Tully burst in: 'Don't come the innocent! If you read his name on the tag, you know his name's Wayne Orrell.'

'If you want access to information you're not entitled to, look for first names,' Chris said. 'They have the greatest manipulative pull.' She looked Tully in the eye. 'It's basic social engineering.'

'Yeah?' His accent became more pronounced as he grew more agitated. 'Well what about knowing them *personally*, like? Don't tell us you didn't recognise him. He's worked for the records office for ten years or more, which means he must of been there at the same time's you.'

Chris shrugged. 'Maybe. It was a long time ago.'

'All right, *Chris*,' Tully said. 'Tell us why you wanted a butcher's at Laura Smith's file.'

Chris smiled, genuinely amused. The Cockney rhyming slang sat uneasily with broad Liverpudlian. 'The trick, Sergeant Tully, is knowing *when* to use a first name,' she said. 'Use it at the wrong time, or in the wrong context, and it becomes merely offensive.'

'We wouldn't want to cause you offence, Dr Radcliffe.' Jameson's careful intonation understated the irony well. 'But we are investigating the murders of people with a direct link to the borough council, and when you turn up, trying to gain access to confidential files, we are naturally . . . curious.'

Chris hesitated. Would it hurt to tell Jameson what she was doing? He had probably worked it out for himself already, after all.

* * *

She was working in her office at the hospital the next morning when the telephone call came. The windows were open, and the nets drifted in a tantalizing breeze which carried with it a faint whiff of grass mowings and melting tarmac. She picked up the receiver on the first ring.

'Dr Radcliffe?'

'Speaking.' Chris finished typing the last few words of a preliminary report, the handset wedged between her shoulder and her ear.

'Alan Jameson.'

For a moment, Chris wondered who Alan Jameson was, then, appreciating the significance of the omission of his title, she said, 'What can I do for you, Alan?'

'I hope I'm not interrupting anything — I tried to catch you at home.'

'Just finished. And my first appointment isn't for another fifteen minutes.'

'I . . . um . . . I wanted to let you know we're following up the names you gave us yesterday. It's already given us some useful lines of inquiry.'

Chris felt she ought to say something, but was, for once, at a loss for words.

'I . . . er . . . I'd like to talk to you about Sunnyside. Not now,' he added, 'I know you're busy, but perhaps we can set up an appointment — I'd appreciate your insights.'

'Of course,' Chris said. 'I'll check with my secretary and get back to you.' She realized that she sounded stiff and formal. The man was trying to make this easy for her, making what could legitimately be conducted as a taped interview into a consultation.

Then she remembered the main item of news that morning and, anxious that Jameson was about to hang up, she called, 'Alan—' When she was sure he was listening, she said, 'I'm sorry I caused you so much trouble yesterday. I didn't know about Jim.' His murder had been reported in the national newspapers that day. There was a silence on the line and Chris was about to ring off when Jameson's voice made her pull the receiver back from its cradle.

'You knew him?' he asked.

'He kept a check on some of the kids in local authority care. I was fond of him. He was a truly decent man.'

Jameson ignored her comment. 'You realize that's the third?'

'Linked with me? Yes. But there must be dozens of people who knew them — their efficiency in doing their jobs hinged upon the variety and usefulness of their contacts within the LEA. How . . .' she began. There was no gentle way to put it. 'How was he killed?'

'A single stab wound to the heart.'

Chris swallowed.

'Have you seen the papers?' she asked. A degree or two of frost formed in the silence that followed.

'If you mean have I seen the *Herald*, the answer is yes.'

* * *

Jameson hung up without another word. He had got into the habit of reading the morning papers every day since the first abduction. A combination of the unrelenting heat and worry about the case had resulted in insomnia, so he jogged across the park to Aigburth Vale each morning, kicking up little mist devils from the dampness, which at five thirty still condensed in swirling pools around his ankles. The exercise fulfilled the dual task of airing the dogs and rousing him sufficiently after a few hours' sleep to perform the necessary ritual of feeding himself and them, before showering and rummaging through the freshly laundered shirts in the airing cupboard for something approaching respectable. More than once he had wondered if he should ask Mrs Delaney to do an extra couple of hours and iron his shirts as well as wash them, but he hadn't got round to leaving her a note, so he had dragged another slightly crumpled shirt from the pile that morning and hoped the creases would fall out with wear.

The byline for the Municipal Murders headline was credited to Ralph Milton. Foster had confirmed that Milton had also tracked down the story on the children's home — and had tagged it as exclusive. Apparently, he had decided to make a career out of the events of the last few weeks, making all kinds of wild connections between the children's home scandal and the murders. His paper had printed the names and ages of Dorothy's two children and this morning's issue had a photograph of them, looking dazed and fretful, being led by the hand to their primary school. He had quoted 'sources' who described Dorothy Hardy as a 'church mouse', and he had somehow unearthed Ann Lee's ex-husband, who had given her a pretty lousy character reference.

* * *

In a small but comfortable hotel on Mount Pleasant, a main thoroughfare which curved downhill from the University of Liverpool campus to the city centre, less than ten minutes' walk away, Ralph Milton was keeping busy. He had, since his liaison with the talented Mr Dixon, become the editor's golden boy, and Milton intended to milk this one for all it was worth. Dixon had initially contacted the news desk to ask if anyone was interested in buying information on institutional child abuse. The background he gave them seemed authentic enough to find out more, and Milton had been sent to investigate Darkest Merseyside. Not that it was put to him as any great honour — no one else had been interested. It wasn't like it was Manchester and possibly worth a flying visit. Somehow, the promise of a week in Liverpool and outlying *Straw Dogs* countryside didn't have the same charm.

Ralph Milton was London born, and held in deep suspicion any town north of Watford. His highly imaginative brain had conjured up images of satanic rituals in crumbling, soot-blackened mansions facing murky canals and derelict docklands. So, he had packed his gear and booked into his present hotel lodgings. Within a week he had a juicy story. Days after that, when the first woman disappeared, he had the story of a lifetime, and a head start on every other newspaper in the UK. And whatever he needed to know, whenever he needed to find something out, the endlessly resourceful Jake Dixon had come up with the goods.

Milton leaned back in his armchair and looked about him. His bag was packed; by two p.m., he would move from his small hotel to the Moat House Hotel, to be nearer the police and the local radio and television studios. He liked to keep his ear to the ground, and since his story had been elevated to national status, the *Herald* had agreed to fund a larger, air-conditioned room in plusher surroundings — a must in this weather. It was also three times as expensive, and Milton was keenly aware of the status that such a concession on his expense account conferred on him. The phone rang and he scooped up the receiver. This was the call he'd been waiting for. He cradled the receiver to his ear and spoke into it with a bonhomie he actually felt. 'Jake, me old mate. Yeah — good pictures. What did you think of the story?' He laughed. 'The public has a right to know, yeah? Listen, what can you give me on a warrant sergeant, name of Jim Bradbury? Retired.'

He heard Dixon at the other end of the line typing Bradbury's name on his keyboard to initiate a search. He asked what Milton wanted on him.

'Nothing much, just a motive for someone wanting to murder him.'

'You sound as if you'd like to claim credit for it yourself,' Dixon said, sounding a bit queasy.

Milton laughed, appreciating the gallows humour. 'You are a card,' he said. 'No, someone else signed the sergeant's death warrant.' He paused, savouring the phrase, filing it away for use. 'But I'd like to be the first to get something *interesting* on him.'

'I'm looking at 252 hits on the screen. It'll take a couple of hours to check through — I'll have to get back to you.'

'OK,' Milton said. 'I got to switch hotels, anyway. You can find me at the Moat House after two o'clock,' he added with a glow of pride.

'Fine. There could be a children's home link, if that's what you're after,' Dixon said, clearly not appreciating the significance of the hotel upgrade.

'That, or anything at all murky in the past,' Milton said, trying not to feel rebuffed. 'Skeletons in cupboards. Disciplinary proceedings. Whatever. You know me, I'm not fussy.'

'Just as long as you get your story, right?'

'Got it in one, mate.'

Milton broke the connection and surveyed the little room for the last time. He might call a cab, get to the hotel early and have a spot of lunch.

* * *

Chris Radcliffe was sitting in her shared office in one of the armchairs adjacent to the mirror. The curtains were closed. Both the window and the door stood open and her feet rested unshod on the coffee table.

'Are you all right?' It was Ted.

'Just trying to keep cool.'

'That's not what I heard.'

Chris opened one eye. 'Irony isn't your strong point, Ted.'

'Fran's in the staffroom, crying.'

Chris sighed, swinging her legs off the table and relishing the brief coolness of the tiles under her feet. 'Fran launched in with something about Philip having "got off" with it. In the next breath, she happened to mention the "he'd" done another one. I assumed she meant Philip. I was wrong.'

Ted knew more than most about Chris's background, and felt the responsibility attendant upon the privilege of a shared confidence. 'How is Philip?'

'A bloody wreck, if I'm honest. He spent most of Monday cleaning and rearranging his flat. He wouldn't let anyone help. He says he feels violated.' She passed a hand over her eyes, feeling weary and helpless. 'I don't know how to . . .' She grappled with a tiredness that almost robbed her of words. 'To be of use to him,' she finished, looking into Ted's eyes and, reading something stronger than compassion, withdrew quickly, adding a brusque, meaningless, 'I suppose he'll find his own way.'

She winced as she said it and saw that Ted was puzzled at the very least.

'He must have survived on his wits all the time the police were looking for him,' Ted said, after a pause.

Chris frowned. 'He won't tell me where he slept. It's like he feels betrayed. Like he can't trust anyone anymore. I worry, you know? I mean how did he find the money for his medication? For food? What if he did hurt someone, Ted?'

'He'll tell you. Give him time.'

Chris bit back a testy remark about platitudes. 'I'd better go and see how Fran is.'

'Leave her. Maybe she'll be more careful who she upsets in future.' She knew that Ted disapproved of Fran's insatiable appetite for gossip and had been known to mutter darkly that such people should be strung up by their wagging tongues.

'I'm afraid I overreacted,' Chris said. 'I was unnecessarily cruel.'

'She's not particularly kind herself when she gets going.'

'I'm sure she didn't mean anything by it,' said Chris, perplexed by her own need to defend the receptionist. 'It was typical Fran, running off at the mouth and not thinking of the consequences.' She pictured Fran, uncomfortable, hot, fiddling with the ice-cube container, trying ineffectually to disgorge the contents into a jug of tap water.

Ted shrugged impatiently. 'Aren't you being a little too generous?'

Chris smiled. 'You may be right. I suppose I'm relieved that Phil is home safe.' Ted's question posed another: was this increased vulnerability, the willingness to accept blame, centred on her own unresolved inner conflicts? 'You think I'm racked with guilt, is that it? Taking the miseries of the world on my shoulders because I had an unhappy childhood?'

'Your flippancy isn't much of a smokescreen,' Ted said. 'You know you'll have to work through your feelings some time.'

'I may choose not to.'

'Then you'll be the worse for it.'

Their eyes locked. Chris knew he was right; she had thought she'd dealt with her alienation from her father a long time ago, but his death last year had generated a whole new crop of feelings she had scarcely been prepared to meet. In an abstract way her book research had been an attempt to purge some of the anger she still felt against both her parents, but she knew in her heart that it was impossible finally to overcome the injuries of her childhood without engaging those emotions she had quelled for so long. Lofty scientific detachment simply would not do.

Ted must have seen her thoughts projected like phantoms behind her eyes. 'Look, if you do need to talk—'

'I don't,' she said, looked away from him, shutting him out.

'I'm trying to help, Chris,' Ted said, without rancour. Chris understood for the first time, in this one small moment of revelation, the depth of his feelings for her, and she found the realization unexpectedly shocking.

Detective Chief Inspector Jameson stared at the tabloid newspaper on his desk. Another article by Milton. Each time he saw the headline he felt a fresh rush of outrage.

DEATH WARRANT
MUNICIPAL MURDERER CLAIMS NEW VICTIM
Sergeant slain in knife attack

He turned the paper face down. The tactless pun was bad enough, but it was the personal details: the fact that he had only recently retired, the use of his nickname, the fact that he had been murdered near the woods where the bodies of the women had been found, an oblique reference to some supposed misuse of his authority in the past. No direct accusation, but a hint that his murder 'may have been' a grudge attack. Jim had been variously described as 'devoted to his duties', 'keen' and 'zealous'. The public was informed that he had pursued his duties with a 'passion' which left little time for home and family and for his other 'abiding obsession', fishing. The judicious placing of an article featuring two officers who had been suspended from duty for alleged brutality in the columns adjacent to this character assassination by insinuation would leave readers in no doubt as to the conclusions they were expected to draw.

Foster knocked and entered without waiting for permission. He held a copy of the same newspaper in his hand. 'You've seen it then,' he said.

Jameson nodded. 'I just hope to God Lily hasn't. Someone has been talking, Foz. I want to know who.'

'D'you want me to find Ralph Milton and shake the little weasel by the tail till he squeaks?'

'And have him do a follow-up — "Intrepid Reporter Refuses to Reveal Sources"? It would only give credence to this bloody lie.' Jameson picked up the paper and slammed it down onto the desk.

After a brief silence, Foster asked, '*Did* Jim Bradbury get his wrist slapped for something?'

Jameson could always trust his sergeant to ask the difficult questions. 'I don't know, Foz. You know what it's like. Some little bastard makes a complaint and it has to be investigated.' He sighed. 'But I suppose I'd better make sure. I'll check on that side of things; you sort out who's giving Milton this garbage.' This time when he picked the paper up he flung it into the wastepaper bin.

* * *

Chris Radcliffe drove through a heavy downpour under a cloudless sky. A dense mist of droplets drifted in the southerly breeze from the potato fields onto the roadway; white spumes cannoned from massive hoses, arching in solid white fountains over the flat landscape. Drought restrictions had not yet been imposed, but it was only a matter of time, and the farmers were getting what they could while it was still available.

The prison squatted low in a natural depression in the parched fields surrounding it. Nondescript rather than ugly. A perimeter fence and high outer wall gave onto a huddle of rustic, red-roofed brick buildings. Less than an hour's drive from Liverpool, Avonlea was located in a Lancashire landscape as level and unsettlingly featureless as the broad, even plains of Norfolk.

She had been ready to strike George Maddox from the list until Nicky told her that Avonlea was an open prison. Maddox was nearing the end of a sentence for GBH and was allowed overnight and weekend passes. An application to the Home Office to visit him in prison might have taken weeks, and then they might refuse — or Maddox himself might. If Maddox was the killer, Chris would bear some of the responsibility if there were further attacks.

She had given Jameson the name after her arrest at the records office, watching carefully for his reaction. There was nothing she could point to, nothing tangible, but instinct told her he was more than casually interested. 'What do you know about him?' he asked.

'What do you?' Chris returned.

Jameson's eyes flickered to a pile of folders stacked untidily on one corner of his desk. 'He's on our list,' he said.

Of course, they would cross-check links with Ann and Dorothy, just as she had. She had underestimated the police, made arrogant assumptions. Chris felt a creeping warmth in her cheeks and glanced away. When she'd looked up Jameson was still gazing at her, and she saw from his thinly veiled amusement that he knew precisely what she was thinking. She began with a synopsis of George Maddox's history, ending with a brief psychological profile. She wanted to meet Maddox face-to-face. If he was the killer, she wanted to know if she was a target and she thought that perhaps she may be able to pick up clues — that he might betray himself. It seemed important to make the first contact from a position of superiority.

'I'll get one of my team onto it,' Jameson said.

Chris almost reacted, but then she saw something in Jameson's face: he was willing to negotiate.

'You should send a woman,' she said, staring past him through the window at the view of Liverpool docks. 'He'll do the tough old lag act if you send a male officer — right to silence, that sort of thing. But George likes to show off to the ladies.' It was difficult to gauge Jameson's reaction. 'He may want to talk about the killings. She shouldn't show shock or fear. He likes to shock, and fear is one of his weapons, so she'll need to be a tough nut or a good actress.' He was listening now; the game element of the exchange had gone. 'And tell her not to ask direct questions,' Chris added. 'He finds them threatening — of course, the fact that it's a police officer posing the questions could be construed as threatening in itself—'

'You're saying we would be better sending someone like a prison visitor or social worker. Or maybe a psychologist, is that it?'

Chris beamed at him. 'I thought you'd never ask.'

It had taken Jameson a day to achieve what might have taken her several weeks. He had asked that Dr Radcliffe be allowed to speak to Maddox on behalf of the Merseyside police force.

Maddox shook hands formally, waiting for her to be seated before taking the sofa opposite. The irony was deadpan, but Chris appreciated it. He must be twenty-five or -six now, but she could not have guessed his age from his inexpressive, immobile face. She glanced around the room, absorbing its main features: two sofas faced each other across a tiled coffee table. A stack of magazines, mainly cars and computing, but with a few women's titles among them, were fanned across one end of the table, and a clean ashtray stood at its centre.

'Like the artwork?' Maddox asked, indicating a huge collage which dominated one wall, swamping the room with its size and vibrancy.

Chris regarded the work with a critical eye. It was a composition of thin brass and copper sheet, cut and welded into shapes which suggested fish. The background shimmered, changing colour as the observer moved.

'In another setting, yes. It's clever, well executed.'

He grimaced. 'Bit overpowering in here, isn't it? But then you don't get an awful lot of space in a prison — even an open one.'

'No,' Chris agreed. 'But that's not likely to be a problem for much longer, at least as far as you're concerned.'

'You mean my release? Does that worry you, Doctor?'

Chris could read nothing in those dark eyes. 'Should it?'

Maddox laughed. 'Don't you people ever switch off?'

She half smiled. 'Sorry,' she said. 'Force of habit.'

'So?'

She paused. 'I don't know if I've any need to be worried,' she said. 'I don't know what your feelings are towards me.'

'We hardly know each other, Doctor.' The insinuation was interwoven with a subtle menace. 'But that's often the — what's the word? — the *rationalization* for violent men, yeah? Don't acknowledge the victim as a person and you don't have to feel any guilt.'

'You seem to have gained an insight into violent behaviour, Mr Maddox. Is that reading or therapy?'

'Bit of both. Therapy mostly. I don't go much for books.'

'And do you believe it?'

He considered. 'Seems too simple to me. What about the ones who beat up their girlfriends, their wives?' He gazed steadily into her eyes. 'Their kids? You're not telling me they don't know them as people. They know their victim all right. Know them and despise them so much it doesn't matter what they do to them.'

'Denying their status as people, you mean?' Chris said. 'So the violence is justified again.' Chris sensed an unaccountable build-up of emotion in the man.

'Vicious circle,' he said, watching her with an intensity which betrayed his inner passion.

'If the victim stands up to the aggressor—'

She was cut short by a shout of angry laughter. 'Think you could do that, Doc? Think you could stand up to fifteen stone of pure hate?' His eyes glittered and his hands balled into fists.

Chris forced herself to hold his angry stare. 'Physically? No,' she said quietly, 'but in other ways.'

Maddox grunted his contempt. 'There is no other way,' he said, but his eyes slid away from hers and he stubbed out his cigarette angrily, lighting another immediately. 'What the fuck do you want anyway?' he demanded. 'I'm on my way out of here. I've got a job fixed up. I don't need no aggro.'

'I know that, Mr Maddox, which is why I'm here and not the police.'

He glanced up sharply, then quickly looked away. It took several moments for him to adjust his position, then he began again, taking a more placatory tone. 'Look, if it's about the . . . transactions I made on leave, they were for personal use only — the shit you get in here can fuck you up good style.'

Chris tried to read his face. Maddox was afraid, that much was evident, and despite the efforts he was making, he was barely in control. He didn't want to wreck his chances of getting out, but was his anxiety really about drugs he had bought on the outside, or was he using them to hide another, more sinister guilt?

Maddox saw her hesitation, registered her bafflement and must have interpreted it as a vulnerability, because in that instant, he relaxed. The faint whiff of fear she had scented on him vanished, and the man's immobile mask was once more in place.

'Heard you on the radio,' he said conversationally, leaning back on the sofa, stretching one arm out along its length.

'Did you?' Chris asked, bracing herself.

'Can't see you as the Agony Aunt type, meself,' he said with a grin.

Chris smiled in return, refusing to be needled into defensiveness.

'I'd forgot about you being in with them others.'

'Which others?'

Maddox looked at her with his dark eyes throwing out little pinpoints of light. A smile that was not a smile flickered over his face like the light from a guttering candle flame. Then, as if losing heart, it died.

'You know the only difference between people like you and people like me?' He took her silence as a tacit confirmation; they understood each other. 'You got away with it and I didn't.'

'Got away with what?' Chris asked, shutting out a vision of grey light on hard steel.

Maddox lowered his lids, shielding her momentarily from his scrutiny. 'Sometimes you get sent down and sometimes you don't,' he said, snaring her once more in his gaze. 'But there's always a price to pay, isn't there, Doc?'

* * *

'Is that it?' Jameson asked. 'Is that all you got?'

'What did you want me to do?' Chris said. 'Ask him straight out if he was carrying out some sort of vendetta against anyone from Calderbank borough council who ever crossed his path? That'd be an open invitation to terrorize for a man like George Maddox.' She wondered irrationally if Jameson had registered Maddox's personal accusation against her. Unwilling to allow him time to think, time to wonder about her own place in all of this, she added, 'He did happen to mention that he'd enjoyed reading the news from home of late. Even said it was always a thrill to see people you know on the telly.'

Jameson swore softly and Chris leaned forward, slipping her notebook onto his desk. She was wearing a short, lemon-coloured A-line linen dress. When she glanced up, she saw Jameson watching her, and thought she saw admiration in the look.

She stared into his eyes, setting her own hard, and he fumbled into a question.

'Is Maddox capable,' he asked, 'of committing murder?'

'That's indisputable,' Chris said. 'He did, after all, kill his own father. But then most of us would do the same, given sufficient provocation and the right opportunity.'

'Let me rephrase,' said Jameson. 'Is he capable of multiple killings?'

She shook her head. 'I honestly don't know. He's a difficult man to read: bitter, damaged, drug dependent. But he was all of that long before the authorities ever got near him.'

'Does he think they — we — should have got to him sooner? Helped him more?'

'Oh yes,' Chris said softly, remembering the conversation they had had just after he had murdered his father. 'But is he angry enough, mad enough or bad enough to do anything about it? I really couldn't say. He desperately wants to get out of prison, but he was willing to jeopardize his chances by buying drugs on the outside and smuggling them back in. Still, I suppose the need to feed a habit transcends all logic and nullifies normal fears. The question is: would his need for vengeance allow him — or force him — to undertake the same level of risk?' She paused. 'I don't know . . .'

She was thinking aloud, and Jameson seemed suddenly impatient. 'Is Maddox a plausible suspect or not?' he demanded.

Chris was mildly surprised by his irritation. Did he imagine that she'd been trying out her radio persona on him?

'I'm trying to clarify in my mind what it is you're trying to say,' he added, and she heard the defensiveness in his tone.

Chris began carefully. 'I suppose what I'm saying is, George Maddox wouldn't think twice about killing if it served his purpose.'

'And what *purpose* have these three murders served?' Jameson demanded.

'We won't know that for sure until you catch your killer, Mr Jameson. Perhaps not even then.'

She hesitated, and Jameson, clearly making a determined effort to control his temper, prompted: 'But if you were to make a guess?'

'If I *were* to hazard a guess, I'd say the motive was revenge. The killer is a man—'

'Or woman.'

She nodded, unconvinced. 'Or woman, who is so eaten up with rage that they don't care if they're caught — as long as they finish the job.'

'Are you ruling out George Maddox?'

'He doesn't answer the description of the man who tried to get into the records office.' An impression flashed into her mind that she knew the mysterious blond man, but as yet, the feeling was no more than a vague niggling. 'But the man at the records office may have nothing to do with the murders.'

'Nothing — or everything,' said Jameson.

'And—' Chris stopped, unwilling to admit to such a lapse in objectivity.

'And?'

She shrugged. 'And George Maddox scares me half to death.'

He regarded her silently, then nodded. 'OK. Is there anyone else?'

Chris nodded again. She had assigned a half day from her private practice to go and see George. On the way back she had called in at Laura Smith's — now Laura Stanford. Social services had traced her at Jameson's request.

Laura kept a large and rowdy houseful of children — six was Chris's estimate, though she assumed that some belonged to the two women Laura had insisted on introducing to her, who sat in her kitchen, sipping coffee and munching steadily through a packet of digestive biscuits. Chris had telephoned ahead, and Laura had agreed to see her, the only stipulation being that Chris would have to take her as she found her. Which was, to all appearances, in considerable disarray.

One child sat on the doorstep, peeling an orange and watching her with large solemn eyes as she rang the doorbell. The front door stood open and Chris could hear the sound of women's voices and laughter over the shouts of children, and the meaningless blare of pop music on a radio somewhere down the hallway. An older child charged to the door, the very image of her mother — she was perhaps five years old, and as dark and pretty as her mother had been at nine. She had evidently been expecting someone else, for she stopped abruptly, eyeing Chris with deep suspicion before yelling over her shoulder, 'Mam! There's someone at the door!'

'Ask them what they want!'

For a moment the voices in the kitchen were hushed, and only the radio could be heard, the DJ's voice jabbering with mindless cheerfulness and echoing up through the empty passage. Chris gave her name and the child relayed it at ear-splitting volume to her mother. Laura came from the kitchen, smiling faintly, laughter at her back from her friends who sat on.

Laura made her way down the narrow hallway, her hips brushing the walls on either side, her movements a little laboured: she seemed to rock from side to side with every step. Chris recognized her instantly, although the face had elongated a little and her hair was longer and permed into waves. She was no more than five foot four inches tall but must have weighed in the region of eighteen stone. Her prettiness was still there, and Chris saw something else which had been absent in the nine-year-old she had tried to counsel: a kind of contentment, not complete — and perhaps a little tenuous — but it was there, nevertheless. Chris extended a hand and Laura took it without eye contact, after a moment's alarm. Her skin was milk-white despite the long weeks of unbroken sunshine. She dropped Chris's hand and, smiling shyly, invited her in.

The little girl stood by her mother's side, clutching a Barbie doll and watching Chris as though she expected her to make a sudden lunge at Laura. 'It's all right, Natalie, she's only come to talk.' Laura reassured her, ruffling the child's hair.

'Her dad told her the men in white coats was coming for me,' she explained to Chris. 'He thinks it's funny.' She shook her head, smiling indulgently. 'Your dad was only joking,' she said to the girl. 'They take everything so literal at this age.' The faint smile, which Chris recognized as a sign of insecurity, had returned. A boy pushed past Laura and her daughter from inside the house and was followed by another, yelling at him to stop. Laura showed her through to the sitting room.

It was tiny, littered with children's toys and with the television set playing the manic action of a cartoon to an empty room. Laura apparently noticed neither the confusion nor the noise, for she simply cleared some of the detritus from one of the armchairs and smiled an invitation for Chris to be seated, then she lowered herself onto the large and well pummelled sofa diagonally opposite. Laura's eyes were frequently drawn to the television set as they talked, and Chris had to resist an urge to stand up and snap the off switch.

'Is it about them poor women?' Laura asked, with a directness which was refreshing after her recent conversation with George Maddox.

'Do you know anything about it?' Chris asked, watching for any indication that the question had been taken at anything deeper than surface value.

'Only what I seen on telly.' Her eyes drifted to the television. 'Shame, that. The first one had kids, didn't she?'

Chris nodded.

'God help them if they go into care,' Laura said earnestly.

* * *

'So, what do you think of Mrs Stanford?' Jameson asked, determined to be more civil this time.

'If you want my honest opinion, I think she's capable of harming no-one but herself, and then only with the insidious assaults of junk food. Her children may be unruly, but they're well cared for and they're loved. Laura may surround herself with noise and clamour because she's afraid of silence, of being alone. She may eat to quell the emptiness inside, but is that so different from thousands of others who keep their nightmares at bay with familiar comforts?'

'Which leaves us where?'

Chris Radcliffe glanced at her watch. 'I don't know where it leaves you, Alan,' she said, and he noted the deliberate use of his given name, 'but it leaves *me* well behind schedule. I promised one of my afternoon appointments that I'd see her this evening. You haven't managed to trace Darren Lewis yet?'

Jameson shook his head. 'We've checked his two properties and with his mother, but there's no sign of him. We're interviewing known associates. Lewis seems to have had quite a number, but they're afraid to talk.'

'He always did have that effect on people.'

Alan Jameson gave her a sharp look, registering the animosity in her tone. The phone on his desk rang. It was his ex-wife. 'Roz. Can't this wait?' he asked coldly, forgetting Dr Radcliffe's acerbic response in his own feelings of bitter resentment. 'I'm in conference here.'

'I thought you might like to discuss your daughter's visit to England during the vacation.'

Holidays! He wanted to yell at her. *Why can't you call them holidays?* 'This is not a good time, Roz,' he said. 'I'm in the middle of a murder investigation.'

'You're always in the middle of *something*, aren't you, Alan? Always were. Still, if you're too busy, I ought to mention that Jack has offered to take us both to Europe — see the sights, do the grand tour.'

Jameson glanced up at the Dr Radcliffe. 'Was there anything else?' he asked.

She seemed startled but not stung by his brusqueness, and he wondered with added resentment if she had gleaned something of his family situation from chatting to the detectives on the team.

'Give me a bell if there's anything more I can do,' she said in answer.

Like she's doing me a favour! Jameson thought, and immediately felt guilty. Talking to Roz made him ungracious; he had directed his anger outwards because Zoe was 4,000 miles away and Roz was with her, able to persuade her against taking the trip home, able to suggest that a trip to Europe was a once-in-a-lifetime opportunity, and Roz, he had discovered, was capable of doing anything to get her own way.

Chris Radcliffe stood, and Jameson was too incensed and too unhappy to be affected by the sinuous grace of her movements, the discreet smoothing of her dress, the way she slid her slim arms into her jacket. She had closed the door quietly behind her, leaving a faint scent of perfume and a vague feeling of regret, before Jameson had sufficiently regained control to speak again into the receiver.

18

Len was smoking feverishly. 'What're you lookin' at?' she demanded.

De Niro, you're not, Chris Radcliffe thought, but didn't say aloud, since she estimated that Len would be about twenty years too young to have seen *Taxi Driver*. She was sitting opposite her patient. Behind the modesty panel of her desk she had kicked off her shoes; she didn't mind the heat as a rule, didn't notice it over-much, but she was tired and she was scared, and being scared made her angry — with herself as well as with the nameless, faceless threat that was making her feel that way.

'In the days when everyone smoked,' she said, 'before my time, believe it or not — you might say a woman smoked seductively or with cool poise. A man might hold his cigarette at a rakish angle.' Len sighed the way that Chris imagined she must do when her parents began one of their lectures. She went on. 'Awareness of the risks of cancer and emphysema has changed all that.' She paused, eyeing the angry, vulnerable face of the girl opposite and wondering how Len would have coped with the problems Laura Smith had been forced to deal with since the age of nine, but perhaps that was unfair. 'In these enlightened times, man or woman, girl or boy, there is always something defiant in the act of smoking.'

'You're saying it's a dead giveaway, right? I smoke because my mum and dad don't want me to?'

'The teenage market seems to be the only one that's expanding in the Western world,' Chris said, leaving Len to draw her own conclusions.

'I can smoke if I want,' Len pouted. 'They don't care if I get cancer. All they're worried about is what their friends think.'

'I think they do care, Len, don't you?'

'I hate them!' Len's face was a tortured mixture of animosity and guilt.

'Lots of people your age hate their parents for a while. It's normal. It doesn't last for ever.'

'I wish *I* could go into care,' said Len, with clear emphasis on the 'I'. She had taken in everything last Wednesday, it seemed, even though she had made no mention of Chief Inspector Jameson's interruption at the time but had continued with the interview as if nothing had happened. '*They* take you because they want you, not because they have to,' Len said. 'You must really — you know — *like* your foster parents. That picture — you looked so happy.'

Chris remembered the photograph, how difficult it had been getting Phil to pose for it, his unease with the close proximity, the physical contact, the day-long tension on Christmas Day that something would conflict with his perception of what should happen on Christmas Day and he wouldn't be able to cope.

'I don't just like them, I love them,' Chris said, smiling inwardly at the girl's embarrassment at the use of so simple a word. 'But it isn't like that for everyone, Len. Foster parents are paid for what they do. They don't have to invest love and money and heartache in a child. They can send you back if they don't get on with you, or if you're too troublesome.' Len flushed slightly. 'If I'd had a family, I'd have stayed with them.'

'But she's always on at me!' Len blurted out. 'She wants me to dress like her, do the same things as her, talk like her. She wants me to *be* her!'

Chris had organized a session with Len's mother and father, and she suspected that Len's assessment of her mother was fairly accurate. 'But you are learning to be yourself,' she said quietly.

'She hates me being myself!' Len sobbed. 'Sometimes I feel like I'm *becoming* her. Not just doing things to please her but—' She struggled for the right words. 'It's like she's inside my head, making me think things. She's there, behind my eyes. Sometimes I'm scared to open my mouth in case her voice comes out!' She began sobbing uncontrollably and covered her face with her ringed hands. The black nail polish she wore was chipped and the nails bitten to the quick. Chris watched her for a while, shocked by what the girl had said. It was hardly surprising that Len had reacted so violently, that her metamorphosis had been so sudden and so complete.

When she was sure Len was calm enough to listen, Chris asked, 'So you changed yourself — your outside appearance — to show her how unlike her you are?'

Len brought her hands away from her face and took a handful of tissues from the proffered box. Her eyeshadow had run, and her make-up had streaked like the face of a sorrowful Pierrette.

Wiping her face, Len said, 'I'm scared of her, Chris. I know it seems stupid, 'cos she's never hit me or locked me in my room or anything, but she makes me feel bad if I do things my way.' She stopped, frowning furiously. 'Not *bad*,' she corrected. 'Bad makes it sound like I feel naughty or something childish like that.' Her face screwed up with frustration at the difficulty she was having in expressing herself. 'It's more than bad. She makes me feel like I'm crazy or unbalanced or ungrateful or *evil* if I go against her.' She uttered a strangled sob and gave up on trying to explain herself.

'And now?' Chris asked. 'Do you still feel that way, after all the changes you've made?'

One shoulder twitched in a half shrug. 'At least I'm not her little darling anymore. I'm not her little puppet, mouthing her words.'

'And is this really you, Len?' Chris asked gently.

Fresh tears sprang to the girl's eyes. 'I don't *know*!' she exclaimed. 'I'm so confused. I hate her!' She buried her face in her hands again and her shoulders heaved silently for some minutes. When the emotion had subsided somewhat, Len was able to say, 'I don't really hate her — well *sometimes* I do, but mostly, it's just that . . .' She heaved both shoulders up to her ears and let them drop in a massive shrug, able neither to understand nor express her feelings.

' . . . It's just that you don't want to *be* her,' Chris said, articulating the girl's confused thoughts for her.

Len stopped twisting the tissues in her hands into strangulated knots. 'Yeah,' she said, wiping her eyes with the heel of her hand.

Chris smiled. 'OK.'

'But I feel so miserable!' Len wailed, ready to begin crying again.

'You know what I think, Len? I think the adolescent years should be taken out of our teens, shredded finely and sprinkled with miserly care throughout our adult lives, so we never get too much turning up all in one day.'

Len looked up, round-eyed, snuffling, puzzled by the notion that adults once might really have been teenagers and might even have gone through some of the traumas she had recently had to face. It must hard for her to imagine that her mother and father in their staid middle age had ever been irritated by their own parents' insensitivity or had ever rebelled against the middle-class values they now held. The revelation was too difficult to assimilate on first disclosure, and she crumpled.

'But what am I going to *do*?' she pleaded.

'You're going to write down all the new things about yourself that you like, and then the things that you don't like or aren't particularly bothered about.'

'Why?' Len asked, wiping her nose.

'First, because it will help you to see which aspects of your character really matter to you, and secondly, it'll provide you with a few bargaining chips.'

Len looked puzzled. 'I get the first bit,' she said, 'but what've I got to bargain with?'

'The bits you don't like. If you ditch them — maybe the cigs for a start, you hate them anyway—'

Len smiled tearfully. She clearly hadn't thought to find an ally in Chris. Puzzlement and surprise were supplanted by a fragile hope in the girl's face.

'It's compromise, Len,' said Chris. 'There's a lot of that in life. Which is fine, so long as you don't compromise the things that really matter to you.'

Chris locked up the office at seven thirty. Nicky had left before she had arrived back from her interview with Jameson; staff from the other practices seemed to have given in to the heat and gone home. The building was deserted. Len's parents had picked her up half an hour earlier, but Chris had remained to write up her notes of the interview. The old building seemed to heave and groan as it cooled, and Chris jumped at a sudden thud over her head. She bent to recover her keys, which had fallen to the polished wood floor. Perhaps someone was working late after all. The stairway disappeared into an amorphous mass of brown shadow. Chris gripped her shoulder bag a little tighter and continued down the creaking staircase, glancing right and left at each landing. At last, with a grateful exhalation, she stepped into the evening light.

* * *

Lewis waited in the deep shadows of an open doorway across the road until he saw her come out. He had to get her while she was alone. A movement to his right checked him, and he watched a tall figure slide out from the driver's seat of a Montego parked a little way down from her office.

'Dr Radcliffe—'

Chris gasped and whirled, her heart thudding. 'Jameson! For Christ's sake! Don't you know better than to pounce on a woman like that?'

The chief inspector apologized and stepped away from her, clearly appalled by his own stupidity, taken aback by the intensity of her fear. 'I'd just arrived,' he said. 'I was on my way home and I wanted to catch you — to apologize for my rudeness earlier.'

Chris was puzzled momentarily. 'Rudeness?' She slowed in her walk to her car. 'Oh, you mean the phone call.'

'Roz — my ex — is threatening to take our daughter, Zoe, to Europe for the summer. She was supposed to be bringing her home — well, here, anyway.'

Chris found his honesty disarming. 'It's a short step from Europe to Britain,' she said. 'Get Roz to put Zoe on a plane. Unless you feel the need to see Roz as well.'

Jameson gave a short laugh. 'I didn't really notice the knot of tension I carried round like a ball in my stomach until she went to the States and it began to unravel. I thought it was the job that made me so damned uptight.' He shook his head. 'Sometimes,' he said, 'it seems our marriage was nothing more than a series of silences punctuated by furious rows.'

Chris studied him for a few moments. If he was on his way home, it wasn't from work. He had changed out of the rumpled suit he had been wearing earlier and was now dressed relatively smartly in pale cream chinos and a short-sleeved shirt. *Is this for me?* she wondered.

'I thought I could make amends by asking you to dinner.' He had followed her into the narrow side street where she had parked. 'I really am sorry I startled you.'

'Not your fault.' She smiled. 'Too much coffee and too little nourishment — and I think maybe I let George Maddox get to me. As for dinner . . .' She checked her watch. If they found somewhere local and stuck with a main course, they would have plenty of time before the radio show.

19

Chris was woken at four a.m. on Thursday morning by the sound of breathing, inches from her face. She groped under her pillow. It was soaked in sweat. Her hand moved wildly and then she found it, gripped it too tightly in her frenzy of panic and caught her thumb on the blade. She whimpered, turning away from him as he reached for the bedclothes. 'No.' In her head she had screamed, but terror of her father robbed her voice of any power, and in reality, it was only whisper. The stink of whisky and a sharper tang — urine or sex — stung her nostrils and made her eyes water. She wanted to retch.

If she didn't move now, he would be on her and she would be defenceless. She slid her arm under the length of the pillow, forcing the knife before it. As it broke free, she saw it glint in the cold grey light of the streetlamp outside her window, heard a ripping sound like old rags followed by the soft yielding of flesh, and then he was bellowing, thrashing about with his right hand, trying to get the knife from her.

The coppery scent of blood and his screams made her feel faint. The room was bleached of colour but for the dark splash of blood and the gaping, mouth-like wound in his upper arm. She struggled against him, but she was weak with fever and he got the knife from her. For a moment she saw with absolute clarity the instant of her death — a slash to her throat and the final leaching of light and life. She almost welcomed it. Then he threw the knife away and his fist smashed into her face and she could smell her own blood and taste it in her mouth and nose and throat.

Then she was really awake, her mouth dry and her heart pounding. She stumbled from her bed, all thought of sleep banished. More than anything she hated him for the dreams, because they reminded her of her helplessness. Whenever she had been tempted to relent and forgive him, whenever she began to consider arranging to meet him, another of those nightmares would visit her and rescue her from the temporary insanity which had made her think she could ever allow him back into her life.

She spent a few hours working on the notes of what might become the second chapter of her new book. Titled 'Daddy's Little Girl', this chapter looked at the long-term psychological effects of physical and sexual abuse of girls by their fathers. She was finding the process difficult and painful. She had spoken to dozens of women and had found similarities with her own situation in each, but in each there were also differences, whether in the mode of 'punishment' or the degree of sophistication with which it was inflicted. Quite often, the most damaged and insecure women were those from whom affection was withdrawn and whose experience of paternal disapproval was a piercingly cold contempt. Chris read over the transcript of a conversation with one woman who had been raped by her father nightly from the age of ten until she fell pregnant at fifteen: *I was never afraid that he would hit me. I can't remember him ever touching me in anger, even when I was little. What I was so scared of was the thought that he wouldn't love me anymore, because if I refused him his 'little treat', as he called it, he would look at me with real burning hatred. There would be these silences across the breakfast table, and I would try to eat, although it nearly choked me, because Mum wasn't ever to know, she mustn't suspect anything. If he caught my eye, he would look right through me and I felt that he could see all the badness in me, all the wickedness of a little girl who was disobedient and would go to Hell. I was in terror because he told me that if I died, God would examine my soul and find a great black chunk like coal in the centre and he would throw me away into the eternal fire because I was a hateful little girl who didn't like to make her daddy happy.*

Chris had decided early in the preparatory work on the book that she would let the women tell their own stories in their own words, keeping her own commentary as unobtrusive as possible, collating and organizing their contributions into themes so that the book retained coherence, but allowing the women to answer, by describing their own experiences, the questions that so many of them had been asked: 'Why didn't you tell anyone?' 'How could you let him do that to you?' 'Don't you have any self-respect?' 'Why didn't you leave him?' 'Why did you go back to him?' 'Do you *like* it, or what?' These questions were to form the headings for the subsequent chapters.

She knew that eventually she would have to think dispassionately about her own part in the 'Daddy's Little Girl' chapter, but for now it was enough to get by, to hold together in a situation which was troubling at best. She felt the same paradoxical and ultimately incomprehensible need for approval as these other women.

The alarm on her watch beeped insistently and Chris turned it off with a muttered curse. She had several morning appointments she could not cancel. She sighed and, after jotting down a few notes in the margin of the transcript, threw down her pen and went through to the hallway to pick up her shoulder bag and car keys.

Nicky looked her up and down as she stepped into the office.

'Last time I saw a gob like that, Liverpool had lost two-nil in the derby,' Nicky said.

It took a few seconds to sink in.

'What? Oh, sorry, Nicky. I'm not sleeping too well.'

'Or eating neither, by the look of you. Get your coat on, we're going to the Everyman.'

Chris glanced at her watch. 'I don't think I have time—'

'Make it,' Nicky ordered. 'Not eating, not sleeping — talk about physician heal thyself!'

The Everyman theatre had a basement bar and restaurant, popular with students and the artistic community of Liverpool. Chris wasn't sure a subterranean setting was such a good idea in the unrelenting heat of the continuing drought, but she went along mainly because she didn't have the energy to argue.

It was crowded with noisy lunchtime business, hushed fleetingly by their entrance — or rather by Nicky's entrance. Today she was wearing a puce blouse unbuttoned to her cleavage and tied in a knot at her midriff. Her black Lycra skirt and high heels showed off her legs to excellent advantage. One man gave a low, appreciative whistle, frozen to a dry exhalation by Nicky's frosty stare. Nicky talked mostly about Chris's radio show, but Chris wasn't really paying attention, and Nicky switched to her plans for the summer holiday — which she was due to take in the next two weeks. They had found places at one of the long tables and were hemmed in on either side. Chris felt oppressed by the din, the press of bodies all around them, and the smell of beer and food. She picked at her meal and pushed it to one side. After a time, she sighed and checked her watch. 'Better go. See if Alan has turned anything up.'

'Alan?' said Nicky.

Chris blinked, aware suddenly that Nicky had been talking for the last twenty minutes, and she had been rudely inattentive. She shook herself, and it felt as though she were coming out of a dream. 'Alan?' she repeated. 'Oh, sorry — DCI Jameson.'

'Oh . . .' Nicky's eyebrows arched.

'*What?*' Chris demanded.

Nicky's face was a studied mask of unconcern. 'Nothing. Just, "Alan", you know . . .' Before Chris could answer, she abruptly changed the subject. 'I got a call just before you finished your last appointment. About that bloke you thought was following you.'

Chris concentrated for a moment. 'Dixon?'

'That's him. One of the flat agencies has got him on their books. Nice flat an' all. Proper contract. Five hundred down against damage and three months' rent in advance.'

Chris knew that Nicky had meant this to be a distraction, but something Wayne had said on Monday evening was trying to surface in her mind. She had telephoned him to apologize after Jameson had released her.

'What?'

'I went to see Wayne on Monday after work,' Chris said.

'Wayne at the council records office? Has he forgiven you for nearly dobbing him in to the police, yet?'

'He was impressed by my mendacity.'

'Men—what?'

Chris smirked. 'Apparently, Mr Jameson believed my story about not knowing Wayne, and was convinced that my visit to the archives on Monday was my first.'

'And I thought *I* was gullible,' Nicky said with a sneer. 'But what's that got to do with Jake Dixon?'

'The bloke who was impersonating Sergeant Tully was tall, quite good looking,' Chris said. 'He had fair hair, cut short. Looked like he could handle himself. And he'd been more than once — only last time, Wayne thinks he showed a council employee ID card.'

'Okaaay . . .'

'Remind me,' Chris went on. 'What was the description we gave to accommodation the agencies for Jake Dixon?'

'Tall, fair, green eyes, spiky haircut,' Nicky said, her eyes popping. 'So, Jake Dixon and the fake Sergeant Tully could be one and the same. But I'd have thought he was no use to you now Phil's home an' that.'

Chris mused. Jake Dixon . . . Moved into the hostel a couple of weeks after Phil's release from prison. Left shortly after Phil had been allocated a flat in warden-controlled premises. Moved out in a hurry when Chris came asking after him. Turned up a week later at the council offices, flashing a fake ID, raking through the files that had been interfered

217

with — files which seemed to be linked in some way with the murders. A clear picture of the corpse on the mortuary slab and the unmistakable whiff of decay assailed her.

'Are you all right?' Nicky asked.

'I was just thinking about Dixon's talent for falsifying documents,' Chris said.

* * *

A row was just coming to the boil as she arrived at the house. It was a pleasant Victorian villa, recently refurbished and gleaming in the afternoon sunshine. Sounds of the argument bubbled over into the street through the open front window. A woman was screaming something and a man's voice, almost sobbing, could be heard pleading with her.

The bells on the front door were neatly labelled, each with its own little printed card, backlit by a miniature bulb. Dixon's bell was inaudible over the screaming and shouting, but the front door stood ajar, so Chris walked up the first flight of stairs and knocked at his flat door. Nicky was right about the quality of the accommodation: the hallway was clean, covered in good quality floor tiles, with not a crack or curl along its length; the lights flicked on automatically as she walked up the stairs, some kind of movement-sensitive device. There was no letter box to rattle — each of the three flats had its own letter box at the side of the entrance downstairs — just a peephole and two locks, one mortise, one Yale. A fire door, which Chris had no doubt conformed to the HSE guidelines.

She knocked again, sensed or imagined a presence listening behind the door. At that moment, the row spilt out into the hallway and the woman ran up the stairs, screaming back at her distraught partner. She afforded Chris no more than a cursory glance before hammering on the door of Dixon's flat.

'He doesn't seem to be answering,' Chris remarked.

The woman ignored her and began beating at the door with the flat of her hands, kicking it with stilettoed feet and leaving small pockmarks in the glossy white paint. 'Open the bloody door!' she yelled.

Chris leaned against the stair rail, arms folded, and watched in startled admiration. The woman could be no more than twenty-five. Slim, elegant, she would have said, but for the steady stream of invective she hurled at Dixon through the door.

It was barely two thirty in the afternoon, but she was dressed for the evening: a strapless dress of peach shot-silk threatened to unharness her breasts as she flung herself at the door with increasing rage.

Her face could not be called pretty, even if it weren't so contorted in her fury, but there was a fierce handsomeness in the high cheekbones and aquiline nose. Her hair was swept back from her face, though a few chestnut-brown strands quivered over her forehead.

She appeared to sense Chris's scrutiny and stopped rattling the door in its frame long enough to ask, 'What the fuck d'you think you're looking at?'

Chris raised her hands to show she meant no harm. The woman muttered a curse and once again resorted to venting her fury on the door. 'Open this *friggin'* door, Dixon!' she yelled, then, lowering her voice to a loud whisper, 'Or I'll tell him what you get up to when he's on nights.'

A brief jingle of a door chain and the door opened. Chris could not see his face, but the smirk was positively audible. 'What *we* get up to, you mean?' It wasn't a local accent; Chris was unable to place it. Northern, she was fairly certain, but she suspected that Mr Dixon had taken as many pains to disguise his origins as he had to falsify his credentials. The woman grunted something Chris did not quite catch, and Dixon said with urbane insouciance, 'I take it you'd like to use my phone.' The woman pushed past him into the flat and he laughed, a low, throaty chuckle.

Chris took a deep breath and stepped up to the door, stopping it with her hand as he made to shut it.

'Aren't I the popular one?' he said, as if noticing her for the first time. His look of approbation made her distinctly uncomfortable. Dixon's mouth curved into a half smile and he opened the door wide. She introduced herself and offered her hand. After a moment's consideration he took it, holding it a moment too long and caressing the soft tissue between her forefinger and thumb.

'If I'd known you were so attractive, Dr Radcliffe, I wouldn't have left the hostel so precipitately.'

The woman, who had been giving instructions to someone at the other end of the line, stopped and asked sharply, '*Doctor?* Sick, are you?'

Dixon smiled. 'Don't worry, Vicky. I haven't given you the clap. She's not *that* kind of doctor.'

Vicky turned suspicious eyes on Chris, who returned a solemn stare and tapped her temple. Vicky's eyebrows lifted just perceptibly, and her eyes darted from Chris to Dixon and back to Chris, then she shrugged, losing interest. 'Five minutes,' she said into the telephone receiver. 'I'll be waiting on the corner.' She tossed the phone, a portable, onto the sofa.

And then she was gone, leaving a void, a silence which cried out to be broken. Seconds later they heard her tittupping out of the front door, the anguished cries of her lover following after her.

'Done his back,' said Dixon, evidently amused. 'A woman with Vicky's libido can't tolerate abstinence, and I can't do anything to ease her suffering while he's here in the house. I may be a cuckolder, but I'm not a sadist.'

Consideration or cowardice? Chris wondered, allowing her gaze to wander about the room as he continued, explaining to her in salacious detail how Vicky's lover had injured his back. It was a well-proportioned flat: the sitting room was large, with a bay window which let in afternoon sunshine and blackbird song along with the distant hum of traffic from the ring road a couple of hundred yards away. A few boxes remained unpacked from Dixon's recent move, but the place was tidy, and the walls were papered with something above the standard-issue woodchip and cheap emulsion which most landlords seemed to buy in job lots.

'Nice, isn't it?' he said, sweeping an arm in a wide semicircle, indicating doors off the sitting room. 'Such luxuries as patterned paper and central heating are relatively rare where an absentee landlord owns the property. Apart from this rather splendid entertaining room, it has a kitchen-diner, two bedrooms, one with walk-in wardrobe, bathroom and shower room.'

'You sound like an estate agent,' Chris said.

'Perhaps that's because I used to be one.' He smiled a secretive, unfathomable smile. 'You looking for somewhere to stay?'

Chris ignored the rather obvious innuendo. 'It *is* nice,' she agreed. 'Which makes me wonder why you found it necessary to stay in a hostel for homeless men?'

He stroked a line from the side of his nose to the corner of his mouth. 'Anyone can be down on his luck.' Chris thought she saw a muted glint of speculation in his eye. 'I blame the Tories.'

'Do you?' Chris asked.

'Don't you?'

'If you're trying to mine my deepest feelings, Mr Dixon, you might show me the courtesy of being a little more subtle.'

'You can sit down if you like,' he said, indicating a sofa, its cream and scarlet stripes still gleaming and stiff with newness. 'Or if you find me too intimidating, do feel free to take one of the armchairs.'

Chris looked from the armchair to Dixon. She sat down on the sofa. Dixon sat next to her. *First point to Dixon,* she thought. *He double bluffed you, Flip. You're letting the little shit manipulate you.*

He half turned to her and she caught his look of triumph. His eyes, an arresting shade of green, gleamed with something on the sinister edge of laughter.

He fished behind him and drew out the telephone, tutting a little as he turned it off and placed it carefully on the pristine glass of the coffee table. 'You can't be here about Phil. You turned him in on Sunday, didn't you?'

Chris smiled. 'Obviously leading questions and crass insults. You really do disappoint me, Mr Dixon. I expected a greater degree of sophistication.'

'*Jake*, please!' he insisted. 'And you may be right. No doubt you did it for his own good.' He allowed the silence to assert its significance.

This is something he does often, Chris thought. This cat-and-mouse game, this intrigue, the careful nuances of speech, the pauses to allow the victim to weave the web which would eventually ensnare them. *How did he use this rather distasteful skill?* She gave herself time to take in the essential features of the room and the word *lucratively* came to mind. Mr Dixon had expensive tastes in hi-fi and computer hardware. A laptop lay open on the coffee table. The table was entirely innocent of fingerprints or coffee stains. Her glance flicked back to the laptop. A screensaver worked mindlessly on, a barrage of flying windows, streaming outwards from some point of infinity.

'You're not rising to the bait, Chris. I cast my lines into the conversational current—'

His voice cut across her thoughts and she replied without thinking, 'But I don't have to bite.'

'A pity. You have such pretty teeth.' His eyes played over her face.

Chris wondered at a sudden pang of anxiety and realized that he had moved closer to her. Offensively close. Attack being the best form of defence, she asked, 'Why did you run away from me, Jake?'

Their eyes locked. Ocean blue into forest green. There was an intensity in the man which manifested itself as a veiled threat — a tense, urgent energy which seemed to warn of imminent danger. It occurred to Chris that they might be the only people in the house besides the crippled lover in the ground floor flat, and he was hardly likely to rush to her rescue.

He held her gaze for some seconds longer and then his expression softened. A wicked grin spread slowly across his face, kindling briefly in his eyes. 'Do you think I've got something to hide, Chris?'

'Have you, Jake?'

'Have I!' The tone was as ambiguous as the words. 'Isn't it your job to find out?'

And is it yours, too? Chris wondered. 'You like to play games, don't you?' she said.

'What sort of games do you like to play, Chris?' The intimidation, she sensed, was a cover for his own uneasiness: since she hadn't responded to his sledgehammer brand of manipulation, he was trying to probe another weakness. Well, she wasn't going to allow herself to be so easily intimidated.

'Oh, I don't know . . . Let's try impersonating a police officer, for instance.'

'Are you into uniforms, Dr Radcliffe?' he asked, but there was a wariness in his eyes. He seemed to become aware of her evaluation of the unease behind his affected unconcern and he stood, stretched and ambled over to a bookshelf. 'Drink?' he asked. She decided on a Glenfiddich and agreed to ice, although she didn't want it because she guessed that he would have to go through to the kitchen for it. While he was out of the room, she took the opportunity to scan the bookshelves. Aside from the three types of malt whisky, the gin, the vodka and the bottle of Malibu (Vicky, she supposed, must have a sweet tooth), there was a selection of hardback books. No fiction, except for a few science-fiction titles, but rows and rows of fat volumes on MS-DOS and Windows, computer manuals and books on programming languages with exotic names like Java and C++. She returned her attention to the laptop on the table in front of her. He came from the kitchen with a tumbler half full of ice and already sweating with condensation. Chris waited for him to pick up the whisky bottle and, while he was occupied with pouring the drinks, she jogged the mouse, and the screensaver was replaced by text. A database. Names, dates of birth, addresses, phone numbers and credit ratings.

He turned away from the drinks tray, perhaps alerted by her silence, and Chris looked up at him, forcing herself to ignore the screen, but Dixon splashed whisky into two glasses and hurried back to Chris.

A little of the whisky had spilt on his hand and he licked it off, standing over her, regarding her pensively.

What is he so scared of? Chris wondered. As he handed her one glass and took a gulp from his own, she allowed herself a quick glance again at the screen. The screensaver had not yet kicked in to hide the text. Then Dixon was sitting next to her, close enough for her to feel the muscles of his thigh against her own. Chris resisted an urge to shuffle away from him and made herself look at him rather than the computer, regulating her breathing.

'So, tell me what you see, Doc.' He plonked his hand, palm up in her lap. She lifted it, feeling the slight moistness, which was not entirely due to the spilt whisky, pleased to feel him tense a little. *Called your bluff, didn't I?* she thought, letting go of his hand, watching it curl in on itself as he placed it rather awkwardly on his knee.

'Conman,' she said aloud. 'Forger.' He was smiling at her. She looked back at the manuals on the shelf. The word *hacker* came into her head. 'Businessman,' she added.

He laughed loudly and explosively. 'You make *that* sound like more of a crime than the other two.'

'It depends on the business,' she said, with a tight smile. 'I think you find things out about people.'

'Rather like you.'

'Not a bit like me.'

'Are you saying you don't get paid for what you do?' He lifted his eyebrows ironically.

'I don't harm people with what I know.' Dixon's gaze fixed on the laptop, then, suspicious, he swivelled the machine so that he could see the screen. Flying windows batted out at him unceasingly.

Chris pushed a lock of her hair over the scar on her eyebrow. Dixon seemed recognize it as a nervous gesture and reached to comb the hair from her forehead, but Chris moved away sharply and he stopped, letting his hand drop.

'Does it help or hinder,' he asked, 'having your background?' A trickle of fear ran down Chris's spine.

'What do you mean, my background?' *You should have ignored that, Chris*, she told herself.

'It must bring a deeper understanding, but don't they say emotional detachment is essential in your line of business?'

'What do you mean, *my background*?' Chris repeated, her voice rising. *He's baiting you. Leave it alone.*

'It's a matter of public record,' he said. 'All laid out in your book. The wife beating, the drunkenness, the verbal humiliations, the little physical cruelties which escalated as he sank deeper into alcoholism after your mother's death.' He paused, looking her full in the face. 'The fight that put you both in hospital.'

Chris stood abruptly, her heart racing. 'I'm sorry to have wasted your time, Mr Dixon.'

'Whoa!' he exclaimed, catching her by the arm as she stood. He fondled the inside of her wrist. 'Surely you're not leaving so soon.'

'I'm afraid so,' Chris said, deliberately relaxing, although her heart was still pounding. She even moved closer to him when her instinct was to pull away. 'I have an appointment.'

'Postpone it.' With his free hand he picked up the telephone and handed it to her.

Chris punched the keypad and spoke quietly. 'This is Dr Radcliffe.' She carefully modulated her voice. 'Could you put me through to Chief Inspector Jameson?'

Dixon released her hand as if burned. Jameson hadn't been available when she left the office, so she had left a message with the police switchboard. He may or may not know where she was. Chris continued the telephone call, cursing the fact that in reality she hadn't had the presence of mind to telephone the police, explaining that she had been delayed talking to Mr Dixon, but that she was on her way to the station right now. Nicky, at the other end of the line, was growing more and more agitated, asking whether she was all right, wondering should she send the police.

'No, there's no need to trouble yourself,' Chris heard herself say airily. 'I should be there within half an hour.'

20

'Dr Radcliffe has just been to see a Jake Dixon,' Jameson told Foster. 'It seems he made a point of getting to know Philip Greer at the hostel where he lived before being allocated a warden-controlled flat.'

Chris had telephoned Jameson from her office. She sounded shaken, convinced that Dixon had seen her personal file. She had relayed the entire conversation to Jameson, holding nothing back.

'He knew things,' she had begun haltingly. 'He said he'd read them in my book, but he couldn't have.' Jameson thought he heard a shuddering breath. 'When my father attacked me — the time I was taken into care — I . . .' Her voice was thick with emotion. Jameson heard a second voice, possibly her secretary. Chris said, 'I'm OK,' as if in answer, then she continued. 'During the attack I stabbed my father. I don't remember much about it, but I'd been sleeping with a knife under my pillow for months before it happened. He was wounded in the shoulder.' She stopped and Jameson was sure she was holding her breath.

'I know,' he said quietly.

An exhalation. 'Of course . . . It was in the reports.' She paused. 'Mr Jameson, I've never told anyone about it. Not then, nor since. Not even my foster mother, Maria, although social services must have told her. But Dixon *knew*. Which means he must have seen my file.' She hesitated. 'I think maybe he planted my father's ID on the body of that poor man to scare me off. Why would he do that?'

'So . . . ?' Foster broke in on Jameson's thoughts.

'Dr Radcliffe seems to think that Dixon is the man who impersonated Sergeant Tully at the records office. She also thinks he may have gained access to our computer records.' For the moment he kept her speculation about faking the ID of the body to himself.

'What makes her think that, then?'

Jameson decided to start from the beginning. 'Philip Greer has a talent for remembering facts, procedures, numbers, that sort of thing. He has an encyclopaedic knowledge of the records and filing procedures of Calderbank borough council.'

'And?'

'Dixon has a lot of high-tech computer equipment in his flat — she got a glimpse of something he was working on — names, salaries, credit ratings, the sort of information finance companies might be interested in.'

Foster seemed sceptical. 'A load of social workers and office clerks on council pay rates?'

'Targeted mailshots,' Jameson said. 'Haven't you ever wondered why the mail-order catalogues seem to come in spurts?'

'Just after you've bought something, yeah. They sell your name, don't they?' said Foster.

'And some go further than that: if they know your family status, they can send carefully selected information on toys, family holidays, clothing. If they know your financial situation as well, they can offer loans, saving schemes, credit cards and so on. It's big business.'

'If it's all on computer he wouldn't need Greer then, would he? All he'd need would be a computer and an internet connection.'

'Except the council haven't put all their paper records onto a computer database as yet — as we know to our cost. When Dixon realized he couldn't access the borough files by computer, he looked for other ways in.'

'Yeah, but how come he knew to try out the hostel? How could he know Greer'd give him the back alley into the council records?'

Jameson shrugged. 'His business is information. He infiltrates wherever he can, gathers what he can and makes use of it. What better way than to befriend those who are hooked into the system, who know its back alleys and rat runs — and which employees are easy to cajole or bully and which not? I doubt if Greer or anyone like him would have been part of his wildest imaginings. He did a bit of prospecting and struck the mother lode in Philip Greer.'

Foster gave him a measured look. 'What, and Radcliffe thinks he was poking about in the borough records office, getting all this stuff on council employees when the abductions happened, started collecting info on Dorothy and Ann and sold what he found to the papers?'

'To Ralph Milton of the "Death Warrant" headline, to be specific.' Jameson looked out of the window for a moment and found himself staring into the maniacal yellow eye of a seagull, drifting lightly on a thermal updraught.

'So how did he get that stuff on Jim Bradbury?' Foster demanded. 'That's not likely to be a matter of council record, is it?'

'Pull Milton. See if you can shake something out of him. A hint that he fits the description of a man we want to question regarding the impersonation of a police officer might loosen him up a bit.'

Foster's eyes gleamed at the prospect.

He left a few moments later, and Jameson tried to put Chris Radcliffe out of his mind so that he could consider how they were going to track down the arsonist, Darren Lewis. He had told the psychologist that the tampered sections of the files all related to six months in 1987, and that the section on her own youth was intact. He agreed with Chris that Jake Dixon must have read her file to know as much as he did about her, and may even have set up the dead vagrant as a threat, but she would be safe from him as soon as they got enough from Milton to arrest Dixon.

Lewis made him more nervous because he was on the loose and, so far, untraceable. He had solid alibis for the nights of the disappearances, but that meant very little, given the character of his alibis. Added to which, he had no alibi for the morning of Jim's murder — which was highly significant. Jameson reached for the phone and requested a roundup of Lewis's friends who had provided alibis. Maybe they could trip one of them into admitting that he was covering for Lewis. Failing that, they might know the arsonist's present whereabouts. There wasn't much hope, but it was better than sitting around waiting for something to happen.

21

The room was silent but for the faint whirr of the tape recorder and the subliminal hum of the air conditioning. Dixon was sitting with his left foot resting on his right thigh, one arm hooked over the back of his chair and the other quite relaxed on the black top of the interview room table.

He eyed Jameson contemptuously, his gaze moving from the chief inspector's face to his crumpled clothing. Finally, he yawned, raising a languid hand to his mouth. 'Sorry, Mr Jameson, but this really is tedious — we must've been over it three times already.'

Dixon had been in custody for two hours. Milton had confirmed that he had paid Dixon for information but had stipulated that he was not aware that the gathering of the information had involved any illegal activity. Dixon had refused to be interviewed without a solicitor present and had been very specific in his choice.

David Alingford, of Alingford Betts LLP, was a man of vast experience amassed during long years of representing the seedier class of businessman. A man of dubious morality and monstrous ego, he was a narcissist so pleased with himself that a constant smirk played about his lips. After twenty years of monetary quest, Alingford was able to afford the luxury of choosing whom he represented, but his reputation was such that he drew an unsavoury, sleazier class of client. If he had been an honest man, which he was not, he would have had to admit that despite his renown (or because of his notoriety, depending on your viewpoint) he wasn't spoiled for choice. The press connection had initially attracted him to the case, and Dixon had had the wit to inform him of it early in their telephone conversation, but it was the man himself who sustained his interest. He *liked* Dixon. Here was a client who knew how to shift for himself, a man with a greater degree of subtlety than the criminals Alingford was used to. There was a coolness, a refinement in Mr Dixon's interactions with the police which Alingford could not but appreciate.

'Once more, Mr Dixon,' Jameson said, 'for the sake of accuracy.'

Alingford made a small explosive sound with his lips. 'My client has already explained to you why he was at the records office. He is a researcher. He admits that he was hoping to gather certain items of information for the press, but since he did not gain access to the records—'

'Your client was impersonating a police officer, Mr Alingford,' Jameson interrupted. 'And the records office clerk is fairly certain that he visited his office on several other occasions.'

'*Fairly* certain!' Alingford laughed gaily, 'And they say policemen have no sense of humour. You should try putting that before the magistrates, Mr Jameson — they don't get many laughs in their line of work.' His voice boomed a little in the confines of the small room.

Jameson seemed disinclined to humour. 'Our witness is willing to swear before a magistrate or a Crown Court, whatever it takes, that your client gained illegal access to sensitive and restricted files. And we have in our possession not one, Mr Alingford, but *two* falsified identity cards, one identifying Mr Dixon as a local authority worker, the other as a CID officer.'

Alingford tensed. Dixon had not mentioned this. He resisted the temptation to steal a glance at his client and

232

instead stared at the man sitting opposite. An examination of Jameson's features revealed no hint of dissimulation. Alingford let his eyes travel over the chief inspector's clothing; he really had let himself go since his wife left him. Alingford despised slovenliness of dress more than he had ever abhorred moral weakness, and Jameson had apparently slipped into the quagmire, judging by his badly pressed shirt and scuffed shoes. His tie was slightly askew and would not have borne close inspection, his hair looked as though it hadn't had a decent cut in months.

'That is a serious allegation, Chief Inspector,' he said, having allowed himself time to overcome an undignified irritation with his client.

Dixon seemed untroubled. 'I worked for the local authority briefly,' he said. 'I forgot to return my ID card when I left. The police identification is a plant,' he added dismissively.

Alingford brought a finger to his mouth to cover a smile. The man was unshakeable! He gauged Jameson's reaction and thought he could discern a slight deflation of his initial authoritative assurance. He permitted himself a glance at his client. 'I'm sure we can settle this amicably, Mr Jameson,' he said.

'So am I.' Jameson produced a document from his inside pocket, which he smoothed out on the table before Dixon. 'This is a warrant, Mr Dixon. It permits a search of your flat. We will be looking for confidential files, documents and other materials — electronic or hard copy. Isn't that what you call it? Hard copy? You see, we hope to glean some *hard facts* about exactly what you've been up to.'

Alingford glanced quickly at the ceiling but chose to reserve comment on the awfulness of the pun.

'We know you've gained illegal access to council records,' he went on. 'We know you've been feeding information to the press about Sunnyside Children's Home and about the two murdered women, as well as Warrant Sergeant Jim Bradbury. We're just not sure how you've gained access to that confidential information. We shall, of course,' he added, raising his voice over Alingford's protestations, 'invite you, Mr Alingford, to observe the search, to witness that it is conducted according to proper procedure.'

Dixon protested, but Jameson waved him down, looking pleased to have that at last ruffled his smooth exterior. 'I should warn you that we are empowered to seize and retain anything which may be relevant to our enquiries.'

'Not my computer!'

'Unless you agree to cooperate and provide us with all relevant information as a printout.'

Alingford half turned to his client. Dixon was pale, barely in control, and with a warning look, Alingford said, 'It's best, if I—'

But Jameson interrupted: 'You see, Mr Milton — the journalist with all the insights — has had an attack of guilt. And he's named you, Mr Dixon, as his source.'

Dixon half rose, and Alingford put a restraining hand on his arm. This was what his clients paid him for: to keep his composure when they lost theirs. 'I should like to speak to my client in private,' he said.

* * *

'If I am to help you, Mr Dixon, you have to be honest with me.'

Amusement flickered over Dixon's face. '*You're* advising *me* to be honest?'

'Dear me, Mr Dixon, you'll have to do better than that if you mean to insult me,' Alingford said, unconsciously echoing the sentiments Chris had voiced earlier in the day. He drew up a chair and placed it at right angles to his client's. They had remained in the interview room, since nowhere else was available. 'I know my reputation.' He raised his eyebrows. 'And so do you — or you would not have appointed me to act on your behalf.'

He sat, complacent, while Dixon studied his tidy figure. Alingford had chosen a pale grey suit and pink bow tie that morning. His well-shod feet were planted neatly together under the table and his hands rested on his knees. He knew that Dixon appraised him as a prim picture of self-possession and self-righteousness, and he saw no reason to apologise for that. He waited for his client to finish his perusal, meeting his gaze without challenge, but with absolute self-assurance.

'All right,' said Dixon, relenting. 'I know your reputation, but why do you need to know more than I already told you?'

'Because,' said Alingford, his manicured fingers digging into the good, summer-weight wool of his trousers, 'I don't like surprises.' He sat back suddenly, flapping his arms listlessly in front of his face and spluttering with counterfeit laughter. 'It's not as if I'm a barrister or a judge.' He leaned forward and tapped Dixon's hand, no more than the light pressure of the pad of one fingertip, a foppish gesture of admonishment. 'I'm here as your representative. But I cannot represent what I do not know, and I can only avoid pitfalls if I have the information necessary to anticipate them.'

There was a silence. Alingford leaned forward in his chair, staring hard at his client. At last Dixon nodded. 'I gather information.'

'Ye-es.' Dixon had already told him that much.

'The easiest — the cleanest — way is via computer records. All you need is a password sniffer, a little skill on the internet and a lot of patience. When you find your trapdoor, you're in and out. Cybercommandos.' He smiled to himself.

'Sorry?' Alingford's bland expression masked an impatience which he could not quite conceal in the querulousness of his tone.

Dixon continued, ignoring the question, apparently unaware of his solicitor's impatience. 'Sometimes direct contact is needed — old filing systems don't respond to computer infiltration. Or if the contractor wants personal information. I can do that, too.'

'Like the background on the murder victims? Do you see yourself as a sort of modern-day private detective?' Alingford asked, his tone gently mocking.

Dixon established and held eye contact and Alingford became so uncomfortable that he almost apologised.

'I don't spy on husbands for jealous wives,' Dixon said. 'I acquire information for financial institutions, employers, anyone who can pay my commission.'

'Financial institutions.' Alingford paused reflectively. 'Banks and loan companies? That sort of financial institution?'

'Occasionally banks, but they mostly like to keep their hands clean.'

Alingford eyed his client beadily. 'And who, precisely, in this instance, does not mind a little dirt beneath the fingernails?'

A slow smile spread over Dixon's face.

'If you are not honest with me, Mr Dixon, I cannot — *cannot* — help you.' He waited while Dixon composed his reply.

'In theory,' Dixon began, 'credit card numbers are good business. With bank account and branch number, it's amazing what you could access via the internet, if you were so minded.'

'But surely you — I beg your pardon,' Alingford corrected himself, 'surely *one* could only use credit card numbers to buy goods.'

'*I* don't use them at all,' said Dixon, amused. 'The security's too lax for my liking. Some have been known to buy large quantities of goods — equipment, toys, whatever — for resale, and then bunk out after a day or so having spent a few thousand pounds. Frankly, that's for thugs who can't find a more elegant way in.'

Alingford nodded appreciatively.

'More useful are the new issues,' Dixon said.

'What issues are these?' Alingford repeated.

Dixon smiled. 'Not "issues" in that sense — I'm talking about newly issued or replacement cards — that sort of thing.'

'And this information is picked up from the accounts departments of large employees?'

'Indirectly. Once you've got bank account names and numbers it's just a case of hacking into the banks concerned. Select someone who's due for a new card: Visa, Connect, Switch, whatever. Zip into their account details and change the mailing address. A rented flat is often given as the drop, used for a few weeks and then they're out. And they can use the cards for withdrawing cash, because the PIN is mailed to the same address.'

'But of course, Calderbank borough council's records weren't all accessible online.' This doggedness of approach was Alingford's way of extracting as much detail as possible. There wouldn't be time for explanations when Jameson resumed the interview if he had misunderstood or misread Dixon's coded messages.

'Which is where *people* can be helpful,' Dixon said. 'They're not as quick as machines and need more in the way of cajoling, but you can generally tunnel your way in if you have the patience and the right password.'

Alingford raised an eyebrow in question.

'Some respond to flattery, some like to be fussed over — so many feel sorely misunderstood, thwarted, undervalued.'

'So — hypothetically, of course — you might identify an individual and speak to them directly?'

A nod.

'Someone like Ann Lee or Dorothy Hardy?'

Dixon made no attempt to disguise his contempt, and Alingford immediately called to mind a pastel-coloured image of Dorothy he had seen in the newspapers. Shy and rather frumpy looking.

'I imagine a woman like Dorothy might be *very* obliging, once a fellow had found her emotional G-spot,' Alingford remarked.

'Don't let the sensible shoes and comfy cardy fool you,' Dixon said. 'A woman like that can be a cauldron of repressed but passionate ambition.'

Alingford's eyebrows twitched; he had imagined passion of a more earthy quality.

'So a "cybercommando" like yourself might extract dates, facts, names, locations — details of the staff and inmates.'

'They might,' Dixon said, with a wry twist of his lips.

Alingford had read Milton's in-depth account of the goings-on at Sunnyside Children's Home in the *Herald*. He'd been supplied with all the names dates and facts any journalist could ever wish for in an investigation. He knew who was sacked, the administrators who narrowly escaped dismissal, the names of children moved into foster care. Dorothy — Dot, as he had come to think of her — working mother, wife, homemaker. Underappreciated, and perhaps depressed, he could imagine that she would be dazzled by his client's flattery — his urbane sophistication. Alingford's ability to imagine such scenarios had served him well in his practice: being able to reconstruct scenarios without requiring a detailed admission of guilt from his clients was one of his great strengths. Now, obliging as ever, Dot was no more than that — a punctuation, a full stop. She had served her purpose, and was now conveniently out of the way. Milton, however, might prove to be a more recalcitrant problem.

'Knowledge is power . . . ' Alingford murmured.

'Knowledge,' Dixon corrected, 'is a saleable commodity. *Money* is power. What people need to know they're willing to pay for. Sometimes handsomely.'

'So, your forays into the borough records office were fact-finding missions?' Alingford said with a disingenuous smile.

'Foray,' Dixon corrected him. 'My for*ay*. I only tried it the once, and I didn't gain access.'

'Quite so,' said Alingford. 'Quite so. Now, how do you propose we convince Chief Inspector Jameson of that, given the fake identification cards you had on your person at the time of your arrest?'

22

Chris Radcliffe stood under the shower, tepid water needling her skin, unwilling to step out because the stifling heat would hit her as soon as she started to dry. With Dixon in custody she felt safer. Perhaps Jameson was right — perhaps he was just a fraudster and hacker, selling information — but he had frightened her badly. Her head was pounding in slow, viscous waves and she remembered that she had not eaten anything since breakfast, and had had nothing to drink but two glasses of whisky. Sighing, she turned off the shower and went downstairs.

The kitchen tiles were cool underfoot, but the towelling robe she had put on already felt too hot, and Chris returned to her bedroom carrying a jingling glass of iced lemonade. The files on her list of suspects were stacked in an unstable pile on her dressing table. An unsettling thought occurred to her: if Jameson *was* right about Dixon, then the killer must still be out there. Chris shed her robe and began dressing, fastening her blouse with one hand, while rummaging through the stack with the other.

Jameson had traced John Emerson — one of the children affected in the scandal. He had moved to Leeds and was working as a driver for a small coach firm, but he had alibis for the nights of both Dorothy's and Ann's disappearances. She picked up the next folder: Laura Smith, that tiny scrap of a girl battling to save her mother from the cancer that devoured her until all that was left were pain and delirium. Fighting everyone who tried to help because they had allowed her mother to die. She had certainly wanted revenge back then. But thinking of her chaotic, happy houseful of children and friends, Chris could not imagine her carrying that grudge into adult life. Laura may have refused help, but she had found her own way in life. And she'd seemed genuinely concerned for Dorothy's children.

George Maddox. George had enough rage in him to kill, but what had he to gain from these deaths? What could they have known that could jeopardize him? She shook her head: she didn't know Dorothy or Ann well enough to speculate. Darren Lewis. His mother had said she was glad to be rid of him and wouldn't think twice about shopping him to the police if he dared show his face at their house again. Unfortunately, he was smarter than that. Was it coincidence that Lewis had vanished the day that Jim Bradbury's body had been found? If she'd only had a chance to speak to him.

She wandered through to the dining room. Her research files, card boxes, folders, notes and pens were littered across the dining table. Simon, who had worked until midnight the previous night, had tagged a number of folders with post-it slips — reminders to telephone contacts or follow up leads. She picked up a document wallet and began leafing through the notes, some written in Simon's clear, neat hand and some in her near-illegible scrawl. Chris felt suddenly guilty that she hadn't talked to Simon about his mother's rejection of him. He had two convictions for arson — and for this, it seemed, his mother had disowned him entirely. Since his release from prison at the age of seventeen Simon had fended for himself, living in bedsits that were far removed from the luxury of Jake Dixon's apartment. If Dixon had, as she believed, been stealing sensitive information on employees and clients of Calderbank borough council, and Dorothy or Ann had found him out, would it be motive enough for murder?

She saw Dorothy smiling, flattered by Dixon's attentions. He would perhaps have taken her out for a meal, complimented her on her clothing, her hair, drawn her out with gentle questions which were calculated to make her feel important, overworked, intelligent. And he would make her laugh — and laughter was the most winning strategy of all.

Had Dorothy told him more than she had meant to about Sunnyside, and then read her own words in Milton's exposé? What would she have done then? Demanded to see him? Then what?

That, Chris told herself firmly, was up to the police to find out. She'd had enough adventure to last her a lifetime — and Nicky had not been pleased with her phone call from Dixon's flat. She would leave the investigation to the police. Philip was safe and Jameson no longer considered her a suspect. She had passed on all she knew to Jameson — except her part in the bloody awful Sunnyside business.

She had discovered recently a need for the chief inspector's good opinion, and she was afraid Sunnyside would diminish her in his eyes. If the murderer's motive was linked to the children's home, wouldn't he have singled out the people who were now on suspension? The people who had established and coordinated the regime of beatings and punishments? Yet those directly responsible were safe, and two relatively obscure administrators were dead.

She returned to her research papers, but a vague, unfocused apprehension prevented her from concentrating. Simon's post-it slips were everywhere. Simon, who had patiently waited for her when she was late, and who worked on into the night when her mind raced and she was unable to switch off, who had listened to her when she had needed to talk about her father. She had failed twice in the eighteen months she had worked for Calderbank borough council. Both failures had affected the lives of children she was paid to protect. If she had heard about the regime of punishments and the misuse of drugs for controlling children at Sunnyside before her suspension, she hoped that she would have had the courage to defy her bosses and go to the press, but four weeks of isolation and the threat of dismissal for unprofessional conduct had made a coward of her. So, she had taken the coward's way out and resigned. Which, in the event, she thought bitterly, turned out very well for her, but not so well for the children at Sunnyside. And very badly for Simon. He had even been sent to Sunnyside, pending psychological assessment. That was after her time, but the regime which perpetrated the abuses was still in operation.

Simon had been subdued during the last week or two, and she had traced the beginnings of his quietness to the work she had asked him to do, typing out her notes on the chapter titled 'Why Didn't You Tell Anyone?'. Chris felt guilt settle like a solid mass in the pit of her stomach. If she knew what it was about the chapter that Simon had found so disturbing, she might be able to help him — maybe a little late — but she hoped he would forgive her that.

So she climbed into the attic and began the search. It took her ten minutes to find Simon's file, carefully logged among the others relating to her tenure at Calderbank borough council. She flipped it open, tilting the page to the dim light of the single naked sixty-watt bulb which hung from the rafters on brown, two-wire twisted flex.

* * *

A brand-new building stood among the solid middle-class 1940s houses in the street. It was half timbered in the Tudor style and the garden had been carefully landscaped for year-round colour, but many of the plants wilted onto the brick-paved driveway, beaten to greying strands by the unrelenting heat, and the buds of the miniature roses were distorted by aphid attack. Chris rang the doorbell, then stepped back to survey the house. All of the windows were shut. Apparently, no one was home. She debated whether to return later but was unwilling to leave. If she had done more for Simon ten years earlier, when the panel of experts had voted to return him to his parents — if she had argued more strongly — perhaps he would not have been sent home, would not have repeated the crime, and would not have gone to prison. Perhaps he would now be pursuing the academic career so suited to his temperament and abilities.

'Can I help you?'

Chris turned. A woman stood on the pavement at the gates to the driveway. A second, younger woman watched from a few yards' distance.

'Mrs Webster?' As Chris stepped towards the woman, she saw her mistake: this woman was much older than Mrs Webster and far too direct, too well fleshed, too confident. Simon's mother had seemed a gentle, respectable woman, but rather scrawny in appearance, and puzzled and distressed by her son's behaviour, there was also a cold glimmer of disgust which had chilled her more than Chris could understand. She recalled that Mrs Webster had looked to her husband before answering any question put to her, as if asking for permission to speak.

The women exchanged glances. Finally, the second woman spoke up. 'She's been gone for some time,' she said. 'How long would you say, Hilda?' The younger woman turned her shiny, round face to her neighbour, deferring to her age and status in matters of detail.

But Hilda was not a founder member of Tennyson Street Homewatch for nothing. 'And you are?' she asked stiffly.

'Chris Radcliffe.' Chris handed her a business card. 'I was hoping to have a chat with Mrs Webster.'

'*Dr* Radcliffe. *Rodney Street*,' the second woman murmured, standing on tiptoe to peer over Hilda's shoulder. Hilda shrugged her off with a gesture curiously reminiscent of a horse twitching its flanks to dislodge troublesome flies. The second woman seemed to crumple slightly, hurt by the dismissal, but she held her peace as Hilda said, 'You won't find her here. She left shortly after the fire.'

'The fire at the school?' Chris asked.

Hilda studied her suspiciously, and several seconds elapsed before the younger woman, apparently unable to contain herself any longer, nodded towards the new house. 'It burned to the ground,' she said. 'Five or six years ago, wasn't it, Hilda?'

'Seven,' said Hilda. 'Let me handle this, Jennifer.'

The younger woman blushed to the roots of her hair and looked as though she would like to bolt for cover, but she remained, shifting from one foot to the other, as if finding the pavement too hot to bear.

Hilda glanced back at the card. 'What's your interest, Dr Radcliffe?'

'Do you know who started the fire?'

'Isn't that obvious?' Hilda asked.

'Simon . . . Do they know why?'

Hilda pursed her lips. 'I don't pry into my neighbours' private affairs,' she said, all virtuous indignation.

Chris reflected that when her father beat and bit and pummelled her, she would not have called kindly intervention 'prying'. And what 'private affair' had driven a teenage boy to set fire to his own home rather than return to it? That was a circumstance well worth prying into, she thought.

'Of course, they rebuilt, but the place wasn't the same for them,' Jennifer said, taking advantage of Hilda's reticence. 'And after Mr Webster died . . .' Here Jennifer trailed off. 'Well, you know how it is. Mrs Webster moved out to Southport.'

Hilda jumped in. 'I think we've said quite enough, Jennifer.'

'How did Mr Webster . . . ?' Chris began, hoping that Jennifer would fill in the blanks.

'Terrible thing. In the garage,' she said, nodding over Chris's shoulder to the house.

Ashamed of herself for exploiting her, but determined to get to the truth, Chris focused her attention on Jennifer, judging that she was unused to being in control of a conversation,

244

and flattered that this stranger — this *doctor* — was asking her opinion. 'How awful,' she murmured.

Jennifer nodded, her eyes huge. 'My John forced the door, but the fumes!'

'Jennifer . . .' Hilda warned.

Jennifer refused to yield to the older woman's protestations. 'He'd only been gone half an hour before he was missed. John did what he could — but it was too late.'

'Really!' Hilda looked as if she would like to take Jennifer by the arm and march her back to her own doorstep, but her bullying did not quite extend to the physical.

'Suicide is a terrible thing,' Chris said, ignoring the older woman. She had to be sure of her facts before she spoke to Mrs Webster.

'Well, with a son like that . . . Never even came to the funeral. Broke her heart, poor thing.'

'I don't suppose you have her address?' Chris asked.

Jennifer had already begun shaking her head when Hilda said, 'If you want to know anything more, I suggest you contact the police, Dr Radcliffe. I'm sure they'll help you if they can.'

Chris drove out to Southport, calling in at the library on her arrival. She borrowed a phone book for the local area and skimmed through the Websters. There were dozens listed, but only a few in the centre of town. She made a list and found a phone box; her fifth call was successful.

'Dr Radcliffe?' The voice sounded distant, enfeebled by illness or worry. 'I don't think I . . .'

'I looked after Simon for a while as an educational psychologist,' Chris explained. 'And before that, I was his English teacher at Wellesthorne School.'

'Oh.' Mrs Webster became flustered, her voice weaker, breathier. 'Oh, I can't! I don't want to talk to you.' She hung up.

Chris took a note of the address and called in at the tourist information office for a map. The house was on the promenade, facing the marine lake. The shouts of children competed with the scream of the gulls.

Chris had walked from the car park, half a mile away, under the elegant Victorian wrought-iron canopies of shops which had succeeded in maintaining a dignity not often seen in seaside towns. The sudden transition, just a few minutes' walk down a side road off the main street, from solid middle-class opulence to tawdry seaside tat came as a surprise. Seaside smells — candy floss and doughnuts, hot dogs and ice cream — nauseatingly overlaid each other, and above all of these the fresher tang of seaweed and salt air transported her to her childhood and to a rare day out with her parents. They had come to Southport, visited the fair and walked the extra half mile or so down to the huge expanse of beach. The sea, as it always was when they visited the seaside, was miles from shore. Her father had bought a newspaper and hired two deckchairs, and her mother and father had sat side by side on the dark, mud-coloured sand in companionable silence, she reading a book, he with his crossword.

Chris remembered with a sudden jolt that there had been good things in her childhood. Most of her adult life she had shut out these good memories along with the bad, had tried to make believe none of it had been, but now she saw it clearly: her father, handsome still, for at first his drinking had been confined to Saturday-night binges, her mother relaxed and pretty in her peach summer frock, glancing up occasionally and smiling encouragement at Chris's attempts to build a sandcastle. Tears pricked the back of her eyes and she blinked rapidly, then turned away from the rail which separated the promenade from the glittering water of the marine lake.

Mrs Webster's flat was in a newly refurbished Victorian house a little further along the sandy roadway, away from the bustle and the vulgar clamour of the amusement arcades. Its red brickwork was sandblasted by the constant scour of the windy seafront, but the window frames were gleaming with fresh white paint. The larger windows on the upper floors had balconies, festooned with pots of geraniums and ivy, splashes of poster-paint colour. The top sashes on the ground floor stood open, and several of the doors onto the

246

balconies had been opened to their fullest extent, but there was no evidence of life within, for behind each dazzling window hung a dense shroud of clean white net. A sea breeze occasionally puffed into the land, catching playfully at the nets and lifting their hems, giving a tantalizing glimpse of the interior of the building. In one room on the second floor the curtain seemed to have caught on some article of furniture and was hitched up at one side, leaving a triangle of darkness. Chris looked up at it as she approached, and the curtain was dropped sharply.

The sleek front door, with its restored stained-glass lights and burnished brass knocker, was firmly shut. Chris peered at the array of bells — there must have been twenty flats in the huge mansion. Most of the bells bore surnames, and one or two included military titles, but half a dozen showed only the flat number, and Chris was wondering whether she should risk the tenants' outrage by ringing each in turn, when a tinny voice squawked at her.

'May I help you?' it asked.

Chris looked up, startled, and noticed for the first time an intercom attached to the wall above the bells. She pressed the button on the intercom and spoke. 'I'm Dr Radcliffe. I'm looking for Mrs Webster.'

There was a pause, then the disembodied voice said, 'Please wait.' The intercom gave an electronic shriek and was silent. Chris stepped back and looked up at the windows again. The curtain at the window she had noticed earlier twitched a little, but it may have been the breeze. Then the door opened, and a man was smiling down at her. He was tall, a little stooped, and bore a faded white moustache clipped to disciplined neatness in a fine line which was not allowed to extend below his upper lip.

'Jones,' he said, by way of introduction. His voice had a high, fluting quality which, with the added distortion of the intercom, she had taken to be female. Mr Jones was dressed formally in a lightweight suit. She pictured him putting on his jacket before answering the door, and she was glad that she had thought to change from shorts into a pair of pale-green linen trousers. Even so, she felt underdressed.

'Chris Radcliffe,' she said, offering her hand.

'*Dr* Radcliffe?'

Chris recognised it as a question. She presented him with her card. His eyebrows, which retained a few black and bristling strands among the white tufts, twitched as he read *psychologist*. He returned her card with a slight lift of the shoulder. 'I do hope you will understand when I ask if you have any other form of identification,' he said.

'My drivers' licence — and credit cards.'

He agreed to her drivers' licence, apologising as she showed it to him. 'One can't be too careful in the terrible moral climate of this degenerate age,' he said, and Chris murmured reassuringly. He scrutinized the details with an assiduousness which seemed to confirm this. 'Might I keep this until you have completed your visit? You see our residents don't like to think of strangers roaming freely about the building.'

'Of course,' Chris said, smiling. 'I'll pick it up on my way out.'

Mr Jones tilted his head with a formality which became almost a bow, then turned away and led Chris into the hallway. The tiling had been restored and buffed to a dull sheen, its pale blues and greyish whites enhanced by the glowing fragments of colour from the stained glass of the front door and the great arched windows of the stairwell.

'Is Mrs Webster expecting you?' he asked.

'I rang earlier,' Chris said, avoiding an outright lie, hoping her blush was disguised by the patterns of colour from the door lights, 'but I didn't think to ask for the flat number.'

'Eleven. On the second floor.'

Mr Jones gave her his own flat number and left Chris to find her own way. The hallway danced with colour and the stairway directly ahead of her gleamed handsomely. Its broad grey steps were edged by a pink granite strip and the banister was supported by a wide mahogany rail, each hand-turned baluster polished to a reddish sheen that seemed to glow with an inner light.

To one side of the stairway stood a lift, lovingly restored. The old-fashioned concertina doors were drawn across and Chris heard it whirring some two floors above. She used the stairway, enjoying the warm spectrum of colour afforded by the windows and smiling to herself at the clattering of her feet on the stone steps — it reminded her of the church she had visited with her mother in her childhood, this light and colour and sound, even the honey-tinted scent of beeswax polish which had been used on the handrail.

Mrs Webster opened the door on the chain. 'I told you, don't want to talk to you,' she said, her voice high and petulant.

'Mrs Webster, I'm—'

'I know who you are! Don't you think I know? If it weren't for you, none of this would have happened. You turned him against us, and Charles never got over it. He'd be alive today if it weren't for you.'

'I'd like to talk to you about Simon, Mrs Webster.'

'Go away! I shall call security. I only have to press my alarm button.'

'I promise I'll go in a moment, but can't you tell me why Simon set fire to your house?'

Chris saw one pale eye through the crack between the door and the jamb. It rolled wildly, and Mrs Webster uttered a piercing screech. 'I've pressed the alarm!' she warned. Then the door slammed.

Chris knocked, her hand bunched into a fist.

'Why won't you talk to me, Mrs Webster?' she yelled, and echoes rebounded like rapid gunfire from the high, tiled walls of the hallway. A hand gripped her shoulder and she wheeled, ready to strike.

Mr Jones fell back, appalled. Chris lowered her fist, muttering an apology, and he recovered his composure enough to say that he was forced to ask her to leave.

'I'm going,' Chris growled, controlling a strong desire to kick the door as Vicky had kicked Dixon's door. Mr Jones returned her driver's licence after she had crossed the thresh-old. 'My passport to the real world,' Chris said.

'A rather acid remark, young lady, and wholly unjustified.'

'D'you think so?'

'Some of us prefer a more civilized interaction with our fellow man,' Jones said.

'Shutting yourself away behind your great doors and your expensive security systems doesn't stop the bad old world from turning.'

'Perhaps not. But if it slows the pace of its revolution, while keeping the more unsavoury elements at bay, then it is worth the added expense.'

Chris began walking away, then she turned and asked, 'What happened to Mr Webster, do you know?'

Jones stiffened, and for a moment his stoop was less pro-nounced. 'I know only that Mrs Webster is a widow. The cir-cumstances of her husband's death are none of my concern.'

Chris drove back to Liverpool in a black mood. She wished she *had* kicked Mrs Webster's pristine, high-gloss, polyurethane-painted door. Kicked it until the stupid bloody woman was forced to answer, to tell her what she wanted to know. On an impulse she pulled off the Southport to Liverpool road at Calderbank and drove back to Tennyson Street. Jennifer was dead-heading roses in her front garden. Chris strolled over, smiling. Jennifer glanced up the street before daring to return her smile. Chris admired the roses and the tangle of violas which so prettily covered the leggi-ness of their stems, and Jennifer positively flushed with pride.

'You couldn't spare a minute, could you?' Chris asked. 'I'd like to ask you a couple of questions.'

Jennifer hesitated a moment, then, wiping the back of her hand across her forehead, she said, 'You'd better come through. I wouldn't want Hilda to see me talking to you.'

They sat in the shade of a lilac tree on Jennifer's back lawn and Jennifer told Chris how Simon's father had killed himself. 'Put a pipe from the exhaust through the car win-dow, closed the garage door and that was it. As I told you earlier, he was only gone half an hour when Mrs Webster started looking for him. She called at our house when she couldn't get into the garage. My John went to help. Of course, they tried to revive him, but it was too late.'

'Why did he do it?' Chris asked.

For a moment Jennifer stared, then she began to understand. 'Oh!' she said. 'You mean a suicide note?' She paused, considering. 'There *was* one. It was addressed to his son. I believe — I mean, I only know what I've been told — it was just one word.'

'And what was that?' Chris asked, allowing Jennifer the dramatic licence which she guessed Hilda had denied her for so long.

Jennifer spread her hands. 'It just said "Sorry".'

23

Chris Radcliffe played back her calls. What good, she wondered, were apologies? What did 'sorry' mean? Who was Mr Webster sorry for? Himself or his son? And for what? All the apologies her father had made had come to nothing — each a further insult in a young life overburdened with insults, both physical and spiritual, because he was only really sorry for how he felt after he had hit her or beaten her up. And yet she had still needed — even craved — his approval and affection. Her father's affection had been grudgingly bestowed, an embarrassed, awkward, non-physical manifestation of love, which was surprising in a man who felt no compunction about expressing his disapproval with a slap or a punch or a kick. Her father's approval had been given on rare occasions, and always provisionally, always qualified, some portion held back, as though love were a finite resource to be carefully husbanded. The thin-lipped reluctance with which he praised her childish successes had demonstrated to her more graphically than his violence her father's innate meanness of spirit.

Chris was distracted from her reverie by Alan Jameson's voice on her recorded messages. He told her that she had been right about Dixon: they had found files, electronic data, false IDs and bugging equipment in his flat. He finished by saying, 'I . . . I hope you're all right.'

'As a matter of fact,' she said aloud, into an awkward silence. 'I'm bloody miserable.'

But Jameson wasn't finished. He took a breath, as if he'd come to a difficult decision. 'I'll phone again, later.'

Chris sighed. She considered phoning Maria or even Hugh — she had a contact number — but dismissed the idea, admitting to herself that she *wanted* to be miserable. She could have stayed with Maria and Pete — and Nicky had also asked her to stay over with her — but she had turned them down, preferring to indulge herself in this depressive mood.

Ted had left a message. 'Give me a buzz if you need to talk.' Bluff, rough-edged, to disguise his real feelings.

There was no message from Simon. She switched off the machine and was attempting an analysis of her profound disappointment at his failure to call, when the telephone rang.

* * *

'Are you sure you want to do this?' Simon asked. He had arrived at her place thirty minutes after he'd made the call. 'I mean, are you sure you don't want to say to hell with it all, and go for a walk or to the pictures or down the local and get rat-arsed?'

He had agreed to come over, despite the fact that it was late and it was hot. He had almost convinced her that there was nothing he would rather do than spend a Thursday evening cooped up with a depressed workaholic typing up notes on a book which promised about as many laughs as Leonard Cohen's greatest hits.

'If I don't do something constructive, I think I'll go out of my mind,' Chris said.

Simon frowned at her, then, affecting a Sigmund Freud accent he said, 'I *sink* zis is an example off der displazement activity, yes?'

Chris smiled. 'That, or avoidance strategy, or denial, denial, denial.' She sensed him looking at her out of the corner of his eye, the way he used to when she had taught him all those years ago, and she looked up. The frown had produced two deep creases, like speech marks, between his almost straight eyebrows. Simon's face was never so unguarded, so eloquently expressive as when he was deep in thought. It had always been so, even when, as a young boy, he had tried to hide his enthusiasm, his enjoyment, his laughter, but most of all the pain behind that bland, immobile blankness which he imposed on his features.

'Avoidance?' he said. 'Denial?' He repeated this word, as she had, but under his breath. 'Denial of your love for him? Avoidance of that fact?'

Chris stared. How had he known that her father was preoccupying her thoughts? Something in his face stopped her from telling him to cut the hobbyist's psychology and mind his own business. How had *he* felt when his father had killed himself? Why hadn't he attended the funeral? Was it for the same reason she had at first resolved not to attend her own father's funeral? She wanted to know.

She sighed. 'The truth is, Simon, I don't know how I feel.'

'Yeah.' The depth of understanding in that one word was profound. 'The problem is, you don't know how you're *supposed* to feel,' Simon murmured. He was staring intently through the open French windows into the garden. The sky had paled to a thin wash of blue and the sun was low over the fields. It caught the fuchsia in a golden spotlight, making the red flowers flare like drops of blood suspended from the tips of each branch. His face, pale and serious, was lit by the same warm rays of sunlight, and she was struck by the fine delineation of his cheekbones and by the length and thickness of his eyelashes. He reminded her of a painting by Caravaggio.

'I mean—' his frown deepened — 'everyone expects you to be upset when your dad dies. But it isn't that straightforward, is it? You hated him, but he's dead, and that changes everything. Suddenly you don't know the rules anymore. Is it OK to go on hating him, now that he's dead? Is that a terrible sin? Or was his sin more terrible, and so it absolves me of mine? Does death bring absolution?' He seemed unaware that he had switched from the second to the first person. 'What I remember feeling most, more than anything else, was relief.'

Chris stirred uneasily but did not interrupt.

'While he was alive, he was like some evil spirit waiting out there. I felt that one day, when I wasn't on my guard, he'd be there, and everything would fall apart, everything I'd built, all that I'd worked for, and it'd be like it always was. Nothing would have changed.' He searched her face, conveying a frantic, desperate need to be understood. 'I knew he couldn't hurt me physically, by then, but—' He broke off, closing his eyes and it seemed for a few moments that he held his breath. 'I was relieved I would never see him again, and all that left me with was—' He shrugged.

'Was guilt,' Chris said.

'Guilt.' He smiled. 'There's nothing quite so potent as Catholic guilt, is there, Chris?'

'Was the guilt all because you were relieved he was dead?'

'Why else?' Simon asked.

'Did you—?' This was a difficult subject for her to broach, even the idea of it made her skin prickle, but she needed to work out how she felt, and she sensed that Simon more than anyone else would be able to help her do that. 'Was it — I mean partly — because . . .' She was afraid to say it in case Simon did not understand, could not share her feelings. 'Because you still needed him, even yearned for him? Or, if not for *him*, then for some idealized image of what a father should be?'

During the silence that followed, Simon's frown grew shallower and his forehead smoothed and cleared. 'Perverse, isn't it?' he said. 'After everything, after all that he did—'

After all that he did. Chris realized she wasn't supposed to know about his father's death. Simon had never even hinted at it before. So why, now, was he telling her all of this? Simon was looking at her expectantly and she felt an obligation to respond, to follow the prepared script. 'Approval is dearly bought from men like your father and mine,' Chris said. It sounded forced, a textbook platitude, but it seemed that all Simon wanted was some indication that she was interested enough to hear him out.

He nodded. 'Mum never understood that. Perhaps that's why she blames me.' He shot her a quick, searching look. 'She thinks he killed himself because he was ashamed of me. She thinks it was my fault.'

'Do you believe that, Simon? That it was your fault?'

A faint smile played over his face and was gone in an instant. 'Guilt got to him, too,' he said. 'It's a dangerous emotion, isn't it, Chris?'

'Almost as destructive as hate,' she said, watching him closely.

'Do you remember what it was like after your mum died?' he asked. 'At home, I mean.'

Chris was silent. She was thinking of the hasty cleaning and ironing after school. Getting her father's dinner ready for six o'clock. Going to her room as soon as he would allow her. And every evening at ten o'clock, well before throwing out time, heaving the big old chest of drawers across the thin green bedroom carpet and jamming it hard against the door. Peeing in a bucket so she didn't have to risk leaving her room when he got home. And the one night she had been too ill and feverish to drag the heavy furniture across to bar the way—

Oh yes, she remembered all right. Simon studied her face for some moments and then nodded as though she had spoken.

'His big, sweaty hands all over you. His stinking breath.' Simon's face twisted with loathing.

'Who are we talking about now, Simon?' she asked.

His head jerked up and he stared at her. His breathing was harsh and uneven. 'I'll bet you were glad he beat you up, because then everyone would know.'

Chris stroked the fine white scar over her eyebrow. She had been terrified, ashamed, lost. But she had also known, somewhere in a part of her that was safe from scrutiny, that because this time he had injured her where it would show, she would not have to go back to him. She hadn't told on him. She hadn't broken her promises to him or to her mother. He had done it himself. He couldn't blame her — she had told no secrets, and somehow that had been important to her.

'Yes,' she said. 'It didn't feel like it at the time — but in a way I *was* glad.'

'You'd've killed him if you could. Making you feel the way you did.'

Chris shut her eyes against the vivid flash of memory; the knife arching up and out as he leaned over her, breathing beer into her face, the warmth of his breath suffocating, smothering, a violation in itself.

Simon gave a strangled cry as though he had shared the vision, and he began pacing the room.

'What he did is not your fault,' Chris said. 'You trusted your father as a child must and should trust a parent. But he didn't care about you. All he cared about was himself. So it's all right to hate him, Simon — it's *safe*, because he can't hurt you anymore.'

Simon stopped abruptly, gazing at her in disbelief. 'He's made me what I am,' he said. 'Chris, he hurts me every waking moment of my life.' He went through to the sitting room and stared out at the gathering gloom at the front of the house.

After a few minutes, Chris joined him.

'You should talk to someone about this,' she said.

He laughed. 'Don't you think it's a bit too late for that?'

'It's never too late.'

His eyes probed hers, assessing her sincerity. 'Who did *you* talk to, Chris?'

'Maria, mostly.'

'That was then, what about now?'

Chris frowned and looked away. 'There's nothing to—'

'First the children's home, then Dorothy, now Ann.' Again, she felt the raking exploration of her features. 'Chris.' He stopped. 'You know on the Monday, when Ann—'

Chris stared. When Ann disappeared and she had spent the evening alone unpacking after her move. Surely, he couldn't think that she—

'I don't need a *confessor*, Simon,' she said, not sure if she should be laughing or outraged.

Simon smiled. He seemed embarrassed and relieved, his eyes tracking restlessly over and around her, still avoiding eye contact. He walked to the bookshelves. 'See this?' He picked up a plastic moulding of the statue of liberty, stuck untidily onto an unpolished marble base. It leaned slightly. 'When I saw this on your bookshelf the other day, I cried.'

Chris smiled. Simon had bought it for her when his parents had taken him on holiday to America. He was eleven years old.

'I found it while I was unpacking,' she explained. 'Hugh moaned so much about it being on display in the flat that I had to put it away.'

'It's just cheap tat,' he said, with a sudden flush of colour.

'You didn't think so then. You thought it was magnificent.'

'And you kept it all these years.' He seemed stunned that anyone should care enough to want to keep a memento of him.

'I'd never seen you so much your real self as when you gave me that little present,' Chris said. 'I'd never seen you so thrilled, so . . . So alive.'

Simon forced his gaze up from the model in his hands and searched her eyes, fearfully, ready to withdraw from her ridicule. Chris's eyes had always fascinated him; her face could be a mask of perfect control, like his, but her eyes often betrayed the anger or amusement she truly felt. He had never seen fear in those eyes — a fear of the boys which some of the newer, younger teachers had telegraphed so clearly despite their furious bravado. But he had seen something in

Chris's eyes, on the few occasions he had conferred on her the compliment of eye contact. It was something old, something which told him that she could see into his heart and soul, could see behind the cold mask and did not despise what she saw, but understood it in a way that only shared experience can understand. And when he had expected her to recoil, disgusted, she had instead felt sorry for him. Not the kind of sympathy which is half revulsion, which repels and insults the recipient, but a sadness which stems from an empathic consciousness of what the other is feeling. At these times he had longed to tell her everything, but his other self would not allow it, and so the silence had remained between them.

'I didn't go to the funeral,' he said flatly. 'I was given the chance, but I didn't want to.' He placed the little ornament carefully on the shelf. 'I wish I had now. It doesn't seem real until you've seen the bastard in the ground.' This was another thing Chris would know, but he felt the need to say it aloud. He needed to purge himself of all the secrets he had been forced to keep for too long. 'I thought I'd feel more secure when he was dead, but sometimes I sense that he's still out there. The threat is still there. I'm not really safe.' He gave an apologetic smile.

'You can't believe that if you think rationally.'

'No. It's like I said, I know he can't do me actual harm, but he's like some disease in my system, lying dormant, waiting to strike.'

'It feels that way because that's how it really is,' Chris said. 'He is in your system, eating away at your unconscious. You're afraid because so much of what harmed you has been locked away, and you're fearful it might get out.'

She was talking like a psychologist, and he was suddenly angry with her. 'Are you telling me I should confront my demons, Doc?'

'Don't be flippant, Simon, I'm serious.'

'Did you confront your dad?' he countered. 'Did *you* tell anyone what he did to you?'

'No.'

259

'Not even when he put you in hospital.' It was a statement, not a question.

Chris smiled, again her finger traced the jagged line of the scar over her eyebrow. 'It was hardly necessary,' she said.

'But you didn't *tell*.' He heard the urgency in his voice, and he looked into her eyes, begging her to understand.

'No,' she said. 'I didn't say a word to anyone. Not then, nor for a long time after.'

'Then you *must* understand why I told nobody.'

She regarded him thoughtfully. 'Yes, I think I do know.'

Hugely relieved, he said, 'I had to do something to get away from him. I couldn't carry on like that.' His mouth was distorted in disgust. 'But I didn't want people to know. Do you see?' His eyes filled with tears and he felt the old disgust for the small boy he had once been, aching for love, desperate for help, but powerless to ask for either.

'Is that why you set the fires?'

He shrugged, palming away a tear that had fallen onto his cheek. 'I don't know what I thought. I suppose I just wanted people to notice, but I couldn't actually tell them . . . what he was . . .' He still couldn't say it, even knowing that Chris had been through — if not the same, then something very close to his own experience.

'When I realized I was looking at a custodial sentence,' he began again. 'I thought at least I was going in on my own terms. As a fire-raiser. Not as a sexually abused child.' He paused, stunned for a few moments by the admission. He stared at the statuette on the bookshelf with frowning concentration, then began again, haltingly, 'I thought it would make a difference — going in with a reputation. They knew what was on my file, the other boys — they always know. I was right about that. First few days it was Pyro-freak. Firebug. Human Torch. But it didn't last. It was like when you looked at me. They could see *me*. They knew what I was just by looking at me.'

'Perhaps we see in each other what we feel in ourselves,' Chris suggested.

He paced the room, prowling its perimeter, touching the walls with the tips of his fingers, moving ornaments and pictures as he passed the bookshelves. 'You can't hide it,' he whispered, barely audibly. 'Not from the lads — the older lads . . . They were as bad as him.'

He paused, feeling tension building up like a static charge, then he lashed out, punching the wall. 'They fucking knew!' he yelled.

Chris gasped, but Simon barely felt the pain of the impact. He walked backwards and forwards across the room, clenching and opening his injured hand. Four bright spots of red oozed from his knuckles. He muttered over and over to himself: 'They *knew*. They *fucking* knew.'

'You weren't to blame, Simon.'

'Who should I blame?' he demanded. 'I should have told someone, right? Any *normal* kid would've told.'

'You didn't know what was normal and what you were allowed to object to.'

He snarled at her. *Platitudes.*

'Simon, you were right about me. I didn't tell anyone about my father, and I was older than you. I should have known better. He scarred my face and I still wouldn't tell. But that's normal — for abused kids — it's *normal.*'

'How did you feel when you saw him on the slab?' Simon said. 'It felt great, didn't it? You wouldn't have to worry about him anymore. He couldn't humiliate you ever again. I mean—' He smiled, but inside he was raging. 'What's the ultimate humiliation if it isn't death?'

24

Frank Garrett was feeling pleased with himself. His lecture that afternoon had gone well, judging by the number of laughs, and Frank was a man whose estimate of success relied heavily on the number and volume of laughs. He was a connoisseur; he liked to build from the polite ripple to the wave of spontaneous hilarity — the good, full-fleshed belly laugh — in a succession from titters to giggles, to frank, open glee in a carefully timed crescendo. And he knew not to rush his audience. He couldn't expect to raise the stiff-necked stuffed shirts he was generally faced with from lugubrious solemnity to levity in a matter of minutes. That was for stand-up comedians with a following and a catchphrase, and although he did like to make people laugh, he also had a serious message to put across, a kind of crusade, you might say. It was an unpalatable message, given that some of these people had spent half their teaching lives believing all the crap the textbooks and the headshrinkers told them. It was a kind of religion to them, and they had chanted the daily mantra of multisensory structured programmes to keep the bogeyman of failure at bay, so he had to sweeten the pill. He showed them the stupidity of the scatter-gun philosophy of multisensory teaching by making them laugh at it.

He paused on the steps of the college, smiling a little to himself, then he stepped out. The evening was comfortably warm, his favourite time of day. He hooked his jacket on his finger and swung it over his shoulder, conscious of the impression he would give, should anyone be watching him. Not that he expected them to be watching; he wasn't a self-obsessed prat. But you never knew for sure, and Frank liked to make an impression. He strolled through a procession of bays, separated by tumbling beds of cotoneaster and dog roses and euonymus. These same bays had been crammed with cars in the afternoon when he had arrived, so that he had been forced to park at the far end of the car park, between the main building and the annexe, but now they were mostly empty.

He enjoyed making people laugh. Kids, teachers, parents, students — it didn't matter. There was nothing like the feeling of getting an audience behind you and making them really *laugh*. He looked at himself, glancing slyly at his reflection in the polished fire doors of the college music block. Sleek, but far away from being fat, his shirt fitted tautly at the waist but did not pull, and his well-chosen tie was still neatly knotted. His short brown hair was brushed back from his face. An intelligent face, he thought.

But an objective observer would see something covert — a suppressed insecurity in the self-satisfied smile which he too readily wore. He walked on unhurriedly. Perhaps he would stop for a drink on the way home, then go for a meal at his favourite restaurant. He had earned it.

A figure in the shadows saw Garrett pat his stomach as he passed by the polished glass doors of one of the buildings. He watched, unnoticed; saw the small man's swagger in his walk, an unconvincing cockiness which irritated and was vaguely ludicrous. Strange that he hadn't seen this before. The sureness, the complacency had been so obtrusive, and he himself was so inexperienced in identifying adult defensive mannerisms that he had imagined the facade to be real. And Frank Garrett had always been able to raise a laugh. But when laughter is provoked, there has to be something — or someone — to laugh at, and Garrett had been indiscriminate in his choice of subject. He didn't care who he hurt if he got the reaction he wanted.

Garrett reflected on the response he had got; he couldn't leave it alone. This is what actors call the buzz, he told himself. Of course, women audiences were easier, they were more willing than men to believe that they had got it all wrong, more amenable to the other's viewpoint, more used to smiling and laughing at other people's jokes. They had lapped it up. When he'd got onto the bit about practice being more important than psychological insights, he had seen heads nodding in agreement. When he had asked them, palms upturned, if an ed. psych. had ever actually told them something they didn't know, there had been an unmistakable ripple of shared understanding, an empathic rush of feeling which the audience created and responded to like the faithful at a revivalist meeting: a soft, collective chortle bubbled up from nowhere and people exchanged smiles. Some even shouted responses. So, when he'd got onto the serious message, the message which had sold his book in its thousands nationwide, they had been ready to listen. '*You* are the experts,' he told them. '*You* can make a difference. You don't need an overpaid, out-of-touch psychologist to tell you what's best for your kids. It doesn't take a doctorate to know that what kids like ours need is practice, and plenty of it!' They had laughed, and this time they had applauded, too — a warm, companionable applause — and he had known that he would make good sales this evening.

He arrived home at eight thirty, having eaten well and drunk just a unit or two over the limit. What the hell — the restaurant was only five minutes' drive from his home, and you could be just a bit too anally retentive about following the rules to the letter. What was five minutes' drive on a drink or two, give or take?

He climbed out of his car in a pleasant haze. No need to lock it in the garage. It wasn't that sort of neighbourhood.

The night air was rich with the scent of grass mowings and barbecue smoke. Next door, by the smell of it, and judging by the shouts of laughter echoing on the warm night air, they hadn't finished yet.

A little further down the road, Dave Lilley was watering his garden. Frank waved, feeling well disposed towards him, even though Dave's cats shat on his rockery and sprayed their foul smell all over his dwarf conifers. But tonight was not a night for such concerns. Tonight he had sold forty-seven books to an audience of seventy people who had already paid six pounds per head to hear him talk, and even after deducting the cost of hire of the lecture hall, and taking into account the miserable percentage his publishers allowed him on each book sale, that still left him 400 to the good. Not bad for an hour's work. Seven pounds a minute. Almost as well paid as the poncey doctors who talked down to everyone so convincingly that everyone thought they had to look up to them. But he would not allow such thoughts to intrude upon his philanthropic mood. The looking-down-looking-up idea might be a good line for a lecture, though. He made a mental note to work on it.

He let himself in, engaging the key in the lock at only his second attempt. He hummed 'We're in the Money' quietly to himself. He wasn't ready to sleep yet and he might be seen in the garden by the neighbours, so he changed into a pair of shorts and a polo shirt and opened a few windows, then poured himself a gin and tonic — lots of ice — and padded outside to his sun lounger and flopped. He rested his drink on a stomach only a *little* swollen by the four-course meal he had just eaten (reducing his profits by £55.92, including tip) and the squeals and laughter from next door blended agreeably with the song of a blackbird proclaiming its territory from the TV aerial of his house. Frank was in his most mellow of moods. He was beginning to drift into a delectable dream, involving a young woman teacher who had been effusive in praise of his lecture, when the doorbell rang.

'Mr Garrett?'

Frank smiled good-humouredly at the young man on the doorstep. 'Yes?' he said.

'I . . . I was wondering . . .' the young man stuttered, 'if you wouldn't mind . . .' He rummaged in a plastic carrier bag. 'If you wouldn't mind signing this.' He presented Frank with a copy of his book.

'Well,' Frank said, mildly surprised.

'It's just that I was at your lecture and I thought it was brilliant, but I'd already bought your book and anyway there was such a queue, and I didn't realize we live in the same street. Practically neighbours! When I saw you pull up a few minutes ago, I recognized you straight away. I don't know why I didn't make the connection from your photo on the dust jacket, but, well, you just don't expect celebrities to live on your own street.' He came to a sudden halt, apparently having run out of things to say, and looked hopefully up at Frank. Frank looked at the book, tilting it so that the gold lettering of his name glinted in the late sunlight.

'I'm terribly sorry,' the young man said, apparently realizing with sudden force the imposition he was making on a complete stranger. 'I shouldn't have bothered you. You must be exhausted after all that work.'

Frank raised a hand to stop the renewed babbling. 'Enough!' he said, laughing. 'I'll do it.' He smirked to himself, fingering the embossed lettering of the title *Expert Ease*. The lettering of the subtitle *How to take control of your child's education* would have been better in a subtler shade of red, but it was a good, strong design, nevertheless. He held out his hand for a pen.

'Oh . . . I forgot to bring a pen. It was sort of spur of the moment. I wouldn't have had the nerve if I'd stopped to think about it.' The young man grinned sheepishly. 'I'm sorry about this.'

'No problem,' Frank said. For this level of adulation he was prepared to be magnanimous. He ambled into the hallway and picked up a biro from the telephone table. Turning, he saw that the young man had stepped into his porch and was grinning nervously. Frank frowned a little at the intrusion but instantly forgot his irritation.

'I wouldn't normally do this sort of thing, it's just that I admire your system so much,' the younger man said.

Garrett smiled back, then signed his name with a flourish. 'Who shall I say?'

'Don't you remember me?' He seemed disappointed, dismayed even that Frank did not know him. Pathetic, really, but disarming. Frank gave him a long, thoughtful look. He had taken out his contact lenses, so the guy's features were a little blurred.

'I'm—'

'No! Don't tell me,' Frank interrupted. 'I never forget a face.' He considered. 'Teacher training, possibly.' The young man smiled and shook his head. 'BTEC conference, London? No? NASEN Conference North West, then?' The blur of fair hair floating around a longish face seemed suddenly familiar, and Frank had a flash of near-recognition. 'Bloody hell! I didn't teach you, did I? Back in the bad old days?'

A glimmer of white appeared as his young fan grinned. 'I—'

'No! Wait. Wait a bit.'

But his guest had half turned and was thumbing over his shoulder. 'I should get back. My girlfriend—'

'Girlfriends, mothers, sisters — they're meant to worry,' Frank said, 'it's their job. And it's our job to keep *them* in a job.'

This remark provoked laughter. 'Still the same old Windy Garrett!' the young man said.

Frank was concentrating so hard on what it was that he recognized about the face that he failed to appreciate he was being insulted. 'Come through and have a drink,' he said. 'It'll come to me. It always does.'

It did. Twenty minutes and several clues later, as they sat in the garden sipping drinks. Nobody heard his one anguished cry above the mingled shouts and conversation and good-natured laughter from the barbecue next door.

25

'Alan? Etherington here.' It took Jameson a second or two to focus his attention sufficiently to remember the Home Office pathologist's name. Etherington swept on, unaware of Jameson's confusion. 'I think we may have another.'

Jameson was speechless for a moment.

'Jameson?'

'Where?' the chief inspector demanded.

Jameson arrived at the address in south Liverpool twenty minutes later. The street, a long, wide, tree-lined avenue, was empty of children, but clusters of adults had gathered at a discreet distance from Frank Garrett's house and now watched Jameson's arrival with undisguised curiosity. A constable had been posted to keep out sightseers. She moved aside as Jameson approached.

'Sergeant Foster arrived a few minutes ago, sir,' she told him.

Jameson nodded his thanks and went inside. The house itself seemed deserted, but he could hear Etherington holding court — in the back garden by the sound of it. He followed the sound of the Home Office pathologist's voice down a wide hallway and through to a large and rather over-furnished dining room. The narrow oak table was decorated at either end with two Gothic candelabra in a greenish-black metal. At the far end of the table lay a neatly folded overall, sealed in a plastic bag. The patio doors were open.

'Ah, Alan!' Etherington exclaimed, seeing him in the doorway. 'Once you're togged up, you'd better come through, I want you to see this.'

Jameson wasn't sure *he* wanted to see, but he donned the overall reluctantly and stepped out into the garden, where Etherington, a SOCO, DS Foster and DC Nolan formed a semi-circle around a sun lounger upon which the body was sprawled. Jameson's first view of the body was the top of its head. He had to edge round the back of the lounger to join the little tableau. He noted, in his careful negotiation of the corpse, that two drinks were set out on the cast iron table and next to them, a book. The body lay with its mouth open, the teeth of its lower jaw just visible, like a premonition of the decay to come. He also noted a look exchanged between his men and Etherington.

'Same MO as the others?' he asked, determined to gain some control of the situation.

'Very likely. Similar, if not the same knife. Similar wound. As I was explaining to your colleagues as you arrived, Alan, the murderer could well have done just as you did, inching around the back of the chair on his way out — or in. He pulls the knife and stabs the victim before he knows what's happening. There's no sign of a struggle,' he added.

So that was the significance of the exchanged glances? Jameson wondered.

'I'm glad I was of use in your little demonstration,' Jameson said, unreasonably irritated. 'Do we have a name for the victim?' He addressed this question to Bob Foster, fixing the sergeant in his line of sight and avoiding looking down at the corpse. He had a sudden urge to close the man's mouth in an attempt to restore some fraction of his dignity among all these dispassionate, professionally detached observers. He suppressed the urge with some difficulty and tried to make himself concentrate on what his sergeant was saying.

'Frank Garrett. A teacher, lecturer and writer. That's his book on the table.'

Jameson dipped into his inside pocket and brought out a pen. He used it to lift the book's front cover. *To . . . with best wishes.* And then his signature,' he read. 'Seems the murderer isn't above a little flattery to get himself where he wants to be.'

'If it's OK with you, sir,' the SOCO said, 'I'll get it off to the lab for fingerprinting.'

'The glasses, too,' said Jameson, stepping back. He let the book cover fall and gestured that he had finished. 'Find out if his name is on file, will you?' he asked Foster. 'Who found him?'

'A neighbour. They were having a barbecue. A teenager hopped over the fence to get a Frisbee back. None of them heard anything.'

The chief inspector turned to Nolan, who, although he had not spoken, had been trying to project an impression of sharp alertness. 'Knock on a few doors, will you?' Jameson said. 'Find out if anyone saw anything.' Nolan left smartly and Jameson returned his attention to the prosaic setting of the murder. 'If the murderer sat chatting while the two of them sipped their gin and tonics, he may have left something behind.'

'We'll not get prints from the glasses,' the SOCO said, indicating the condensate, pooling onto the table.

'I suppose not,' Jameson agreed.

'Want me to organize a fingertip search of the garden?' Foster asked.

Jameson nodded. He would have to clear it with Compton, but he was confident he would be allocated the staff he needed for this particular search. Meanwhile he wanted to satisfy himself that all was well with Chris Radcliffe. He'd been struggling with a niggling worry over her ever since Etherington's phone call. He dispatched Foster to check Garrett against the files and then arranged by telephone for the search of the garden. Superintendent Compton had taken little persuasion, and it was agreed that the search would begin at first light. Police constables were posted at the front and back of the house and were already having to keep press photographers and ghouls at bay.

Garrett's car was missing from the driveway and the police helicopter had been deployed to help in the search for it. A neighbour — Dave Lilley as it turned out — had been able to give them a description of the man who had driven it away.

* * *

It was ten thirty. Chris had lit a small cluster of candles, her only concession to the fading light. Simon was in the kitchen washing his bleeding knuckles, having refused her assistance.

The candle flames, unwavering in the breathless air, made opalescent circles of overlapping creamy light, enough to cheer, but not to draw the gathering darkness inward. Chris listened to Simon moving about in the kitchen. She had left him some gauze and a light bandage — Maria had bought her a first aid kit, declaring that she would have use of it, being so isolated. Chris heard a soft exclamation and then something quieter, like a sob. She felt like she was eavesdropping. Swearing under her breath, she snatched up the TV control and flicked irritably through the channels. She was no bloody use to him — a trained psychologist and supposed friend and she couldn't ease his suffering.

The regional news bulletin was just ending: ' . . . was last seen alive parking his car at the front of his house.' The reporter stood in front of a modern, semi-detached property, making the most of her unexpected good fortune. It wasn't every day that the regional news team got a story like this. Too late for the ten o'clock news, it had just made the regional slot and Tanya Maldrake had been ready.

'Police,' Tanya went on, trying not to seem too eager, nor thrilled by the news, 'are refusing to confirm that the body is that of Frank Garrett, a writer and lecturer in education.'

'Frank!' Chris said, her eyes widening. She leaned forward in her seat, then half turned to the kitchen door, but without taking her eyes from the screen. 'Simon—'

'I see it,' he said quietly.

'Earlier today, police issued a photograph and description of a man they want to interview in connection with the so-called Municipal Murders. Darren Lewis—' a photograph of Lewis appeared on the screen — 'was questioned last weekend but later released without charge. It isn't clear at this stage whether the killing is connected with the murders of Dorothy Hardy and Ann Lee, although unconfirmed reports do seem to point to similarities between this and the brutal murders of the two council workers and of retired police sergeant Jim Bradbury on Monday.'

Chris looked into Simon's bloodless face. 'You know something about this, don't you?' she said.

Simon would not look at her.

'Simon, you said you'd help me, if I needed it. I'm asking for your help now. He has to be stopped. If you know where Darren Lewis is you *have* to tell me.'

* * *

Jameson walked to Garrett's front door, braced himself, then stepped, blinking, into the glare of halogen lamps and the whirring motors of automatic camera winds. A cacophony of calls vied for his attention. The reporters had been kept out of the front garden by the competent young PC who had greeted him on his arrival. The gates across the driveway had been closed, but reporters leaned across the garden fence and the gates, anywhere they could find a space, and aimed cameras and microphones at him, each shouting to be heard above the rest.

'Can you confirm the name of the victim?'

'What is Mr Garrett's connection with Calderbank borough council?'

'Did he know the other victims?'

'Is there a link with the Municipal Murders?'

272

Jameson glanced sharply in the direction of this particular questioner. Milton. Jameson had to admire the man's resilience. He had apparently returned directly to business after his release from the cells. The chief inspector held up his hands for silence. 'I can't give you a definite answer as to the identity of the victim, and I can't say if this death is linked to the terrible events of the past few weeks. But—' he raised his voice over a groan of protest — '*but* I can tell you that we are looking for a white male, aged between twenty and twenty-five. He has fair hair and was wearing jeans and a light-coloured T-shirt.'

A few mutters of 'Lewis' and a nodding of heads, then someone shouted, 'Are you looking for Darren Lewis in connection with this murder?'

'We wish to interview Mr Lewis. I can't comment beyond that. The man seen talking to the victim shortly before he was found may be driving a car which was stolen from the driveway of this house.' Jameson spoke slowly and carefully, allowing those taking notes to take down the description accurately. 'It is a metallic-blue Vauxhall Astra, registration 1 FG — it's a personalized number plate and very distinctive.' There was a flurry of excitement, as the assembled media inferred his admission that the victim was, indeed, Mr Frank Garrett. 'If any member of the public sees this car, they should dial 999 immediately — and on no account should they tackle the man driving it. He may be armed and extremely dangerous.' *That should keep them busy for the rest of the night*, Jameson thought with a degree of satisfaction. Then the gabble of questions began again. 'You will have a full statement at a press conference tomorrow. Thank you, ladies and gentlemen.' He ignored all requests for further information and strode to his car. He had just turned out of the avenue when his mobile phone rang. The call was from Superintendent Compton, who had been watching the late news.

'What the hell do you think you're doing, giving out the victim's car registration before you've had his identity confirmed?' he demanded.

'Sir, we're looking for someone who coolly knocked on Mr Garrett's door, charmed the poor bastard into offering him drinks and cold-bloodedly stabbed him to death. The media already knew the victim's name; I didn't bluff them with my refusal to confirm it, and it seemed sensible to use them to help us enlist the help of a few million extra pairs of eyes in trying to find his killer. Garrett, we think, was found minutes after the attack, which means the killer might still be in the area, driving a very distinctive car—'

'Well you'd just better hope none of your vigilante recruits gets hurt trying to make a citizen's arrest,' Compton said, but the fury had drained out of his voice and Jameson felt it safe to continue.

'If there are any inaccuracies in what I said, they can be put right at the press conference tomorrow morning.'

'You mean I can carry the can for any of your bloody gaffes? Well, I'll tell you what, DCI Jameson, if there's anything to be "put right", as you call it, you can have the spotlight all to yourself.'

'Thank you, sir,' Jameson said solemnly, but he grinned into the mouthpiece. Two minutes later, his mobile rang again. 'Christ almighty!' he muttered. 'What now?' he pulled over to the kerbside.

'Foster here, boss.' The sergeant sounded strained, even apprehensive. 'I've got the results of the cross-check on Garrett. He worked in the same school as Dr Radcliffe for a while — as head of the Special Needs department. A place called Wellesthorne. It's closed now. He had contacts with Dorothy and Ann on a number of referrals for special school placements.' There was an awkward pause. 'He also worked with Dr Radcliffe when she went into the educational psychology service. Sir—'

'Has anyone managed to contact Dr Radcliffe?'

'No sir, but—'

'Get a car round to her house then. Call out the local force if no one's available. I want her warned.'

'Sir — that's what I've been trying to say. We got a call from her foster mother. She'd been trying to reach Dr

Radcliffe all evening. In the end she drove over. The house is deserted. Doors and windows open. A lot of her files have been burned to ashes in the hearth and—' Foster broke off.

Jameson felt suddenly cold. The roadway outside the car seemed to recede from him. 'And?' he demanded, his heart thudding.

'There's blood, sir. On one of the walls and on an ornament, a sort of statuette.'

Jameson covered the mouthpiece with his hand. A terrible dread seized him, and he realized for the first time how much he had grown to anticipate each meeting with Chris Radcliffe. She had been slippery, obstinate, antagonistic and devious by turns, but she had succeeded in giving him an optimism for the future which he had thought impossible since Roz left him. Yes, she was difficult, but she was also compassionate and humorous and courageous. He had begun, almost without knowing it, to think of Chris as a friend and to hope for more.

'Boss?'

Jameson coughed. 'Put out a description of her,' he said, his voice noticeably hoarse. 'Merseyside, Wirral and Cheshire. Get photos of her into as many of the morning papers as you can. Have the scene of crime lot picked up anything useful?'

'They're typing the bloods. A few fingerprints — about half a dozen different types, they think. I've asked Mrs Stevens and her family to provide us with prints for elimination, and we're running any that don't match through NAFIS.'

'Good. Keep me posted. Where are you?'

'Still at Dr Radcliffe's house, sir.'

'Wait there for me. I'm on my way. Can you get someone to cross-reference Garrett and Dr Radcliffe against those with convictions — see if they were taught by the two of them?'

'It'll mean getting someone out of bed — but sure.'

* * *

275

Jameson used his siren from Liverpool right through to the narrow Cheshire B-road on which Chris Radcliffe's cottage stood. It was nearly midnight when he arrived. 'Christ, Foz, this is a bloody nightmare.' He was staring at the drying bloodstains on the wall of Chris Radcliffe's sitting room. The ornament, a heavy statuette of the Statue of Liberty, had already been bagged and taken away. A little blood had spattered onto the wood floor and had been carefully marked, photographed and videotaped.

Foster shifted uneasily, then cleared his throat, preparatory to speaking, but when Jameson looked up at him, he seemed to lose heart and glanced away.

Jameson sat down and put his head in his hands. He roused himself a few seconds later when he realized he was in danger of falling asleep.

'You should go home, Bob,' he said. 'We've done all we can here. Alison will be wondering what's happened to you.' Foster followed him from the room. 'Cheshire Police'll make this place secure for the night. If anything happens, I'll call you.' Outside, he noticed DC Nolan for the first time. 'Where's your car?' Jameson asked.

'I'm parked out on the verge, sir.' Nolan almost snapped to attention, still overdoing the formality since the bollocking Jameson had given him over Greer.

'Drive me back to the station, would you?' Jameson asked. 'I keep mistaking postboxes for pedestrians, and when the postboxes start waving you down, you know it's time to stop.'

'Of course, sir. It'd be a pleasure.'

Jameson fixed Nolan with a curious stare. Was he really so carved up about the way he and Flynn had botched Philip Greer's arrest?

The constable smiled nervously under Jameson's scrutiny. 'Gets you like that after a long day, sometimes.'

Had Jameson remained awake, he would have remarked that Nolan drove back to Liverpool with all the care and precision of an examinee on their advanced driving test.

But Jameson dozed through the entire journey. At times of extreme tiredness, he would fall into immediate dreaming sleep.

Chris Radcliffe, dressed as the Statue of Liberty, was standing barefoot on a cliff's edge, the wind riffling her tunic. Her right arm was raised and carried, not a torch, but a knife which dripped blood in dark rivulets onto her hand and down her arm into the lovely concavity of her oxter. She was grey as death. Jameson felt a strong conviction that he was at home in his living room, watching this as though on a screen, but simultaneously he could feel the cool buffeting of the wind which tugged at Chris's tunic and played in her hair.

'You see?' Roz was saying. 'This is your fault. Another casualty of your goddamned job. Another sacrifice on the altar of Law and Order.' The figure on the cliff turned slowly and Jameson felt a devastating sense of responsibility and a terrible dread of looking into that face. He jolted awake.

If he had cried out, Nolan was tactfully ignoring it, and for this Jameson was grateful. He was beginning to see the keen young DC in a new light. In this heightened state of benevolence, he wondered whether it hadn't been unfair to team him up with Quinn, who was, at best, a lazy copper and would hardly give the right sort of guidance and encouragement. He would think about a change of staff groupings when this lunacy was finally over. He arrived home at two a.m., dispirited and exhausted.

When the phone by his bed rang two hours later, he made a few tentative assaults on his alarm clock before his confused and tired mind located the true source of the noise and he fumbled the receiver from its cradle.

It was a DI from Cheshire police. 'We've got someone you've been looking for,' he said. Jameson felt a fraction of a second of soaring optimism, then the officer went on. 'Darren Lee Lewis. Caught him round the back of Dr Radcliffe's house.'

Jameson took a moment to adjust to this new emotion, and an almost overpowering need to hit someone hard, then he arranged for Lewis to be brought to Merseyside HQ. He debated whether to wake Foster up but decided that Sergeant Ryman would be more useful in the interview because she had the background on the case.

* * *

Lewis sat slumped in his chair, throbbing with anger and terror. Jameson could smell it on him. Despite the air conditioning, Lewis was sweating and his T-shirt was stained in two wide arcs under the arms. He smoked fretfully, flicking in a compulsive action at the tipped end of his cigarette, his mouth twisted unconsciously into a snarl.

They had found a duty brief for him, a dark-haired innocent of no more than twenty-five. She looked pale, half asleep and bemused by the whole procedure.

'Where is Dr Radcliffe?' Jameson asked.

'I don't know, do I?'

'What were you doing at her house?'

Lewis focused his attention on the metal ashtray he had been provided with, shuttling it backwards and forwards between his hands. He stopped suddenly and placed the crimped metal disk dead centre of the table. 'I just wanted to talk to her.' Beneath the table, his foot tapped incessantly.

'About what?'

He threw a furious look at Jameson. 'Nothing.'

'You were going to break in.'

'No, I wasn't!'

'Then why were you sneaking around the back of the house?'

Lewis took three short puffs on his cigarette. 'I was just sussing the place out. I wanted to make sure she was on her own.'

'So that you could abduct her.'

'What?' Lewis sat back suddenly and slapped both hands on the table. 'No! I just wanted to talk to her.'

'At four in the morning?'

Lewis shrugged, scowling, stubbed out his cigarette and began to rap with his knuckles on the tabletop. He picked up his cigarette pack, set it down, picked it up again and took one, lighting it and taking the same jabbing drags on it as before.

Jameson wondered that anyone could carry around so much rage without self-combusting. 'You'd been there earlier, hadn't you, Darren?' he asked.

'No.'

'You set fire to some papers.'

'You wha'?'

'Some hadn't completely burned. Your name was on them.'

'If I'd done it, there wouldn't be nothin' to show.' It seemed that the suggestion hurt Lewis's professional pride.

'You're good at fires, aren't you, Darren?'

Lewis's brief shot him an anxious glance, but he smiled, the snarl becoming more pronounced. 'Who says?'

'*You* just did. And one or two of your mates have decided to be a bit more helpful.'

Lewis looked away, the smile wavered, but only just. It seemed he was still confident his friends wouldn't shop him.

'Abduction is a very serious charge, Darren. And there are limits to how far even friends will go.'

'Add to that the fact that the squatter who got burned is on the critical list.' He clicked his tongue. 'Situations like this, friends are apt to fade away like mist on a summer's day,' Ryman added.

'Look,' Lewis jabbed a finger at Jameson. 'I never touched her! I heard her on the radio, and I thought she might help, I didn't wanna get done for someone else's shit. But I never laid a finger on her.'

They were interrupted by a knock at the door. When Jameson returned to the table, he terminated the interview.

'You'll be returned to the cells until someone from Toxteth arrives,' Jameson explained. 'They have a few questions they would like to ask you.'

26

Chris woke, frightened and disorientated. It was pitch dark. She tried to move and discovered that her hands and feet were tied. She struggled, whimpering, until nausea and the pain in her head made her feel faint. There was a musty smell, a dry, dusty odour that reminded her of the loft in her new home — dust and age and fibreglass insulation. But this was a much bigger space, judging by the whispering echoes which had come back at her in mocking ripples as she had struggled. Creaks, the intermittent splash of dripping water, the faint but unmistakable shudder and groan of settling foundations. Beneath and above these sounds, woven like threads in the greater pattern, were furtive movements, scampering sounds, the occasional squeak.

She called for help, but her voice was as dry as the suffocating air around her, and all that echoed back at her was a hoarse croak. The back of her head ached abominably. It felt tight and sore and she could feel something warm and oily oozing down behind her right ear and finding the crevice between her jawline and her neck.

Oh God, I'm going to die in this terrible place, she thought, and began to cry. Hurried footsteps overhead made her stop and draw breath sharply. There. Again. She ran her tongue around her parched mouth, trying to coax the salivary glands into action.

'Help!' she cried, this time louder, but the effort triggered a spasm of coughing which seemed to tear at the tight place at the back of her skull.

'Chris?' A torchlight flashed in her face and Chris felt an indescribable sense of relief.

'Thank God!' she said, as the coughing subsided. 'Help me.'

Strong hands straightened her up against the supporting pillar of what seemed to be a large basement. Wide heating pipes and electrical conduits filled the space between the floor and the low ceiling and Chris felt suddenly claustrophobic.

'You're bleeding.' As he turned from her, she saw for the first time that it was Simon.

* * *

'Why'd you stop the interview, sir?' Ryman asked. 'He was just beginning to warm up.'

'The fingerprint lab has come up with something — a partial print on Garrett's book which matches a print on the statuette — which matches to a convicted arsonist,' he said. 'One Simon Webster.' Jameson remembered that he had met Webster and was swamped by a wave of regret that he hadn't checked more closely, then he recalled that Simon had been given a glowing character reference by Chris herself.

He made a few hurried phone calls: one of which was to persuade a local regional intelligence officer to come in and run a search for the last known address of Simon Webster.

He was running his electric razor half-heartedly over his chin for something to do while he waited for the result of the computer search, when an idea struck him. Cursing himself for not having thought of it before, he dialled the switchboard and asked for the telephone number of Chris's secretary. Minutes later, Nicky's voice piped down the line. He asked his question and she was silent a moment.

'I don't know offhand,' she said, 'but Chris'll have it in her files. I'll meet you at the office.'

He waited in the deserted roadway, in the early hours, his nerves jangling. Nicky arrived in tightly cut jeans and a T-shirt, the morning already being hot. Her hair was a flattened mat and she had pulled it back into a ponytail. She wore no make-up and he was surprised that her skin was remarkably pale and faintly freckled. She caught his appraising look as she opened the front door to the building. 'Me morning face,' she said with a wan smile.

He smiled back, warming to her. The pallid vulnerability made an unexpectedly strong impression on him, and he became aware that she had not slept and was desperately worried about Chris, but was determined to keep herself in check for her friend's sake.

She tackled the office alarm, then went straight to one of a bank of filing cabinets and found the file in seconds. The address was in Old Swan, and he quickly dispatched a squad car. Another two phone calls secured him a warrant and a courier to pick it up and bring it to him. For this task he chose Bob Foster.

The flat was in a crumbling yellow-brick building which had once been a small family house. The front wall bulged ominously towards the pavement and the gateposts leaned at converging angles. The tenant of the downstairs flat opened the front door, preparing to be crabby with them, but when they showed their warrant cards he stepped back in alarm, clutching a grubby towelling dressing gown to his scrawny chest.

'Nothing to worry about,' Jameson said, grim faced. 'Go inside, now.' The man fled, slamming his flat door behind him.

A plasterboard partition had been built to separate the upstairs and downstairs living space and across the stairwell was a flimsy door. They punched a hole in the plasterboard to the left of the door and reached in to open the latch. The door swung outwards.

The stairway was uncarpeted but clean, and on the landing an array of bookshelves cramped the already narrow space. There was one bedroom, which was tiny, the bed neatly made up with one lightweight blanket and the corners were box-turned, a mark of an ex-serviceman or someone with experience of youth custody, Jameson reflected. The wardrobe held a few shirts and pairs of jeans, one suit, one pair of shoes — all clean, all neatly arranged.

The living room contained more bookshelves — homemade but carefully finished — a sofa and chairs, covered with patterned throws, and a radio. There was no TV, but several prints of Monets and a couple more disturbing images by Bacon were clustered on the wall. An ancient Dansette portable record player occupied one corner of the room. It gleamed like new.

Jameson's eyes skimmed the bookshelves and found a neat pile of buff document wallets. He leafed through them. Some seemed to be research notes, but there were several which were jammed with torn out pages of documents bearing the Calderbank council logo. Many mentioned Chris Radcliffe or Dorothy or Ann. All related to Simon Webster.

'Bingo,' Jameson muttered.

* * *

Simon struck a match and lit a hurricane lamp, flicking off the torch to save the batteries. He worked busily, avoiding Chris's eye, opening a one-gallon container and tipping it to wet a pad of cotton wool. Then he pulled her forward, making her yelp with pain. He apologized and began dabbing at the wound at the back of her head. Chris was too faint with pain and sickness to resist. He worked carefully for some minutes, then put some form of padding onto the cleaned cut and wrapped a makeshift bandage around her head. He lowered her gently so that her back was supported by the pillar once more, then leaned back on his heels.

Chris stared at him sullenly. She was afraid and confused, but mostly she was angry. Angry at the helplessness he had forced on her, angry with herself for not having seen that it was Simon who had followed her in the blue Fiesta — he had even told her once that someone in the workshops in youth custody had shown him how to get into a car and hot-wire it in less than five minutes, and yet she had never suspected him. Simon had watched her from the shrubbery, had dogged her, anxious that she would discover it was he who had killed and killed again.

'Let me go,' she said.

He avoided her gaze. 'I can't.' He chewed his lower lip. 'I'm sorry. I never meant to hurt anyone. I was only trying to stop them finding out.'

'And now you're trying to stop me.' Her voice sounded cracked and old and she was forced to stop. He turned away and poured her a drink into a plastic cup. She wished she had the resolve to refuse it but she was desperately thirsty, and as she drank greedily he began to talk.

'I hung around the council offices for days, trying to get the nerve up to talk to them. I saw them both, Mrs Lee and Mrs Hardy, and they saw me. Then I followed Mrs Hardy home one night. I thought she'd talk to me. I wanted—' For a moment he paused, focusing on something above her, and she caught a glint of light reflected in the grey blue of his eyes. 'I wanted her to explain *why*,' he said. 'I sat outside her house for hours. I was about to give it up when she came out. She walked to the community centre for her keep-fit class. I plucked up the courage when she was on the way home, but she freaked out, screaming and calling for help. I swear to you — all I wanted to do was talk. I didn't know what to do. I panicked.'

Chris waited for him to go on, but he sat staring at his hands for some minutes. 'Ann?' said Chris, finding her voice. 'Did you panic over her, too? And Jim Bradbury — what about him?'

'I can't go back,' he said, as if he hadn't heard her questions. 'I won't go back to prison.' Another calm statement of fact. 'Mrs Lee — Ann — had seen me, talked to me. She might have told the police. The policeman saw me coming back from the woods where I'd left her. Where I'd left both of them. He was on his way to the ponds. He even spoke to me. He was the warrant sergeant who used to check on me after I got let out. He didn't recognise me, but I couldn't risk the chance of him suddenly remembering.'

'Christ!' Chris's voice cracked. 'We're talking about people's lives here, and you're making it sound like you had to make a few tricky decisions on a party invitation list. They didn't mean to hurt you, and they didn't deserve to die because of it. *I'm* more to blame than they were. I knew more than any of them that you should have been taken away from your parents — from your father, anyway.'

He smiled faintly. 'I thought you psychologists weren't supposed to take on other people's problems. I know how far you pushed it. I know you got yourself suspended over me.' He chewed his lower lip.

Chris recalled how she had telephoned Simon's mother to try and persuade her that Simon would be better placed in a boarding situation, and Mrs Webster had complained to the borough education office. That had resulted in the four-week suspension.

'I'm not the hero you think I am,' she said.

'Mum tried to get him to send me to boarding school. It must've been after you phoned her. He wouldn't listen. He was near to tears.

'So, you burned your house.'

'It wasn't mine,' he said quickly. 'It was never mine. It was theirs — his really. Home is a place where you go to feel safe, loved. Looked after.'

Chris softened towards him. 'Robert Frost said, "Home is the place where, when you have to go there, they have to take you in."'

Unexpectedly, Simon smiled and relaxed a little. 'Like prison,' he said.

'In many ways, just like prison,' said Chris, but she couldn't return his smile. Then, with more daring than she thought she possessed, she asked, 'Why waste your life on useless revenge?'

His face smoothed to a mask of expressionlessness, which was more frightening, more unnerving than his rage or his tears. 'My life ended when my father raped me when I was nine years old.'

'No. It didn't. You could have made something of yourself.'

'Like what?' he snarled. 'What could I do, after everything they did to me? My father, the lads in youth custody. They knew what I was. They could smell it on me. They used me like he did. How could I ever ask a girl out? She'd see what I was before the second date. A prison *fag*. Less than human.'

'No, Simon. No . . . It didn't have to be this way.'

He seemed to flinch, then looked away.

'It was only the predators who ever saw me,' he said. 'To everyone else, I was invisible.'

'Except when you tried to set fire to the school and you succeeded in burning down your parents' house.'

He nodded, accepting her reasoning.

'But, Simon, surely you didn't kill four people so that you would be *noticed*?'

Simon's face creased in pain and he reached out to her, but she flinched violently and he let his hand drop. Chris watched him shift position slowly and cautiously to avoid alarming her. He uncurled his legs from under him and moved to a more comfortable cross-legged sitting position.

'I *won't* hurt you,' he said, making it sound more like a resolution than a reassurance. 'And I won't go back. It's got to stop. Dorothy was an accident. I didn't mean her any harm. I only wanted answers to questions. *You* know how important that is.' There was an imploring note in this last statement which sounded like a question.

'Sometimes there are no good reasons,' Chris said. 'Sometimes things happen because they just *do*.'

Simon frowned, looking up as if he had been distracted by a movement. Cobwebs hung in dusty festoons from the pipes above their heads. 'I suppose I wanted an apology for all the years of abuse I went through after they turned down your recommendation for a residential placement. It wasn't so much to ask, was it?'

'Did you really expect an apology from Frank Garrett?'

'Garrett was a bully and a sadist.'

'He was a pathetic, insecure little prick. All right, he was a bully. But is that reason enough to kill him?'

'He was a systematic, monstrous sadist and he humiliated me more times than I can remember. I knocked on his door — not a flicker of recognition. I even called him "Windy Garrett" — you remember, all the boys called him that — he still didn't recognize me.'

'Untie me!' Chris yelled, filled with a sudden disgust for his wallowing self-pity. She struggled with her bonds, feeling a mounting fury. 'Untie me and I'll kick your self-absorbed, bastard arse!'

He blinked at her, dismayed. 'You'll hurt yourself,' he warned with genuine concern.

The ropes tightened as she struggled and she screamed with rage, too incensed to be afraid anymore. 'Is that it?' she demanded. 'Is that what this is all about?' She gave up with a cry of frustration and lay where she had fallen, panting, staring balefully up at him.

'I'm trying to explain.'

'God! I don't *believe* this! You're asking for pity from a woman you've hit over the head and dragged to this rat-infested hole, trussed hand and foot. Those people made a stupid *mistake*, Simon! A costly one for you — I'll grant you that — but a mistake, nevertheless. Sad, friendless Windy Garrett didn't even have anything to do with it. I don't want to hear your explanations or your whining excuses.'

Simon poured himself a cup of water. It was stiflingly hot in the basement and she could see in the yellow light of the lamp that the front of his T-shirt was damp, the bloodstains beginning to brown already. 'I don't have to listen to this,' he said.

'No, *I'm* the one who's tied up. *You* can walk away if you want to.' She paused, allowing him chance to leave, but he remained. 'OK,' she began, 'let me give *you* an explanation. The first real feelings of power you ever experienced were when you set the fire in school.' She saw him nod almost imperceptibly.

'Then you started working for me and things looked up. You discovered you had a brain and a possible route out of the hole your parents dug for you.' His eyes raked hers hungrily. The lamp had burned low and he flicked on the torch before blowing out the flame and carefully refilling the reservoir from a plastic container. The air reeked of paraffin and Chris felt a surge of nausea. He carried the lamp away from a pool of spilt fuel in order to relight it, and Chris went on. 'This is where I come in. This is *my* mistake. When you offered to move my junk up to the loft, I let you. Which was stupid, because my files were in among that junk, and your file was one of them, and you didn't just move them, you read them. I *really* screwed up there. I let you read my notes. Instead of taking the time off work I was entitled to for moving house, I gave you access to files, which you should never have seen.'

Simon shrugged and began to speak.

'No excuses, Simon. It was wrong of me. I didn't mean for anything bad to happen, any more than Ann or Dorothy did, but I shouldn't have given you virtually unrestricted access to confidential, sensitive files. Still, I'm alive and they're dead — where's the justice in that?'

'You weren't the cause.'

'Neither were they, Simon. Your *father* was the cause — and your mother, for not having done anything to prevent it. But he's dead, so you decided to punish some poor scapegoats who made an error of judgement.' She pushed on, feeling faint and suddenly cold. 'This is about revenge and justification. You've taken your revenge for a whole lifetime of misery, but on the people who were mere spectators. And now you're trying to justify it by saying you had to *protect* yourself!'

288

'No!' He jumped up and blundered into the darkness. Chris could hear him tripping over pipes and rubbish just outside the range of the lamp.

'Dorothy was harmless. Why didn't you just run away? If you hadn't touched her what could she say? That you frightened her? Dorothy was frightened of her own shadow! You can't go to prison for *talking* to someone.' She could hear him breathing, sobbing in the darkness beyond the little smudge of light.

'How do you know Ann saw you? *If* she saw you, how do you know she recognized you? And Jim. He must have seen thousands of delinquent boys in his time. What made you think he'd know you after one or two meetings? Face it, Simon. It wasn't fear they *would* recognize you; it was rage that they *didn't*. Rage that you, who had suffered so because of their incompetence, were nobody to them — nothing, an unknown.'

'Stop it.' His voice growled from somewhere behind her.

'What was it you said about Frank Garrett? He humiliated you, and he didn't even know you when he met you face to face. Even though you're a *celebrity* now. What is it the tabloids call you? "The Municipal Murderer". But it's an anonymous kind of fame, isn't it?'

Suddenly his face was in hers, contorted with rage and pain. 'Stop it, Chris, please! I don't—' he took a few ragged breaths — 'I don't want to hurt you.'

She closed her eyes until she felt steadier and then asked, in a voice which sounded small and afraid, 'Am I to be your way to make your name?'

There was a speechless, breathless silence, and when at last Chris opened her eyes, he was standing in front of her, and she saw that he was astounded, hurt.

'You haven't understood at all, have you?'

'Haven't I?' Chris asked, falling back on an old ploy because she was too exhausted and sick to argue.

'I've looked after you all along.'

Chris stared into his eyes. 'If you were trying to protect me, why all this now?'

'Because I need you to understand why. You were right about one thing. I did kill Garrett for revenge. But not the others. When you went to see my mum, I thought she'd told you. I thought you *knew*.' So, he had followed her there, too.

'You thought she told me *what*? Are you saying that your mother knew about the murders?' His response was to sit down and cover his face with his hands. She watched him sobbing silently until she thought she could stand it no longer, and then, slowly, he began to speak.

'I went to see her after I'd read the files. She knew all along about what he was doing. She *knew* what was going on and she did nothing to stop it.' He paused, crouched on his haunches, peering into her face. 'She wouldn't talk to me. But I made her listen. And I told her I was going to get answers to questions.'

Chris closed her eyes. *She knew and she said nothing . . . ?* It made sense. Those furtive little glances from Mrs Webster to her husband, testing his reaction. Simon's introversion, the barrier of cold detachment he'd put up to protect himself, because there was no one in his little boy's world who would help or protect him.

'The guilt's going to finish her, like it finished my father and yours,' he murmured. 'I should have told someone. That was my guilt. But she was guiltiest of all.'

'What are you saying, Simon?' But he was no longer listening. He was exploring some inner landscape which she could not comprehend and where she could not follow.

'I shouldn't have had to say anything — *you* knew I had to get away from him. You knew what I needed. If they'd listened to you . . . But they didn't. They sent me back, when I was screaming—' He grabbed the front of his T-shirt and twisted it. 'In here. I was *screaming*, and you're the only one who listened to me.'

'I don't have magical powers,' Chris said, and was inexpressibly relieved that her voice was comparatively steady. 'I can't read minds. I knew you were deeply unhappy. We all knew that. And I thought you were afraid of your father, but

I didn't know why. I didn't know until you told me in this room, tonight. I saw a lonely, frightened child who needed help. But I couldn't read your mind, Simon. Any more than they could.'

He stared at his hands, confused by what she had said. 'You tried to get me away from him. If they'd listened to you—' He glanced up.

'And they didn't. But it was a *mistake*, Simon,' the repetition made her weary and profoundly sad.

He smiled, and there was compassion and regret in it. 'I've read the notes, Chris,' he said. 'It was a financial decision. You said as much to them. I was too costly to save. I never meant for any of this to happen,' he went on, pinching and squeezing compulsively at the bandage on his hand until the knuckles began to bleed afresh. 'I swear I never meant any of it. I was mixed up, angry when I read your notes.'

She made herself speak calmly. 'You know you have to let me go, don't you, Simon?'

He muttered something and she had to ask him to repeat it.

'I can't.' He looked up at her and his face was glistening with tears. Fear flashed in his eyes. 'I *can't*,' he repeated, as if trying to persuade himself.

'But this can't go on,' Chris said.

'It isn't finished yet.'

'It's gone too far already.'

A muscle twitched in Simon's jaw. 'Not far enough.'

'Is your mother . . . Is she safe?' She watched him, her eyes fixed on him, her attention focused only on what he was preparing to tell her. Then he had her under the arms and was hauling her to her feet. Chris screamed at the pain in her wrists and ankles.

'You'll see,' he shouted. 'I'll make you understand.'

He carried her up the basement steps and out into a rubble-strewn corridor. Vandals had bent stair rails, broken windows, torn doors from their hinges, and everywhere there was graffiti, but she recognized it as Wellesthorne School, where she had taught, briefly, and where Simon had been a pupil for four years. Simon pushed down the bar of the fire door and carried her out into the sunlight. Chris yelped at the sudden blinding flash of light, then she was dumped onto the back seat of a car.

She must have blacked out for a few minutes, perhaps longer, for when she opened her eyes again, they were driving on an open road with a great expanse of sky and occasional clumps of trees sliding dizzyingly past the car windows.

'You know what I despise most about my father?' Simon demanded.

Chris did not answer. She could not, because during her blackout Simon had taped her mouth with masking tape and she was concentrating her efforts on not throwing up. A few inches from her face she could smell paraffin, could hear it sloshing in its container somewhere unseen.

'What I Despise Most about My Father,' said Simon, laughing with genuine amusement. 'Sounds like the title of an English homework exercise, doesn't it?' He began again, relishing the words: '*What I most despise about my father is:* the way he killed himself. Finishing his cowardly life in a fume-filled car. Crawling away quietly and waiting for the end. A footnote in the local rag. Sadly missed. Epitaph to a nobody.' He drove recklessly, sending the car into skids at the bends. A car horn blared and Chris heard its tires squealing, then a soft *thud*, as Simon drove on.

'Not me. I won't go like that. People will see me. Maybe for the first time. And I'll make sure they remember for a long, long time.'

He parked in the residential car park at the back of the mansions where his mother lived, choosing the dense shade of an overhanging sycamore. 'I'll leave the window open, so you won't suffocate,' he said. 'Someone'll find you eventually.'

Chris struggled to be heard through the gag.

'The time for talking is over,' he said without rancour. 'I don't blame you for this,' he said. 'It was their fault. Mum's and Dad's. A family matter. And now she's going to pay.' He lifted a damp lock of hair from Chris's eyes and smoothed it back. 'I never would have hurt you.' He frowned at her as if he wanted to say more but didn't know how to frame the words. Then he was gone.

* * *

Jameson drove fast through the traffic, flashing his lights and sounding his horn to move sluggish lane-hoggers. A car fitting the description of Garrett's had been reported after a Volvo was driven off the Southport road. The police helicopter deployed to look for the stolen car had been redirected, and they followed at a distance, relaying his movements to Lancashire police. Their instructions were to observe only — Chris Radcliffe was a suspected hostage.

The chief inspector arrived at the mansions ten minutes after Webster had followed the gardener in, actually holding the door for him as he brought his tools into the storage cupboard he had been forced to use ever since his tool shed had been vandalized.

'You don't mind, do you?' Webster said. 'It saves me trekking round to the front of the building. Mum's expecting me, and I'm a bit late.' He grimaced, lifting a carrier bag brimming with shopping. The gardener, who knew all about demanding elderly parents, muttered that it made no difference to him, and Webster was inside.

Jameson spoke to the two detectives at the front of the building. 'No sign, sir. The helicopter lost him in the town centre. There's so much bloody traffic today, with the school holidays just starting.'

'Well, keep your eyes open. I'll check the back.' The newly surfaced car park reeked of tar and shimmered in the early afternoon heat. The doors at the rear of the building were secure. Jameson quickly scanned the car park, almost missing the metallic-blue Vauxhall Astra parked in the shade of a tree at the far side of the yard. It was parked at right angles to him, so he had to walk in a semicircle to check the registration. 1 FG. The windows were open a fraction. Jameson approached the car at an oblique angle, every muscle tensed. He edged closer and peered in.

'Chris!' The door was locked but he forced the window down, reached in and released the lever. She was unconscious. Her hair was plastered to her scalp and matted at the back with blood. A dirty bandage had been wound round her head. She was deathly pale, but she was still breathing. He gingerly removed the masking tape from her mouth and untied the rope which bound her feet and hands. She stirred and groaned. He dug into his pocket for his mobile phone.

'He's inside,' he said. 'I need an ambulance. No sirens. Dr Radcliffe is here. Head wound. I can't tell how serious, but she's unconscious. Patch me through to the caretaker's office and contact the local nick just in case he's rung through to tell them there's been a break-in at Mrs Webster's flat. Tell them to do nothing. We do not want to panic him.'

Chris gave a startled cry, then she coughed and cried out again, this time in pain.

'It's OK,' Jameson said, crouching beside her. 'It's all right, Chris. Lie still, I've sent for an ambulance.'

Chris muttered something through parched and swollen lips. 'Stop . . .'

'We've got him, he won't get away.'

Chris moaned, a frustrated frown on her face. She articulated something faintly — it sounded like 'fool'. 'His mother has been taken somewhere out of reach,' Jameson said, guessing wildly at what was troubling her. 'You're safe now.'

Chris slumped, semi-conscious, in his arms.

* * *

His mother was gone. Simon had known, somehow, that she would not be there to witness this final act. He could see the grey Sierra which had followed Chris for several days parked outside on the promenade. He thought he even recognized one of the plain-clothes officers who loitered with his back to the rail, watching the mansions.

He dialled out on his mother's phone. Perhaps it was best this way. Since she was to be allowed to live, she would begin her purgatory today and it would go on for all eternity. For Simon, purgatory was a real place. He felt he had been there most of his life, and now it would be her turn.

An ambulance crept quietly into the car park and Chris was lifted gently and expertly, still mumbling in protest, inside. Jameson watched it leave before going to the front of the house. Mr Jones let him in without demur and he was followed by the two DCs who had been on duty. They knocked at Mrs Webster's door and Simon screamed at them to leave him alone. 'I'll kill myself, I swear!' They backed off, and Jameson left one DC outside the door while he telephoned HQ to ask for a negotiating team.

* * *

Behind the flat door Simon's face was an expressionless mask. He walked from room to room, touching each ornament, fingering the tablecloth in the dining room, playing a few desultory notes on the baby grand piano, drinking in the smells which were so uniquely her: Imperial Leather talcum powder and rose water, clothing dried outside on the washing line, starched into compliance. He sat in one of his mother's pale cream armchairs and stretched his feet out on the dusty pink and green embossed surface of the Chinese rug, absorbing the genteel, if rather pallid colours and style which had typified her, knowing with certainty and with profound satisfaction that for her this place would be for ever tainted.

It took an hour for the media representatives who had been encamped in Liverpool to remove to the sunny seaside town. Jameson, who was in the middle of deploying the local uniformed branch to clear the prom of the public, stopped to ask, 'Who the *fuck* told them?'

Simon heard them arrive. He had been waiting for some time, but he was used to waiting. They had taken him seriously because he had asked to speak to Milton himself and had given details which only the police and the Municipal Murderer would know. Perhaps Milton had cross-checked first. It didn't matter. They had come, all of them, as he knew they would, and they were waiting for him. Sipping a long, cool glass of lemonade, he watched them set up their tripods and still cameras, their boom microphones and hand-held TV cameras, their arc lights and gizmos and waited until he heard the generators power up. He opened the French windows and flared his nostrils as the first faint whiffs of diesel smoke and ozone drifted in, and he was reminded of fun fairs and big-wheel rides. 'Soon,' he murmured. 'Very soon.' He glanced contemptuously at the door, through which the negotiator was trying to talk to him, since he had pulled out the telephone wire.

Simon ignored the noise outside and focused on his breathing. He checked his watch. Six p.m. It was time. He unpacked the groceries from the top of the bag, pulled out the plastic container of pink fuel and opened the cap. He drew out the lighter he had bought along with the groceries and set it to maximum, then flicked the trigger. A flame six inches high leaped with a roar from the nozzle. He walked to the balcony, leaning a little to the left with the weight of the paraffin. The public had been cleared from the promenade, but the media were there in force. His eyes watered slightly in the glare of the sunlight and the arc lights and the million dancing points of light on the marina water. He stepped out onto the balcony, locking the doors behind him, then he unscrewed the top of the container and listened, pleased by the sudden collective intake of breath from the audience below him. He tipped the paraffin over his head, shutting his eyes tightly against the stinging liquid. A gasp of dismay went up from the media. He imagined them leaning back, away from the possible danger, taking a few shuffling steps in retreat, torn between self-preservation and a good story.

He reached into his pocket for a handkerchief and wiped his eyes before opening them. He placed both hands on the ledge of the balcony, like a statesman about to deliver an address, and spoke in a clear voice. 'I am the Municipal Murderer,' he said. 'My name is Simon Webster.' He held the lighter to his face and hit the trigger.

EPILOGUE

Chris sighed, looking up at the neat figure who sat at the head of the table. 'I've been drifting again, haven't I?' she said. Sister Aloysius had turned up on the doorstep, unannounced. Chris suspected that Maria had covertly set up a rota of visitors whom she felt would do Chris good, and who could be relied upon to assess her state of mind.

Sister Aloysius nodded. 'Understandable,' she replied.

'I was just thinking that before all this happened, I was going to dedicate my book to him.'

'You can hardly do that now,' said Sister Aloysius, with only the slightest lifting of the eyebrows.

'I should have seen it.'

'Why?'

'Because I failed him. I knew he should be taken away from his father and I didn't make it happen. Because I was closest to him. Because I knew something was troubling him, but it just never occurred to me—'

'And why should it?'

Chris shook her head, unable to find a suitable answer.

'Do you think he's in Hell?'

The nun seemed startled by the question. 'I didn't think you believed in Hell.'

'You're right,' said Chris, smiling faintly, 'I don't. Good job you were here to remind me.' The doorbell rang and Chris went to answer it, thinking that Maria had slipped up this time: usually her visitors came at conveniently spaced intervals.

'Oh,' she said, 'I thought—' She looked uncertainly over her shoulder.

Sister Aloysius, who had followed her into the hallway, looked past her at the tall, smartly dressed and attractively athletic figure on the doorstep.

'Chief Inspector Jameson, I was just on my way,' she said, a mischievous smile answering Chris's hot look of accusation. She had been avoiding this meeting for weeks.

'I was worried about you,' he said, as he thrust flowers into Chris's hand. 'And since you wouldn't take my calls, I thought I might as well come round. Maybe we could go for a walk?'

'It's going to rain,' Sister Aloysius warned as she unlocked her car.

'God, I hope so.' The earnestness with which he spoke surprised a smile from Chris, and he brightened appreciably.

Chris set the flowers down on the hall stand, took her jacket from the rail by the door. She stepped outside as the first fat droplets spattered the clay on the pathway, sending up small explosions of dust.

THE END

ACKNOWLEDGEMENTS

My thanks to Tony Baldwin of the Child Development Unit, Alder Hey Hospital, Liverpool, for his time and patience in answering my questions and for giving me an insight into an educational psychologist's work.

This is the ninth of my novels to be relaunched by Joffe Books in the past year. In a year of lockdowns and restrictions, anxiety, disappointments, constraints, and personal loss, these nine books have been a steady beacon of light in my life, reaching new audiences and exciting readers in a way I had scarcely dreamed possible. The enthusiasm, professionalism and hard work of the small but tireless team at Joffe Books is simply magnificent. My sincere thanks to Jasper Joffe for welcoming me into the fold, and to Emma, Laura, Nina, Annie, Bev and Jill, who have all, according to their specialist superpowers, given these books their second life. Thanks also to Darja at DeeDee Book Covers, who designed this striking new cover for *The Darkest Hours*.

Thank you for reading this book.

If you enjoyed it please leave feedback on Amazon or Goodreads, and if there is anything we missed or you have a question about, then please get in touch. We appreciate you choosing our book.

Founded in 2014 in Shoreditch, London, we at Joffe Books pride ourselves on our history of innovative publishing. We were thrilled to be shortlisted for Independent Publisher of the Year at the British Book Awards.

www.joffebooks.com

We're very grateful to eagle-eyed readers who take the time to contact us. Please send any errors you find to corrections@joffebooks.com. We'll get them fixed ASAP.

Made in the USA
Las Vegas, NV
27 March 2021

20290323R00184